William Wilkie Collins (8 January 1824 – 23 September 1889) was an English novelist, playwright, and short story writer, best known for The Woman in White (1859), No Name (1862), Armadale (1866) and The Moonstone (1868). The last has been called the first modern English detective novel. Born to the family of painter William Collins in London, he grew up in Italy and France, learning French and Italian. He began work as a clerk for a tea merchant. After his first novel, Antonina, appeared in 1850, he met Charles Dickens, who became a close friend and mentor. Some of Collins's works appeared first in Dickens's journals All the Year Round and Household Words and they collaborated on drama and fiction. Collins published his best known works in the 1860s, achieving financial stability and an international following. However, he began suffering from gout. Taking opium for the pain developed into an addiction. In the 1870s and 1880s the quality of his writing declined along with his health. Collins was critical of the institution of marriage: he split his time between Caroline Graves, except for a two-year separation, and his common-law wife Martha Rudd, with whom he had three children. (Source: Wikipedia)

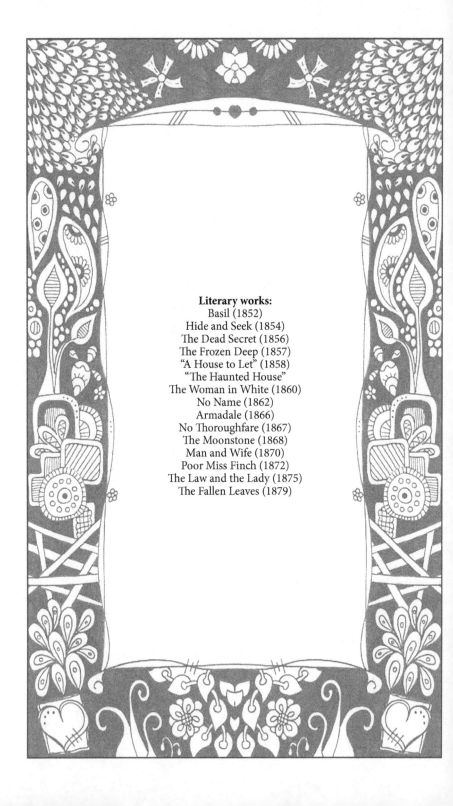

Literary works:
Basil (1852)
Hide and Seek (1854)
The Dead Secret (1856)
The Frozen Deep (1857)
"A House to Let" (1858)
"The Haunted House"
The Woman in White (1860)
No Name (1862)
Armadale (1866)
No Thoroughfare (1867)
The Moonstone (1868)
Man and Wife (1870)
Poor Miss Finch (1872)
The Law and the Lady (1875)
The Fallen Leaves (1879)

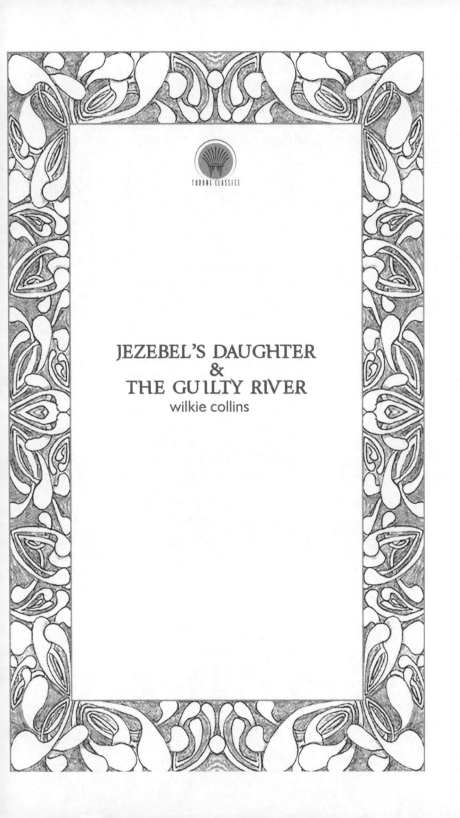

JEZEBEL'S DAUGHTER
&
THE GUILTY RIVER

wilkie collins

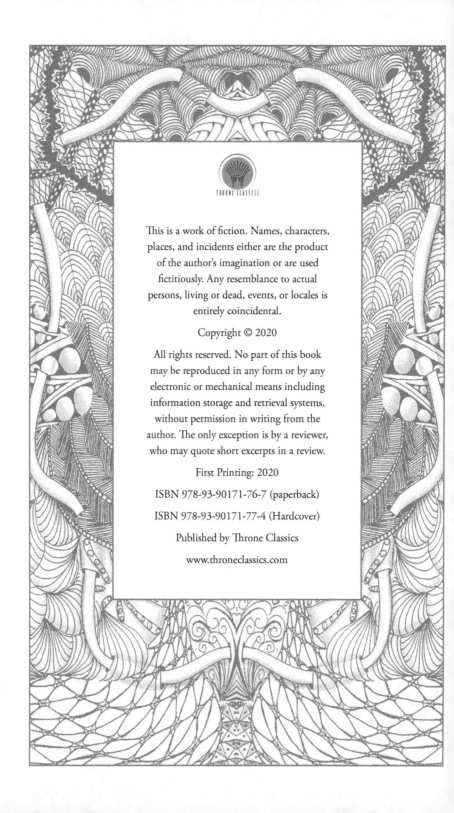

Copyright © 2020

First Printing: 2020

ISBN 978-93-90171-76-7 (paperback)

ISBN 978-93-90171-77-4 (Hardcover)

Published by Throne Classics

www.throneclassics.com

Contents

JEZEBEL'S DAUGHTER
&
THE GUILTY RIVER

JEZEBEL'S DAUGHTER

TO ALBERTO CACCIA

Let me begin by informing you, that this new novel does not present the proposed sequel to my last work of fiction—"The Fallen Leaves."

The first part of that story has, through circumstances connected with the various forms of publications adopted thus far, addressed itself to a comparatively limited class of readers in England. When the book is finally reprinted in its cheapest form—then, and then only, it will appeal to the great audience of the English people. I am waiting for that time, to complete my design by writing the second part of "The Fallen Leaves."

Why?

Your knowledge of English Literature—to which I am indebted for the first faithful and intelligent translation of my novels into the Italian language—has long since informed you, that there are certain important social topics which are held to be forbidden to the English novelist (no matter how seriously and how delicately he may treat them), by a narrow-minded minority of readers, and by the critics who flatter their prejudices. You also know, having done me the honor to read my books, that I respect my art far too sincerely to permit limits to be wantonly assigned to it, which are imposed in no other civilized country on the face of the earth. When my work is undertaken with a pure purpose, I claim the same liberty which is accorded to a writer in a newspaper, or to a clergyman in a pulpit; knowing, by previous experience, that the increase of readers and the lapse of time will assuredly do me justice, if I have only written well enough to deserve it.

In the prejudiced quarters to which I have alluded, one of the characters in "The Fallen Leaves" offended susceptibilities of the sort felt by Tartuffe, when he took out his handkerchief, and requested Dorine to cover her bosom. I not only decline to defend myself, under such circumstances as these—I say plainly, that I have never asserted a truer claim to the best and noblest sympathies of Christian readers than in presenting to them, in my last novel, the character of the innocent victim of infamy, rescued and purified from the contamination of the streets. I remember what the nasty posterity of Tartuffe, in this country, said of "Basil," of "Armadale," of "The New Magdalen," and I know that the wholesome audience of the nation at large has done liberal justice to those books. For this reason, I wait to write the second part of "The Fallen Leaves," until the first part of the story has found its way to the people.

Turning for a moment to the present novel, you will (I hope) find two interesting studies of humanity in these pages.

In the character called "Jack Straw," you have the exhibition of an enfeebled intellect, tenderly shown under its lightest and happiest aspect, and used as a means of relief in some of the darkest scenes of terror and suspense occurring in this story. Again, in "Madame Fontaine," I have endeavored to work out the interesting moral problem, which takes for its groundwork the strongest of all instincts in a woman, the instinct of maternal love, and traces to its solution the restraining and purifying influence of this one virtue over an otherwise cruel, false, and degraded nature.

The events in which these two chief personages play their parts have been combined with all possible care, and have been derived, to the best of my ability, from natural and simple causes. In view of the distrust which certain readers feel, when a novelist builds his fiction on a foundation of fact, it may not be amiss to mention (before I close these lines), that the accessories of the scenes in the Deadhouse of Frankfort have been studied on the spot. The published rules and ground-plans of that curious mortuary establishment have also been laid on my desk, as aids to memory while I was writing the closing passages of the story.

With this, I commend "Jezebel's Daughter" to my good friend and brother in the art—who will present this last work also to the notice of Italian readers.

W. C.

Gloucester Place, London:

February 9, 1880.

PART I

MR. DAVID GLENNEY CONSULTS HIS MEMORY AND OPENS THE STORY

CHAPTER I

In the matter of Jezebel's Daughter, my recollections begin with the deaths of two foreign gentlemen, in two different countries, on the same day of the same year.

They were both men of some importance in their way, and both strangers to each other.

Mr. Ephraim Wagner, merchant (formerly of Frankfort-on-the-Main), died in London on the third day of September, 1828.

Doctor Fontaine—famous in his time for discoveries in experimental chemistry—died at Wurzburg on the third day of September, 1828.

Both the merchant and the doctor left widows. The merchant's widow (an Englishwoman) was childless. The doctor's widow (of a South German family) had a daughter to console her.

At that distant time—I am writing these lines in the year 1878, and looking back through half a century—I was a lad employed in Mr. Wagner's office. Being his wife's nephew, he most kindly received me as a member of his household. What I am now about to relate I saw with my own eyes and heard with my own ears. My memory is to be depended on. Like other old men, I recollect events which happened at the beginning of my career far more clearly than events which happened only two or three years since.

Good Mr. Wagner had been ailing for many months; but the doctors had no immediate fear of his death. He proved the doctors to be mistaken; and took the liberty of dying at a time when they all declared that there was every reasonable hope of his recovery. When this affliction fell upon his wife, I was absent from the office in London on a business errand to our branch-establishment at Frankfort-on-the-Main, directed by Mr. Wagner's partners. The day of my return happened to be the day after the funeral. It was also the occasion chosen for the reading of the will. Mr. Wagner, I should add, had been a naturalized British citizen, and his will was drawn by an English lawyer.

The fourth, fifth, and sixth clauses of the will are the only portions of the document which it is necessary to mention in this place.

The fourth clause left the whole of the testator's property, in lands and in money, absolutely to his widow. In the fifth clause he added a new proof of his implicit confidence in her—he appointed her sole executrix of his will.

The sixth and last clause began in these words:—

"During my long illness, my dear wife has acted as my secretary and representative. She has made herself so thoroughly well acquainted with the system on which I have conducted my business, that she is the fittest person to succeed me. I not only prove the fullness of my trust in her and the sincerity of my gratitude towards her, but I really act in the best interests of the firm of which I am the head, when I hereby appoint my widow as my sole successor in the business, with all the powers and privileges appertaining thereto."

The lawyer and I both looked at my aunt. She had sunk back in her chair; her face was hidden in her handkerchief. We waited respectfully until she might be sufficiently recovered to communicate her wishes to us. The expression of her husband's love and respect, contained in the last words of the will, had completely overwhelmed her. It was only after she had been relieved by a burst of tears that she was conscious of our presence, and was composed enough to speak to us.

"I shall be calmer in a few days' time," she said. "Come to me at the end of the week. I have something important to say to both of you."

The lawyer ventured on putting a question. "Does it relate in any way to the will?" he inquired.

She shook her head. "It relates," she answered, "to my husband's last wishes."

She bowed to us, and went away to her own room.

The lawyer looked after her gravely and doubtfully as she disappeared. "My long experience in my profession," he said, turning to me, "has taught me many useful lessons. Your aunt has just called one of those lessons to my mind.

"May I ask what it is, sir?"

"Certainly." He took my arm and waited to repeat the lesson until we had left the house; "Always distrust a man's last wishes on his death-bed—unless they are communicated to his lawyer, and expressed in his will."

At the time, I thought this rather a narrow view to take. How could I foresee that coming events in the future life of my aunt would prove the lawyer to be right? If she had only been content to leave her husband's plans and projects where he had left them at his death, and if she had never taken that rash journey to our branch office at Frankfort—but what is the use of speculating on what might or might not have happened? My business in these pages is to describe what did happen. Let me return to my business.

CHAPTER II

At the end of the week we found the widow waiting to receive us.

To describe her personally, she was a little lady, with a remarkably pretty figure, a clear pale complexion, a broad low forehead, and large, steady, brightly-intelligent gray eyes. Having married a man very much older than herself, she was still (after many years of wedded life) a notably attractive woman. But she never seemed to be conscious of her personal advantages, or vain of the very remarkable abilities which she did unquestionably possess. Under ordinary circumstances, she was a singularly gentle, unobtrusive creature. But let the occasion call for it, and the reserves of resolution in her showed themselves instantly. In all my experience I have never met with such a firm woman, when she was once roused.

She entered on her business with us, wasting no time in preliminary words. Her face showed plain signs, poor soul, of a wakeful and tearful night. But she claimed no indulgence on that account. When she spoke of her dead husband—excepting a slight unsteadiness in her voice—she controlled herself with a courage which was at once pitiable and admirable to see.

"You both know," she began, "that Mr. Wagner was a man who thought for himself. He had ideas of his duty to his poor and afflicted fellow-creatures which are in advance of received opinions in the world about us. I love and revere his memory—and (please God) I mean to carry out his ideas."

The lawyer began to look uneasy. "Do you refer, madam, to Mr. Wagner's political opinions?" he inquired.

Fifty years ago, my old master's political opinions were considered to be nothing less than revolutionary. In these days—when his Opinions have been sanctioned by Acts of Parliament, with the general approval of the nation— people would have called him a "Moderate Liberal," and would have set him down as a discreetly deliberate man in the march of modern progress.

"I have nothing to say about politics," my aunt answered. "I wish to speak to you, in the first place, of my husband's opinions on the employment of women."

Here, again, after a lapse of half a century, my master's heresies of the year 1828 have become the orthodox principles of the year 1878. Thinking the subject over in his own independent way, he had arrived at the conclusion that there were many employments reserved exclusively for men, which might with perfect propriety be also thrown open to capable and deserving women. To recognize the claims of justice was, with a man of Mr. Wagner's character, to act on his convictions without a moment's needless delay. Enlarging his London business at the time, he divided the new employments at his disposal impartially between men and women alike. The scandal produced in the city by this daring innovation is remembered to the present day by old men like me. My master's audacious experiment prospered nevertheless, in spite of scandal.

"If my husband had lived," my aunt continued, "it was his intention to follow the example, which he has already set in London, in our house at Frankfort. There also our business is increasing, and we mean to add to the number of our clerks. As soon as I am able to exert myself, I shall go to Frankfort, and give German women the same opportunities which my husband has already given to English women in London. I have his notes on the best manner of carrying out this reform to guide me. And I think of sending you, David," she added, turning to me, "to our partners in Frankfort, Mr. Keller and Mr. Engelman, with instructions which will keep some of the vacant situations in the office open, until I can follow you." She paused, and looked at the lawyer. "Do you see any objection to what I propose?" she said.

"I see some risks," he answered, cautiously.

"What risks?"

"In London, madam, the late Mr. Wagner had special means of investigating the characters of the women whom he took into his office. It may not be so easy for you, in a strange place like Frankfort, to guard against the danger——" He hesitated, at a loss for the moment to express himself with sufficient plainness and sufficient delicacy.

My aunt made no allowances for his embarrassment.

"Don't be afraid to speak out, sir," she said, a little coldly. "What danger are you afraid of?"

"Yours is a generous nature, madam: and generous natures are easily imposed upon. I am afraid of women with bad characters, or, worse still, of other women——"

He stopped again. This time there was a positive interruption. We heard a knock at the door.

Our head-clerk was the person who presented himself at the summons to come in. My aunt held up her hand. "Excuse me, Mr. Hartrey—I will attend to you in one moment." She turned to the lawyer. "What other women are likely to impose on me?" she asked.

"Women, otherwise worthy of your kindness, who may be associated

17

with disreputable connections," the lawyer replied. "The very women, if I know anything of your quick sympathies, whom you would be most anxious to help, and who might nevertheless be a source of constant trouble and anxiety, under pernicious influences at home."

My aunt made no answer. For the moment, the lawyer's objections seemed to annoy her. She addressed herself to Mr. Hartrey; asking rather abruptly what he had to say to her.

Our head-clerk was a methodical gentleman of the old school. He began by confusedly apologizing for his intrusion; and ended by producing a letter.

"When you are able to attend to business, madam, honor me by reading this letter. And, in the meantime, will you forgive me for taking a liberty in the office, rather than intrude on your grief so soon after the death of my dear and honored master?" The phrases were formal enough; but there was true feeling in the man's voice as he spoke. My aunt gave him her hand. He kissed it, with the tears in his eyes.

"Whatever you have done has been well done, I am sure," she said kindly. "Who is the letter from?"

"From Mr. Keller, of Frankfort, madam."

My aunt instantly took the letter from him, and read it attentively. It has a very serious bearing on passages in the present narrative which are yet to come. I accordingly present a copy of it in this place:

"Private and confidential.

"Dear Mr. Hartrey,—It is impossible for me to address myself to Mrs. Wagner, in the first days of the affliction that has fallen on her. I am troubled by a pressing anxiety; and I venture to write to you, as the person now in charge at our London office.

"My only son Fritz is finishing his education at the university of Wurzburg. He has, I regret to say, formed an attachment to a young woman, the daughter of a doctor at Wurzburg, who has recently died. I believe the girl to be a perfectly reputable and virtuous young person. But her father has not only left her in poverty, he has done worse—he has died in debt. Besides this, her mother's character does not stand high in the town. It is said, among other things, that her extravagance is mainly answerable for her late husband's debts. Under these circumstances, I wish to break off the connection while the two young people are separated for the time by the event of the doctor's recent death. Fritz has given up the idea of entering the medical profession, and has accepted my proposal that he shall succeed me in our business. I have decided on sending him to London, to learn something of commercial affairs, at headquarters, in your office.

"My son obeys me reluctantly; but he is a good and dutiful lad—and he yields to his father's wishes. You may expect him in a day or two after receipt of these lines. Oblige me by making a little opening for him in one of your official departments, and by keeping him as much as possible under your own eye, until I can venture on communicating directly with Mrs. Wagner— to whom pray convey the expression of my most sincere and respectful sympathy."

My aunt handed back the letter. "Has the young man arrived yet?" she asked.

"He arrived yesterday, madam."

"And have you found some employment for him?"

"I have ventured to place him in our corresponding department," the head-clerk answered. "For the present he will assist in copying letters; and, after business-hours, he will have a room (until further orders) in my house. I hope you think I have done right, madam?"

"You have done admirably, Mr. Hartrey. At the same time, I will relieve you of some of the responsibility. No grief of mine shall interfere with my duty to my husband's partner. I will speak to the young man myself. Bring him here this evening, after business-hours. And don't leave us just yet; I want to put a question to you relating to my husband's affairs, in which I am deeply interested." Mr. Hartrey returned to his chair. After a momentary hesitation, my aunt put her question in terms which took us all three by surprise.

19

CHAPTER III

"My husband was connected with many charitable institutions," the widow began. "Am I right in believing that he was one of the governors of Bethlehem Hospital?"

At this reference to the famous asylum for insane persons, popularly known among the inhabitants of London as "Bedlam," I saw the lawyer start, and exchange a look with the head-clerk. Mr. Hartrey answered with evident reluctance; he said, "Quite right, madam"—and said no more. The lawyer, being the bolder man of the two, added a word of warning, addressed directly to my aunt.

"I venture to suggest," he said, "that there are circumstances connected with the late Mr. Wagner's position at the Hospital, which make it desirable not to pursue the subject any farther. Mr. Hartrey will confirm what I say, when I tell you that Mr. Wagner's proposals for a reformation in the treatment of the patients——"

"Were the proposals of a merciful man," my aunt interposed "who abhorred cruelty in all its forms, and who held the torturing of the poor mad patients by whips and chains to be an outrage on humanity. I entirely agree with him. Though I am only a woman, I will not let the matter drop. I shall go to the Hospital on Monday morning next—and my business with you to-day is to request that you will accompany me."

"In what capacity am I to have the honor of accompanying you?" the lawyer asked, in his coldest manner.

"In your professional capacity," my aunt replied. "I may have a proposal to address to the governors; and I shall look to your experience to express it in the proper form."

The lawyer was not satisfied yet. "Excuse me if I venture on making another inquiry," he persisted. "Do you propose to visit the madhouse in consequence of any wish expressed by the late Mr. Wagner?"

"Certainly not! My husband always avoided speaking to me on that

20

melancholy subject. As you have heard, he even left me in doubt whether he was one of the governing body at the asylum. No reference to any circumstance in his life which might alarm or distress me ever passed his lips." Her voice failed her as she paid that tribute to her husband's memory. She waited to recover herself. "But, on the night before his death," she resumed, "when he was half waking, half dreaming, I heard him talking to himself of something that he was anxious to do, if the chance of recovery had been still left to him. Since that time I have looked at his private diary; and I have found entries in it which explain to me what I failed to understand clearly at his bedside. I know for certain that the obstinate hostility of his colleagues had determined him on trying the effect of patience and kindness in the treatment of mad people, at his sole risk and expense. There is now in Bethlehem Hospital a wretched man—a friendless outcast, found in the streets—whom my noble husband had chosen as the first subject of his humane experiment, and whose release from a life of torment he had the hope of effecting through the influence of a person in authority in the Royal Household. You know already that the memory of my husband's plans and wishes is a sacred memory to me. I am resolved to see that poor chained creature whom he would have rescued if he had lived; and I will certainly complete his work of mercy, if my conscience tells me that a woman should do it."

Hearing this bold announcement—I am almost ashamed to confess it, in these enlightened days—we all three protested. Modest Mr. Hartrey was almost as loud and as eloquent as the lawyer, and I was not far behind Mr. Hartrey. It is perhaps to be pleaded as an excuse for us that some of the highest authorities, in the early part of the present century, would have been just as prejudiced and just as ignorant as we were. Say what we might, however, our remonstrances produced no effect on my aunt. We merely roused the resolute side of her character to assert itself.

"I won't detain you any longer," she said to the lawyer. "Take the rest of the day to decide what you will do. If you decline to accompany me, I shall go by myself. If you accept my proposal, send me a line this evening to say so."

In that way the conference came to an end.

Early in the evening young Mr. Keller made his appearance, and was

21

introduced to my aunt and to me. We both took a liking to him from the first. He was a handsome young man, with light hair and florid complexion, and with a frank ingratiating manner—a little sad and subdued, in consequence, no doubt, of his enforced separation from his beloved young lady at Wurzburg. My aunt, with her customary kindness and consideration, offered him a room next to mine, in place of his room in Mr. Hartrey's house. "My nephew David speaks German; and he will help to make your life among us pleasant to you." With those words our good mistress left us together.

Fritz opened the conversation with the easy self-confidence of a German student.

"It is one bond of union between us that you speak my language," he began. "I am good at reading and writing English, but I speak badly. Have we any other sympathies in common? Is it possible that you smoke?"

Poor Mr. Wagner had taught me to smoke. I answered by offering my new acquaintance a cigar.

"Another bond between us," cried Fritz. "We must be friends from this moment. Give me your hand." We shook hands. He lit his cigar, looked at me very attentively, looked away again, and puffed out his first mouthful of smoke with a heavy sigh.

"I wonder whether we are united by a third bond?" he said thoughtfully. "Are you a stiff Englishman? Tell me, friend David, may I speak to you with the freedom of a supremely wretched man?"

"As freely as you like," I answered. He still hesitated.

"I want to be encouraged," he said. "Be familiar with me. Call me Fritz."

I called him "Fritz." He drew his chair close to mine, and laid his hand affectionately on my shoulder. I began to think I had perhaps encouraged him a little too readily.

"Are you in love, David?" He put the question just as coolly as if he had asked me what o'clock it was.

I was young enough to blush. Fritz accepted the blush as a sufficient answer. "Every moment I pass in your society," he cried with enthusiasm, "I like you better—find you more eminently sympathetic. You are in love. One word more—are there any obstacles in your way?"

There were obstacles in my way. She was too old for me, and too poor for me—and it all came to nothing in due course of time. I admitted the obstacles; abstaining, with an Englishman's shyness, from entering into details. My reply was enough, and more than enough, for Fritz. "Good Heavens!" he exclaimed; "our destinies exactly resemble each other! We are both supremely wretched men. David, I can restrain myself no longer; I must positively embrace you!"

I resisted to the best of my ability—but he was the stronger man of the two. His long arms almost strangled me; his bristly mustache scratched my cheek. In my first involuntary impulse of disgust, I clenched my fist. Young Mr. Keller never suspected (my English brethren alone will understand) how very near my fist and his head were to becoming personally and violently acquainted. Different nations—different customs. I can smile as I write about it now.

Fritz took his seat again. "My heart is at ease; I can pour myself out freely," he said. "Never, my friend, was there such an interesting love-story as mine. She is the sweetest girl living. Dark, slim, gracious, delightful, desirable, just eighteen. The image, I should suppose, of what her widowed mother was at her age. Her name is Minna. Daughter and only child of Madame Fontaine. Madame Fontaine is a truly grand creature, a Roman matron. She is the victim of envy and scandal. Would you believe it? There are wretches in Wurzburg (her husband the doctor was professor of chemistry at the University)—there are wretches, I say, who call my Minna's mother 'Jezebel,' and my Minna herself 'Jezebel's Daughter!' I have fought three duels with my fellow-students to avenge that one insult. Alas, David, there is another person who is influenced by those odious calumnies!—a person sacred to me—the honored author of my being. Is it not dreadful? My good father turns tyrant in this one thing; declares I shall never marry 'Jezebel's Daughter;' exiles me, by his paternal commands, to this foreign country; and perches me on a high stool to copy letters. Ha! he little knows my heart. I am my Minna's and my

Minna is mine. In body and soul, in time and in eternity, we are one. Do you see my tears? Do my tears speak for me? The heart's relief is in crying freely. There is a German song to that effect. When I recover myself, I will sing it to you. Music is a great comforter; music is the friend of love. There is another German song to that effect." He suddenly dried his eyes, and got on his feet; some new idea had apparently occurred to him. "It is dreadfully dull here," he said; "I am not used to evenings at home. Have you any music in London? Help me to forget Minna for an hour or two. Take me to the music."

Having, by this time, heard quite enough of his raptures, I was eager on my side for a change of any kind. I helped him to forget Minna at a Vauxhall Concert. He thought our English orchestra wanting in subtlety and spirit. On the other hand, he did full justice, afterwards, to our English bottled beer. When we left the Gardens he sang me that German song, 'My heart's relief is crying freely,' with a fervor of sentiment which must have awakened every light sleeper in the neighborhood.

Retiring to my bedchamber, I found an open letter on my toilet-table. It was addressed to my aunt by the lawyer; and it announced that he had decided on accompanying her to the madhouse—without pledging himself to any further concession. In leaving the letter for me to read, my aunt had written across it a line in pencil: "You can go with us, David, if you like."

My curiosity was strongly aroused. It is needless to say I decided on being present at the visit to Bedlam.

CHAPTER IV

On the appointed Monday we were ready to accompany my aunt to the madhouse.

Whether she distrusted her own unaided judgment, or whether she wished to have as many witnesses as possible to the rash action in which she was about to engage, I cannot say. In either case, her first proceeding was to include Mr. Hartrey and Fritz Keller in the invitation already extended to the lawyer and myself.

They both declined to accompany us. The head-clerk made the affairs of the office serve for his apology, it was foreign post day, and he could not possibly be absent from his desk. Fritz invented no excuses; he confessed the truth, in his own outspoken manner. "I have a horror of mad people," he said, "they so frighten and distress me, that they make me feel half mad myself. Don't ask me to go with you—and oh, dear lady, don't go yourself."

My aunt smiled sadly—and led the way out.

We had a special order of admission to the Hospital which placed the resident superintendent himself at our disposal. He received my aunt with the utmost politeness, and proposed a scheme of his own for conducting us over the whole building; with an invitation to take luncheon with him afterwards at his private residence.

"At another time, sir, I shall be happy to avail myself of your kindness," my aunt said, when he had done. "For the present, my object is to see one person only among the unfortunate creatures in this asylum."

"One person only?" repeated the superintendent. "One of our patients of the higher rank, I suppose?"

"On the contrary," my aunt replied, "I wish to see a poor friendless creature, found in the streets; known here, as I am informed, by no better name than Jack Straw."

The superintendent looked at her in blank amazement.

"Good Heavens, madam!" he exclaimed; "are you aware that Jack Straw is one of the most dangerous lunatics we have in the house?"

"I have heard that he bears the character you describe," my aunt quietly admitted.

"And yet you wish to see him?"

"I am here for that purpose—and no other."

The superintendent looked round at the lawyer and at me, appealing to us silently to explain, if we could, this incomprehensible desire to see Jack Straw. The lawyer spoke for both of us. He reminded the superintendent of the late Mr. Wagner's peculiar opinions on the treatment of the insane, and of the interest which he had taken in this particular case. To which my aunt added: "And Mr. Wagner's widow feels the same interest, and inherits her late husband's opinions." Hearing this, the superintendent bowed with his best grace, and resigned himself to circumstances. "Pardon me if I keep you waiting for a minute or two," he said, and rang a bell.

A man-servant appeared at the door.

"Are Yarcombe and Foss on duty on the south side?" the superintendent asked.

"Yes, sir."

"Send one of them here directly."

We waited a few minutes—and then a gruff voice became audible on the outer side of the door. "Present, sir," growled the gruff voice.

The superintendent courteously offered his arm to my aunt. "Permit me to escort you to Jack Straw," he said, with a touch of playful irony in his tone.

We left the room. The lawyer and I followed my aunt and her escort. A man, whom we found posted on the door-mat, brought up the rear. Whether he was Yarcombe or whether he was Foss, mattered but little. In either case he was a hulking, scowling, hideously ill-looking brute. "One of our assistants," we heard the superintendent explain. "It is possible, madam, that we may want two of them, if we are to make things pleasant at your introduction to Jack Straw."

We ascended some stairs, shut off from the lower floor by a massive locked door, and passed along some dreary stone passages, protected by more doors. Cries of rage and pain, at one time distant and at another close by, varied by yelling laughter, more terrible even than the cries, sounded on either side of us. We passed through a last door, the most solid of all, which shut out these dreadful noises, and found ourselves in a little circular hall. Here the superintendent stopped, and listened for a moment. There was dead silence. He beckoned to the attendant, and pointed to a heavily nailed oaken door.

26

"Look in," he said.

The man drew aside a little shutter in the door, and looked through the bars which guarded the opening.

"Is he waking or sleeping?" the superintendent asked.

"Waking, sir."

"Is he at work?"

"Yes, sir."

The superintendent turned to my aunt.

"You are fortunate, madam—you will see him in his quiet moments. He amuses himself by making hats, baskets, and table-mats, out of his straw. Very neatly put together, I assure you. One of our visiting physicians, a man with a most remarkable sense of humor, gave him his nickname from his work. Shall we open the door?"

My aunt had turned very pale; I could see that she was struggling with violent agitation. "Give me a minute or two first," she said; "I want to compose myself before I see him."

She sat down on a stone bench outside the door. "Tell me what you know about this poor man?" she said. "I don't ask out of idle curiosity—I have a better motive than that. Is he young or old?"

"Judging by his teeth," the superintendent answered, as if he had been speaking of a horse, "he is certainly young. But his complexion is completely gone, and his hair has turned gray. So far as we have been able to make out (when he is willing to speak of himself), these peculiarities in his personal appearance are due to a narrow escape from poisoning by accident. But how the accident occurred, and where it occurred, he either cannot or will not tell us. We know nothing about him, except that he is absolutely friendless. He speaks English—but it is with an odd kind of accent—and we don't know whether he is a foreigner or not. You are to understand, madam, that he is here on sufferance. This is a royal institution, and, as a rule, we only receive lunatics of the educated class. But Jack Straw has had wonderful luck. Being too mad, I suppose, to take care of himself, he was run over in one of the streets in our neighborhood by the carriage of an exalted personage, whom it would be an indiscretion on my part even to name. The personage (an illustrious lady, I may inform you) was so distressed by the accident—without the slightest need, for the man was not seriously hurt—that she actually had him brought here in her carriage, and laid her commands on us to receive him. Ah, Mrs. Wagner, her highness's heart is worthy of her highness's rank. She occasionally sends to inquire after the lucky lunatic who rolled under her horse's feet. We don't tell her what a trouble and expense he is to us. We have had irons specially invented to control him; and, if I am not mistaken," said the superintendent, turning to the assistant, "a new whip was required only last week."

The man put his hand into the big pocket of his coat, and produced a horrible whip, of many lashes. He exhibited this instrument of torture with every appearance of pride and pleasure. "This is what keeps him in order, my lady," said the brute, cheerfully. "Just take it in your hand."

My aunt sprang to her feet. She was so indignant that I believe she would have laid the whip across the man's shoulders, if his master had not pushed him back without ceremony. "A zealous servant," said the superintendent, smiling pleasantly. "Please excuse him."

My aunt pointed to the cell door.

"Open it," she said, "Let me see anything, rather than set eyes on that monster again!"

The firmness of her tone evidently surprised the superintendent. He knew nothing of the reserves of resolution in her, which the mere sight of the whip had called forth. The pallor had left her face; she trembled no longer; her fine gray eyes were bright and steady. "That brute has roused her," said the lawyer, looking back at the assistant, and whispering to me; "nothing will restrain her, David—she will have her way now."

CHAPTER V

The superintendent opened the cell door with his own hand.

We found ourselves in a narrow, lofty prison, like an apartment in a tower. High up, in one corner, the grim stone walls were pierced by a grated opening, which let in air and light. Seated on the floor, in the angle formed by the junction of two walls, we saw the superintendent's "lucky lunatic" at work, with a truss of loose straw on either side of him. The slanting rays of light from the high window streamed down on his prematurely gray hair, and showed us the strange yellow pallor of his complexion, and the youthful symmetry of his hands, nimbly occupied with their work. A heavy chain held him to the wall. It was not only fastened round his waist, it also fettered his legs between the knee and the ankle. At the same time, it was long enough to allow him a range of crippled movement, within a circle of five or six feet, as well as I could calculate at the time. Above his head, ready for use if required, hung a small chain evidently intended to confine his hands at the wrists. Unless I was deceived by his crouching attitude, he was small in stature. His ragged dress barely covered his emaciated form. In other and happier days, he must have been a well-made little man; his feet and ankles, like his hands, were finely and delicately formed. He was so absorbed in his employment that he had evidently not heard the talking outside his cell. It was only when the door was banged to by the assistant (who kept behind us, at a sign from the superintendent) that he looked up. We now saw his large vacantly-patient brown eyes, the haggard outline of his face, and his nervously sensitive lips. For a moment, he looked from one to the other of the visitors with a quiet childish curiosity. Then his wandering glances detected the assistant, waiting behind us with the whip still in his hand.

In an instant the whole expression of the madman's face changed. Ferocious hatred glittered in his eyes; his lips, suddenly retracted, showed his teeth like the teeth of a wild beast. My aunt perceived the direction in which he was looking, and altered her position so as to conceal from him the hateful figure with the whip, and to concentrate his attention on herself. With startling abruptness, the poor creature's expression changed once more. His eyes softened, a faint sad smile trembled on his lips. He dropped the straw

29

which he had been plaiting, and lifted his hands with a gesture of admiration. "The pretty lady!" he whispered to himself. "Oh, the pretty lady!"

He attempted to crawl out from the wall, as far as his chain would let him. At a sign from the superintendent he stopped, and sighed bitterly. "I wouldn't hurt the lady for the world," he said; "I beg your pardon, Mistress, if I have frightened you."

His voice was wonderfully gentle. But there was something strange in his accent—and there was perhaps a foreign formality in his addressing my aunt as "Mistress." Englishmen in general would have called her "ma'am."

We men kept our places at a safe distance from his chain. My aunt, with a woman's impulsive contempt of danger when her compassion is strongly moved, stepped forward to him. The superintendent caught her by the arm and checked her. "Take care," he said. "You don't know him as well as we do."

Jack's eyes turned on the superintendent, dilating slowly. His lips began to part again—I feared to see the ferocious expression in his face once more. I was wrong. In the very moment of another outbreak of rage, the unhappy man showed that he was still capable, under strong internal influence, of restraining himself. He seized the chain that held him to the wall in both hands, and wrung it with such convulsive energy that I almost expected to see the bones of his fingers start through the skin. His head dropped on his breast, his wasted figure quivered. It was only for an instant. When he looked up again, his poor vacant brown eyes turned on my aunt, dim with tears. She instantly shook off the superintendent's hold on her arm. Before it was possible to interfere, she was bending over Jack Straw, with one of her pretty white hands laid gently on his head.

"How your head burns, poor Jack!" she said simply. "Does my hand cool it?"

Still holding desperately by the chain, he answered like a timid child. "Yes, Mistress; your hand cools it. Thank you."

She took up a little straw hat on which he had been working when his door was opened. "This is very nicely done, Jack," she went on. "Tell me how you first came to make these pretty things with your straw."

He looked up at her with a sudden accession of confidence; her interest in the hat had flattered him.

"Once," he said, "there was a time when my hands were the maddest things about me. They used to turn against me and tear my hair and my flesh. An angel in a dream told me how to keep them quiet. An angel said, "Let them work at your straw." All day long I plaited my straw. I would have gone on all night too, if they would only have given me a light. My nights are bad, my nights are dreadful. The raw air eats into me, the black darkness frightens me. Shall I tell you what is the greatest blessing in the world? Daylight! Daylight!! Daylight!!!"

At each repetition of the word his voice rose. He was on the point of breaking into a scream, when he took a tighter turn of his chain and instantly silenced himself. "I am quiet, sir," he said, before the superintendent could reprove him.

My aunt added a word in his favor. "Jack has promised not to frighten me; and I am sure he will keep his word. Have you never had parents or friends to be kind to you, my poor fellow?" she asked, turning to him again.

He looked up at her. "Never," he said, "till you came here to see me." As he spoke, there was a flash of intelligence in the bright gratitude of his eyes. "Ask me something else," he pleaded; "and see how quietly I can answer you."

"Is it true, Jack, that you were once poisoned by accident, and nearly killed by it?"

"Yes!"

"Where was it?"

"Far away in another country. In the doctor's big room. In the time when I was the doctor's man."

"Who was the doctor?"

He put his hand to his head, "Give me more time," he said. "It hurts me

31

when I try to remember too much. Let me finish my hat first. I want to give you my hat when it's done. You don't know how clever I am with my fingers and thumbs. Just look and see!"

He set to work on the hat; perfectly happy while my aunt was looking at him. The lawyer was the unlucky person who produced a change for the worse. Having hitherto remained passive, this worthy gentleman seemed to think it was due to his own importance to take a prominent part in the proceedings. "My professional experience will come in well here," he said; "I mean to treat him as an unwilling witness; you will see we shall get something out of him in that way. Jack!"

The unwilling witness went on impenetrably with his work. The lawyer (keeping well out of reach of the range of the chain) raised his voice. "Hullo, there!" he cried, "you're not deaf, are you?"

Jack looked up, with an impish expression of mischief in his eyes. A man with a modest opinion of himself would have taken warning, and would have said no more. The lawyer persisted.

"Now, my man! let us have a little talk. 'Jack Straw' can't be your proper name. What is your name?"

"Anything you like," said Jack. "What's yours?"

"Oh, come! that won't do. You must have had a father and mother."

"Not that I know of."

"Where were you born?"

"In the gutter."

"How were you brought up?"

"Sometimes with a cuff on the head."

"And at other times?"

"At other times with a kick. Do be quiet, and let me finish my hat."

The discomfited lawyer tried a bribe as a last resource. He held up a shilling. "Do you see this?"

"No, I don't. I see nothing but my hat."

This reply brought the examination to an end. The lawyer looked at the superintendent, and said, "A hopeless case, sir." The superintendent looked at the lawyer, and answered, "Perfectly hopeless."

Jack finished his hat, and gave it to my aunt. "Do you like it, now it's done?" he asked.

"I like it very much," she answered: "and one of these days I shall trim it with ribbons, and wear it for your sake."

She appealed to the superintendent, holding out the hat to him.

"Look," she said. "There is not a false turn anywhere in all this intricate plaiting. Poor Jack is sane enough to fix his attention to this subtle work. Do you give him up as incurable, when he can do that?"

The superintendent waved away the question with his hand. "Purely mechanical," he replied. "It means nothing."

Jack touched my aunt. "I want to whisper," he said. She bent down to him, and listened.

I saw her smile, and asked, after we had left the asylum, what he had said. Jack had stated his opinion of the principal officer of Bethlehem Hospital in these words: "Don't you listen to him, Mistress; he's a poor half-witted creature. And short, too—not above six inches taller than I am!"

But my aunt had not done with Jack's enemy yet.

"I am sorry to trouble you, sir," she resumed—"I have something more to say before I go, and I wish to say it privately. Can you spare me a few minutes?"

The amiable superintendent declared that he was entirely at her service. She turned to Jack to say good-bye. The sudden discovery that she was about to leave him was more than he could sustain; he lost his self-control.

33

"Stay with me!" cried the poor wretch, seizing her by both hands. "Oh, be merciful, and stay with me!"

She preserved her presence of mind—she would permit no interference to protect her. Without starting back, without even attempting to release herself, she spoke to him quietly.

"Let us shake hands for to-day," she said; "you have kept your promise, Jack—you have been quiet and good. I must leave you for a while. Let me go."

He obstinately shook his head, and still held her.

"Look at me," she persisted, without showing any fear of him. "I want to tell you something. You are no longer a friendless creature, Jack. You have a friend in me. Look up."

Her clear firm tones had their effect on him; he looked up. Their eyes met.

"Now, let me go, as I told you."

He dropped her hand, and threw himself back in his corner and burst out crying.

"I shall never see her again," he moaned to himself. "Never, never, never again!"

"You shall see me to-morrow," she said.

He looked at her through his tears, and looked away again with an abrupt change to distrust. "She doesn't mean it," he muttered, still speaking to himself; "she only says it to pacify me."

"You shall see me to-morrow," my aunt reiterated; "I promise it."

He was cowed, but not convinced; he crawled to the full length of his chain, and lay down at her feet like a dog. She considered for a moment—and found her way to his confidence at last.

"Shall I leave you something to keep for me until I see you again?"

The idea struck him like a revelation: he lifted his head, and eyed her with breathless interest. She gave him a little ornamental handbag, in which she was accustomed to carry her handkerchief, and purse, and smelling-bottle.

"I trust it entirely to you, Jack: you shall give it back to me when we meet to-morrow."

Those simple words more than reconciled him to her departure—they subtly flattered his self-esteem.

"You will find your bag torn to pieces, to-morrow," the superintendent whispered, as the door was opened for us to go out.

"Pardon me, sir," my aunt replied; "I believe I shall find it quite safe."

The last we saw of poor Jack, before the door closed on him, he was hugging the bag in both arms, and kissing it.

CHAPTER VI

On our return to home, I found Fritz Keller smoking his pipe in the walled garden at the back of the house.

In those days, it may not be amiss to remark that merchants of the old-fashioned sort still lived over their counting-houses in the city. The late Mr. Wagner's place of business included two spacious houses standing together, with internal means of communication. One of these buildings was devoted to the offices and warehouses. The other (having the garden at the back) was the private residence.

Fritz advanced to meet me, and stopped, with a sudden change in his manner. "Something has happened," he said—"I see it in your face! Has the madman anything to do with it?"

"Yes. Shall I tell you what has happened, Fritz?"

"Not for the world. My ears are closed to all dreadful and distressing narratives. I will imagine the madman—let us talk of something else."

"You will probably see him, Fritz, in a few weeks' time."

"You don't mean to tell me he is coming into this house?"

"I am afraid it's likely, to say the least of it."

Fritz looked at me like a man thunderstruck. "There are some disclosures," he said, in his quaint way, "which are too overwhelming to be received on one's legs. Let us sit down."

He led the way to a summer-house at the end of the garden. On the wooden table, I observed a bottle of the English beer which my friend prized so highly, with glasses on either side of it.

"I had a presentiment that we should want a consoling something of this sort," said Fritz. "Fill your glass, David, and let out the worst of it at once, before we get to the end of the bottle."

I let out the best of it first—that is to say, I told him what I have related in the preceding pages. Fritz was deeply interested: full of compassion for Jack Straw, but not in the least converted to my aunt's confidence in him.

"Jack is supremely pitiable," he remarked; "but Jack is also a smoldering volcano—and smoldering volcanos burst into eruption when the laws of nature compel them. My only hope is in Mr. Superintendent. Surely he will not let this madman loose on us, with nobody but your aunt to hold the chain? What did she really say, when you left Jack, and had your private talk in the reception-room? One minute, my friend, before you begin," said Fritz, groping under the bench upon which we were seated. "I had a second presentiment that we might want a second bottle—and here it is! Fill your glass; and let us establish ourselves in our respective positions—you to administer, and I to sustain, a severe shock to the moral sense. I think, David, this second bottle is even more deliciously brisk than the first. Well, and what did your aunt say?"

My aunt had said much more than I could possibly tell him.

In substance it had come to this:—After seeing the whip, and seeing the chains, and seeing the man—she had actually determined to commit herself to the perilous experiment which her husband would have tried, if he had lived! As to the means of procuring Jack Straw's liberation from the Hospital, the powerful influence which had insisted on his being received by the Institution, in defiance of rules, could also insist on his release, and could be approached by the intercession of the same official person, whose interest in the matter had been aroused by Mr. Wagner in the last days of his life. Having set forth her plans for the future in these terms, my aunt appealed to the lawyer to state the expression of her wishes and intentions, in formal writing, as a preliminary act of submission towards the governors of the asylum.

"And what did the lawyer say to it?" Fritz inquired, after I had reported my aunt's proceedings thus far.

"The lawyer declined, Fritz, to comply with her request. He said, 'It would be inexcusable, even in a man, to run such a risk—I don't believe there is another woman in England who would think of such a thing.' Those were his words."

"Did they have any effect on her?"

"Not the least in the world. She apologized for having wasted his valuable time, and wished him good morning. 'If nobody will help me,' she said, quietly, 'I must help myself.' Then she turned to me. 'You have seen how carefully and delicately poor Jack can work,' she said; 'you have seen him tempted to break out, and yet capable of restraining himself in my presence. And, more than that, on the one occasion when he did lose his self-control, you saw how he recovered himself when he was calmly and kindly reasoned with. Are you content, David, to leave such a man for the rest of his life to the chains and the whip?' What could I say? She was too considerate to press me; she only asked me to think of it. I have been trying to think of it ever since—and the more I try, the more I dread the consequences if that madman is brought into the house."

Fritz shuddered at the prospect.

"On the day when Jack comes into the house, I shall go out of it," he said. The social consequences of my aunt's contemplated experiment suddenly struck him while he spoke. "What will Mrs. Wagner's friends think?" he asked piteously. "They will refuse to visit her—they will say she's mad herself."

"Don't let that distress you, gentlemen—I shan't mind what my friends say of me."

We both started in confusion to our feet. My aunt herself was standing at the open door of the summer-house with a letter in her hand.

"News from Germany, just come for you, Fritz."

With those words, she handed him the letter, and left us.

We looked at each other thoroughly ashamed of ourselves, if the truth must be told. Fritz cast an uneasy glance at the letter, and recognized the handwriting on the address. "From my father!" he said. As he opened the envelope a second letter enclosed fell out on the floor. He changed color as he picked it up, and looked at it. The seal was unbroken—the postmark was Wurzburg.

CHAPTER VII

Fritz kept the letter from Wurzburg unopened in his hand.

"It's not from Minna," he said; "the handwriting is strange to me. Perhaps my father knows something about it." He turned to his father's letter; read it; and handed it to me without a word of remark.

Mr. Keller wrote briefly as follows:—

"The enclosed letter has reached me by post, as you perceive, with written instructions to forward it to my son. The laws of honor guide me just as absolutely in my relations with my son as in my relations with any other gentleman. I forward the letter to you exactly as I have received it. But I cannot avoid noticing the postmark of the city in which the Widow Fontaine and her daughter are still living. If either Minna or her mother be the person who writes to you, I must say plainly that I forbid your entering into any correspondence with them. The two families shall never be connected by marriage while I live. Understand, my dear son, that this is said in your own best interests, and said, therefore, from the heart of your father who loves you."

While I was reading these lines Fritz had opened the letter from

Wurzburg. "It's long enough, at any rate," he said, turning over the closely-written pages to find the signature at the end.

"Well?" I asked.

"Well," Fritz repeated, "it's an anonymous letter. The signature is 'Your Unknown Friend.'"

"Perhaps it relates to Miss Minna, or to her mother," I suggested. Fritz turned back to the first page and looked up at me, red with anger. "More abominable slanders! More lies about Minna's mother!" he burst out. "Come here, David. Look at it with me. What do you say? Is it the writing of a woman or a man?"

The writing was so carefully disguised that it was impossible to answer his question. The letter (like the rest of the correspondence connected with this narrative) has been copied in duplicate and placed at my disposal. I reproduce it here for reasons which will presently explain themselves—altering nothing, not even the vulgar familiarity of the address.

"My good fellow, you once did me a kindness a long time since. Never mind what it was or who I am. I mean to do you a kindness in return. Let that be enough.

"You are in love with 'Jezebel's Daughter.' Now, don't be angry! I know you believe Jezebel to be a deeply-injured woman; I know you have been foolish enough to fight duels at Wurzburg in defense of her character.

"It is enough for you that she is a fond mother, and that her innocent daughter loves her dearly. I don't deny that she is a fond mother; but is the maternal instinct enough of itself to answer for a woman? Why, Fritz, a cat is a fond mother; but a cat scratches and swears for all that! And poor simple little Minna, who can see no harm in anybody, who can't discover wickedness when it stares her in the face—is she a trustworthy witness to the widow's character? Bah!

"Don't tear up my letter in a rage; I am not going to argue the question with you any further. Certain criminal circumstances have come to my knowledge, which point straight to this woman. I shall plainly relate those circumstances, out of my true regard for you, in the fervent hope that I may open your eyes to the truth.

"Let us go back to the death of Doctor-Professor Fontaine, at his apartments in the University of Wurzburg, on the 3rd of September, in the present year 1828.

"The poor man died of typhoid fever, as you know—and died in debt, through no extravagance on his own part, as you also know. He had outlived all his own relatives, and had no pecuniary hopes or expectations from anyone. Under these circumstances, he could only leave the written expression of his last wishes, in place of a will.

"This document committed his widow and child to the care of his widow's relations, in terms of respectful entreaty. Speaking next of himself, he directed that he should be buried with the strictest economy, so that he might cost the University as little as possible. Thirdly, and lastly, he appointed one of his brother professors to act as his sole executor, in disposing of those contents of his laboratory which were his own property at the time of his death.

"The written instructions to his executor are of such serious importance that I feel it my duty to copy them for you, word for word.

"Thus they begin:—

"'I hereby appoint my dear old friend and colleague, Professor Stein—now absent for a while at Munich, on University business—to act as my sole representative in the disposal of the contents of my laboratory, after my death. The various objects used in my chemical investigations, which are my own private property, will be all found arranged on the long deal table that stands between the two windows. They are to be offered for sale to my successor, in the first instance. If he declines to purchase them, they can then be sent to Munich, to be sold separately by the manufacturer, as occasion may offer. The furniture of the laboratory, both movable and stationary, belongs entirely to the University, excepting the contents of an iron safe built into the south wall of the room. As to these, which are my own sole property, I seriously enjoin my executor and representative to follow my instructions to the letter:—

"'(1) Professor Stein will take care to be accompanied by a competent witness, when he opens the safe in the wall.

"'(2) The witness will take down in writing, from the dictation of Professor Stein, an exact list of the contents of the safe. These are:—Bottles containing drugs, tin cases containing powders, and a small medicine-chest, having six compartments, each occupied by a labeled bottle, holding a liquid preparation.

"'(3) The written list being complete, I desire Professor Stein to empty every one of the bottles and cases, including the bottles in the medicine-chest, into the laboratory sink, with his own hands. He is also to be especially careful to destroy the labels on the bottles in the medicine-chest. These things done, he will sign the list, stating that the work of destruction is accomplished; and the witness present will add his signature. The document, thus attested, is to be placed in the care of the Secretary to the University.

"'My object in leaving these instructions is simply to prevent the dangerous results which might follow any meddling with my chemical preparations, after my death.

"'In almost every instance, these preparations are of a poisonous nature. Having made this statement, let me add, in justice to myself, that the sole motive for my investigations has been the good of my fellow-creatures.

"'I have been anxious, in the first place, to enlarge the list of curative medicines having poison for one of their ingredients. I have attempted, in the second place, to discover antidotes to the deadly action of those poisons, which (in cases of crime or accident) might be the means of saving life.

"'If I had been spared for a few years longer, I should so far have completed my labors as to have ventured on leaving them to be introduced to the medical profession by my successor. As it is—excepting one instance, in which I ran the risk, and was happily enabled to preserve the life of a poisoned man—I have not had time so completely to verify my theories, by practical experiment, as to justify me in revealing my discoveries to the scientific world for the benefit of mankind.

"'Under these circumstances, I am resigned to the sacrifice of my ambition—I only desire to do no harm. If any of my preparations, and more particularly those in the medicine-chest, fell into ignorant or wicked hands, I tremble when I think of the consequences which might follow. My one regret is, that I have not strength enough to rise from my bed, and do the good work of destruction myself. My friend and executor will take my place.

"'The key of the laboratory door, and the key of the safe, will be secured this day in the presence of my medical attendant, in a small wooden box. The box will be sealed (before the same witness) with my own seal. I shall keep it under my pillow, to give it myself to Professor Stein, if I live until he returns from Munich.

"'If I die while my executor is still absent, my beloved wife is the one person in the world whom I can implicitly trust to take charge of the sealed box. She will give it to Professor Stein, immediately on his return to Wurzburg; together with these instructions, which will be placed in the box along with the keys.'"

"There are the instructions, friend Fritz! They are no secret now. The Professor has felt it his duty to make them public in a court of law, in consequence of the events which followed Doctor Fontaine's death. You are interested in those events, and you shall be made acquainted with them before I close my letter.

"Professor Stein returned from Munich too late to receive the box from the hands of his friend and colleague. It was presented to him by the Widow Fontaine, in accordance with her late husband's wishes.

"The Professor broke the seal. Having read his Instructions, he followed them to the letter, the same day.

"Accompanied by the Secretary to the University, as a witness, he opened the laboratory door. Leaving the sale of the objects on the table to be provided for at a later date, he proceeded at once to take the list of the bottles and cases, whose contents he was bound to destroy. On opening the safe, these objects were found as the Instructions led him to anticipate: the dust lying thick on them vouched for their having been left undisturbed. The list being completed, the contents of the bottles and cases were thereupon thrown away by the Professor's own hand.

"On looking next, however, for the medicine-chest, no such thing was to be discovered in the safe. The laboratory was searched from end to end, on the chance that some mistake had been made. Still no medicine-chest was to be found.

"Upon this the Widow Fontaine was questioned. Did she know what had become of the medicine-chest? She was not even aware that such a thing existed. Had she been careful to keep the sealed box so safely that no other person could get at it? Certainly! She had kept it locked in one of her drawers, and the key in her pocket.

"The lock of the drawer, and the locks of the laboratory door and the safe, were examined. They showed no sign of having been tampered with. Persons employed in the University, who were certain to know, were asked if duplicate keys existed, and all united in answering in the negative. The medical attendant was examined, and declared that it was physically impossible for Doctor Fontaine to have left his bed, and visited the laboratory, between the time of writing his Instructions and the time of his death.

"While these investigations were proceeding, Doctor Fontaine's senior assistant obtained leave to examine through a microscope the sealing-wax left on the box which had contained the keys.

"The result of this examination, and of the chemical analyses which followed, proved that two different kinds of sealing-wax (both of the same red color, superficially viewed) had been used on the seal of the box—an undermost layer of one kind of wax, and an uppermost layer of another, mingled with the undermost in certain places only. The plain inference followed that the doctor's sealing-wax had been softened by heat so as to allow of the opening of the box, and that new sealing-wax had been afterwards added, and impressed by the Doctor's seal so that the executor might suspect nothing. Here, again, the evidence of the medical attendant (present at the time) proved that Doctor Fontaine had only used one stick of sealing-wax to secure the box. The seal itself was found in the possession of the widow; placed carelessly in the china tray in which she kept her rings after taking them off for the night.

"The affair is still under judicial investigation. I will not trouble you by reporting the further proceedings in detail.

"Of course, Widow Fontaine awaits the result of the investigation with the composure of conscious innocence. Of course, she has not only submitted to an examination of her lodgings, but has insisted on it. Of course, no red sealing-wax and no medicine-chest have been found. Of course, some thief unknown, for some purpose quite inconceivable, got at the box and the seal, between the Doctor's death and the return of the Professor from Munich, and read the Instructions and stole the terrible medicine-chest. Such is the theory adopted by the defense. If you can believe it—then I have written in vain. If, on the other hand, you are the sensible young man I take you to be, follow my advice. Pity poor little Minna as much as you please, but look out for another young lady with an unimpeachable mother; and think yourself lucky to have two such advisers as your excellent father, and Your Unknown Friend."

CHAPTER VIII

"I will lay any wager you like," said Fritz, when we had come to the end of the letter, "that the wretch who has written this is a woman."

"What makes you think so?"

"Because all the false reports about poor Madame Fontaine, when I was at Wurzburg, were traced to women. They envy and hate Minna's mother. She is superior to them in everything; handsome, distinguished, dresses to perfection, possesses all the accomplishments—a star, I tell you, a brilliant star among a set of dowdy domestic drudges. Isn't it infamous, without an atom of evidence against her, to take it for granted that she is guilty? False to her dead husband's confidence in her, a breaker of seals, a stealer of poisons— what an accusation against a defenseless woman! Oh, my poor dear Minna! how she must feel it; she doesn't possess her mother's strength of mind. I shall fly to Wurzburg to comfort her. My father may say what he pleases; I can't leave these two persecuted women without a friend. Suppose the legal decision goes against the widow? How do I know that judgment has not been pronounced already? The suspense is intolerable. Do you mean to tell me I am bound to obey my father, when his conduct is neither just nor reasonable?"

"Gently, Fritz—gently!"

"I tell you, David, I can prove what I say. Just listen to this. My father has never even seen Minna's mother; he blindly believes the scandals afloat about her—he denies that any woman can be generally disliked and distrusted among her neighbors without some good reason for it. I assure you, on my honor, he has no better excuse for forbidding me to marry Minna than that. Is it just, is it reasonable, to condemn a woman without first hearing what she has to say in her own defense? Ah, now indeed I feel the loss of my own dear mother! If she had been alive she would have exerted her influence, and have made my father ashamed of his own narrow prejudices. My position is maddening; my head whirls when I think of it. If I go to Wurzburg, my father will never speak to me again. If I stay here, I shall cut my throat."

There was still a little beer left in the bottom of the second bottle. Fritz poured it out, with a gloomy resolution to absorb it to the last drop.

I took advantage of this momentary pause of silence to recommend the virtue of patience to the consideration of my friend. News from Wurzburg, I reminded him, might be obtained in our immediate neighborhood by consulting a file of German journals, kept at a foreign coffee-house. By way of strengthening the good influence of this suggestion, I informed Fritz that I expected to be shortly sent to Frankfort, as the bearer of a business communication addressed to Mr. Keller by my aunt; and I offered privately to make inquiries, and (if possible) even to take messages to Wurzburg—if he would only engage to wait patiently for the brighter prospects that might show themselves in the time to come.

I had barely succeeded in tranquilizing Fritz, when my attention was claimed by the more serious and pressing subject of the liberation of Jack Straw. My aunt sent to say that she wished to see me.

I found her at her writing-table, with the head-clerk established at the desk opposite.

Mr. Hartrey was quite as strongly opposed as the lawyer to any meddling with the treatment of mad people on the part of my aunt. But he placed his duty to his employer before all other considerations; and he rendered, under respectful protest, such services as were required of him. He was now engaged in drawing out the necessary memorials and statements, under the instructions of my aunt. Her object in sending for me was to inquire if I objected to making fair copies of the rough drafts thus produced. In the present stage of the affair, she was unwilling to take the clerks at the office into her confidence. As a matter of course, I followed Mr. Hartrey's example, and duly subordinated my own opinions to my aunt's convenience.

On the next day, she paid her promised visit to poor Jack.

The bag which she had committed to his care was returned to her without the slightest injury. Naturally enough, she welcomed this circumstance as offering a new encouragement to the design that she had in view. Mad Jack could not only understand a responsibility, but could prove himself worthy of it. The superintendent smiled, and said, in his finely ironical way, "I never denied, madam, that Jack was cunning."

From that date, my aunt's venturesome enterprise advanced towards completion with a rapidity that astonished us.

Applying, in the first instance, to the friend of her late husband, holding a position in the Royal Household, she was met once more by the inevitable objections to her design. She vainly pleaded that her purpose was to try the experiment modestly in the one pitiable case of Jack Straw, and that she would willingly leave any further development of her husband's humane project to persons better qualified to encounter dangers and difficulties than herself. The only concession that she could obtain was an appointment for a second interview, in the presence of a gentleman whose opinion it would be important to consult. He was one of the physicians attached to the Court, and he was known to be a man of liberal views in his profession. Mrs. Wagner would do well, in her own interests, to be guided by his disinterested advice.

Keeping this second appointment, my aunt provided herself with a special means of persuasion in the shape of her husband's diary, containing his unfinished notes on the treatment of insanity by moral influence.

As she had anticipated, the physician invited to advise her was readier to read the notes than to listen to her own imperfect explanation of the object in view. He was strongly impressed by the novelty and good sense of the ideas that her husband advocated, and was candid enough openly to acknowledge it. But he, too, protested against any attempt on the part of a woman to carry out any part of the proposed reform, even on the smallest scale. Exasperated by these new remonstrances, my aunt's patience gave way. Refusing to submit herself to the physician's advice, she argued the question boldly from her own point of view. The discussion was at its height, when the door of the room was suddenly opened from without. A lady in walking-costume appeared, with two ladies in attendance on her. The two gentlemen started to their feet, and whispered to my aunt, "The Princess!"

This was the exalted personage whom the superintendent at Bethlehem had been too discreet to describe more particularly as a daughter of George the Third. Passing the door on her way to the Palace-gardens, the Princess had heard the contending voices, and the name of Jack distinctly pronounced in a woman's tones. Inheriting unusually vigorous impulses of curiosity from her august father, her Highness opened the door and joined the party without ceremony.

"What are you quarreling about?" inquired the Princess. "And who is this lady?"

Mrs. Wagner was presented, to answer for herself. She made the best of the golden opportunity that had fallen into her hands. The Princess was first astonished, then interested, then converted to my aunt's view of the case. In the monotonous routine of Court life, here was a romantic adventure in which even the King's daughter could take some share. Her Highness quoted Boadicea, Queen Elizabeth, and Joan of Arc, as women who had matched the men on their own ground—and complimented Mrs. Wagner as a heroine of the same type.

"You are a fine creature," said the Princess, "and you may trust to me to help you with all my heart. Come to my apartments tomorrow at this time—and tell poor Jack that I have not forgotten him."

Assailed by Royal influence, all the technical obstacles that lawyers, doctors, and governors could raise to the liberation of Jack Straw were set aside by an ingenious appeal to the letter of the law, originating in a suggestion made by the Princess herself.

"It lies in a nutshell, my dear," said her Highness to my aunt. "They tell me I broke the rules when I insisted on having Jack admitted to the Hospital. Now, your late husband was one of the governors; and you are his sole executor. Very good. As your husband's representative, complain of the violation of the rules, and insist on the discharge of Jack. He occupies a place which ought to be filled by an educated patient in a higher rank of life. Oh, never mind me! I shall express my regret for disregarding the regulations—and, to prove my sincerity, I shall consent to the poor creature's dismissal, and assume the whole responsibility of providing for him myself. There is the way out of our difficulty. Take it—and you shall have Jack whenever you want him."

In three weeks from that time, the "dangerous lunatic" was free (as our friend the lawyer put it) to "murder Mrs. Wagner, and to burn the house down."

How my aunt's perilous experiment was conducted—in what particulars it succeeded and in what particulars it failed—I am unable to state as an eyewitness, owing to my absence at the time. This curious portion of the narrative will be found related by Jack himself, on a page still to come. In the meanwhile, the course of events compels me to revert to the circumstances which led to my departure from London.

While Mrs. Wagner was still in attendance at the palace, a letter reached her from Mr. Keller, stating the necessity of increasing the number of clerks at the Frankfort branch of our business. Closely occupied as she then was, she found time to provide me with those instructions to her German partners, preparing them for the coming employment of women in their office, to which she had first alluded when the lawyer and I had our interview with her after the reading of the will.

"The cause of the women," she said to me, "must not suffer because I happen to be just now devoted to the cause of poor Jack. Go at once to Frankfort, David. I have written enough to prepare my partners there for a change in the administration of the office, and to defer for the present the proposed enlargement of our staff of clerks. The rest you can yourself explain from your own knowledge of the plans that I have in contemplation. Start on your journey as soon as possible—and understand that you are to say No positively, if Fritz proposes to accompany you. He is not to leave London without the express permission of his father."

Fritz did propose to accompany me, the moment he heard of my journey. I must own that I thought the circumstances excused him.

On the previous evening, we had consulted the German newspapers at the coffee-house, and had found news from Wurzburg which quite overwhelmed my excitable friend.

Being called upon to deliver their judgment, the authorities presiding at the legal inquiry into the violation of the seals and the loss of the medicine-chest failed to agree in opinion, and thus brought the investigation to a most unsatisfactory end. The moral effect of this division among the magistrates was unquestionably to cast a slur on the reputation of Widow Fontaine. She was not pronounced to be guilty—but she was also not declared to be innocent. Feeling, no doubt, that her position among her neighbors had now become unendurable, she and her daughter had left Wurzburg. The newspaper narrative added that their departure had been privately accomplished. No information could be obtained of the place of their retreat.

But for this last circumstance, I believe Fritz would have insisted on traveling with me. Ignorant of what direction to begin the search for Minna and her mother, he consented to leave me to look for traces of them in Germany, while he remained behind to inquire at the different foreign hotels, on the chance that they might have taken refuge in London.

The next morning I started for Frankfort.

My spirits were high as I left the shores of England. I had a young man's hearty and natural enjoyment of change. Besides, it flattered my self-esteem to feel that I was my aunt's business-representative; and I was almost equally proud to be Fritz's confidential friend. Never could any poor human creature have been a more innocent instrument of mischief in the hands of Destiny than I was, on that fatal journey. The day was dark, when the old weary way of traveling brought me at last to Frankfort. The unseen prospect, at the moment when I stepped out of the mail-post-carriage, was darker still.

CHAPTER IX

I had just given a porter the necessary directions for taking my portmanteau to Mr. Keller's house, when I heard a woman's voice behind me asking the way to the Poste Restante—or, in our roundabout English phrase, the office of letters to be left till called for.

The voice was delightfully fresh and sweet, with an undertone of sadness, which made it additionally interesting. I did what most other young men in my place would have done—I looked round directly.

Yes! the promise of the voice was abundantly kept by the person. She was quite a young girl, modest and ladylike; a little pale and careworn, poor thing, as if her experience of life had its sad side already. Her face was animated by soft sensitive eyes—the figure supple and slight, the dress of the plainest material, but so neatly made and so perfectly worn that I should have doubted her being a German girl, if I had not heard the purely South-German accent in which she put her question. It was answered, briefly and civilly, by the conductor of the post-carriage in which I had traveled. But, at that hour, the old court-yard of the post-office was thronged with people arriving and departing, meeting their friends and posting their letters. The girl was evidently not used to crowds. She was nervous and confused. After advancing a few steps in the direction pointed out to her, she stopped in bewilderment, hustled by busy people, and evidently in doubt already about which way she was to turn next.

If I had followed the strict line of duty, I suppose I should have turned my steps in the direction of Mr. Keller's house. I followed my instincts instead, and offered my services to the young lady. Blame the laws of Nature and the attraction between the sexes. Don't blame me.

"I heard you asking for the post-office," I said. "Will you allow me to show you the way?"

She looked at me, and hesitated. I felt that I was paying the double penalty of being a young man, and of being perhaps a little too eager as well.

"Forgive me for venturing to speak to you," I pleaded. "It is not very pleasant for a young lady to find herself alone in such a crowded place as this. I only ask permission to make myself of some trifling use to you."

She looked at me again, and altered her first opinion.

"You are very kind, sir; I will thankfully accept your assistance."

"May I offer you my arm?"

She declined this proposal—with perfect amiability, however. "Thank you, sir, I will follow you, if you please."

I pushed my way through the crowd, with the charming stranger close at my heels. Arrived at the post-office, I drew aside to let her make her own inquiries. Would she mention her name? No; she handed in a passport, and asked if there was a letter waiting for the person named in it. The letter was found; but was not immediately delivered. As well as I could understand, the postage had been insufficiently paid, and the customary double-rate was due. The young lady searched in the pocket of her dress—a cry of alarm escaped her. "Oh!" she exclaimed, "I have lost my purse, and the letter is so important!"

It occurred to me immediately that she had had her pocket picked by some thief in the crowd. The clerk thought so too. He looked at the clock. "You must be quick about it if you return for the letter," he said, "the office closes in ten minutes."

She clasped her hands in despair. "It's more than ten minutes' walk," she said, "before I can get home."

51

I immediately offered to lend her the money. "It is such a very small sum," I reminded her, "that it would be absurd to consider yourself under any obligation to me."

Between her eagerness to get possession of the letter, and her doubt of the propriety of accepting my offer, she looked sadly embarrassed, poor soul.

"You are very good to me," she said confusedly; "but I am afraid it might not be quite right in me to borrow money of a stranger, however little it may be. And, even if I did venture, how am I——?" She looked at me shyly, and shrank from finishing the sentence.

"How are you to pay it back?" I suggested.

"Yes, sir."

"Oh, it's not worth the trouble of paying back. Give it to the first poor person you meet with to-morrow." I said this, with the intention of reconciling her to the loan of the money. It had exactly the contrary effect on this singularly delicate and scrupulous girl. She drew back a step directly.

"No, I couldn't do that," she said. "I could only accept your kindness, if——" She stopped again. The clerk looked once more at the clock. "Make up your mind, Miss, before it's too late."

In her terror of not getting the letter that day, she spoke out plainly at last. "Will you kindly tell me, sir, to what address I can return the money when I get home?"

I paid for the letter first, and then answered the question.

"If you will be so good as to send it to Mr. Keller's house——"

Before I could add the name of the street, her pale face suddenly flushed. "Oh!" she exclaimed impulsively, "do you know Mr. Keller?"

A presentiment of the truth occurred to my mind for the first time.

"Yes," I said; "and his son Fritz too."

She trembled; the color that had risen in her face left it instantly; she looked away from me with a pained, humiliated expression. Doubt was no longer possible. The charming stranger was Fritz's sweetheart—and "Jezebel's Daughter."

My respect for the young lady forbade me to attempt any concealment of the discovery that I had made. I said at once, "I believe I have the honor of speaking to Miss Minna Fontaine?"

She looked at me in wonder, not unmixed with distrust.

"How do you know who I am?" she asked.

"I can easily tell you, Miss Minna. I am David Glenney, nephew of Mrs. Wagner, of London. Fritz is staying in her house, and he and I have talked about you by the hour together."

The poor girl's face, so pale and sad the moment before, became radiant with happiness. "Oh!" she cried innocently, "has Fritz not forgotten me?"

Even at this distance of time, my memory recalls her lovely dark eyes riveted in breathless interest on my face, as I spoke of Fritz's love and devotion, and told her that she was still the one dear image in his thoughts by day, in his dreams by night. All her shyness vanished. She impulsively gave me her hand. "How can I be grateful enough to the good angel who has brought us together!" she exclaimed. "If we were not in the street, I do believe, Mr. David, I should go down on my knees to thank you! You have made me the happiest girl living." Her voice suddenly failed her; she drew her veil down. "Don't mind me," she said; "I can't help crying for joy."

Shall I confess what my emotions were? For the moment, I forgot my own little love affair in England—and envied Fritz from the bottom of my heart.

The chance-passengers in the street began to pause and look at us. I offered Minna my arm, and asked permission to attend her on the way home.

"I should like it," she answered, with a friendly frankness that charmed me. "But you are expected at Mr. Keller's—you must go there first."

"May I call and see you to-morrow?" I persisted, "and save you the trouble of sending my money to Mr. Keller's?"

She lifted her veil and smiled at me brightly through her tears. "Yes," she said; "come to-morrow and be introduced to my mother. Oh! how glad my dear mother will be to see you, when I tell her what has happened! I am a selfish wretch; I have not borne my sorrow and suspense as I ought; I have made her miserable about me, because I was miserable about Fritz. It's all over now. Thank you again and again. There is our address on that card. No, no, we must say good-bye till to-morrow. My mother is waiting for her letter; and Mr. Keller is wondering what has become of you." She pressed my hand warmly and left me.

On my way alone to Mr. Keller's house, I was not quite satisfied with myself. The fear occurred to me that I might have spoken about Fritz a little too freely, and might have excited hopes which could never be realized. The contemplation of the doubtful future began to oppress my mind. Minna might have reason to regret that she had ever met with me.

I was received by Mr. Keller with truly German cordiality. He and his partner Mr. Engelman—one a widower, the other an old bachelor—lived together in the ancient building, in Main Street, near the river, which served for house and for offices alike.

The two old gentlemen offered the completest personal contrast imaginable. Mr. Keller was lean, tall, and wiry—a man of considerable attainments beyond the limits of his business, capable (when his hot temper was not excited) of speaking sensibly and strongly on any subject in which he was interested. Mr. Engelman, short and fat, devoted to the office during the hours of business, had never read a book in his life, and had no aspiration beyond the limits of his garden and his pipe. "In my leisure moments," he used to say, "give me my flowers, my pipe, and my peace of mind—and I ask no more." Widely as they differed in character, the two partners had the truest regard for one another. Mr. Engelman believed Mr. Keller to be the most accomplished and remarkable man in Germany. Mr. Keller was as firmly persuaded, on his side, that Mr. Engelman was an angel in sweetness of temper, and a model of modest and unassuming good sense. Mr. Engelman listened to Mr. Keller's learned talk with an ignorant admiration which knew no limit. Mr. Keller, detesting tobacco in all its forms, and taking no sort of interest in horticulture, submitted to the fumes of Mr. Engelman's pipe, and passed hours in Mr. Engelman's garden without knowing the names of nine-tenths of the flowers that grew in it. There are still such men to be found in Germany and in England; but, oh! dear me, the older I get the fewer I find there are of them.

The two old friends and partners were waiting for me to join them at their early German supper. Specimens of Mr. Engelman's flowers adorned the table in honor of my arrival. He presented me with a rose from the nosegay when I entered the room.

"And how did you leave dear Mrs. Wagner?" he inquired.

"And how is my boy Fritz?" asked Mr. Keller.

I answered in terms which satisfied them both, and the supper proceeded gaily. But when the table was cleared, and Mr. Engelman had lit his pipe, and I had kept him company with a cigar, then Mr. Keller put the fatal question. "And now tell me, David, do you come to us on business or do you come to us on pleasure?"

I had no alternative but to produce my instructions, and to announce the contemplated invasion of the office by a select army of female clerks. The effect produced by the disclosure was highly characteristic of the widely different temperaments of the two partners.

Mild Mr. Engelman laid down his pipe, and looked at Mr. Keller in helpless silence.

Irritable Mr. Keller struck his fist on the table, and appealed to Mr. Engelman with fury in his looks.

"What did I tell you," he asked, "when we first heard that Mr. Wagner's widow was appointed head-partner in the business? How many opinions of philosophers on the moral and physical incapacities of women did I quote? Did I, or did I not, begin with the ancient Egyptians, and end with Doctor

Bernastrokius, our neighbor in the next street?"

Poor Mr. Engelman looked frightened.

"Don't be angry, my dear friend," he said softly.

"Angry?" repeated Mr. Keller, more furiously than ever. "My good Engelman, you never were more absurdly mistaken in your life! I am delighted. Exactly what I expected, exactly what I predicted, has come to pass. Put down your pipe! I can bear a great deal—but tobacco smoke is beyond me at such a crisis as this. And do for once overcome your constitutional indolence. Consult your memory; recall my own words when we were first informed that we had a woman for head-partner."

"She was a very pretty woman when I first saw her," Mr. Engelman remarked.

"Pooh!" cried Mr. Keller.

"I didn't mean to offend you," said Mr. Engelman. "Allow me to present you with one of my roses as a peace-offering."

"Will you be quiet, and let me speak?"

"My dear Keller, I am always too glad to hear you speak! You put ideas into my poor head, and my poor head lets them out, and then you put them in again. What noble perseverance! If I live a while longer I do really think you will make a clever man of me. Let me put the rose in your buttonhole for you. And I say, I wish you would allow me to go on with my pipe."

Mr. Keller made a gesture of resignation, and gave up his partner in despair. "I appeal to you, David," he said, and poured the full flow of his learning and his indignation into my unlucky ears.

Mr. Engelman, enveloped in clouds of tobacco-smoke, enjoyed in silence the composing influence of his pipe. I said, "Yes, sir," and "No, sir," at the right intervals in the flow of Mr. Keller's eloquence. At this distance of time, I cannot pretend to report the long harangue of which I was made the victim. In substance, Mr. Keller held that there were two irremediable vices in the composition of women. Their dispositions presented, morally speaking, a disastrous mixture of the imitativeness of a monkey and the restlessness of a child. Having proved this by copious references to the highest authorities, Mr. Keller logically claimed my aunt as a woman, and, as such, not only incapable of "letting well alone," but naturally disposed to imitate her husband on the most superficial and defective sides of his character. "I predicted, David, that the fatal disturbance of our steady old business was now only a question of time—and there, in Mrs. Wagner's ridiculous instructions, is the fulfillment of my prophecy!"

Before we went to bed that night, the partners arrived at two resolutions. Mr. Keller resolved to address a written remonstrance to my aunt. Mr. Engelman resolved to show me his garden the first thing in the morning.

CHAPTER X

On the afternoon of the next day, while my two good friends were still occupied by the duties of the office, I stole out to pay my promised visit to Minna and Minna's mother.

It was impossible not to arrive at the conclusion that they were indeed in straitened circumstances. Their lodgings were in the cheap suburban quarter of Frankfort on the left bank of the river. Everything was scrupulously neat, and the poor furniture was arranged with taste—but no dexterity of management could disguise the squalid shabbiness of the sitting-room into which I was shown. I could not help thinking how distressed Fritz would feel, if he could have seen his charming Minna in a place so unworthy of her as this.

The rickety door opened, and the "Jezebel" of the anonymous letter (followed by her daughter) entered the room.

There are certain remarkable women in all countries who, whatever sphere they may be seen in, fill that sphere as completely as a great actor fills the stage. Widow Fontaine was one of these noteworthy persons. The wretched little room seemed to disappear when she softly glided into it; and even the pretty Minna herself receded into partial obscurity in her mother's presence. And yet there was nothing in the least obtrusive in the manner of Madame Fontaine, and nothing remarkable in her stature. Her figure, reaching to no more than the middle height, was the well-rounded figure of a woman approaching forty years of age. The influence she exercised was, in part, attributable, as I suppose, to the supple grace of all her movements; in part, to the commanding composure of her expression and the indescribable witchery of her manner. Her dark eyes, never fully opened in my remembrance, looked at me under heavy overhanging upper eyelids. Her enemies saw something sensual in their strange expression. To my mind it was rather something furtively cruel—except when she looked at her daughter. Sensuality shows itself most plainly in the excessive development of the lower part of the face. Madame Fontaine's lips were thin, and her chin was too small. Her profuse black hair was just beginning to be streaked with gray. Her complexion wanted color. In spite of these drawbacks, she was still a striking, I might almost say a startling, creature, when you first looked at her. And, though she only wore the plainest widow's weeds, I don't scruple to assert that she was the most perfectly dressed woman I ever saw.

Minna made a modest attempt to present me in due form. Her mother put her aside playfully, and held out both her long white powerful hands to me as cordially as if we had known each other for years.

"I wait to prove other people before I accept them for my friends," she said. "Mr. David, you have been more than kind to my daughter—and you are my friend at our first meeting."

I believe I repeat the words exactly. I wish I could give any adequate idea of the exquisite charm of voice and manner which accompanied them.

And yet, I was not at my ease with her—I was not drawn to her irresistibly, as I had felt drawn to her daughter. Those dark, steady, heavy-lidded eyes of hers seemed to be looking straight into my heart, and surprising all my secrets. To say that I actually distrusted and disliked her would be far from the truth. Distrust and dislike would have protected me, in some degree at least, from feeling her influence as I certainly did feel it. How that influence was exerted—whether it was through her eyes, or through her manner, or, to speak the jargon of these latter days, through some "magnetic emanation" from her, which invisibly overpowered me—is more than I can possibly say.

I can only report that she contrived by slow degrees to subject the action of my will more and more completely to the action of hers, until I found myself answering her most insidious questions as unreservedly as if she had been in very truth my intimate and trusted friend.

"And is this your first visit to Frankfort, Mr. David?" she began.

"Oh, no, madam! I have been at Frankfort on two former occasions."

"Ah, indeed? And have you always stayed with Mr. Keller?"

"Always."

She looked unaccountably interested when she heard that reply, brief as it was.

"Then, of course, you are intimate with him," she said. "Intimate enough, perhaps, to ask a favor or to introduce a friend?"

I made a futile attempt to answer this cautiously.

"As intimate, madam, as a young clerk in the business can hope to be with a partner," I said.

"A clerk in the business?" she repeated. "I thought you lived in London, with your aunt."

Here Minna interposed for the first time.

"You forget, mamma, that there are three names in the business. The inscription over the door in Main Street is Wagner, Keller, and Engelman. Fritz once told me that the office here in Frankfort was only the small office— and the grand business was Mr. Wagner's business in London. Am I right, Mr. David?"

"Quite right, Miss Minna. But we have no such magnificent flower-garden at the London house as Mr. Engelman's flower-garden here. May I offer you a nosegay which he allowed me to gather?"

I had hoped to make the flowers a means of turning the conversation to more interesting topics. But the widow resumed her questions, while Minna was admiring the flowers.

"Then you are Mr. Wagner's clerk?" she persisted.

"I was Mr. Wagner's clerk. Mr. Wagner is dead."

"Ha! And who takes care of the great business now?"

Without well knowing why, I felt a certain reluctance to speak of my aunt and her affairs. But Widow Fontaine's eyes rested on me with a resolute expectation in them which I felt myself compelled to gratify. When she understood that Mr. Wagner's widow was now the chief authority in the business, her curiosity to hear everything that I could tell her about my aunt became all but insatiable. Minna's interest in the subject was, in quite another way, as vivid as her mother's. My aunt's house was the place to which cruel Mr. Keller had banished her lover. The inquiries of the mother and daughter followed each other in such rapid succession that I cannot pretend to remember them now. The last question alone remains vividly impressed on my memory, in connection with the unexpected effect which my answer produced. It was put by the widow in these words:

"Your aunt is interested, of course, in the affairs of her partners in this place. Is it possible, Mr. David, that she may one day take the journey to Frankfort?"

"It is quite likely, madam, that my aunt may be in Frankfort on business before the end of the year."

As I replied in those terms the widow looked round slowly at her daughter. Minna was evidently quite as much at a loss to understand the look as I was. Madame Fontaine turned to me again, and made an apology.

"Pardon me, Mr. David, there is a little domestic duty that I had forgotten." She crossed the room to a small table, on which writing-materials were placed, wrote a few lines, and handed the paper, without enclosing it, to Minna. "Give that, my love, to our good friend downstairs—and, while you are in the kitchen, suppose you make the tea. You will stay and drink tea with us, Mr. David? It is our only luxury, and we always make it ourselves."

My first impulse was to find an excuse for declining the invitation. There was something in the air of mystery with which Madame Fontaine performed her domestic duties that was not at all to my taste. But Minna pleaded with me to say Yes. "Do stay with us a little longer," she said, in her innocently frank way, "we have so few pleasures in this place." I might, perhaps, have even resisted Minna—but her mother literally laid hands on me. She seated herself, with the air of an empress, on a shabby little sofa in the corner of the room, and beckoning me to take my place by her side, laid her cool firm hand persuasively on mine. Her touch filled me with a strange sense of disturbance, half pleasurable, half painful—I don't know how to describe it. Let me only record that I yielded, and that Minna left us together.

"I want to tell you the whole truth," said Madame Fontaine, as soon as we were alone; "and I can only do so in the absence of my daughter. You must have seen for yourself that we are very poor?"

Her hand pressed mine gently. I answered as delicately as I could—I said I was sorry, but not surprised, to hear it.

"When you kindly helped Minna to get that letter yesterday," she went on, "you were the innocent means of inflicting a disappointment on me— one disappointment more, after others that had gone before it. I came here to place my case before some wealthy relatives of mine in this city. They refused to assist me. I wrote next to other members of my family, living in Brussels. The letter of yesterday contained their answer. Another refusal! The landlady of this house is an afflicted creature, with every claim on my sympathies; she, too, is struggling with poverty. If I failed to pay her, it would be too cruel. Only yesterday I felt it my hard duty to give her notice of our departure in a week more. I have just written to recall that notice. The reason is, that I see a gleam of hope in the future—and you, Mr. David, are the friend who has shown it to me."

I was more than surprised at this. "May I ask how?" I said.

She patted my hand with a playful assumption of petulance.

"A little more patience," she rejoined; "and you shall soon hear. If I had only myself to think of, I should not feel the anxieties that now trouble me. I could take a housekeeper's place to-morrow. Yes! I was brought up among surroundings of luxury and refinement; I descended in rank when I married— but for all that, I could fill a domestic employment without repining my lot, without losing my self-respect. Adversity is a hard teacher of sound lessons, David. May I call you David? And if you heard of a housekeeper's place vacant, would you tell me of it?"

I could hardly understand whether she was in jest or in earnest. She went on without waiting for me to reply.

"But I have my daughter to think of," she resumed, "and to add to my anxieties my daughter has given her heart to Mr. Keller's son. While I and my dear Minna had only our own interests to consider, we might have earned our daily bread together; we might have faced the future with courage. But what might once have been the calm course of our lives is now troubled by a third person—a rival with me in my daughter's love—and, worse still, a man who is forbidden to marry her. Is it wonderful that I feel baffled, disheartened, helpless? Oh, I am not exaggerating! I know my child's nature. She is too delicate, too exquisitely sensitive, for the rough world she lives in. When she loves, she loves with all her heart and soul. Day by day I have seen her pining and fading under her separation from Fritz. You have revived her hopes for the moment—but the prospect before her remains unaltered. If she loses Fritz she will die of a broken heart. Oh, God! the one creature I love—and how I am to help her and save her I don't know!"

For the first time, I heard the fervor of true feeling in her voice. She turned aside from me, and hid her face with a wild gesture of despair that was really terrible to see. I tried, honestly tried, to comfort her.

"Of one thing at least you may be sure," I said. "Fritz's whole heart is given to your daughter. He will be true to her, and worthy of her, through all trials."

"I don't doubt it," she answered sadly, "I have nothing to say against my girl's choice. Fritz is good, and Fritz is true, as you say. But you forget his father. Personally, mind, I despise Mr. Keller." She looked round at me with unutterable contempt flashing through the tears that filled her eyes. "A man who listens to every lie that scandal can utter against the character of a helpless woman—who gives her no opportunity of defending herself (I have written to him and received no answer)—who declares that his son shall never marry my daughter (because we are poor, of course); and who uses attacks on my reputation which he has never verified, as the excuse for his brutal conduct—can anybody respect such a man as that? And yet on this despicable creature my child's happiness and my child's life depend! For her sake, no matter what my own feeling may be, I must stoop to defend myself. I must make my opportunity of combating his cowardly prejudice, and winning his good opinion in spite of himself. How am I to get a hearing? how am I to approach him? I understand that you are not in a position to help me. But you have done wonders for me nevertheless, and God bless you for it!"

She lifted my hand to her lips. I foresaw what was coming; I tried to speak. But she gave me no opportunity; her eloquent enthusiasm rushed into a new flow of words.

"Yes, my best of friends, my wisest of advisers," she went on; "you have suggested the irresistible interference of a person whose authority is supreme. Your excellent aunt is the head of the business; Mr. Keller must listen to his charming chief. There is my gleam of hope. On that chance, I will sell the last few valuables I possess, and wait till Mrs. Wagner arrives at Frankfort. You start, David! What is there to alarm you? Do you suppose me capable of presuming on your aunt's kindness—of begging for favors which it may not be perfectly easy for her to grant? Mrs. Wagner knows already from Fritz what our situation is. Let her only see my Minna; I won't intrude on her myself. My daughter shall plead for me; my daughter shall ask for all I want—an interview with Mr. Keller, and permission to speak in my own defense. Tell me, honestly, am I expecting too much, if I hope that your aunt will persuade Fritz's father to see me?"

It sounded modestly enough in words. But I had my own doubts, nevertheless.

I had left Mr. Keller working hard at his protest against the employment of women in the office, to be sent to my aunt by that day's post. Knowing them both as I did, I thought it at least probable that a written controversy might be succeeded by a personal estrangement. If Mr. Keller proved obstinate, Mrs. Wagner would soon show him that she had a will of her own. Under those circumstances, no favors could be asked, no favors could be granted—and poor Minna's prospects would be darker than ever.

This was one view of the case. I must own, however, that another impression had been produced on me. Something in Madame Fontaine's manner suggested that she might not be quite so modest in her demands on my aunt, when they met at Frankfort, as she had led me to believe. I was vexed with myself for having spoken too unreservedly, and was quite at a loss to decide what I ought to say in answer to the appeal that had been made to me. In this state of perplexity I was relieved by a welcome interruption. Minna's voice reached us from the landing outside. "I have both hands engaged," she said; "please let me in."

I ran to the door. The widow laid her finger on her lips. "Not a word, mind, to Minna!" she whispered. "We understand each other—don't we?"

I said, "Yes, certainly." And so the subject was dropped for the rest of the evening.

The charming girl came in carrying the tea-tray. She especially directed my attention to a cake which she had made that day with her own hands. "I can cook," she said, "and I can make my own dresses—and if Fritz is a poor man when he marries me, I can save him the expense of a servant." Our talk at the tea-table was, I dare say, too trifling to be recorded. I only remember that I enjoyed it. Later in the evening, Minna sang to me. I heard one of those simple German ballads again, not long since, and the music brought the tears into my eyes.

The moon rose early that night. When I looked at my watch, I found that it was time to go. Minna was at the window, admiring the moonlight. "On such a beautiful night," she said, "it seems a shame to stay indoors. Do let us walk a part of the way back with Mr. David, mamma! Only as far as the bridge, to see the moon on the river."

Her mother consented, and we three left the house together.

Arrived at the bridge, we paused to look at the view. But the clouds were rising already, and the moonlight only showed itself at intervals. Madame Fontaine said she smelt rain in the air, and took her daughter's arm to go home. I offered to return with them as far as their own door; but they positively declined to delay me on my way back. It was arranged that I should call on them again in a day or two.

Just as we were saying good-night, the fitful moonlight streamed out brightly again through a rift in the clouds. At the same moment a stout old gentleman, smoking a pipe, sauntered past us on the pavement, noticed me as he went by, stopped directly, and revealed himself as Mr. Engelman. "Good-night, Mr. David," said the widow. The moon shone full on her as she gave me her hand; Minna standing behind her in the shadow. In a moment more the two ladies had left us.

Mr. Engelman's eyes followed the smoothly gliding figure of the widow, until it was lost to view at the end of the bridge. He laid his hand eagerly on my arm. "David!" he said, "who is that glorious creature?"

"Which of the two ladies do you mean?" I asked, mischievously.

"The one with the widow's cap, of course!"

"Do you admire the widow, sir?"

"Admire her!" repeated Mr. Engelman. "Look here, David!" He showed me the long porcelain bowl of his pipe. "My dear boy, she has done what no woman ever did with me yet—she has put my pipe out!"

CHAPTER XI

There was something so absurd in the association of Madame Fontaine's charms with the extinction of Mr. Engelman's pipe, that I burst out laughing. My good old friend looked at me in grave surprise.

"What is there to laugh at in my forgetting to keep my pipe alight?" he asked. "My whole mind, David, was absorbed in that magnificent woman the instant I set eyes on her. The image of her is before me at this moment—

an image of an angel in moonlight. Am I speaking poetically for the first time in my life? I shouldn't wonder. I really don't know what is the matter with me. You are a young man, and perhaps you can tell. Have I fallen in love, as the saying is?" He took me confidentially by the arm, before I could answer this formidable question. "Don't tell friend Keller!" he said, with a sudden outburst of alarm. "Keller is an excellent man, but he has no mercy on sinners. I say, David! couldn't you introduce me to her?"

Still haunted by the fear that I had spoken too unreservedly during my interview with the widow, I was in the right humor to exhibit extraordinary prudence in my intercourse with Mr. Engelman.

"I couldn't venture to introduce you," I said; "the lady is living here in the strictest retirement."

"At any rate, you can tell me her name," pleaded Mr. Engelman. "I dare say you have mentioned it to Keller?"

"I have done nothing of the sort. I have reasons for saying nothing about the lady to Mr. Keller."

"Well, you can trust me to keep the secret, David. Come! I only want to send her some flowers from my garden. She can't object to that. Tell me where I am to send my nosegay, there's a dear fellow."

I dare say I did wrong—indeed, judging by later events, I know I did wrong. But I could not view the affair seriously enough to hold out against Mr. Engelman in the matter of the nosegay. He started when I mentioned the widow's name.

"Not the mother of the girl whom Fritz wants to marry?" he exclaimed.

"Yes, the same. Don't you admire Fritz's taste? Isn't Miss Minna a charming girl?"

"I can't say, David. I was bewitched—I had no eyes for anybody but her mother. Do you think Madame Fontaine noticed me?"

"Oh, yes. I saw her look at you."

"Turn this way, David. The effect of the moonlight on you seems to make you look younger. Has it the same effect on me? How old should you guess me to be to-night? Fifty or sixty?"

"Somewhere between the two, sir."

(He was close on seventy. But who could have been cruel enough to say so, at that moment?)

My answer proved to be so encouraging to the old gentleman that he ventured on the subject of Madame Fontaine's late husband. "Was she very fond of him, David? What sort of man was he?"

I informed him that I had never even seen Dr. Fontaine; and then, by way of changing the topic, inquired if I was too late for the regular supper-hour at Main Street.

"My dear boy, the table was cleared half an hour ago. But I persuaded our sour-tempered old housekeeper to keep something hot for you. You won't find Keller very amiable to-night, David. He was upset, to begin with, by writing that remonstrance to your aunt—and then your absence annoyed him. 'This is treating our house like an hotel; I won't allow anybody to take such liberties with us.' Yes! that was really what he said of you. He was so cross, poor fellow, that I left him, and went out for a stroll on the bridge. And met my fate," added poor Mr. Engelman, in the saddest tones I had ever heard fall from his lips.

My reception at the house was a little chilly.

"I have written my mind plainly to your aunt," said Mr. Keller; "you will probably be recalled to London by return of post. In the meantime, on the next occasion when you spend the evening out, be so obliging as to leave word to that effect with one of the servants." The crabbed old housekeeper (known in the domestic circle as Mother Barbara) had her fling at me next. She set down the dish which she had kept hot for me, with a bang that tried the resisting capacity of the porcelain severely. "I've done it this once," she said. "Next time you're late, you and the dog can sup together."

The next day, I wrote to my aunt, and also to Fritz, knowing how anxious he must be to hear from me.

To tell him the whole truth would probably have been to bring him to Frankfort as fast as sailing-vessels and horses could carry him. All I could venture to say was, that I had found the lost trace of Minna and her mother, and that I had every reason to believe there was no cause to feel any present anxiety about them. I added that I might be in a position to forward a letter secretly, if it would comfort him to write to his sweetheart.

In making this offer, I was, no doubt, encouraging my friend to disobey the plain commands which his father had laid on him.

But, as the case stood, I had really no other alternative. With Fritz's temperament, it would have been simply impossible to induce him to remain in London, unless his patience was sustained in my absence by a practical concession of some kind. In the interests of peace, then—and I must own in the interests of the pretty and interesting Minna as well—I consented to become a medium for correspondence, on the purely Jesuitical principle that the end justified the means. I had promised to let Minna know of it when I wrote to Fritz. My time being entirely at my own disposal, until the vexed question of the employment of women was settled between Mr. Keller and my aunt, I went to the widow's lodgings, after putting my letters in the post.

Having made Minna happy in the anticipation of hearing from Fritz, I had leisure to notice an old china punch-bowl on the table, filled to overflowing with magnificent flowers. To anyone who knew Mr. Engelman as well as I did, the punch-bowl suggested serious considerations. He, who forbade the plucking of a single flower on ordinary occasions, must, with his own hands, have seriously damaged the appearance of his beautiful garden.

"What splendid flowers!" I said, feeling my way cautiously. "Mr. Engelman himself might be envious of such a nosegay as that."

The widow's heavy eyelids drooped lower for a moment, in unconcealed contempt for my simplicity.

"Do you really think you can mystify me?" she asked ironically. "Mr. Engelman has done more than send the flowers—he has written me a too-flattering note. And I," she said, glancing carelessly at the mantelpiece, on which a letter was placed, "have written the necessary acknowledgment. It would be absurd to stand on ceremony with the harmless old gentleman who met us on the bridge. How fat he is! and what a wonderful pipe he carries—almost as fat as himself!"

Alas for Mr. Engelman! I could not resist saying a word in his favor—she spoke of him with such cruelly sincere contempt.

"Though he only saw you for a moment," I said, "he is your ardent admirer already."

"Is he indeed?" She was so utterly indifferent to Mr. Engelman's admiration that she could hardly take the trouble to make that commonplace reply. The next moment she dismissed the subject. "So you have written to Fritz?" she went on. "Have you also written to your aunt?"

"Yes, by the same post."

"Mainly on business, no doubt? Is it indiscreet to ask if you slipped in a little word about the hopes that I associate with Mrs. Wagner's arrival at Frankfort?"

This seemed to give me a good opportunity of moderating her "hopes," in mercy to her daughter and to herself.

"I thought it undesirable to mention the subject—for the present, at least," I answered. "There is a serious difference of opinion between Mrs. Wagner and Mr. Keller, on a subject connected with the management of the office here. I say serious, because they are both equally firm in maintaining their convictions. Mr. Keller has written to my aunt by yesterday's post; and I fear it may end in an angry correspondence between them."

I saw that I had startled her. She suddenly drew her chair close to mine.

"Do you think the correspondence will delay your aunt's departure from England?" she asked.

"On the contrary. My aunt is a very resolute person, and it may hasten her departure. But I am afraid it will indispose her to ask any favors of Mr. Keller, or to associate herself with his personal concerns. Any friendly intercourse between them will indeed be impossible, if she asserts her authority as head-partner, and forces him to submit to a woman in a matter of business."

She sank back in her chair. "I understand," she said faintly.

While we had been talking, Minna had walked to the window, and had remained there looking out. She suddenly turned round as her mother spoke.

"Mamma! the landlady's little boy has just gone out. Shall I tap at the window and call him back?"

The widow roused herself with an effort. "What for, my love?" she asked, absently.

Minna pointed to the mantelpiece. "To take your letter to Mr. Engelman, mamma." Madame Fontaine looked at the letter—paused for a moment—and answered, "No, my dear; let the boy go. It doesn't matter for the present."

She turned to me, with an abrupt recovery of her customary manner.

"I am fortunately, for myself, a sanguine person," she resumed. "I always did hope for the best; and (feeling the kind motive of what you have said to me) I shall hope for the best still. Minna, my darling, Mr. David and I have been talking on dry subjects until we are tired. Give us a little music." While her daughter obediently opened the piano, she looked at the flowers. "You are fond of flowers, David?" she went on. "Do you understand the subject? I ignorantly admire the lovely colors, and enjoy the delicious scents—and I can do no more. It was really very kind of your old friend Mr. Engelman. Does he take any part in this deplorable difference of opinion between your aunt and Mr. Keller?"

What did that new allusion to Mr. Engelman mean? And why had she declined to despatch her letter to him, when the opportunity offered of sending it by the boy?

Troubled by the doubts which these considerations suggested, I committed an act of imprudence—I replied so reservedly that I put her on her guard. All I said was that I supposed Mr. Engelman agreed with Mr. Keller, but that I was not in the confidence of the two partners. From that moment she saw through me, and was silent on the subject of Mr. Engelman. Even Minna's singing had lost its charm, in my present frame of mind. It was a relief to me when I could make my excuses, and leave the house.

On my way back to Main Street, when I could think freely, my doubts began to develop into downright suspicion. Madame Fontaine could hardly hope, after what I had told her, to obtain the all-important interview with Mr. Keller, through my aunt's intercession. Had she seen her way to trying what Mr. Engelman's influence with his partner could do for her? Would she destroy her formal acknowledgment of the receipt of his flowers, as soon as my back was turned, and send him a second letter, encouraging him to visit her? And would she cast him off, without ceremony, when he had served her purpose?

These were the thoughts that troubled me on my return to the house. When we met at supper, some hours later, my worst anticipations were realized. Poor innocent Mr. Engelman was dressed with extraordinary smartness, and was in the highest good spirits. Mr. Keller asked him jestingly if he was going to be married. In the intoxication of happiness that possessed him, he was quite reckless; he actually retorted by a joke on the sore subject of the employment of women! "Who knows what may happen," he cried gaily, "when we have young ladies in the office for clerks?" Mr. Keller was so angry that he kept silence through the whole of our meal. When Mr. Engelman left the room I slipped out after him.

"You are going to Madame Fontaine's," I said.

He smirked and smiled. "Just a little evening visit, David. Aha! you young men are not to have it all your own way." He laid his hand tenderly on the left breast-pocket of his coat. "Such a delightful letter!" he said. "It is here, over my heart. No, a woman's sentiments are sacred; I mustn't show it to you."

I was on the point of telling him the whole truth, when the thought of Minna checked me for the time. My interest in preserving Mr. Engelman's tranquillity was in direct conflict with my interest in the speedy marriage of my good friend Fritz. Besides, was it likely that anything I could say would have the slightest effect on the deluded old man, in the first fervor of his infatuation? I thought I would give him a general caution, and wait to be guided by events.

"One word, sir, for your private ear," I said. "Even the finest women have their faults. You will find Madame Fontaine perfectly charming; but don't be too ready to believe that she is in earnest."

Mr. Engelman felt infinitely flattered, and owned it without the slightest reserve.

"Oh, David! David!" he said, "are you jealous of me already?"

He put on his hat (with a jaunty twist on one side), and swung his stick gaily, and left the room. For the first time, in my experience of him, he went out without his pipe; and (a more serious symptom still) he really did not appear to miss it.

CHAPTER XII

Two days passed, and I perceived another change in Mr. Engelman.

He was now transformed into a serious and reticent man. Had he committed indiscretions which might expose him to ridicule if they were known? Or had the widow warned him not to be too ready to take me into his confidence? In any case, he said not one word to me about Madame Fontaine's reception of him, and he left the house secretly when he paid his next visit to her. Having no wish to meet him unexpectedly, and feeling (if the truth be told) not quite at ease about the future, I kept away from Minna and her mother, and waited for events.

On the third day, an event happened. I received a little note from Minna:—

"Dear Mr. David,—If you care to see mamma and me, stay at home this evening. Good Mr. Engelman has promised to show us his interesting old house, after business hours."

There was nothing extraordinary in making an exhibition of "the old house." It was one among the many picturesque specimens of the domestic architecture of bygone days, for which Frankfort is famous; and it had been sketched by artists of all nations, both outside and in. At the same time, it was noticeable (perhaps only as a coincidence) that the evening chosen for showing the house to the widow, was also the evening on which Mr. Keller had an engagement with some friends in another part of the city.

As the hour approached for the arrival of the ladies, I saw that Mr. Engelman looked at me with an expression of embarrassment.

"Are you not going out this evening, David?" he asked.

"Am I in the way, sir?" I inquired mischievously.

"Oh, no!"

"In that case then, I think I shall stay at home."

He said no more, and walked up and down the room with an air of annoyance. The bell of the street-door rang. He stopped and looked at me again.

"Visitors?" I said.

He was obliged to answer me. "Friends of mine, David, who are coming to see the house."

I was just sufficiently irritated by his persistence in keeping up the mystery to set him the example of speaking plainly.

"Madame Fontaine and her daughter?" I said.

He turned quickly to answer me, and hesitated. At the same moment, the door was opened by the sour old housekeeper, frowning suspiciously at the two elegantly-dressed ladies whom she ushered into the room.

If I had been free to act on my own impulse, I should certainly (out of regard for Mr. Engelman) have refrained from accompanying the visitors when they were shown over the house. But Minna took my arm. I had no choice but to follow Mr. Engelman and her mother when they left the room.

Minna spoke to me as confidentially as if I had been her brother.

"Do you know," she whispered, "that nice old gentleman and mamma are like old friends already. Mamma is generally suspicious of strangers. Isn't it odd? And she actually invites him to bring his pipe when he comes to see us! He sits puffing smoke, and admiring mamma—and mamma does all the talking. Do come and see us soon! I have nobody to speak to about Fritz. Mamma and Mr. Engelman take no more notice of me than if I was a little dog in the room."

As we passed from the ground floor to the first floor, Madame Fontaine's admiration of the house rose from one climax of enthusiasm to another. Among the many subjects that she understood, the domestic architecture of the seventeenth century seemed to be one, and the art of water-color painting soon proved to be another.

"I am not quite contemptible as a lady-artist," I heard her say to Mr. Engelman; "and I should so like to make some little studies of these beautiful old rooms—as memorials to take with me when I am far away from Frankfort. But I don't ask it, dear Mr. Engelman. You don't want enthusiastic ladies with sketch-books in this bachelor paradise of yours. I hope we are not intruding on Mr. Keller. Is he at home?"

"No," said Mr. Engelman; "he has gone out."

Madame Fontaine's flow of eloquence suddenly ran dry. She was silent as we ascended from the first floor to the second. In this part of the house our bedrooms were situated. The chamber in which I slept presented nothing particularly worthy of notice. But the rooms occupied by Mr. Keller and Mr. Engelman contained some of the finest carved woodwork in the house.

It was beginning to get dark. Mr. Engelman lit the candles in his own room. The widow took one of them from him, and threw the light skillfully on the different objects about her. She was still a little subdued; but she showed her knowledge of wood-carving by picking out the two finest specimens in the room—a wardrobe and a toilet-table.

"My poor husband was fond of old carving," she explained modestly;

"what I know about it, I know from him. Dear Mr. Engelman, your room is a picture in itself. What glorious colors! How simple and how grand! Might we——" she paused, with a becoming appearance of confusion. Her voice dropped softly to lower tones. "Might we be pardoned, do you think, if we ventured to peep into Mr. Keller's room?"

She spoke of "Mr. Keller's room" as if it had been a shrine, approachable only by a few favored worshippers. "Where is it?" she inquired, with breathless interest. I led the way out into the passage, and threw open the door without ceremony. Madame Fontaine looked at me as if I had committed an act of sacrilege.

Mr. Engelman, following us with one of his candles, lit an ancient brass lamp which hung from the middle of the ceiling. "My learned partner," he explained, "does a great deal of his reading in his bedroom, and he likes plenty of light. You will have a good view when the lamp has burnt up. The big chimney-piece is considered the finest thing of that sort in Frankfort."

The widow confronted the chimney-piece, and clasped her hands in silent rapture. When she was able to speak, she put her arm round Minna's waist.

"Let me teach you, my love, to admire this glorious work," she said, and delivered quite a little lecture on the merits of the chimney-piece. "Oh, if I could but take the merest sketch of it!" she exclaimed, by way of conclusion. "But no, it is too much to ask." She examined everything in the room with the minutest attention. Even the plain little table by the bed-side, with a jug and a glass on it, did not escape her observation. "Is that his drink?" she asked, with an air of respectful curiosity. "Do you think I might taste it?"

Mr. Engelman laughed. "It's only barley-water, dear lady," he said. "Our rheumatic old housekeeper makes as few journeys as possible up and down stairs. When she sets the room in order in the evening, she takes the night-drink up with her, and so saves a second journey."

"Taste it, Minna," said the widow, handing the glass to her daughter. "How refreshing! how pure!"

Mr. Engelman, standing on the other side of her, whispered in her ear. I was just behind them, and could not help hearing him. "You will make me jealous," he said; "you never noticed my night-drink—I have beer."

The widow answered him by a look; he heaved a little sigh of happiness. Poor Mr. Engelman!

Minna innocently broke in on this mute scene of sentiment.

She was looking at the pictures in the room, and asked for explanations of them which Mr. Engelman only could afford. It struck me as odd that her mother's artistic sympathies did not appear to be excited by the pictures. Instead of joining her daughter at the other end of the room, she stood by the bedside with her hand resting on the little table, and her eyes fixed on the jug of barley-water, absorbed in thought. On a sudden, she started, turned quickly, and caught me observing her. I might have been deceived by the lamp-light; but I thought I saw a flash of expression under her heavy eyelids, charged with such intensity of angry suspicion that it startled me. She was herself again, before I could decide whether to trust my own strong impression or not.

"Do I surprise you, David?" she asked in her gentlest tones. "I ought to be looking at the pictures, you think? My friend! I can't always control my own sad recollections. They will force themselves on me—sometimes when the most trifling associations call them up. Dear Mr. Engelman understands me. He, no doubt, has suffered too. May I sit down for a moment?"

She dropped languidly into a chair, and sat looking at the famous chimney-piece. Her attitude was the perfection of grace. Mr. Engelman hurried through his explanation of the pictures, and placed himself at her side, and admired the chimney-piece with her.

"Artists think it looks best by lamplight," he said. "The big pediment between the windows keeps out the light in the daytime."

Madame Fontaine looked round at him with a softly approving smile. "Exactly what I was thinking myself, when you spoke," she said. "The effect by this light is simply perfect. Why didn't I bring my sketch-book with me?

76

I might have stolen some little memorial of it, in Mr. Keller's absence." She turned towards me when she said that.

"If you can do without colors," I suggested, "we have paper and pencils in the house."

The clock in the corridor struck the hour.

Mr. Engelman looked uneasy, and got up from his chair. His action suggested that the time had passed by us unperceived, and that Mr. Keller's return might take place at any moment. The same impression was evidently produced on Minna. For once in her life, the widow's quick perception seemed to have deserted her. She kept her seat as composedly as if she had been at home.

"I wonder whether I could manage without my colors?" she said placidly. "Perhaps I might try."

Mr. Engelman's uneasiness increased to downright alarm. Minna perceived the change, as I did, and at once interfered.

"I am afraid, mamma, it is too late for sketching to-night," she said. "Suppose Mr. Keller should come back?"

Madame Fontaine rose instantly, with a look of confusion. "How very stupid of me not to think of it!" she exclaimed. "Forgive me, Mr. Engelman—I was so interested, so absorbed—thank you a thousand times for your kindness!" She led the way out, with more apologies and more gratitude. Mr. Engelman recovered his tranquillity. He looked at her lovingly, and gave her his arm to lead her down-stairs.

On this occasion, Minna and I were in front. We reached the first landing, and waited there. The widow was wonderfully slow in descending the stairs. Judging by what we heard, she was absorbed in the old balusters now. When she at last joined us on the landing, the doors of the rooms on the first floor delayed her again: it was simply impossible, she said, to pass them without notice. Once more, Minna and I waited on the ground floor. Here, there was another ancient brass lamp which lighted the hall; and, therefore, another object of beauty which it was impossible to pass over in a hurry.

"I never knew mamma to behave so oddly before," said Minna. "If such a thing wasn't impossible, in our situation, one would really think she wanted Mr. Keller to catch us in the house!"

There was not the least doubt in my mind (knowing as I did, how deeply Madame Fontaine was interested in forcing her acquaintance on Mr. Keller) that this was exactly what she did want. Fortune is proverbially said to favor the bold; and Fortune offered to the widow the perilous opportunity of which she had been in search.

While she was still admiring the lamp, the grating sound became audible of a key put into the street door.

The door opened, and Mr. Keller walked into the hall.

He stopped instantly at the sight of two ladies who were both strangers to him, and looked interrogatively at his partner. Mr. Engelman had no choice but to risk an explanation of some kind. He explained, without mentioning names.

"Friends of mine, Keller," he said confusedly, "to whom I have been showing the house."

Mr. Keller took off his hat, and bowed to the widow. With a boldness that amazed me, under the circumstances, she made a low curtsey to him, smiled her sweetest smile, and deliberately mentioned her name.

"I am Madame Fontaine, sir," she said. "And this is my daughter, Minna."

CHAPTER XIII

Mr. Keller fixed his eyes on the widow in stern silence; walked past her to the inner end of the hall; and entered a room at the back of the house, closing the door behind him. Even if he had felt inclined to look at Minna, it would not have been possible for him to see her. After one timid glance at him, the poor girl hid herself behind me, trembling piteously. I took her hand to encourage her. "Oh, what hope is there for us," she whispered, "with such a man as that?"

Madame Fontaine turned as Mr. Keller passed her, and watched his progress along the hall until he disappeared from view. "No," she said quietly to herself, "you don't escape me in that way."

As if moved by a sudden impulse, she set forth on the way by which Mr. Keller had gone before her; walking, as he had walked, to the door at the end of the hall.

I had remained with Minna, and was not in a position to see how her mother looked. Mr. Engelman's face, as he stretched out his hands entreatingly to stop Madame Fontaine, told me that the fierce passions hidden deep in the woman's nature had risen to the surface and shown themselves. "Oh, dear lady! dear lady!" cried the simple old man, "Don't look like that! It's only Keller's temper—he will soon be himself again."

Without answering him, without looking at him, she lifted her hand, and put him back from her as if he had been a troublesome child. With her firm graceful step, she resumed her progress along the hall to the room at the end, and knocked sharply at the door.

Mr. Keller's voice answered from within, "Who is there?"

"Madame Fontaine," said the widow. "I wish to speak to you."

"I decline to receive Madame Fontaine."

"In that case, Mr. Keller, I will do myself the honor of writing to you."

"I refuse to read your letter."

"Take the night to think of it, Mr. Keller, and change your mind in the morning."

She turned away, without waiting for a reply, and joined us at the outer end of the hall.

Minna advanced to meet her, and kissed her tenderly. "Dear, kind mamma, you are doing this for my sake," said the grateful girl. "I am ashamed that you should humble yourself—it is so useless!"

"It shall not be useless," her mother answered. "If fifty Mr. Kellers threatened your happiness, my child, I would brush the fifty out of your way. Oh, my darling, my darling!"

Her voice—as firm as the voice of a man, while she declared her resolution—faltered and failed her when the last words of endearment fell from her lips. She drew Minna to her bosom, and embraced in silent rapture the one creature whom she loved. When she raised her head again she was, to my mind, more beautiful than I had ever yet seen her. The all-ennobling tears of love and grief filled her eyes. Knowing the terrible story that is still to be told, let me do that miserable woman justice. Hers was not a wholly corrupted heart. It was always in Minna's power to lift her above her own wickedness. When she held out the hand that had just touched her daughter to Mr. Engelman, it trembled as if she had been the most timid woman living.

"Good night, dear friend," she said to him; "I am sorry to have been the innocent cause of this little embarrassment."

Simple Mr. Engelman put his handkerchief to his eyes; never, in all his life, had he been so puzzled, so frightened, and so distressed. He kissed the widow's hand. "Do let me see you safe home!" he said, in tones of the tenderest entreaty.

"Not to-night," she answered. He attempted a faint remonstrance. Madame Fontaine knew perfectly well how to assert her authority over him— she gave him another of those tender looks which had already become the charm of his life. Mr. Engelman sat down on one of the hall chairs completely overwhelmed. "Dear and admirable woman!" I heard him say to himself softly.

Taking leave of me in my turn, the widow dropped my hand, struck, to all appearance, by a new idea.

"I have a favor to ask of you, David," she said. "Do you mind going back with us?"

As a matter of course I took my hat, and placed myself at her service. Mr. Engelman got on his feet, and lifted his plump hands in mute and melancholy protest. "Don't be uneasy," Madame Fontaine said to him, with a faint smile of contempt. "David doesn't love me!"

I paused for a moment, as I followed her out, to console Mr. Engelman. "She is old enough to be my mother, sir," I whispered; "and this time, at any rare, she has told you the truth."

Hardly a word passed between us on our way through the streets and over the bridge. Minna was sad and silent, thinking of Fritz; and whatever her mother might have to say to me, was evidently to be said in private. Arrived at the lodgings, Madame Fontaine requested me to wait for her in the shabby little sitting-room, and graciously gave me permission to smoke. "Say good night to David," she continued, turning to her daughter. "Your poor little heart is heavy to-night, and mamma means to put you to bed as if you were a child again. Ah! me, if those days could only come back!"

After a short absence the widow returned to me, with a composed manner and a quiet smile. The meeting with Mr. Keller seemed to have been completely dismissed from her thoughts, in the brief interval since I had seen her last.

"We often hear of parents improving their children," she said. "It is my belief that the children quite as often improve the parents. I have had some happy minutes with Minna—and (would you believe it?) I am already disposed to forgive Mr. Keller's brutality, and to write to him in a tone of moderation, which must surely have its effect. All Minna's doing—and my sweet girl doesn't in the least suspect it herself! If you ever have children of your own, David, you will understand me and feel for me. In the meantime, I must not detain you by idle talk—I must say plainly what I want of you." She opened her writing-desk and took up a pen. "If I write to Mr. Keller under your own eye, do you object to take charge of my letter?"

I hesitated how to answer. To say the least of it, her request embarrassed me.

"I don't expect you to give it to Mr. Keller personally," she explained. "It is of very serious importance to me" (she laid a marked emphasis on those words) "to be quite sure that my letter has reached him, and that he has really

81

had the opportunity of reading it. If you will only place it on his desk in the office, with your own hand, that is all I ask you to do. For Minna's sake, mind; not for mine!"

For Minna's sake, I consented. She rose directly, and signed to me to take her place at the desk.

"It will save time," she said, "if you write the rough draft of the letter from my dictation. I am accustomed to dictate my letters, with Minna for secretary. Of course, you shall see the fair copy before I seal it."

She began to walk up and down the little room, with her hands crossed behind her in the attitude made famous by the great Napoleon. After a minute of consideration, she dictated the draft as follows:

"Sir,—I am well aware that scandalous reports at Wurzburg have prejudiced you against me. Those reports, so far as I know, may be summed up under three heads.

"(First.) That my husband died in debt through my extravagance.

"(Second.) That my respectable neighbors refuse to associate with me.

"(Third.) That I entrapped your son Fritz into asking for my daughter's hand in marriage, because I knew his father to be a rich man.

"To the first calumny I reply, that the debts are due to expensive chemical experiments in which my late husband engaged, and that I have satisfied the creditors to the last farthing. Grant me an audience, and I will refer you to the creditors themselves.

"To the second calumny I reply, that I received invitations, on my arrival in Wurzburg after my marriage, from every lady of distinguished social position in the town. After experience of the society thus offered to me, I own to having courteously declined subsequent invitations, and having devoted myself in retirement to my husband, to my infant child, and to such studies in literature and art as I had time to pursue. Gossip and scandal, with an eternal accompaniment of knitting, are not to my taste; and, while I strictly attend to domestic duties, I do not consider them as constituting, in connection with

82

tea-drinking, the one great interest of a woman's life. I plead guilty to having been foolish enough to openly acknowledge these sentiments, and to having made bitter enemies everywhere as the necessary consequence. If this plain defense of myself fails to satisfy you, grant me an audience, and I will answer your questions, whatever they may be.

"To the third calumny, I reply, that if you had been a Prince instead of a merchant, I would still have done everything in my power to keep your son away from my daughter—for this simple reason, that the idea of parting with her to any man fills me with grief and dismay. I only yielded to the marriage engagement, when the conviction was forced upon me that my poor child's happiness depended on her union with your son. It is this consideration alone which induces me to write to you, and to humiliate myself by pleading for a hearing. As for the question of money, if through some unexpected misfortune you became a bankrupt to-morrow, I would entreat you to consent to the marriage exactly as I entreat you now. Poverty has no terrors for me while I have health to work. But I cannot face the idea of my child's life being blighted, because you choose to believe the slanders that are spoken of her mother. For the third time I ask you to grant me an audience, and to hear me in my own defense."

There she paused, and looked over my shoulder.

"I think that is enough," she said. "Do you see anything objectionable in my letter?"

How could I object to the letter? From beginning to end, it was strongly, and yet moderately, expressed. I resigned my place at the desk, and the widow wrote the fair copy, with her own hand. She made no change whatever, except by adding these ominous lines as a postscript:

"I implore you not to drive me to despair. A mother who is pleading for her child's life—it is nothing less, in this case—is a woman who surely asserts a sacred claim. Let no wise man deny it."

"Do you think it quite discreet," I ventured to ask, "to add those words?"

She looked at me with a moment's furtive scrutiny, and only answered after she had sealed the letter, and placed it in my hands.

"I have my reasons," she replied. "Let the words remain."

Returning to the house at rather a late hour for Frankfort, I was surprised to find Mr. Keller waiting to see me.

"I have had a talk with my partner," he said. "It has left (for the time only, I hope), a painful impression on both sides—and I must ask you to do me a service, in the place of Mr. Engelman—who has an engagement to-morrow, which prevents him from leaving Frankfort."

His tone indicated plainly enough that the "engagement" was with Madame Fontaine. Hard words must have passed between the two old friends on the subject of the widow. Even Mr. Engelman's placid temper had, no doubt, resented Mr. Keller's conduct at the meeting in the hall.

"The service I ask of you," he resumed, "will be easily rendered. The proprietor of a commercial establishment at Hanau is desirous of entering into business-relations with us, and has sent references to respectable persons in the town and neighborhood, which it is necessary to verify. We are so busy in the office that it is impossible for me to leave Frankfort myself, or to employ our clerks on this errand. I have drawn out the necessary instructions—and Hanau, as you are aware, is within an easy distance of Frankfort. Have you any objection to be the representative of the house in this matter?"

It is needless to say that I was gratified by the confidence that had been placed in me, and eager to show that I really deserved it. We arranged that I should leave Frankfort by the earliest conveyance the next morning.

On our way upstairs to our bed-chambers, Mr. Keller detained me for a moment more.

"I have no claim to control you in the choice of your friends," he said; "but I am old enough to give you a word of advice. Don't associate yourself too readily, David, with the woman whom I found here to-night."

He shook hands cordially, and left me. I thought of Madame Fontaine's letter in my pocket, and felt a strong conviction that he would persist in his refusal to read it.

The servants were the only persons stirring in the house, when I rose the next morning. Unobserved by anyone, I placed the letter on the desk in Mr. Keller's private room. That done, I started on my journey to Hanau.

CHAPTER XIV

Thanks to the instructions confided to me, my errand presented no difficulties. There were certain persons to whom I was introduced, and certain information to be derived from them, which it was my duty to submit to Mr. Keller on my return. Fidelity was required of me, and discretion was required of me—and that was all.

At the close of my day's work, the hospitable merchant, whose references I had been engaged in verifying, refused to permit me to return to the hotel. His dinner-hour had been put off expressly to suit my convenience. "You will only meet the members of my family," he said, "and a cousin of my wife's who is here with her daughter, on a visit to us—Frau Meyer, of Wurzburg."

I accepted the invitation, feeling privately an Englishman's reluctance to confronting an assembly of strangers, and anticipating nothing remarkable in reference to Frau Meyer, although she did come from Wurzburg. Even when I was presented to the ladies in due form, as "the honored representative of Mr. Keller, of Frankfort," I was too stupid, or too much absorbed in the business on which I had been engaged, to be much struck by the sudden interest with which Frau Meyer regarded me. She was a fat florid old lady, who looked coarsely clever and resolute; and she had a daughter who promised to resemble her but too faithfully, in due course of time. It was a relief to me, at dinner, to find myself placed between the merchant's wife and her eldest son. They were far more attractive neighbors at table, to my thinking, than Frau Meyer.

Dinner being over, we withdrew to another room to take our coffee. The merchant and his son, both ardent musicians in their leisure hours, played a sonata for pianoforte and violin. I was at the opposite extremity of the room, looking at some fine proof impressions of prints from the old masters, when a voice at my side startled me by an unexpected question.

"May I ask, sir, if you are acquainted with Mr. Keller's son?"

I looked round, and discovered Frau Meyer.

"Have you seen him lately?" she proceeded, when I had acknowledged that I was acquainted with Fritz. "And can you tell me where he is now?"

I answered both these questions. Frau Meyer looked thoroughly well satisfied with me. "Let us have a little talk," she said, and seated herself, and signed to me to take a chair near her.

"I feel a true interest in Fritz," she resumed, lowering her voice so as not to be heard by the musicians at the other end of the room. "Until to-day, I have heard nothing of him since he left Wurzburg. I like to talk about him—he once did me a kindness a long time since. I suppose you are in his confidence? Has he told you why his father sent him away from the University?"

My reply to this was, I am afraid, rather absently given. The truth is, my mind was running on some earlier words which had dropped from the old lady's lips. "He once did me a kindness a long time since." When had I last heard that commonplace phrase? and why did I remember it so readily when I now heard it again?

"Ah, his father did a wise thing in separating him from that woman and her daughter!" Frau Meyer went on. "Madame Fontaine deliberately entrapped the poor boy into the engagement. But perhaps you are a friend of hers? In that case, I retract and apologize."

"Quite needless," I said.

"You are not a friend of Madame Fontaine?" she persisted.

This cool attempt to force an answer from me failed in its object. It was like being cross-examined in a court of law; and, in our common English phrase, "it set my back up." In the strict sense of the word, Madame Fontaine might be termed an acquaintance, but certainly not a friend, of mine. For once, I took the prudent course, and said, No.

Frau Meyer's expansive bosom emitted a hearty sigh of relief. "Ah!" she said, "now I can talk freely—in Fritz's interest, mind. You are a young man like himself, he will be disposed to listen to you. Do all you can to back his father's influence, and cure him of his infatuation. I tell you plainly, his marriage would be his ruin!"

"You speak very strongly, madam. Do you object to the young lady?"

"Not I; a harmless insignificant creature—nothing more and nothing less. It's her vile mother that I object to."

"As I have heard, Frau Meyer, there are two sides to that question. Fritz is persuaded that Madame Fontaine is an injured woman. He assures me, for instance, that she is the fondest of mothers."

"Bah! What does that amount to? It's as much a part of a woman's nature to take to her child when she has got one, as it is to take to her dinner when she is hungry. A fond mother? What stuff! Why, a cat is a fond mother!—What's the matter?"

A cat is a fond mother. Another familiar phrase—and this time a phrase remarkable enough to lead my memory back in the right direction. In an instant I recollected the anonymous letter to Fritz. In an instant I felt the conviction that Frau Meyer, in her eagerness to persuade me, had unconsciously repeated two of the phrases which she had already used, in her eagerness to persuade Fritz. No wonder I started in my chair, when I felt that I was face to face with the writer of the anonymous letter!

I made some excuse—I forget what—and hastened to resume the conversation. The opportunity of making discoveries which might be invaluable to Fritz (to say nothing of good Mr. Engelman) was not an opportunity to be neglected. I persisted in quoting Fritz's authority; I repeated his assertion relative to the love of scandal at Wurzburg, and the envy of Madame Fontaine's superior attractions felt among the ladies. Frau Meyer laughed disdainfully.

"Poor Fritz!" she said. "An excellent disposition—but so easily persuaded, so much too amiable. Our being all envious of Widow Fontaine is too ridiculous. It is a mere waste of time to notice such nonsense. Wait a little, Mr. David, and you will see. If you and Mr. Keller can only keep Fritz out of the widow's way for a few months longer, his eyes will be opened in spite of himself. He may yet come back to us with a free heart, and he may choose his future wife more wisely next time."

As she said this her eyes wandered away to her daughter, at the other end of the room. Unless her face betrayed her, she had evidently planned, at some past time, to possess herself of Fritz as a son-in-law, and she had not resigned the hope of securing him yet. Madame Fontaine might be a deceitful and dangerous woman. But what sort of witness against her was this abusive old lady, the unscrupulous writer of an anonymous letter? "You prophesy very confidently about what is to come in the future," I ventured to say.

Frau Meyer's red face turned a shade redder. "Does that mean that you don't believe me?" she asked.

"Certainly not, madam. It only means that you speak severely of Doctor Fontaine's widow—without mentioning any facts that justify you."

"Oh! you want facts, do you? I'll soon show you whether I know what I am talking about or not. Has Fritz mentioned that among Madame Fontaine's other virtues, she has paid her debts? I'll tell you how she has paid them— as an example, young gentleman, that I am not talking at random. Your admirable widow, sir, is great at fascinating old men; they are always falling in love with her, the idiots! A certain old man at Wurzburg—close on eighty, mind—was one of her victims. I had a letter this morning which tells me that he was found dead in his bed, two days since, and that his nephew is the sole heir to all that he leaves behind him. Examination of his papers has shown that he paid the widow's creditors, and that he took a promissory note from her—ha! ha! ha!—a promissory note from a woman without a farthing!—in payment of the sum that he had advanced. The poor old man would, no doubt, have destroyed the note if he had known that his end was so near. His sudden death has transferred it to the hands of his heir. In money-matters, the nephew is reported to be one of the hardest men living. When that note falls due, he will present it for payment. I don't know where Madame Fontaine is now. No matter! Sooner or later, she is sure to hear of what has happened— and she must find the money, or see the inside of a debtor's prison. Those are the facts that I had in my mind, Mr. David, when I spoke of events opening

Fritz's eyes to the truth."

I submitted with all possible humility to the lady's triumph over me. My thoughts were with Minna. What a prospect for the innocent, affectionate girl! Assuming the statement that I had just heard to be true, there was surely a chance that Madame Fontaine (with time before her) might find the money. I put this view of the case to Frau Meyer.

"If I didn't know Mr. Keller to be a thoroughly resolute man," she answered, "I should say she might find the money too. She has only to succeed in marrying her daughter to Fritz, and Mr. Keller would be obliged to pay the money for the sake of the family credit. But he is one of the few men whom she can't twist round her finger. If you ever fall in with her, take care of yourself. She may find your influence with Fritz an obstacle in her way—and she may give you reason to remember that the mystery of her husband's lost chest of poisons is not cleared up yet. It was all in the German newspapers— you know what I mean."

This seemed to me to be passing all bounds of moderation. "And you know, madam," I answered sharply, "that there was no evidence against her— nothing whatever to associate her with the robbery of the medicine chest."

"Not even suspicion, Mr. David?"

"Not even suspicion."

I rose from my chair as I spoke. Minna was still in my thoughts; I was not merely unwilling, I was almost afraid to hear more.

"One minute," said Frau Meyer. "Which of the two hotels here are you staying at? I want to send you something to read to-night, after you have left us."

I told her the name of the hotel; and we joined our friends at the other end of the room. Not long afterwards I took my leave. My spirits were depressed; a dark cloud of uncertainty seemed to hang over the future. Even the prospect of returning to Frankfort, the next day, became repellent to me. I was almost inclined to hope that my aunt might (as Mr. Keller had predicted) recall me to London.

CHAPTER XV

From these reflections I was roused by the appearance of a waiter, with a letter for me. The envelope contained a slip cut from a German newspaper, and these lines of writing, signed by Frau Meyer:—

"You are either a very just, or a very obstinate young man. In either case, it will do you no harm to read what I enclose. I am not such a scandal-mongering old woman as you seem to think. The concealment of the names will not puzzle you. Please return the slip. It belongs to our excellent host, and forms part of his collection of literary curiosities."

Such was the introduction to my reading. I translate it from the German newspaper into English as literally as I can.

The Editor's few prefatory words were at the top of the column, bearing the date of September 1828.

"We have received, in strictest confidence, extracts from letters written by a lady to a once-beloved female friend. The extracts are dated and numbered, and are literally presented in this column—excepting the obviously necessary precaution of suppressing names, places, and days of the month. Taken in connection with a certain inquiry which is just now occupying the public mind, these fragments may throw some faint glimmer of light on events which are at present involved in darkness."

Number I. 1809.—"Yes, dearest Julie, I have run the grand risk. Only yesterday, I was married to Doctor ———. The people at the church were our only witnesses.

"My father declares that I have degraded his noble blood by marrying a medical man. He forbade my mother to attend the ceremony. Poor simple soul! She asked me if I loved my young doctor, and was quite satisfied when I said Yes. As for my father's objections, my husband is a man of high promise in his profession. In his country—I think I told you in my last letter that he was a Frenchman—a famous physician is ennobled by the State. I shall leave no stone unturned, my dear, to push my husband forward. And when he is made a Baron, we shall see what my father will say to us then."

Number II. 1810.—"We have removed, my Julie, to this detestably dull old German town, for no earthly reason but that the University is famous as a medical school.

"My husband informs me, in his sweetest manner, that he will hesitate at no sacrifice of our ordinary comforts to increase his professional knowledge. If you could see how the ladies dress in this lost hole of a place, if you could hear the twaddle they talk, you would pity me. I have but one consolation—a lovely baby, Julie, a girl: I had almost said an angel. Were you as fond of your first child, I wonder, as I am of mine? And did you utterly forget your husband, when the little darling was first put into your arms? Write and tell me."

Number III. 1811.—"I have hardly patience to take up my pen But I shall do something desperate, if I don't relieve my overburdened mind in some way.

"After I wrote to you last year, I succeeded in getting my husband away from the detestable University. But he persisted in hanging about Germany, and conferring with moldy old doctors (whom he calls "Princes of Science"!) instead of returning to Paris, taking a handsome house, and making his way to the top of the tree with my help. I am the very woman to give brilliant parties, and to push my husband's interests with powerful people of all degrees. No; I really must not dwell on it. When I think of what has happened since, it will drive me mad.

"Six weeks ago, a sort of medical congress was announced to be at the University. Something in the proposed discussion was to be made the subject of a prize-essay. The doctor's professional interest in this matter decided him on trying for the prize—and the result is our return to the hateful old town and its society.

"Of course, my husband resumes his professional studies; of course, I am thrown once more among the dowdy gossiping women. But that is far from being the worst of it. Among the people in the School of Chemistry here, there is a new man, who entered the University shortly after we left it last year. This devil—it is the only right word for him—has bewitched my weak husband; and, for all I can see to the contrary, has ruined our prospects in life.

"He is a Hungarian. Small, dirty, lean as a skeleton, with hands like claws, eyes like a wild beast's, and the most hideously false smile you ever saw in a human face. What his history is, nobody knows. The people at the medical school call him the most extraordinary experimental chemist living. His ideas astonish the Professors themselves. The students have named him 'The new Paracelsus.'

"I ventured to ask him, one day, if he believed he could make gold. He looked at me with his frightful grin, and said, "Yes, and diamonds too, with time and money to help me." He not only believes in The Philosopher's Stone; he says he is on the trace of some explosive compound so terrifically destructive in its effect, that it will make war impossible. He declares that he will annihilate time and space by means of electricity; and that he will develop steam as a motive power, until travelers can rush over the whole habitable globe at the rate of a mile in a minute.

"Why do I trouble you with these ravings? My dear, this boastful adventurer has made himself master of my husband, has talked him out of his senses, has reduced my influence over him to nothing. Do you think I am exaggerating? Hear how it has ended. My husband absolutely refuses to leave this place. He cares no longer even to try for the prize. The idea of medical practice has become distasteful to him, and he has decided on devoting his life to discovery in chemical science.

"And this is the man whom I married with the sincerest belief in the brilliant social career that was before him! For this contemptible creature I have sacrificed my position in the world, and alienated my father from me for ever. I may look forward to being the wife of a poor Professor, who shows experiments to stupid lads in a school. And the friends in Paris, who, to my certain knowledge, are now waiting to give him introductions to the Imperial Court itself, may transfer their services to some other man.

"No words can tell you what I feel at this complete collapse of all my hopes and plans. The one consideration of my child is all that restrains me

92

from leaving my husband, never to see him again. As it is, I must live a life of deceit, and feign respect and regard for a man whom I despise with my whole heart.

"Power—oh, if I had the power to make the fury that consumes me felt! The curse of our sex is its helplessness. Every day, Julie, the conviction grows on me that I shall end badly. Who among us knows the capacity for wickedness that lies dormant in our natures, until the fatal event comes and calls it forth?

"No! I am letting you see too much of my tortured soul. Let me close my letter, and play with my child."

Number IV. 1812.—"My heartfelt congratulations, dearest, on your return to Germany, after your pleasant visit to the United States. And more congratulations yet on the large addition to your income, due to your husband's intelligence and spirit of enterprise on American ground. Ah, you have married a Man! Happy woman! I am married to a Machine.

"Why have I left your kind letters from America without reply? My Julie, I have constantly thought of you; but the life I lead is slowly crushing my energies. Over and over again, I have taken up my pen; and over and over again, I have laid it aside, recoiling from the thought of myself and my existence; too miserable (perhaps too proud) to tell you what a wretched creature I am, and what thoughts come to me sometimes in the wakeful hours of the night.

"After this confession, you wonder, perhaps, why I write to you now.

"I really believe it is because I have been threatened with legal proceedings by my creditors, and have just come victoriously out of a hard struggle to appease them for the time. This little fight has roused me from my apathy; it has rallied my spirits, and made me feel like my old self again. I am no longer content with silently loving my dearest friend; I open my heart and write to her.

"'Oh, dear, how sad that she should be in debt!' I can hear you say this, and sigh to yourself—you who have never known what it was to be in want of money since you were born. Shall I tell you what my husband earns at the University? No: I feel the blood rushing into my face at the bare idea of revealing it.

"Let me do the Professor justice. My Animated Mummy has reached the height of his ambition at last—he is Professor of Chemistry, and is perfectly happy for the rest of his life. My dear, he is as lean, and almost as dirty, as the wretch who first perverted him. Do you remember my once writing to you about a mysterious Hungarian, whom we found in the University? A few years since, this man died by suicide, as mysteriously as he had lived. They found him in the laboratory, with a strange inscription traced in chalk on the wall by which he lay dead. These were the words:—'After giving it a fair trial, I find that life is not worth living for. I have decided to destroy myself with a poison of my own discovery. My chemical papers and preparations are hereby bequeathed to my friend Doctor ——, and my body is presented as a free gift to the anatomy school. Let a committee of surgeons and analysts examine my remains. I defy them to discover a trace of the drug that has killed me.' And they did try, Julie—and discovered nothing. I wonder whether the suicide has left the receipt for that poison, among his other precious legacies, to his 'friend Doctor ——.'

"Why do I trouble you with these nauseous details? Because they are in no small degree answerable for my debts. My husband devotes all his leisure hours to continuing the detestable experiments begun by the Hungarian; and my yearly dress-money for myself and my child has been reduced one half, to pay the chemical expenses.

"Ought I, in this hard case, to have diminished my expenditure to the level of my reduced income?

"If you say Yes, I answer that human endurance has its limits. I can support the martyrdom of my life; the loss of my dearest illusions and hopes; the mean enmity of our neighbors; the foul-mouthed jealousy of the women; and, more than all, the exasperating patience of a husband who never resents the hardest things I can say to him, and who persists in loving and admiring me as if we were only married last week. But I cannot see my child in a stuff frock, on promenade days in the Palace Gardens, when other people's children are wearing silk. And plain as my own dress may be, I must and will have the best material that is made. When the wife of the military commandant (a woman sprung from the people) goes out in an Indian shawl with Brussels lace in her bonnet, am I to meet her and return her bow, in a camelot cloak and a beaver hat? No! When I lose my self-respect let me lose my life too. My husband may sink as low as he pleases. I always have stood above him, and I always will!

"And so I am in debt, and my creditors threaten me. What does it matter? I have pacified them, for the time, with some small installments of money, and a large expenditure of smiles.

"I wish you could see my darling little Minna; she is the loveliest and sweetest child in the world—my pride at all times, and my salvation in my desperate moods. There are moments when I feel inclined to set fire to the hateful University, and destroy all the moldy old creatures who inhabit it. I take Minna out and buy her a little present, and see her eyes sparkle and her color rise, and feel her innocent kisses, and become, for awhile, quite a good woman again. Yesterday, her father—no, I shall work myself up into a fury if I tell you about it. Let me only say that Minna saved me as usual. I took her to the jeweler's and bought her a pair of pearl earrings. If you could have heard her, if you could have seen her, when the little angel first looked at herself in the glass! I wonder when I shall pay for the earrings?

"Ah, Julie, if I only had such an income as yours, I would make my power felt in this place. The insolent women should fawn on me and fear me. I would have my own house and establishment in the country, to purify me after the atmosphere of the Professor's drugs. I would—well! well! never mind what else I would have.

"Talking of power, have you read the account of the execution last year of that wonderful criminal, Anna Maria Zwanziger? Wherever she went, the path of this terrific woman is strewed with the dead whom she has poisoned. She appears to have lived to destroy her fellow-creatures, and to have met her doom with the most undaunted courage. What a career! and what an end! (1)

"The foolish people in Wurzburg are at a loss to find motives for some of the murders she committed, and try to get out of the difficulty by declaring that she must have been a homicidal maniac. That is not my explanation. I can understand the murderess becoming morally intoxicated with the sense of her own tremendous power. A mere human creature—only a woman, Julie!—armed with the means of secretly dealing death with her, wherever she goes—meeting with strangers who displease her, looking at them quietly, and saying to herself, "I doom you to die, before you are a day older"—is there no explanation, here, of some of Zwanziger's poisonings which are incomprehensible to commonplace minds?

"I put this view, in talking of the trial, to the military commandant a few days since. His vulgar wife answered me before he could speak. 'Madame Fontaine,' said this spitfire, 'my husband and I don't feel your sympathy with poisoners!' Take that as a specimen of the ladies of Wurzburg—and let me close this unmercifully long letter. I think you will acknowledge, my dear, that, when I do write, I place a flattering trust in my friend's patient remembrance of me."

There the newspaper extracts came to an end.

As a picture of a perverted mind, struggling between good and evil, and slowly losing ground under the stealthy influence of temptation, the letters certainly possessed a melancholy interest for any thoughtful reader. But (not being a spiteful woman) I failed to see, in these extracts, the connection which Frau Meyer had attempted to establish between the wickedness of Madame Fontaine and the disappearance of her husband's medicine chest.

At the same time, I must acknowledge that a vague impression of distrust was left on my mind by what I had read. I felt a certain sense of embarrassment at the prospect of renewing my relations with the widow, on my return to Frankfort; and I was also conscious of a decided increase of anxiety to hear what had been Mr. Keller's reception of Madame Fontaine's letter. Add to this, that my brotherly interest in Minna was sensibly strengthened—and the effect on me of the extracts in the newspaper is truly stated, so far as I can remember it at this distant time.

On the evening of the next day, I was back again at Frankfort.

(1) The terrible career of Anna Maria Zwanziger, sentenced to death at Bamberg in the year 1811, will be found related in Lady Duff-Gordon's translation of Feuerbach's "Criminal Trials."

CHAPTER XVI

Mr. Keller and Mr. Engelman were both waiting to receive me. They looked over my written report of my inquiries at Hanau, and expressed the warmest approval of it. So far, all was well.

But, when we afterwards sat down to our supper, I noticed a change in the two partners, which it was impossible to see without regret. On the surface they were as friendly towards each other as ever. But a certain constraint of look and manner, a palpable effort, on either side, to speak with the old unsought ease and gaiety, showed that the disastrous discovery of Madame Fontaine in the hall had left its evil results behind it. Mr. Keller retired, when the meal was over, to examine my report minutely in all its details.

When we were alone, Mr. Engelman lit his pipe. He spoke to me once more with the friendly familiarity of past days—before he met the too-fascinating widow on the bridge.

"My dear boy, tell me frankly, do you notice any change in Keller?"

"I see a change in both of you," I answered: "you are not such pleasant companions as you used to be."

Mr. Engelman blew out a mouthful of smoke, and followed it by a heavy sigh.

"Keller has become so bitter," he said. "His hasty temper I never complained of, as you know. But in these later days he is hard—hard as stone. Do you know what he did with dear Madame Fontaine's letter? A downright insult, David—he sent it back to her!"

"Without explanation or apology?" I asked.

"With a line on the envelope. 'I warned you that I should refuse to read

97

your letter. You see that I am a man of my word.' What a message to send to a poor mother, who only asks leave to plead for her child's happiness! You saw the letter. Enough to melt the heart of any man, as I should have thought. I spoke to Keller on the subject; I really couldn't help it."

"Wasn't that rather indiscreet, Mr. Engelman?"

"I said nothing that could reasonably offend him. 'Do you know of some discreditable action on the part of Madame Fontaine, which has not been found out by anyone else?' I asked. 'I know the character she bears in Wurzburg,' he said; 'and the other night I saw her face. That is all I know, friend Engelman, and that is enough for me.' With those sour words, he walked out of the room. What lamentable prejudice! What an unchristian way of thinking! The name of Madame Fontaine will never be mentioned between us again. When that much-injured lady honors me with another visit, I can only receive her where she will be protected from insult, in a house of my own."

"Surely you are not going to separate yourself from Mr. Keller?" I said.

"Not for the present. I will wait till your aunt comes here, and brings that restless reforming spirit of hers into the business. Changes are sure to follow—and my change of residence may pass as one of them."

He got up to leave the room, and stopped at the door.

"I wish you would come with me, David, to Madame Fontaine's. She is very anxious to see you." Feeling no such anxiety on my side, I attempted to excuse myself; but he went on without giving me time to speak—"Nice little Miss Minna is very dull, poor child. She has no friend of her own age here at Frankfort, excepting yourself. And she has asked me more than once when Mr. David would return from Hanau."

My excuses failed me when I heard this. Mr. Engelman and I left the house together.

As we approached the door of Madame Fontaine's lodgings, it was opened from within by the landlady, and a stranger stepped out into the street. He was sufficiently well dressed to pass for a gentleman—but there were obstacles in his face and manner to a successful personation of the character. He cast a peculiarly furtive look at us both, as we ascended the house-steps. I thought he was a police spy. Mr. Engelman set him down a degree lower in the social scale.

"I hope you are not in debt, ma'am," he said to the landlady; "that man looks to me like a bailiff in disguise."

"I manage to pay my way, sir, though it is a hard struggle," the woman replied. "As for the gentleman who has just gone out, I know no more of him than you do."

"May I ask what he wanted here?"

"He wanted to know when Madame Fontaine was likely to quit my apartments. I told him my lodger had not appointed any time for leaving me yet."

"Did he mention Madame Fontaine's name?"

"Yes, sir."

"How did he know that she lived here?"

"He didn't say."

"And you didn't think of asking him?"

"It was very stupid of me, sir—I only asked him how he came to know that I let apartments. He said, 'Never mind, now; I am well recommended, and I'll call again, and tell you about it.' And then I opened the door for him, as you saw."

"Did he ask to see Madame Fontaine?"

"No, sir."

"Very odd!" said Mr. Engelman, as we went upstairs. "Do you think we ought to mention it?"

I thought not. There was nothing at all uncommon in the stranger's inquiries, taken by themselves. We had no right, that I could see, to alarm the widow, because we happened to attach purely fanciful suspicions to a man of whom we knew nothing. I expressed this opinion to Mr. Engelman; and he agreed with me.

The same subdued tone which had struck me in the little household in Main Street, was again visible in the welcome which I received in Madame Fontaine's lodgings. Minna looked weary of waiting for the long-expected letter from Fritz. Minna's mother pressed my hand in silence, with a melancholy smile. Her reception of my companion struck me as showing some constraint. After what had happened on the night of her visit to the house, she could no longer expect him to help her to an interview with Mr. Keller. Was she merely keeping up appearances, on the chance that he might yet be useful to her, in some other way? The trifling change which I observed did not appear to present itself to Mr. Engelman. I turned away to Minna. Knowing what I knew, it grieved me to see that the poor old man was fonder of the widow, and prouder of her than ever.

It was no very hard task to revive the natural hopefulness of Minna's nature. Calculating the question of time in the days before railroads, I was able to predict the arrival of Fritz's letter in two, or at most three days more. This bright prospect was instantly reflected in the girl's innocent face. Her interest in the little world about her revived. When her mother joined us, in our corner of the room, I was telling her all that could be safely related of my visit to Hanau. Madame Fontaine seemed to be quite as attentive as her daughter to the progress of my trivial narrative—to Mr. Engelman's evident surprise.

"Did you go farther than Hanau?" the widow asked.

"No farther."

"Were there any guests to meet you at the dinner-party?"

"Only the members of the family."

"I lived so long, David, in dull old Wurzburg, that I can't help feeling a certain interest in the town. Did the subject turn up? Did you hear of anything that was going on there?"

I answered this as cautiously as I had answered the questions that had gone before it. Frau Meyer had, I fear, partially succeeded in perverting my sense of justice. Before my journey to Hanau, I might have attributed the widow's inquiries to mere curiosity. I believed suspicion to be the ruling motive with her, now.

Before any more questions could be asked, Mr. Engelman changed the topic to a subject of greater interest to himself. "I have told David, dear lady, of Mr. Keller's inhuman reception of your letter."

"Don't say 'inhuman,'" Madame Fontaine answered gently; "it is I alone who am to blame. I have been a cause of estrangement between you and your partner, and I have destroyed whatever little chance I might once have had of setting myself right in Mr. Keller's estimation. All due to my rashness in mentioning my name. If I had been less fond of my little girl here, and less eager to seize the first opportunity of pleading for her, I should never have committed that fatal mistake."

So far, this was sensibly said—and, as an explanation of her own imprudence, was unquestionably no more than the truth.

I was less favorably impressed by what followed, when she went on;

"Pray understand, David, that I don't complain. I feel no ill-will towards Mr. Keller. If chance placed the opportunity of doing him a service in my hands, I should be ready and willing to make use of it—I should be only too glad to repair the mischief that I have so innocently done."

She raised her handkerchief to her eyes. Mr. Engelman raised his handkerchief to his eyes. Minna took her mother's hand. I alone sat undemonstrative, with my sympathies in a state of repose. Frau Meyer again! Nothing but the influence of Frau Meyer could have hardened me in this way!

"I have entreated our sweet friend not to leave Frankfort in despair," Mr. Engelman explained in faltering tones. "Although my influence with Keller is, for the present, a lost influence in this matter, I am more than willing—I am eager—to speak to Mrs. Wagner on Madame Fontaine's behalf. My advice is, Wait for Mrs. Wagner's arrival, and trust to my zeal, and my position in the firm. When both his partners summon him to do justice to an injured woman, even Keller must submit!"

The widow's eyes were still hidden behind her handkerchief. But the lower part of her face was visible. Unless I completely misinterpreted the mute language of her lips, she had not the faintest belief in the fulfillment of Mr. Engelman's prediction. Whatever reason she might have for remaining in Frankfort, after the definite rejection of her too-confident appeal to Mr. Keller's sympathies, was thus far undoubtedly a reason known only to herself. That very night, after we had left her, an incident occurred which suggested that she had some motive for ingratiating herself with one of the servants in Mr. Keller's house.

Our domestic establishment indoors consisted of the sour-tempered old housekeeper (who was perfectly unapproachable); of a little kitchen-maid (too unimportant a person to be worth conciliating); and of the footman Joseph, who performed the usual duties of waiting on us at table, and answering the door. This last was a foolish young man, excessively vain of his personal appearance—but a passably good servant, making allowance for these defects.

Having occasion to ring for Joseph, to do me some little service, I noticed that the loose ends of his necktie were connected by a smart new pin, presenting a circle of malachite set in silver.

"Have you had a present lately," I asked, "or are you extravagant enough to spend your money on buying jewelry?"

Joseph simpered in undisguised satisfaction with himself. "It's a present, sir, from Madame Fontaine. I take her flowers almost every day from Mr. Engelman, and I have done one or two trifling errands for her in the town. She was pleased with my attention to her wishes. 'I have very little money, Mr. Joseph,' she said; 'oblige me by accepting this pin in return for the trouble I have given you.' And she took the pin out of the beautiful white lace round her neck, and made me a present of it with her own hand. A most liberal lady, isn't she, sir?"

"Liberal indeed, Joseph, considering the small services which you seem to have rendered to her. Are you quite sure that she doesn't expect something more of you?"

"Oh, quite sure, sir." He blushed as he said that—and rather hurriedly left the room. How would Frau Meyer have interpreted Joseph's blushes, and the widow's liberality? I went to bed without caring to pursue that question.

A lapse of two days more brought with it two interesting events: the opening night of a traveling opera company on a visit to Frankfort, and the arrival by a late post of our long-expected letters from London.

The partners (both of them ardent lovers of music) had taken a box for the short season, and, with their usual kindness, had placed a seat at my disposal. We were all three drinking our coffee before going to the theater, and Joseph was waiting on us, when the rheumatic old housekeeper brought in the letters, and handed them to me, as the person who sat nearest to the door.

"Why, my good creature, what has made you climb the stairs, when you might have rung for Joseph?" asked kind-hearted Mr. Engelman.

"Because I have got something to ask of my masters," answered crabbed Mother Barbara. "There are your letters, to begin with. Is it true that you are, all three of you, going to the theater to-night?"

She never used any of the ordinary terms of respect. If she had been their mother, instead of their housekeeper, she could not have spoken more familiarly to the two old gentlemen who employed her.

"Well," she went on, "my daughter is in trouble about her baby, and wants my advice. Teething, and convulsions, and that sort of thing. As you are all going out for the evening, you don't want me, after I have put your bedrooms tidy. I can go to my daughter for an hour or two, I suppose—and Joseph (who isn't of much use, heaven knows) can take care of the house."

Mr. Keller, refreshing his memory of the opera of the night (Gluck's

"Armida") by consulting the book, nodded, and went on with his reading. Mr. Engelman said, "Certainly, my good soul; give my best wishes to your daughter for the baby's health." Mother Barbara grunted, and hobbled out of the room.

I looked at the letters. Two were for me—from my aunt and Fritz. One was for Mr. Keller—addressed also in the handwriting of my aunt. When I handed it to him across the table, he dropped "Armida" the moment he looked at the envelope. It was the answer to his remonstrance on the subject of the employment of women.

For Minna's sake, I opened Fritz's letter first. It contained the long-expected lines to his sweetheart. I went out at once, and, enclosing the letter in an envelope, sent Joseph away with it to the widow's lodgings before Mother Barbara's departure made it necessary for him to remain in the house.

Fritz's letter to me was very unsatisfactory. In my absence, London was unendurably dull to him, and Minna was more necessary to the happiness of his life than ever. He desired to be informed, by return of post, of the present place of residence of Madame Fontaine and her daughter. If I refused to comply with this request, he could not undertake to control himself, and he thought it quite likely that he might "follow his heart's dearest aspirations," and set forth on the journey to Frankfort in search of Minna.

My aunt's letter was full of the subject of Jack Straw.

In the first place she had discovered, while arranging her late husband's library, a book which had evidently suggested his ideas of reformation in the treatment of the insane. It was called, "Description of the Retreat, an institution near York for insane persons of the Society of Friends. Written by Samuel Tuke." She had communicated with the institution; had received the most invaluable help; and would bring the book with her to Frankfort, to be translated into German, in the interests of humanity. (1)

(1) Tuke's Description of the Retreat near York is reviewed by Sydney Smith in a number of the "Edinburgh Review," for 1814.

As for her merciful experiment with poor Jack, it had proved to be completely successful—with one serious drawback. So long as he was under her eye, and in daily communication with her, a more grateful, affectionate, and perfectly harmless creature never breathed the breath of life. Even Mr. Hartrey and the lawyer had been obliged to confess that they had been in the wrong throughout, in the view they had taken of the matter. But, when she happened to be absent from the house, for any length of time, it was not to be denied that Jack relapsed. He did nothing that was violent or alarming— he merely laid himself down on the mat before the door of her room, and refused to eat, drink, speak, or move, until she returned. He heard her outside the door, before anyone else was aware that she was near the house; and his joy burst out in a scream which did certainly recall Bedlam. That was the drawback, and the only drawback; and how she was to take the journey to Frankfort, which Mr. Keller's absurd remonstrance had rendered absolutely necessary, was more than my aunt's utmost ingenuity could thus far discover. Setting aside the difficulty of disposing of Jack, there was another difficulty, represented by Fritz. It was in the last degree doubtful if he could be trusted to remain in London in her absence. "But I shall manage it," the resolute woman concluded. "I never yet despaired of anything—and I don't despair now."

Returning to the sitting-room, when it was time to go to the theater, I found Mr. Keller with his temper in a flame, and Mr. Engelman silently smoking as usual.

"Read that!" cried Mr. Keller, tossing my aunt's reply to him across the table. "It won't take long."

It was literally a letter of four lines! "I have received your remonstrance. It is useless for two people who disagree as widely as we do, to write to each other. Please wait for my answer, until I arrive at Frankfort."

"Let's go to the music!" cried Mr. Keller. "God knows, I want a composing influence of some kind."

At the end of the first act of the opera, a new trouble exhausted his small stock of patience. He had been too irritated, on leaving the house, to remember his opera-glass; and he was sufficiently near-sighted to feel the want of it. It is needless to say that I left the theater at once to bring back the glass in time for the next act.

My instructions informed me that I should find it on his bedroom-table.

I thought Joseph looked confused when he opened the house-door to me. As I ran upstairs, he followed me, saying something. I was in too great a hurry to pay any attention to him.

Reaching the second floor by two stairs at a time, I burst into Mr. Keller's bedroom, and found myself face to face with—Madame Fontaine!

CHAPTER XVII

The widow was alone in the room; standing by the bedside table on which Mr. Keller's night-drink was placed. I was so completely taken by surprise, that I stood stock-still like a fool, and stared at Madame Fontaine in silence.

On her side she was, as I believe, equally astonished and equally confounded, but better able to conceal it. For the moment, and only for the moment, she too had nothing to say. Then she lifted her left hand from under her shawl. "You have caught me, Mr. David!" she said—and held up a drawing-book as she spoke.

"What are you doing here?" I asked.

She pointed with the book to the famous carved mantelpiece.

"You know how I longed to make a study of that glorious work," she answered. "Don't be hard on a poor artist who takes her opportunity when she finds it."

"May I ask how you came to know of the opportunity, Madame Fontaine?"

"Entirely through your kind sympathy, my friend," was the cool reply.

"My sympathy? What do you mean?"

"Was it not you, David, who considerately thought of Minna when the post came in? And did you not send the man-servant to us, with her letter from Fritz?"

The blubbering voice of Joseph, trembling for his situation, on the landing outside, interrupted me before I could speak again.

"I'm sure I meant no harm, sir. I only said I was in a hurry to get back, because you had all gone to the theater, and I was left (with nobody but the kitchen girl) to take care of the house. When the lady came, and showed me her drawing-book——"

"That will do, friend Joseph," said the widow, signing to him to go downstairs in her easy self-possessed way. "Mr. David is too sensible to take notice of trifles. There! there! go down," She turned to me, with an expression of playful surprise. "How very serious you look!" she said gaily.

"It might have been serious for you, Madame Fontaine, if Mr. Keller had returned to the house to fetch his opera-glass himself."

"Ah! he has left his opera-glass behind him? Let me help you to look for it. I have done my sketch; I am quite at your service." She forestalled me in finding the opera-glass. "I really had no other chance of making a study of the chimney-piece," she went on, as she handed the glass to me. "Impossible to ask Mr. Engelman to let me in again, after what happened on the last occasion. And, if I must confess it, there is another motive besides my admiration for the chimney-piece. You know how poor we are. The man who keeps the picture-shop in the Zeil is willing to employ me. He can always sell these memorials of old Frankfort to English travelers. Even the few forms he gives me will find two half-starved women in housekeeping money for a week."

It was all very plausible; and perhaps (in my innocent days before I met with Frau Meyer) I might have thought it quite likely to be true. In my present frame of mind, I only asked the widow if I might see her sketch.

She shook her head, and sheltered the drawing-book again under her shawl.

"It is little better than a memorandum at present," she explained. "Wait

107

till I have touched it up, and made it saleable—and I will show it to you with pleasure. You will not make mischief, Mr. David, by mentioning my act of artistic invasion to either of the old gentlemen? It shall not be repeated—I give you my word of honor. There is poor Joseph, too. You don't want to ruin a well-meaning lad, by getting him turned out of his place? Of course not! We part as friends who understand each other, don't we? Minna would have sent her love and thanks, if she had known I was to meet you. Good-night."

She ran downstairs, humming a little tune to herself, as blithe as a young girl. I heard a momentary whispering with Joseph in the hall. Then the house-door closed—and there was an end of Madame Fontaine for that time.

After no very long reflection, I decided that my best course would be to severely caution Joseph, and to say nothing to the partners of what had happened—for the present, at least. I should certainly do mischief, by setting the two old friends at variance again on the subject of the widow, if I spoke; to say nothing (as another result) of the likelihood of Joseph's dismissal by Mr. Keller. Actuated by these reasonable considerations, I am bound frankly to add that I must have felt some vague misgivings as well. Otherwise, why did I carefully examine Mr. Keller's room (before I returned to the theater), without any distinct idea of any conceivable discovery that I might make? Not the vestige of a suspicious appearance rewarded my search. The room was in its customary state of order, from the razors and brushes on the toilet-table to the regular night-drink of barley-water, ready as usual in the jug by the bedside.

I left the bedchamber at last. Why was I still not at my ease? Why was I rude enough, when I thought of the widow, to say to myself, "Damn her!" Why did I find Gluck's magnificent music grow wearisome from want of melody as it went on? Let the learned in such things realize my position, and honor me by answering those questions for themselves.

We were quite gay at supper; the visit to the theater had roused the spirits of the two partners, by means of a wholesome break in the monotony of their lives. I had seldom seen Mr. Keller so easy and so cheerful. Always an abstemious man, he exercised his usual moderation in eating and drinking;

and he was the first to go to bed. But, while he was with us, he was, in the best sense of the word, a delightful companion; and he looked forward to the next opera night with the glee of a schoolboy looking forward to a holiday.

CHAPTER XVIII

The breakfast-room proved to be empty when I entered it the next morning. It was the first time in my experience that I had failed to find Mr. Keller established at the table. He had hitherto set the example of early rising to his partner and to myself. I had barely noticed his absence, when Mr. Engelman followed me into the room with a grave and anxious face, which proclaimed that something was amiss.

"Where is Mr. Keller?" I asked.

"In bed, David."

"Not ill, I hope?"

"I don't know what is the matter with him, my dear boy. He says he has passed a bad night, and he can't leave his bed and attend to business as usual. Is it the close air of the theater, do you think?"

"Suppose I make him a comfortable English cup of tea?" I suggested.

"Yes, yes! And take it up yourself. I should like to know what you think of him."

Mr. Keller alarmed me in the first moment when I looked at him. A dreadful apathy had possessed itself of this naturally restless and energetic man. He lay quite motionless, except an intermittent trembling of his hands as they rested on the counterpane. His eyes opened for a moment when I spoke to him—then closed again as if the effort of looking at anything wearied him. He feebly shook his head when I offered him the cup of tea, and said in a fretful whisper, "Let me be!" I looked at his night-drink. The jug and glass were both completely empty. "Were you thirsty in the night?" In the same fretful whisper he answered, "Horribly!" "Are you not thirsty now?" He only repeated the words he had first spoken—"Let me be!" There he lay, wanting nothing, caring for nothing; his face looking pinched and wan already, and the intermittent trembling still at regular intervals shaking his helpless hands.

We sent at once for the physician who had attended him in trifling illnesses at former dates.

The doctor who is not honest enough to confess it when he is puzzled, is a well-known member of the medical profession in all countries. Our present physician was one of that sort. He pronounced the patient to be suffering from low (or nervous) fever—but it struck Mr. Engelman, as it struck me, that he found himself obliged to say something, and said it without feeling sure of the correctness of his own statement. He prescribed, and promised to pay us a second visit later in the day. Mother Barbara, the housekeeper, was already installed as nurse. Always a domestic despot, she made her tyranny felt even in the sick-room. She declared that she would leave the house if any other woman presumed to enter it as nurse. "When my master is ill," said Mother Barbara, "my master is my property." It was plainly impossible that a woman, at her advanced age, could keep watch at the bedside by day and night together. In the interests of peace we decided on waiting until the next day. If Mr. Keller showed no signs of improvement by that time, I undertook to inquire at the hospital for a properly qualified nurse.

Later in the day, our doubts of the doctor were confirmed. He betrayed his own perplexity in arriving at a true "diagnosis" of the patient's case, by bringing with him, at his second visit, a brother-physician, whom he introduced as Doctor Dormann, and with whom he asked leave to consult at the bedside.

The new doctor was the younger, and evidently the firmer person of the two.

His examination of the sick man was patient and careful in the extreme. He questioned us minutely about the period at which the illness had begun; the state of Mr. Keller's health immediately before it; the first symptoms noticed; what he had eaten, and what he had drunk; and so on. Next, he desired to see all the inmates of the house who had access to the bed-chamber; looking with steady scrutiny at the housekeeper, the footman, and the maid, as they followed each other into the room—and dismissing them again without remark. Lastly, he astounded his old colleague by proposing to administer an emetic. There was no prevailing on him to give his reasons. "If I prove to be right, you shall hear my reasons. If I prove to be wrong, I have only to say so, and no reasons will be required. Clear the room, administer the emetic, and keep the door locked till I come back."

With those parting directions he hurried out of the house.

"What can he mean?" said Mr. Engelman, leading the way out of the bedchamber.

The elder doctor left in charge heard the words, and answered them, addressing himself, not to Mr. Engelman, but to me. He caught me by the arm, as I was leaving the room in my turn.

"Poison!" the doctor whispered in my ear. "Keep it a secret; that's what he means."

I ran to my own bedchamber and bolted myself in. At that one word, "Poison," the atrocious suggestion of Frau Meyer, when she had referred to Doctor Fontaine's lost medicine-chest, instantly associated itself in my memory with Madame Fontaine's suspicious intrusion into Mr. Keller's room. Good God! had I not surprised her standing close by the table on which the night-drink was set? and had I not heard Doctor Dormann say, "That's unlucky," when he was told that the barley-water had been all drunk by the patient, and the jug and glass washed as usual? For the first few moments, I really think I must have been beside myself, so completely was I overpowered by the horror of my own suspicions. I had just sense enough to keep out of Mr. Engelman's way until I felt my mind restored in some degree to its customary balance.

Recovering the power of thinking connectedly, I began to feel ashamed of the panic which had seized on me.

What conceivable object had the widow to gain by Mr. Keller's death? Her whole interest in her daughter's future centered, on the contrary, in his living long enough to be made ashamed of his prejudices, and to give his consent to the marriage. To kill him for the purpose of removing Fritz from the influence of his father's authority would be so atrocious an act in itself, and would so certainly separate Minna and Fritz for ever, in the perfectly possible event of a discovery, that I really recoiled from the contemplation of this contingency as I might have recoiled from deliberately disgracing myself. Doctor Dormann had rashly rushed at a false conclusion—that was the one comforting reflection that occurred to me. I threw open my door again in a frenzy of impatience to hear the decision, whichever way it might turn.

The experiment had been tried in my absence. Mr. Keller had fallen into a broken slumber. Doctor Dormann was just closing the little bag in which he had brought his testing apparatus from his own house. Even now there was no prevailing on him to state his suspicions plainly.

"It's curious," he said, "to see how all mortal speculations on events, generally resolve themselves into threes. Have we given the emetic too late? Are my tests insufficient? Or have I made a complete mistake?" He turned to his elder colleague. "My dear doctor, I see you want a positive answer. No need to leave the room, Mr. Engelman! You and the young English gentleman, your friend, must not be deceived for a single moment so far as I am concerned. I see in the patient a mysterious wasting of the vital powers, which is not accompanied by the symptoms of any disease known to me to which I can point as a cause. In plain words, I tell you, I don't understand Mr. Keller's illness."

It was perhaps through a motive of delicacy that he persisted in making a needless mystery of his suspicions. In any case he was evidently a man who despised all quackery from the bottom of his heart. The old doctor looked at him with a frown of disapproval, as if his frank confession had violated the unwritten laws of medical etiquette.

"If you will allow me to watch the case," he resumed, "under the superintendence of my respected colleague, I shall be happy to submit to approval any palliative treatment which may occur to me. My respected colleague knows that I am always ready to learn."

His respected colleague made a formal bow, looked at his watch, and hastened away to another patient. Doctor Dormann, taking up his hat, stopped to look at Mother Barbara, fast asleep in her easy chair by the bedside.

"I must find you a competent nurse to-morrow," he said. "No, not one of the hospital women—we want someone with finer feelings and tenderer hands than theirs. In the meantime, one of you must sit up with Mr. Keller to-night. If I am not wanted before, I will be with you to-morrow morning."

I volunteered to keep watch; promising to call Mr. Engelman if any alarming symptoms showed themselves. The old housekeeper, waking after her first sleep, characteristically insisted on sending me to bed, and taking my place. I was too anxious and uneasy (if I may say it of myself) to be as compliant as usual. Mother Barbara, for once, found that she had a resolute person to deal with. At a less distressing time, there would have been something irresistibly comical in her rage and astonishment, when I settled the dispute by locking her out of the room.

Soon afterwards Joseph came in with a message. If there was no immediate necessity for his presence in the bedchamber, Mr. Engelman would go out to get a breath of fresh air, before he retired for the night. There was no necessity for his presence; and I sent a message downstairs to that effect.

An hour later Mr. Engelman came in to see his old friend, and to say good-night. After an interval of restlessness, the sufferer had become composed, and was dozing again under the influence of his medicine. Making all allowances for the sorrow and anxiety which Mr. Engelman must necessarily feel under the circumstances, I thought his manner strangely absent and confused. He looked like a man with some burden on his mind which he was afraid to reveal and unable to throw off.

"Somebody must be found, David, who does understand the case," he said, looking at the helpless figure on the bed.

"Who can we find?" I asked.

He bade me good-night without answering. It is no exaggeration to say that I passed my night at the bedside in a miserable state of indecision and suspense. The doctor's experiment had failed to prove absolutely that the doctor's doubts were without foundation. In this state of things, was it my bounden duty to tell the medical men what I had seen, when I went back to the house to look for Mr. Keller's opera-glass? The more I thought of it, the more I recoiled from the idea of throwing a frightful suspicion on Minna's mother which would overshadow an innocent woman for the rest of her life. What proof had I that she had lied to me about the sketch and the mantlepiece? And, without proof, how could I, how dare I, open my lips? I succeeded in deciding firmly enough for the alternative of silence, during the intervals when my attendance on the sick man was not required. But, when he wanted his medicine, when his pillows needed a little arrangement, when I saw his poor eyes open, and look at me vacantly—then my resolution failed me; my indecision returned; the horrid necessity of speaking showed itself again, and shook me to the soul. Never in the trials of later life have I passed such a night as that night at Mr. Keller's bedside.

When the light of the new day shone in at the window, it was but too plainly visible that the symptoms had altered for the worse.

The apathy was more profound, the wan pinched look of the face had increased, the intervals between the attacks of nervous trembling had grown shorter and shorter. Come what might of it, when Dr. Dormann paid his promised visit, I felt I was now bound to inform him that another person besides the servants and ourselves had obtained access secretly to Mr. Keller's room.

I was so completely worn out by agitation and want of sleep—and I showed it, I suppose, so plainly—that good Mr. Engelman insisted on my leaving him in charge, and retiring to rest. I lay down on my bed, with the door of my room ajar, resolved to listen for the doctor's footsteps on the stairs, and to speak to him privately after he had seen the patient.

If I had been twenty years older, I might have succeeded in carrying out my intention. But, with the young, sleep is a paramount necessity, and nature insists on obedience to its merciful law. I remember feeling drowsy; starting up from the bed, and walking about my room, to keep myself awake; then lying down again from sheer fatigue; and after that—total oblivion! When I woke, and looked at my watch, I found that I had been fast asleep for no less

114

than six hours!

Bewildered and ashamed of myself—afraid to think of what might have happened in that long interval—I hurried to Mr. Keller's room, and softly knocked at the door.

A woman's voice answered me, "Come in!"

I paused with my hand on the door—the voice was familiar to me. I had a moment's doubt whether I was mad or dreaming. The voice softly repeated, "Come in!" I entered the room.

There she was, seated at the bedside, smiling quietly and lifting her finger to her lips! As certainly as I saw the familiar objects in the room, and the prostrate figure on the bed, I saw—Madame Fontaine!

"Speak low," she said. "He sleeps very lightly; he must not be disturbed."

I approached the bed and looked at him. There was a faint tinge of color in his face; there was moisture on his forehead; his hands lay as still on the counterpane, in the blessed repose that possessed him, as the hands of a sleeping child. I looked round at Madame Fontaine.

She smiled again; my utter bewilderment seemed to amuse her. "He is left entirely to me, David," she said, looking tenderly at her patient. "Go downstairs and see Mr. Engelman. There must be no talking here."

She lightly wiped the perspiration from his forehead; lightly laid her fingers on his pulse—then reclined in the easy chair, with her eyes fixed in silent interest on the sleeping man. She was the very ideal of the nurse with fine feelings and tender hands, contemplated by Doctor Dormann when I had last seen him. Any stranger looking into the room at that moment would have said, "What a charming picture! What a devoted wife!"

CHAPTER XIX

"A tumbler of the old Marcobrunner, David, and a slice of the game pie—before I say one word about what we owe to that angel upstairs. Off with the wine, my dear boy; you look as pale as death!"

With those words Mr. Engelman lit his pipe, and waited in silence until the good eating and drinking had done their good work.

"Now carry your mind back to last night," he began. "You remember my going out to get a breath of fresh air. Can you guess what that meant?"

I guessed of course that it meant a visit to Madame Fontaine.

"Quite right, David. I promised to call on her earlier in the day; but poor Keller's illness made that impossible. She wrote to me under the impression that something serious must have happened to prevent me, for the first time, from keeping an appointment that I had made with her. When I left you I went to answer her note personally. She was not only distressed to hear of Mr. Keller's illness, she was interested enough in my sad news to ask particularly in what form the illness declared itself. When I mentioned what the symptoms were, she showed an agitation which took me quite by surprise. 'Do the doctors understand what is the matter with him?' she asked. I told her that one of the doctors was evidently puzzled, and that the other had acknowledged that the malady was so far incomprehensible to him. She clasped her hands in despair—she said, 'Oh, if my poor husband had been alive!' I naturally asked what she meant. I wish I could give her explanation, David, in her own delightful words. It came in substance to this. Some person in her husband's employment at the University of Wurzburg had been attacked by a malady presenting exactly the same symptoms from which Mr. Keller was suffering. The medical men had been just as much at a loss what to do as our medical men. Alone among them Doctor Fontaine understood the case. He made up the medicine that he administered with his own hand. Madame Fontaine, under her husband's instructions, assisted in nursing the sick man, and in giving the nourishment prescribed when he was able to eat. His extraordinary recovery is remembered in the University to this day."

I interrupted Mr. Engelman at that point. "Of course you asked her for the prescription?" I said. "I begin to understand it now."

"No, David; you don't understand it yet. I certainly asked her for the prescription. No such thing was known to be in existence—she reminded me that her husband had made up the medicine himself. But she remembered that the results had exceeded his anticipations, and that only a part of the

116

remedy had been used. The bottle might still perhaps be found at Wurzburg. Or it might be in a small portmanteau belonging to her husband, which she had found in his bedroom, and had brought away with her, to be examined at some future time. 'I have not had the heart to open it yet,' she said; 'but for Mr. Keller's sake, I will look it over before you go away.' There is a Christian woman, David, if ever there was one yet! After the manner in which poor Keller had treated her, she was as eager to help him as if he had been her dearest friend. Minna offered to take her place. 'Why should you distress yourself, mamma?' she said. 'Tell me what the bottle is like, and let me try if I can find it.' No! It was quite enough for Madame Fontaine that there was an act of mercy to be done. At any sacrifice of her own feelings, she was prepared to do it."

I interrupted him again, eager to hear the end.

"And she found the bottle?" I said.

"She found the bottle," Mr. Engelman resumed. "I can show it to you, if you like. She has herself requested me to keep it under lock and key, so long as it is wanted in this house."

He opened an old cabinet, and took out a long narrow bottle of dark-blue glass. In form, it was quaintly and remarkably unlike any modern bottle that I had ever seen. The glass stopper was carefully secured by a piece of leather, for the better preservation, I suppose, of the liquid inside. Down one side of the bottle ran a narrow strip of paper, notched at regular intervals to indicate the dose that was to be given. No label appeared on it; but, examining the surface of the glass carefully, I found certain faintly-marked stains, which suggested that the label might have been removed, and that some traces of the paste or gum by which it had been secured had not been completely washed away. I held the bottle up to the light, and found that it was still nearly half full. Mr. Engelman forbade me to remove the stopper. It was very important, he said, that no air should be admitted to the bottle, except when there was an actual necessity for administering the remedy.

"I took it away with me the same night," he went on. "And a wretched state of mind I was in, between my anxiety to give the medicine to poor dear Keller immediately, and my fear of taking such a serious responsibility entirely on myself. Madame Fontaine, always just in her views, said, 'You had better wait and consult the doctors.' She made but one condition (the generous creature!) relating to herself. 'If the remedy is tried,' she said, 'I must ask you to give it a fair chance by permitting me to act as nurse; the treatment of the patient when he begins to feel the benefit of the medicine is of serious importance. I know this from my husband's instructions, and it is due to his memory (to say nothing of what is due to Mr. Keller) that I should be at the bedside.' It is needless to say that I joyfully accepted the offered help. So the night passed. The next morning, soon after you fell asleep, the doctors came. You may imagine what they thought of poor Keller, when I tell you that they recommended me to write instantly to Fritz in London summoning him to his father's bedside. I was just in time to catch the special mail which left this morning. Don't blame me, David. I could not feel absolutely sure of the new medicine; and, with time of such terrible importance, and London so far off, I was really afraid to miss a post."

I was far from blaming him—and I said so. In his place I should have done what he did. We arranged that I should write to Fritz by that night's mail, on the chance that my announcement of the better news might reach him before he left London.

"My letter despatched," Mr. Engelman continued, "I begged both the doctors to speak with me before they went away, in my private room. There I told them, in the plainest words I could find, exactly what I have told you. Doctor Dormann behaved like a gentleman. He said, 'Let me see the lady, and speak to her myself, before the new remedy is tried.' As for the other, what do you think he did? Walked out of the house (the old brute!) and declined any further attendance on the patient. And who do you think followed him out of the house, David, when I sent for Madame Fontaine? Another old brute—Mother Barbara!"

After what I had seen myself of the housekeeper's temper on the previous evening, this last piece of news failed to surprise me. To be stripped of her authority as nurse in favor of a stranger, and that stranger a handsome lady, was an aggravation of the wrong which Mother Barbara had contemplated,

118

when she threatened us with the alternative of leaving the house.

"Well," Mr. Engelman resumed, "Doctor Dormann asked his questions, and smelt and tasted the medicine, and with Madame Fontaine's full approval took away a little of it to be analyzed. That came to nothing! The medicine kept its own secret. All the ingredients but two set analysis at defiance! In the meantime we gave the first dose. Half an hour since we tried the second. You have seen the result with your own eyes. She has saved his life, David, and we have you to thank for it. But for you we might never have known Madame Fontaine."

The door opened as he spoke, and I found myself confronted by a second surprise. Minna came in, wearing a cook's apron, and asked if her mother had rung for her yet. Under the widow's instructions, she was preparing the peculiar vegetable diet which had been prescribed by Doctor Fontaine as part of the cure. The good girl was eager to make herself useful to us in any domestic capacity. What a charming substitute for the crabbed old housekeeper who had just left us!

So here were Madame Fontaine and Minna actually established as inmates under the same roof with Mr. Keller! What would Fritz think, when he knew of it? What would Mr. Keller say when he recognized his nurse, and when he heard that she had saved his life? "All's well that ends well" is a good proverb. But we had not got as far as that yet. The question in our case was, How will it end?

CHAPTER XX

When, late that night, I entered my bedroom again, how I blessed the lucky accident of my six hours' sleep, after a night's watching at Mr. Keller's bedside!

If I had spoken to Doctor Dormann as I had positively resolved to speak, he would, beyond all doubt, have forbidden the employment of Madame Fontaine's remedy; Mr. Keller would have died; and the innocent woman who had saved his life would have been suspected, perhaps even tried, on a charge of murdering him. I really trembled when I looked back on the terrible consequences which must have followed, if I had succeeded that morning in

119

keeping myself awake.

The next day, the doses of the wonderful medicine were renewed at the regular intervals; and the prescribed vegetable diet was carefully administered. On the day after, the patient was so far advanced on the way to recovery, that the stopper of the dark-blue bottle was permanently secured again under its leather guard. Mr. Engelman told me that nearly two doses of it were still left at the bottom. He also mentioned, on my asking to look at it again, that the widow had relieved him of the care of the bottle, and had carefully locked it up in her own room.

Late on this day also, the patient being well-enough to leave his bed and to occupy the armchair in his room, the inevitable disclosure took place; and Madame Fontaine stood revealed in the character of the Good Samaritan who had saved Mr. Keller's life.

By Doctor Dormann's advice, those persons only were permitted to enter the bedroom whose presence was absolutely necessary. Besides Madame Fontaine and the doctor himself, Mr. Engelman and Minna were the other witnesses of the scene. Mr. Engelman had his claim to be present as an old friend; and Minna was to be made useful, at her mother's suggestion, as a means of gently preparing Mr. Keller's mind for the revelation that was to come. Under these circumstances, I can only describe what took place, by repeating the little narrative with which Minna favored me, after she had left the room.

"We arranged that I should wait downstairs," she said, "until I heard the bedroom bell ring—and then I myself was to take up Mr. Keller's dinner of lentils and cream, and put it on his table without saying a word."

"Exactly like a servant!" I exclaimed.

Gentle sweet-tempered Minna answered my foolish interruption with her customary simplicity and good sense.

"Why not?" she asked. "Fritz's father may one day be my father; and I am happy to be of the smallest use to him, whenever he wants me. Well, when I went in, I found him in his chair, with the light let into the room, and with plenty of pillows to support him. Mr. Engelman and the doctor were on either side of him; and poor dear mamma was standing back in a corner behind the bed, where he could not see her. He looked up at me, when I came in with my tray. 'Who's this?' he asked of Mr. Engelman—'is she a new servant?' Mr. Engelman, humoring him, answered, 'Yes.' 'A nice-looking girl,' he said; 'but what does Mother Barbara say to her?' Upon this, Mr. Engelman told him how the housekeeper had left her place and why. As soon as he had recovered his surprise, he looked at me again. 'But who has been my nurse?' he inquired; 'surely not this young girl?' 'No, no; the young girl's mother has nursed you,' said Mr. Engelman. He looked at the doctor as he spoke; and the doctor interfered for the first time. 'She has not only nursed you, sir,' he said; 'I can certify medically that she has saved your life. Don't excite yourself. You shall hear exactly how it happened.' In two minutes, he told the whole story, so clearly and beautifully that it was quite a pleasure to hear him. One thing only he concealed—the name. 'Who is she?' Mr. Keller cried out. 'Why am I not allowed to express my gratitude? Why isn't she here?' 'She is afraid to approach you, sir,' said the doctor; 'you have a very bad opinion of her.' 'A bad opinion,' Mr. Keller repeated, 'of a woman I don't know? Who is the slanderer who has said that of me?' The doctor signed to Mr. Engelman to answer. 'Speak plainly,' he whispered, behind the chair. Mr. Engelman did speak plainly. 'Pardon me, my dear Keller, there is no slanderer in this matter. Your own action has spoken for you. A short time since—try if you cannot remember it yourself—a lady sent a letter to you; and you sent the letter back to her, refusing to read it. Do you know how she has returned the insult? That noble creature is the woman to whom you owe your life.' When he had said those words, the doctor crossed the room, and returned again to Mr. Keller, leading my mother by the hand."

Minna's voice faltered; she stopped at the most interesting part of her narrative.

"What did Mr. Keller say?" I asked.

"There was silence in the room," Minna answered softly. "I heard nothing except the ticking of the clock."

"But you must have seen something?"

121

"No, David. I couldn't help it—I was crying. After a while, my mother put her arm round me and led me to Mr. Keller. I dried my eyes as well as I could, and saw him again. His head was bent down on his breast—his hands hung helpless over the arms of the chair—it was dreadful to see him so overwhelmed by shame and sorrow! 'What can I do?' he groaned to himself. 'God help me, what can I do?' Mamma spoke to him—so sweetly and so prettily—'You can give this poor girl of mine a kiss, sir; the new servant who has waited on you is my daughter Minna.' He looked up quickly, and drew me to him. 'I can make but one atonement, my dear,' he said—and then he kissed me, and whispered, 'Send for Fritz.' Oh, don't ask me to tell you any more, David; I shall only begin crying again—and I am so happy!"

She left me to write to Fritz by that night's post. I tried vainly to induce her to wait a little. We had no electric telegraphs at our disposal, and we were reduced to guessing at events. But there was certainly a strong probability that Fritz might have left London immediately on the receipt of Mr. Engelman's letter, announcing that his father was dangerously ill. In this case, my letter, despatched by the next mail to relieve his anxiety, would be left unopened in London; and Fritz might be expected to arrive (if he traveled without stopping) in the course of the next day or two. I put this reasonable view of the matter to Minna, and received a thoroughly irrational and womanly reply.

"I don't care, David; I shall write to him, for all that."

"Why?"

"Because I like writing to him.

"What! whether he receives your letter or not?"

"Whether he receives it or not," she answered saucily, "I shall have the pleasure of writing to him—that is all I want."

She covered four pages of note-paper, and insisted on posting them herself.

The next morning Mr. Keller was able, with my help and Mr. Engelman's, to get downstairs to the sitting-room. We were both with him, when Madame

Fontaine came in.

"Well," he asked, "have you brought it with you?"

She handed to him a sealed envelope, and then turned to explain herself to me.

"The letter that you put on Mr. Keller's desk," she said pleasantly. "This time, David, I act as my own postman—at Mr. Keller's request."

In her place, I should certainly have torn it up. To keep it, on the bare chance of its proving to be of some use in the future, seemed to imply either an excessive hopefulness or an extraordinary foresight, on the widow's part. Without in the least comprehending my own state of mind, I felt that she had, in some mysterious way, disappointed me by keeping that letter. As a matter of course, I turned to leave the room, and Mr. Engelman (from a similar motive of delicacy) followed me to the door. Mr. Keller called us both back.

"Wait, if you please," he said, "until I have read it."

Madame Fontaine was looking out of the window. It was impossible for us to discover whether she approved of our remaining in the room or not.

Mr. Keller read the closely written pages with the steadiest attention. He signed to the widow to approach him, and took her hand when he had arrived at the last words.

"Let me ask your pardon," he said, "in the presence of my partner and in the presence of David Glenney, who took charge of your letter. Madame Fontaine, I speak the plain truth, in the plainest words, when I tell you that I am ashamed of myself."

She dropped on her knees before him, and entreated him to say no more. Mr. Engelman looked at her, absorbed in admiration. Perhaps it was the fault of my English education—I thought the widow's humility a little overdone. What Mr. Keller's opinion might be, he kept to himself. He merely insisted on her rising, and taking a chair by his side.

"To say that I believe every word of your letter," he resumed, "is only to do you the justice which I have too long delayed. But there is one passage which I must feel satisfied that I thoroughly understand, if you will be pleased to give me the assurance of it with your own lips. Am I right in concluding, from what is here written of your husband's creditors, that his debts (which have now, in honor, become your debts) have been all actually paid to the last farthing?"

"To the last farthing!" Madame Fontaine answered, without a moment's hesitation. "I can show you the receipts, sir, if you like."

"No, madam! I take your word for it—I require nothing more. Your title to my heart-felt respect is now complete. The slanders which I have disgraced myself by believing would never have found their way to my credulity, if they had not first declared you to have ruined your husband by your debts. I own that I have never been able to divest myself of my inbred dislike and distrust of people who contract debts which they are not able to pay. The light manner in which the world is apt to view the relative positions of debtor and creditor is abhorrent to me. If I promise to pay a man money, and fail to keep my promise, I am no better than a liar and a cheat. That always has been, and always will be, my view." He took her hand again as he made that strong declaration. "There is another bond of sympathy between us," he said warmly; "you think as I do."

Good Heavens, if Frau Meyer had told me the truth, what would happen when Madame Fontaine discovered that her promissory note was in the hands of a stranger—a man who would inexorably present it for payment on the day when it fell due? I tried to persuade myself that Frau Meyer had not told me the truth. Perhaps I might have succeeded—but for my remembrance of the disreputable-looking stranger on the door-step, who had been so curious to know if Madame Fontaine intended to leave her lodgings.

CHAPTER XXI

The next day, my calculation of possibilities in the matter of Fritz turned out to be correct.

Returning to Main Street, after a short absence from the house, the door was precipitately opened to me by Minna. Before she could say a word, her face told me the joyful news. Before I could congratulate her, Fritz himself burst headlong into the hall, and made one of his desperate attempts at embracing me. This time I succeeded (being the shorter man of the two) in slipping through his arms in the nick of time.

"Do you want to kiss me," I exclaimed, "when Minna is in the house!"

"I have been kissing Minna," Fritz answered with perfect gravity, until we are both of us out of breath. "I look upon you as a sort of safety-valve."

At this, Minna's charming face became eloquent in another way. I only waited to ask for news of my aunt before I withdrew. Mrs. Wagner was already on the road to Frankfort, following Fritz by easy stages.

"And where is Jack Straw?" I inquired.

"Traveling with her," said Fritz.

Having received this last extraordinary piece of intelligence, I put off all explanations until a fitter opportunity, and left the lovers together until dinner-time.

It was one of the last fine days of the autumn. The sunshine tempted me to take a turn in Mr. Engelman's garden.

A shrubbery of evergreens divided the lawn near the house from the flower-beds which occupied the further extremity of the plot of ground. While I was on one side of the shrubbery, I heard the voices of Mr. Keller and Madame Fontaine on the other side. Then, and then only, I remembered that the doctor had suggested a little walking exercise for the invalid, while the sun was at its warmest in the first hours of the afternoon. Madame Fontaine was in attendance, in the absence of Mr. Engelman, engaged in the duties of the office.

I had just turned back again towards the house, thinking it better not to disturb them, when I heard my name on the widow's lips. Better men than I, under stress of temptation, have been known to commit actions unworthy of them. I was mean enough to listen; and I paid the proverbial penalty for gratifying my curiosity—I heard no good of myself.

"You have honored me by asking my advice, sir," I heard Madame Fontaine say. "With regard to young David Glenney, I can speak quite impartially. In a few days more, if I can be of no further use to you, I shall have left the house."

Mr. Keller interrupted her there.

"Pardon me, Madame Fontaine; I can't let you talk of leaving us. We are without a housekeeper, as you know. You will confer a favor on me and on Mr. Engelman, if you will kindly undertake the direction of our domestic affairs—for the present, at least. Besides, your charming daughter is the light of our household. What will Fritz say, if you take her away just when he has come home? No! no! you and Minna must stay with us."

"You are only too good to me, sir! Perhaps I had better ascertain what Mr. Engelman's wishes are, before we decide?"

Mr. Keller laughed—and, more extraordinary still, Mr. Keller made a little joke.

"My dear madam, if you don't know what Mr. Engelman's wishes are likely to be, without asking him, you are the most unobservant lady that ever lived! Speak to him, by all means, if you think it formally necessary—and let us return to the question of taking David Glenney into our office here. A letter which he has lately received from Mrs. Wagner expresses no intention of recalling him to London—and he has managed so cleverly in a business matter which I confided to him, that he would really be an acquisition to us. Besides (until the marriage takes place), he would be a companion for Fritz."

"That is exactly where I feel a difficulty," Madame Fontaine replied. "To my mind, sir, Mr. David is not at all a desirable companion for your son. The admirable candor and simplicity of Fritz's disposition might suffer by association with a person of Mr. David's very peculiar character."

"May I ask, Madame Fontaine, in what you think his character peculiar?"

"I will endeavor to express what I feel, sir. You have spoken of his cleverness. I venture to say that he is too clever And I have observed that he is—for a young man—far too easily moved to suspect others. Do I make myself understood?"

"Perfectly. Pray go on."

"I find, Mr. Keller, that there is something of the Jesuit about our young friend. He has a way of refining on trifles, and seeing under the surface, where nothing is to be seen. Don't attach too much importance to what I say! It is quite likely that I am influenced by the popular prejudice against 'old heads on young shoulders.' At the same time, I confess I wouldn't keep him here, if I were in your place. Shall we move a little further on?"

Madame Fontaine was, I daresay, perfectly right in her estimate of me. Looking back at the pages of this narrative, I discover some places in which I certainly appear to justify her opinion. I even justified it at the time. Before she and Mr. Keller were out of my hearing, I began to see "under the surface," and "to refine" on what she had said.

Was it Jesuitical to doubt the disinterestedness of her advice? I did doubt it. Was it Jesuitical to suspect that she privately distrusted me, and had reasons of her own for keeping me out of her way, at the safe distance of London? I did suspect it.

And yet she was such a good Christian! And yet she had so nobly and so undeniably saved Mr. Keller's life! What right had I to impute self-seeking motives to such a woman as this? Mean! mean! there was no excuse for me.

I turned back to the house, with my head feeling very old on my young shoulders.

Madame Fontaine's manner to me was so charming, when we all met at the dinner-table, that I fell into a condition of remorseful silence. Fortunately, Fritz took most of the talking on himself, and the general attention was diverted from me. His high spirits, his boisterous nonsense, his contempt for all lawful forms and ceremonies which placed impediments in the way of his speedy marriage, were amusingly contrasted by Mr. Engelman's courteous simplicity in trying to argue the question seriously with his reckless young friend.

"Don't talk to me about the customary delays and the parson's duty!" cried Fritz. "Tell me this: does he do his duty without being paid for it?"

"We must all live," pleaded good Mr. Engelman; "the parson must pay the butcher and the baker, like the rest of us."

"That's shirking the question, my dear sir! Will the parson marry Minna and me, without being paid for it?"

"In all civilized countries, Fritz, there are fees for the performance of the marriage ceremony."

"Very well. Now follow my train of reasoning, Mr. Engelman! On your own showing, the whole affair is a matter of money. The parson gets his fee for making Minna my wife, after the customary delays."

There Minna modestly interposed. "Why do you object to the customary delays, dear Fritz?"

"I'll tell you, my angel, when we are married. In the meantime, I resume my train of reasoning, and I entreat Mr. Engelman not to forget that this is a matter of money. Make it worth the parson's while to marry us, without the customary delays. Double his fee, treble his fee—give him ten times his fee. It's merely a question of what his reverence can resist. My father is a rich man. Favor me with a blank cheque, papa—and I will make Minna Mrs. Keller before the end of the week!"

The father, hitherto content to listen and be amused, checked the son's flow of nonsense at this point.

"There is a time for everything, Fritz," he said. "We have had laughing enough. When you talk of your marriage, I am sorry to observe that you entirely pass over the consideration which is due to your father's only surviving relative."

Madame Fontaine laid down her knife and fork as if her dinner had come to an end. The sudden appearance in the conversation of the "surviving relative," had evidently taken her by surprise. Mr. Keller, observing her, turned away from his son, and addressed himself exclusively to the widow when he spoke next.

"I referred, Madame Fontaine, to my elder sister," he said. "She and I are the sole survivors of a large family."

"Does the lady live in this city, sir?" the widow inquired.

"No, she still lives in our birthplace—Munich."

"May I ask another question?"

"As many questions, dear madam, as you like."

"Is your sister married?"

"My sister has never been married."

"Not for want of suitors," said courteous Mr. Engelman. "A most majestic person. Witty and accomplished. Possessed of an enviable little fortune, entirely at her own disposal."

Mr. Keller gently reproved this latter allusion to the question of money.

"My good friend, Madame Fontaine has a mind above all mercenary considerations. My sister's place in her esteem and regard will not be influenced by my sister's fortune, when they meet (as I hope they will meet) at Fritz's marriage."

At this, Fritz burst into the conversation in his usual headlong way.

"Oh, dear me, papa, have some consideration for us! If we wait for my aunt, we shall never be married on this side of eternity."

"Fritz!"

"Don't be angry, sir, I meant no harm. I was thinking of my aunt's asthma. At her age, she will never take the long journey from Munich to Frankfort. Permit me to offer a suggestion. Let us be married first, and then pay her a visit in the honeymoon."

Mr. Keller passed his son's suggestion over without notice, and addressed himself once more to Madame Fontaine.

"I propose writing to my sister in a day or two," he resumed, "to inform her of the contemplated marriage. She already knows your name through Mr. Engelman, who kindly wrote to allay her anxiety about my illness."

"And to tell her," Mr. Engelman interposed, "to whose devotion he owes his recovery."

The widow received this tribute with eyes fixed modestly on her plate. Her black dress, rising and falling over her bosom, betrayed an agitation, which her enemies at Wurzburg might have attributed to the discovery of the rich sister at Munich. Mr. Keller went on—

"I am sure I may trust to your womanly sympathies to understand the affection which binds me to my last living relative. My sister's presence at the marriage will be an inexpressible comfort and happiness to me. In spite of what my son has said (you are sadly given to talking at random, Fritz), I believe she will not shrink from the journey to Frankfort, if we only make it easier to her by consulting her health and convenience. Our young people have all their lives before them—our young people can wait."

"Certainly, sir."

She gave that short answer very quietly, with her eyes still on her plate. It was impossible to discover in what frame of mind she viewed the prospect of delay, involved in Mr. Keller's consideration for his sister. For the moment, Fritz was simply confounded. He looked at Minna—recovered himself—and favored his father with another suggestion.

"I have got it now!" he exclaimed. "Why not spare my aunt the fatigue of the journey? Let us all start for Bavaria to—morrow, and have the marriage at Munich!"

"And leave the business at Frankfort to take care of itself, at the busiest time of the year!" his father added ironically. "When you open your mouth again, Fritz, put food and drink into it—and confine yourself to that."

With those words the question of the marriage was closed for the time.

When dinner was over, Mr. Keller retired, to take some rest in his own room. Fritz and his sweetheart left the house together, on an errand in which they were both equally interested—the purchase of the ring which was to typify Minna's engagement. Left alone with Mr. Engelman and the widow, I felt that I might be an obstacle to confidential conversation, and withdrew to the office. Though not regularly employed as one of the clerks, I had been admitted to serve as a volunteer, since my return from Hanau. In this way, I improved my experience of the details of our business, and I made some small return for the hospitable welcome which I had received from the two partners.

Half an hour or more had passed, when some papers arrived from the bank, which required the signature of the firm. Mr. Engelman being still absent, the head-clerk, at my suggestion, proceeded to the dining-room with the papers in his charge.

He came back again immediately, looking very much alarmed.

"Pray go into the dining-room!" he said to me. "I am afraid something is seriously wrong with Mr. Engelman."

"Do you mean that he is ill?" I asked.

"I can hardly say. His arms are stretched out on the table, and his face is hidden on them. He paid no attention to me. I am almost afraid he was crying."

Crying? I had left him in excellent spirits, casting glances of the tenderest admiration at Madame Fontaine. Without waiting to hear more, I ran to the dining-room.

He was alone—in the position described by the clerk—and, poor old man, he was indeed weeping bitterly! I put my hand with all possible gentleness on his shoulder, and said, with the tenderness that I really felt for him: "Dear Mr. Engelman, what has happened to distress you?"

At the sound of my voice he looked up, and caught me fervently by the hand.

"Stay here with me a little while, David," he said. "I have got my deathblow."

I sat down by him directly. "Try and tell me what has happened," I went on. "I left you here with Madame Fontaine——"

His tears suddenly ceased; his hand closed convulsively on mine. "Don't speak of her," he cried, with an outburst of anger. "You were right about her, David. She is a false woman." As the words passed his lips, he changed again. His voice faltered; he seemed to be frightened by his own violent language. "Oh, what am I talking about! what right have I to say that of her! I am a brute—I am reviling the best of women. It was all my fault, David—I have acted like a madman, like a fool. Oh, my boy! my boy!—would you believe it?—I asked her to marry me!"

It is needless to say that I wanted no further explanation. "Did she encourage you to ask her?" I inquired.

"I thought she did, David—I thought I would be clever and seize the opportunity. She said she wanted to consult me. She said: 'Mr. Keller has asked me to stay here, and keep house for you; I have not given my answer yet, I have waited to know if you approved it.' Upon that, I said the rash words. I asked her to be more than our housekeeper—to be my wife. I am naturally stupid," said the poor simple gentleman; "whenever I try to do anything clever I always fail. She was very forbearing with me at first; she said No, but she said it considerately, as if she felt for me. I presumed on her kindness, like a fool; I couldn't help it, David, I was so fond of her. I pressed her to say why she refused me. I was mad enough to ask if there was some other man whom she preferred. Oh, she said some hard things to me in her anger! And, worse still, when I went down on my knees to her, she said, 'Get up, you old fool!'—and laughed—and left me. Take me away somewhere, David; I am too old to get over it, if I stay here. I can never see her or speak to her again. Take me to England with you—and, oh, don't tell Keller!"

He burst into another fit of tears. It was dreadful to see and hear him.

I tried to think of some consoling words. Before I could give expression to my thought, the door of the room was gently opened; and Madame Fontaine herself stood before us. Her eyes looked at Mr. Engelman from under their heavy lids, with a quiet and scornful compassion. The poor wretch was of no further use to her. Quite needless to be on her best behavior with him now!

"There is not the least occasion, sir, to disturb yourself," she said. "It is my duty to leave the house—and I will do it."

Without waiting to be answered, she turned back to the door, and left us.

CHAPTER XXII

"For heaven's sake, sir, allow me to go!"

"On no account, Madame Fontaine. If you won't remain here, in justice to yourself, remain as a favor to me."

When I opened my bedroom door the next morning, the widow and Mr. Keller were on the landing outside, and those were the words exchanged between them.

Mr. Keller approached, and spoke to me.

"What do you know, David, about the disappearance of Mr. Engelman?"

"Disappearance?" I repeated. "I was with him yesterday evening—and I bade him good-night in his own room."

"He must have left the house before the servants were up this morning," said Mr. Keller. "Read that."

He handed me a morsel of paper with writing on it in pencil:—

"Forgive me, dear friend and partner, for leaving you without saying good-bye; also for burdening you with the direction of business, before you are perhaps strong enough to accept the charge. My mind is in such a state of confusion that I should be worse than useless in the office. While I write this, my poor weak head burns as if there was fire in it. I cannot face her, I cannot face you—I must go, before I lose all control over myself. Don't attempt to trace me. If change and absence restore me to myself I will return. If not, a man at my age and in my state of mind is willing to die. Please tell Madame

Fontaine that I ask her pardon with all my heart. Good-bye—and God bless and prosper you."

I was unaffectedly distressed. There was something terrible in this sudden break-up of poor Engelman's harmless life—something cruel and shocking in the passion of love fixing its relentless hold on an innocent old man, fast nearing the end of his days. There are hundreds of examples of this deplorable anomaly in real life; and yet, when we meet with it in our own experience, we are always taken by surprise, and always ready to express doubt or derision when we hear of it in the experience of others.

Madame Fontaine behaved admirably. She sat down on the window-seat at the end of the landing, and wrung her hands with a gesture of despair.

"Oh!" she said, "if he had asked me for anything else! If I could have made any other sacrifice to him! God knows I never dreamed of it; I never gave him the smallest encouragement. We might have all been so happy together here—and I, who would have gone to the world's end to serve Mr. Keller and Mr. Engelman, I am the unhappy creature who has broken up the household!"

Mr. Keller was deeply affected. He sat down on the window-seat by Madame Fontaine.

"My dear, dear lady," he said, "you are entirely blameless in this matter. Even my unfortunate partner feels it, and asks your pardon. If inquiries can discover him, they shall be set on foot immediately. In the meantime, let me entreat you to compose yourself. Engelman has perhaps done wisely, to leave us for a time. He will get over his delusion, and all may be well yet."

I went downstairs, not caring to hear more. All my sympathies, I confess, were with Mr. Engelman—though he was a fat simple old man. Mr. Keller seemed to me (here is more of the "old head on young shoulders!") to have gone from one extreme to the other. He had begun by treating the widow with unbecoming injustice; and he was now flattering her with unreasonable partiality.

For the next few days there was tranquillity, if not happiness, in the house. Mr. Keller wrote to his sister in Munich, inviting her to mention the earliest date at which it might suit her convenience to be present at the marriage of his son. Madame Fontaine assumed the regular management of our domestic affairs. Fritz and Minna found sufficient attraction in each other's society. The new week was just beginning, and our inquiries after Mr. Engelman had thus far led to no result—when I received a letter containing news of the fugitive, confided to me under strict reserve.

The writer of the letter proved to be a married younger brother of Mr. Engelman, residing at Bingen, on the Rhine.

"I write to you, dear sir, at my brother's request. My wife and I are doing all that we can to relieve and comfort him, but his mind has not yet sufficiently recovered to enable him to write to you himself. He desires to thank you heartily for your sympathy, at the most trying period of his life; and he trusts to your kindness to let him hear, from time to time, of Mr. Keller's progress towards recovery, and of the well-being of the business. In addressing your letters to me at Bingen, you will be pleased to consider the information of my brother's whereabouts herein afforded to you as strictly confidential, until you hear from me to the contrary. In his present frame of mind, it would be in the last degree painful to him to be made the subject of inquiries, remonstrances, or entreaties to return."

The arrival of this sad news proved to be not the only noteworthy event of the day. While I was still thinking of poor Mr. Engelman, Fritz came into the office with his hat in his hand.

"Minna is not in very good spirits this morning," he said. "I am going to take her out for half an hour to look at the shops. Can you come with us?"

This invitation rather surprised me. "Does Minna wish it?" I asked.

Fritz dropped his voice so that the clerks in the room could not hear his reply. "Minna has sent me to you," he answered. "She is uneasy about her mother. I can make nothing of it—and she wants to ask your advice."

It was impossible for me to leave my desk at that moment. We arranged to put off the walk until after dinner. During the meal, I observed that not

Minna only, but her mother also, appeared to be out of spirits. Mr. Keller and Fritz probably noticed the change as I did. We were all of us more silent than usual. It was a relief so find myself with the lovers, out in the cheerful street.

Minna seemed to want to be encouraged before she could speak to me. I was obliged to ask in plain words if anything had happened to annoy her mother and herself.

"I hardly know how to tell you," she said. "I am very unhappy about my mother."

"Begin at the beginning," Fritz suggested; "tell him where you went, and what happened yesterday."

Minna followed her instructions. "Mamma and I went to our lodgings yesterday," she began. "We had given notice to leave when it was settled we were to live in Mr. Keller's house. The time was nearly up; and there were some few things still left at the apartments, which we could carry away in our hands. Mamma, who speaks considerately to everybody, said she hoped the landlady would soon let the rooms again. The good woman answered: 'I don't quite know, madam, whether I have not let them already.'—Don't you think that rather a strange reply?"

"It seems to require some explanation, certainly. What did the landlady say?"

"The landlady's explanation explained nothing," Fritz interposed. "She appears to have spoken of a mysterious stranger, who had once before inquired if Madame Fontaine was likely to leave the lodgings—and who came yesterday to inquire again. You tell him the rest of it, Minna."

Before she could speak, I had already recognized the suspicious-looking personage whom Mr. Engelman and I had some time since encountered on the door-step. I inquired what the man had said when he heard that the lodgings were to let.

"There is the suspicious part of it," cried Fritz. "Be very particular, Minna, to leave nothing out."

Fritz's interruptions seemed only to confuse Minna. I begged him to be silent, and did my best to help her to find the lost thread of her story.

"Did the man ask to see the lodgings?" I said.

"No."

"Did he talk of taking the lodgings?"

"He said he wished to have the refusal of them until the evening," Minna replied; "and then he asked if Madame Fontaine had left Frankfort. When the landlady said No, he had another question ready directly. He wanted to know in what part of Frankfort Madame Fontaine was now living."

"And the old fool of a landlady actually told him the address," said Fritz, interrupting again.

"And, I am afraid, did some serious mischief by her folly," Minna added. "I saw mamma start and turn pale. She said to the landlady, 'How long ago did this happen?' 'About half an hour ago,' the landlady answered. 'Which way did he turn when he left you—towards Mr. Keller's house or the other way?' The landlady said, 'Towards Mr. Keller's house.' Without another word, mamma took me by the arm. 'It's time we were home again,' she said—and we went back at once to the house."

"You were too late, of course, to find the man there?"

"Yes, David—but we heard of him. Mamma asked Joseph if anyone had called while we were out. Joseph said a stranger had called, and had inquired if Madame Fontaine was at home. Hearing that she was out, he had said, 'I think I had better write to her. She is here for a short time only, I believe?' And innocent Joseph answered, 'Oh, dear no! Madame Fontaine is Mr. Keller's new housekeeper.' 'Well?' mamma asked, 'and what did he say when he heard that?' 'He said nothing,' Joseph answered, 'and went away directly.'"

"Was that all that passed between your mother and Joseph?"

"All," Minna replied. "My mother wouldn't even let me speak to her. I only tried to say a few words of sympathy—and I was told sharply to be silent. 'Don't interrupt me,' she said, 'I want to write a letter.'"

"Did you see the letter?"

"Oh, no! But I was so anxious and uneasy that I did peep over her shoulder while she was writing the address."

"Do you remember what it was?"

"I only saw the last word on it. The last word was 'Wurzburg.'"

"Now you know as much as we do," Fritz resumed. "How does it strike you, David? And what do you advise?"

How could I advise? I could only draw my own conclusions privately. Madame Fontaine's movements were watched by somebody; possibly in the interests of the stranger who now held the promissory note. It was, of course, impossible for me to communicate this view of the circumstances to either of my two companions. I could only suggest a patient reliance on time, and the preservation of discreet silence on Minna's part, until her mother set the example of returning to the subject.

My vaguely-prudent counsels were, naturally enough, not to the taste of my young hearers. Fritz openly acknowledged that I had disappointed him; and Minna turned aside her head, with a look of reproach. Her quick perception had detected, in my look and manner, that I was keeping my thoughts to myself. Neither she nor Fritz made any objection to my leaving them, to return to the office before post-time. I wrote to Mr. Engelman before I left my desk that evening.

Recalling those memorable days of my early life, I remember that a strange and sinister depression pervaded our little household, from the time when Mr. Engelman left us.

In some mysterious way the bonds of sympathy, by which we had been hitherto more or less united, seemed to slacken and fall away. We lived on perfectly good terms with one another; but there was an unrecognized decrease of confidence among us, which I for one felt sometimes almost painfully. An unwholesome atmosphere of distrust enveloped us. Mr. Keller only believed, under reserve, that Madame Fontaine's persistent low spirits were really attributable, as she said, to nothing more important than nervous headaches. Fritz began to doubt whether Mr. Keller was really as well satisfied as he professed to be with the choice that his son had made of a portionless bride. Minna, observing that Fritz was occasionally rather more subdued and silent than usual, began to ask herself whether she was quite as dear to him, in the time of their prosperity, as in the time of their adversity. To sum up all, Madame Fontaine had her doubts of me—and I had my doubts (although she had saved Mr. Keller's life) of Madame Fontaine.

From this degrading condition of dullness and distrust, we were roused, one morning, by the happy arrival of Mrs. Wagner, attended by her maid, her courier—and Jack Straw.

CHAPTER XXIII

Circumstances had obliged my aunt to perform the last stage of her journey to Frankfort by the night mail. She had only stopped at our house on her way to the hotel; being unwilling to trespass on the hospitality of her partners, while she was accompanied by such a half-witted fellow as Jack. Mr. Keller, however, refused even to hear of the head partner in the business being reduced to accept a mercenary welcome at an hotel. One whole side of the house, situated immediately over the offices, had been already put in order in anticipation of Mrs. Wagner's arrival. The luggage was then and there taken off the carriage; and my aunt was obliged, by all the laws of courtesy and good fellowship, to submit.

This information was communicated to me by Joseph, on my return from an early visit to one of our warehouses at the riverside. When I asked if I could see my aunt, I was informed that she had already retired to rest in her room, after the fatigue of a seven hours' journey by night.

"And where is Jack Straw?" I asked.

"Playing the devil already, sir, with the rules of the house," Joseph answered.

Fritz's voice hailed me from the lower regions.

"Come down, David; here's something worth seeing!"

I descended at once to the servants' offices. There, crouched up in a corner of the cold stone corridor which formed the medium of communication between the kitchen and the stairs, I saw Jack Straw again—in the very position in which I had found him at Bedlam; excepting the prison, the chains, and the straw.

But for his prematurely gray hair and the strange yellow pallor of his complexion, I doubt if I should have recognized him again. He looked fat and happy; he was neatly and becomingly dressed, with a flower in his button-hole and rosettes on his shoes. In one word, so far as his costume was concerned, he might have been taken for a lady's page, dressed under the superintendence of his mistress herself.

"There he is!" said Fritz, "and there he means to remain, till your aunt wakes and sends for him."

"Upsetting the women servants, on their way to their work," Joseph added, with an air of supreme disgust—"and freezing in that cold corner, when he might be sitting comfortably by the kitchen fire!"

Jack listened to this with an ironical expression of approval. "That's very well said, Joseph," he remarked. "Come here; I want to speak to you. Do you see that bell?" He pointed to a row of bells running along the upper wall of the corridor, and singled out one of them which was numbered ten. "They tell me that's the bell of Mistress's bedroom," he resumed, still speaking of my aunt by the name which he had first given to her on the day when they met in the madhouse. "Very well, Joseph! I don't want to be in anybody's way; but no person in the house must see that bell ring before me. Here I stay till Mistress rings—and then you will get rid of me; I shall move to the mat outside her door, and wait till she whistles for me. Now you may go. That's a poor half-witted creature," he said as Joseph retired. "Lord! what a lot of them there are in this world!" Fritz burst out laughing. "I'm afraid you're another of them," said Jack, looking at him with an expression of the sincerest compassion.

"Do you remember me?" I asked.

Jack nodded his head in a patronizing way. "Oh, yes—Mistress has been talking of you. I know you both. You're David, and he's Fritz. All right! all right!"

"What sort of journey from London have you had?" I inquired next.

He stretched out his shapely little arms and legs, and yawned. "Oh, a pretty good journey. We should have been better without the courier and the maid. The courier is a tall man. I have no opinion of tall men. I am a man myself of five foot—that's the right height for a courier. I could have done all the work, and saved Mistress the money. Her maid is another tall person; clumsy with her fingers. I could dress Mistress's hair a deal better than the maid, if she would only let me. The fact is, I want to do everything for her myself. I shall never be quite happy till I'm the only servant she has about her."

"Ah, yes," said Fritz, good-naturedly sympathizing with him. "You're a grateful little man; you remember what Mrs. Wagner has done for you."

"Remember?" Jack reported scornfully. "I say, if you can't talk more sensibly than that, you had better hold your tongue." He turned and appealed to me. "Did you ever hear anything like Fritz? He seems to think it wonderful that I remember the day when she took me out of Bedlam!"

"Ah, Jack, that was a great day in your life, wasn't it?"

"A great day? Oh, good Lord in Heaven! where are there words that are big enough to speak about it?" He sprang to his feet, wild with the sudden tumult of his own recollections. "The sun—the warm, golden, glorious, beautiful sun—met us when we came out of the gates, and all but drove me stark-staring-mad with the joy of it! Forty thousand devils—little straw-colored, lively, tempting devils—(mind, I counted them!)—all crawled over me together. They sat on my shoulders—and they tickled my hands—and they scrambled in my hair—and they were all in one cry at me like a pack of dogs. 'Now, Jack! we are waiting for you; your chains are off, and the sun's shining, and Mistress's carriage is at the gate—join us, Jack, in a good yell; a fine, tearing, screeching, terrifying, mad yell!' I dropped on my knees, down in the bottom of the carriage; and I held on by the skirts of Mistress's dress. 'Look at me!' I said; 'I won't burst out; I won't frighten you, if I die for it. Only help me with your eyes! only look at me!' And she put me on the front seat of the carriage, opposite her, and she never took her eyes off me all the way through the streets till we got to the house. 'I believe in you, Jack,' she said. And I wouldn't even open my lips to answer her—I was so determined to be quiet. Ha! ha! how you two fellows would have yelled, in my place!" He sat down again in his corner, delighted with his own picture of the two fellows who would have yelled in his place.

"And what did Mistress do with you when she brought you home?" I asked.

His gaiety suddenly left him. He lifted one of his hands, and waved it to and fro gently in the air.

"You are too loud, David," he said. "All this part of it must be spoken softly—because all this part of it is beautiful, and kind, and good. There was a picture in the room, of angels and their harps. I wish I had the angels and the harps to help me tell you about it. Fritz there came in with us, and called it a bedroom. I knew better than that; I called it Heaven. You see, I thought of the prison and the darkness and the cold and the chains and the straw—and I named it Heaven. You two may say what you please; Mistress said I was right."

He closed his eyes with a luxurious sense of self-esteem, and appeared to absorb himself in his own thoughts. Fritz unintentionally roused him by continuing the story of Jack's introduction to the bedroom.

"Our little friend," Fritz began confidentially, "did the strangest things when he found himself in his new room. It was a cold day; and he insisted on letting the fire out. Then he looked at the bedclothes, and——"

Jack solemnly opened his eyes again, and stopped the narrative at that point.

"You are not the right person to speak of it," he said. "Nobody must speak of it but a person who understands me. You shan't be disappointed,

142

David. I understand myself—I'll tell you about it. You saw what sort of place I lived in and slept in at the madhouse, didn't you?"

"I saw it, Jack—and I can never forget it."

"Now just think of my having a room, to begin with. And add, if you please, a fire—and a light—and a bed—and blankets and sheets and pillows—and clothes, splendid new clothes, for Me! And then ask yourself if any man could bear it, all pouring on him at once (not an hour after he had left Bedlam), without going clean out of his senses and screeching for joy? No, no. If I have a quality, it's profound common sense. Down I went on my knees before her again! 'If you have any mercy on me, Mistress, let me have all this by a bit at a time. Upon my soul, I can't swallow it at once!' She understood me. We let the fire out—and surprised that deficient person, Fritz. A little of the Bedlam cold kept me nice and quiet. The bed that night if you like—but Heaven defend me from the blankets and the sheets and the pillows till I'm able to bear them! And as to putting on coat, waistcoat, and breeches, all together, the next morning—it was as much as I could do, when I saw myself in my breeches, to give the word of command in the voice of a gentleman— 'Away with the rest of them! The shirt for to-morrow, the waistcoat for next day, and the coat—if I can bear the sight of it without screaming—the day after!' A gradual process, you see, David. And every morning Mistress helped me by saying the words she said in the carriage, 'I believe in you, Jack.' You ask her, when she gets up, if I ever once frightened her, from the day when she took me home." He looked again, with undiminished resentment, at Fritz. "Now do you understand what I did when I got into my new room? Is Fritz in the business, David? He'll want a deal of looking after if he is. Just step this way—I wish to speak to you."

He got up again, and taking my arm with a look of great importance, led me a few steps away—but not far enough to be out of sight of my aunt's bell.

"I say," he began, "I've heard they call this place Frankfort. Am I right?"

"Quite right!"

"And there's a business here, like the business in London?"

"Certainly."

"And Mistress is Mistress here, like she is in London?"

"Yes."

"Very well, then, I want to know something. What about the Keys?"

I looked at him, entirely at a loss to understand what this last question meant. He stamped his foot impatiently.

"Do you mean to say, David, you have never heard what situation I held in the London office?"

"Never, Jack!"

He drew himself up and folded his arms, and looked at me from the immeasurable height of his own superiority.

"I was Keeper of the Keys in London!" he announced. "And what I want to know is—Am I to be Keeper of the Keys here?"

It was now plain enough that my aunt—proceeding on the wise plan of always cultivating the poor creature's sense of responsibility—had given him some keys to take care of, and had put him on his honor to be worthy of his little trust. I could not doubt that she would find some means of humoring him in the same way at Frankfort.

"Wait till the bells rings," I answered "and perhaps you will find the Keys waiting for you in Mistress' room."

He rubbed his hands in delight. "That's it!" he said. "Let's keep watch on the bell."

As he turned to go back again to his corner, Madame Fontaine's voice reached us from the top of the kitchen stairs. She was speaking to her daughter. Jack stopped directly and waited, looking round at the stairs.

"Where is the other person who came here with Mrs. Wagner?" the widow asked. "A man with an odd English name. Do you know, Minna, if they have found a room for him?"

She reached the lower stair as she spoke—advanced along the corridor—and discovered Jack Straw. In an instant, her languid indifferent manner disappeared. Her eyes opened wildly under their heavy lids. She stood motionless, like a woman petrified by surprise—perhaps by terror.

"Hans Grimm!" I heard her say to herself. "God in heaven! what brings him here?"

CHAPTER XXIV

Almost instantaneously Madame Fontaine recovered her self-control.

"I really couldn't help feeling startled," she said, explaining herself to Fritz and to me. "The last time I saw this man, he was employed in a menial capacity at the University of Wurzburg. He left us one day, nobody knew why. And he suddenly appears again, without a word of warning, in this house."

I looked at Jack. A smile of mischievous satisfaction was on his face. He apparently enjoyed startling Madame Fontaine. His expression changed instantly for the better, when Minna approached and spoke to him.

"Don't you remember me, Hans?" she said.

"Oh, yes, Missie, I remember you. You are a good creature. You take after your papa. He was a good creature—except when he had his beastly medical bottles in his hand. But, I say, I mustn't be called by the name they gave me at the University! I was a German then—I am an Englishman now. All nations are alike to me. But I am particular about my name, because it's the name Mistress knew me by. I will never have another. 'Jack Straw,' if you please. There's my name, and I am proud of it. Lord! what an ugly little hat you have got on your head! I'll soon make you a better one." He turned on Madame Fontaine, with a sudden change to distrust.

"I don't like the way you spoke of my leaving the University, just now. I had a right to go, if I liked—hadn't I?"

"Oh, yes, Hans."

"Not Hans! Didn't you hear what I mentioned just now? Say Jack."

She said it, with a ready docility which a little surprised me.

"Did I steal anything at the University?" Jack proceeded.

"Not that I know of."

"Then speak respectfully of me, next time. Say, 'Mr. Jack retired from the University, in the exercise of his discretion.'" Having stated this formula with an air of great importance, he addressed himself to me. "I appeal to you," he said. "Suppose you had lost your color here" (he touched his cheek), "and your color there" (he touched his hair); "and suppose it had happened at the University—would you" (he stood on tip-toe, and whispered the next words in my ear) "would you have stopped there, to be poisoned again? No!" he cried, raising his voice once more, "you would have drifted away like me. From Germany to France; from France to England—and so to London, and so under the feet of her Highness's horses, and so to Bedlam, and so to Mistress. Oh, Lord help me, I'm forgetting the bell! good-bye, all of you. Let me be in my corner till the bell rings."

Madame Fontaine glanced at me compassionately, and touched her bead.

"Come to my sitting-room, Jack," she said, "and have something to eat and drink, and tell me your adventures after you left Wurzburg."

She favored him with her sweetest smile, and spoke in her most ingratiating tones. That objectionable tendency of mine to easily suspect others was, I suppose, excited once more. At any rate, I thought the widow showed a very remarkable anxiety to conciliate Jack. He was proof, however, against all attempts at fascination—he shook his head obstinately, and pointed to the bell. We went our several ways, and left the strange little man crouched up in his corner.

In the afternoon, I was sent for to see my aunt.

I found Jack at his post; established in a large empty wardrobe, on the landing outside his mistress's door. His fingers were already busy with the framework of the new straw hat which he had promised to make for Minna.

"All right, David!" he said, patronizing me as indulgently as ever.

"Mistress has had her good sleep and her nice breakfast, and she looks lovely. Go in, and see her—go in!"

I thought myself that she looked perhaps a little worn, and certainly thinner than when I had seen her last. But these were trifles. It is not easy to describe the sense of relief and pleasure that I felt—after having been accustomed to the sleepy eyes and serpentine graces of Madame Fontaine—when I looked again at the lithe active figure and the bright well-opened gray eyes of my dear little English aunt.

"Tell me, David," she began, as soon as the first greetings were over, "what do you think of Jack Straw? Was my poor dear husband not right? and have I not done well to prove it?"

I could, and did, honestly congratulate her on the result of the visit to Bedlam.

"And now about the people here," she went on. "I find Fritz's father completely changed on the subject of Fritz's marriage. And when I ask what it means, I am told that Madame Fontaine has set everything right, in the most wonderful manner, by saving Mr. Keller's life. Is this true?"

"Quite true. What do you think of Madame Fontaine?"

"Ask me that, David, to-morrow or the next day. My head is muddled by traveling—I have not made up my mind yet."

"Have you seen Minna?"

"Seen her, and kissed her too! There's a girl after my own heart. I consider our scatter-brained friend Fritz to be the luckiest young fellow living."

"If Minna was not going to be married," I suggested, "she would just do for one of your young-lady clerks, wouldn't she?"

My aunt laughed. "Exactly what I thought myself, when I saw her. But you are not to make a joke of my young-lady clerks. I am positively determined to carry out that useful reform in the office here. However, as Mr. Keller has been so lately ill, and as we are sure to have a fight about it, I will act considerately towards my opponent—I won't stir in the matter until he is quite himself again. In the meantime, I must find somebody, while I am away, to take my place in the London house. The business is now under the direction of Mr. Hartrey. He is perfectly competent to carry it on; but, as you know, our excellent head-clerk has his old—fashioned prejudices. According to strict rule, a partner ought always to be in command, at the London business—and Hartrey implores me (if Mr. Keller is not well enough to take the journey) to send Mr. Engelman to London. Where is Mr. Engelman? How is it that I have neither heard nor seen anything of him?"

This was a delicate and difficult question to answer—at least, to my way of thinking. There was little prospect of keeping the poor old gentleman's sad secret. It was known to Fritz and Minna, as well as to Mr. Keller. Still, I felt an unconquerable reluctance to be the first person who revealed the disaster that had befallen him.

"Mr. Engelman is not in good health and spirits," I said. "He has gone away for a little rest and change."

My aunt looked astonished.

"Both the partners ill!" she exclaimed. "I remember Mr. Engelman, in the days when I was first married. He used to boast of never having had a day's illness in his life. Not at all a clever man—but good as gold, and a far more sensitive person than most people gave him credit for being. He promised to be fat as years grew on him. Has he kept his promise? What is the matter with him?"

I hesitated. My aunt eyed me sharply, and put another question before I had quite made up my mind what to say.

"If you can't tell me what is the matter with him, can you tell me where he is? I may want to write to him."

I hesitated again. Mr. Engelman's address had been confidentially communicated to me, for reasons which I was bound to respect. "I am afraid I can't answer that question either," I said awkwardly enough.

"Good heavens!" cried my aunt, "what does all this mystery mean? Has

148

Mr. Engelman killed a man in a duel? or run away with an opera-dancer? or squandered the whole profits of the business at the gambling-table? or what? As she put these bold views of the case, we heard voices outside, followed by a gentle knock at the door. Minna entered the room with a message.

"Mamma has sent me, Mrs. Wagner, to ask at what time you would like to dine."

"My dear, I am much obliged to your mother. I have only just breakfasted, and I can wait quite well till supper-time comes. Stop a minute! Here is my nephew driving me to the utmost verge of human endurance, by making a mystery of Mr. Engelman's absence from Frankfort. Should I be very indiscreet if I asked—Good gracious, how the girl blushes! You are evidently in the secret too, Miss Minna. Is it an opera-dancer? Leave us together, David."

This made Minna's position simply unendurable. She looked at me appealingly. I did at last, what I ought to have done at first—I spoke out plainly.

"The fact is, aunt," I said, "poor Mr. Engelman has left us for awhile, sadly mortified and distressed. He began by admiring Madame Fontaine; and he ended in making her an offer of marriage."

"Mamma was indeed truly sorry for him," Minna added; "but she had no other alternative than to refuse him, of course."

"Upon my word, child, I see no 'of course' in the matter!" my aunt answered sharply.

Minna was shocked. "Oh, Mrs. Wagner! Mr. Engelman is more than twenty years older than mamma—and (I am sure I pity him, poor man)—and so fat!"

"Fat is a matter of taste," my aunt remarked, more and more resolute in taking Mr. Engelman's part. "And as for his being twenty years older than your mother, I can tell you, young lady, that my dear lost husband was twenty years my senior when he married me—and a happier couple never lived. I

149

know more of the world than you do; and I say Madame Fontaine has made a great mistake. She has thrown away an excellent position in life, and has pained and humiliated one of the kindest-hearted men living. No! no! I am not going to argue the matter with you now; I'll wait till you are married to Fritz. But I own I should like to speak to your mother about it. Ask her to favor me by stepping this way for a few minutes, when she has nothing to do."

Minna seemed to think this rather a high-handed method of proceeding, and entered a modest protest accordingly.

"Mamma is a very sensitive person," she began with dignity.

My aunt stopped her with a pat on the cheek.

"Good child! I like you for taking your mother's part. Mamma has another merit, my dear. She is old enough to understand me better than you do. Go and fetch her."

Minna left us, with her pretty little head carried high in the air. "Mrs. Wagner is a person entirely without sentiment!" she indignantly whispered to me in passing, when I opened the door for her.

"I declare that girl is absolute perfection!" my aunt exclaimed with enthusiasm. "The one thing she wanted, as I thought, was spirit—and I find she has got it. Ah! she will take Fritz in hand, and make something of him. He is one of the many men who absolutely need being henpecked. I prophesy confidently—their marriage will be a happy one."

"I don't doubt it, aunt. But tell me, what are you going to say to Madame Fontaine?"

"It depends on circumstances. I must know first if Mr. Engelman has really set his heart on the woman with the snaky movements and the sleepy eyes. Can you certify to that?"

"Positively. Her refusal has completely crushed him."

"Very well. Then I mean to make Madame Fontaine marry him—always supposing there is no other man in his way."

"My dear aunt, how you talk! At Madame Fontaine's age! With a grown-up daughter!"

"My dear nephew, you know absolutely nothing about women. Counting by years, I grant you they grow old. Counting by sensations, they remain young to the end of their days. Take a word of advice from me. The evidence of their gray hair may look indisputable; the evidence of their grown-up children may look indisputable. Don't believe it! There is but one period in the women's lives when you may feel quite certain that they have definitely given the men their dismissal—the period when they are put in their coffins. Hush! What's that outside? When there is a noisy silk dress and a silent foot on the stairs, in this house, I know already what it means. Be off with you!"

She was quite right. Madame Fontaine entered, as I rose to leave the room.

The widow showed none of her daughter's petulance. She was sweet and patient; she saluted Mrs. Wagner with a sad smile which seemed to say, "Outrage my most sacred feelings, dear madam; they are entirely at your disposal." If I had believed that my aunt had the smallest chance of carrying her point, I should have felt far from easy about Mr. Engelman's prospects. As it was, I left the two ladies to their fruitless interview, and returned composedly to my work.

CHAPTER XXV

When supper was announced, I went upstairs again to show my aunt the way to the room in which we took our meals.

"Well?" I said.

"Well," she answered coolly, "Madame Fontaine has promised to reconsider it."

I confess I was staggered. By what possible motives could the widow have been animated? Even Mr. Engelman's passive assistance was now of no further importance to her. She had gained Mr. Keller's confidence; her daughter's marriage was assured; her employment in the house offered her a liberal salary, a respectable position, and a comfortable home. Why should she consent to reconsider the question of marrying a man, in whom she could not be said to feel any sort of true interest, in any possible acceptation of the words? I began to think that my aunt was right, and that I really did know absolutely nothing about women.

At supper Madame Fontaine and her daughter were both unusually silent. Open-hearted Minna was not capable of concealing that her mother's concession had been made known to her in some way, and that the disclosure had disagreeably surprised her. However, there was no want of gaiety at the table—thanks to my aunt, and to her faithful attendant.

Jack Straw followed us into the room, without waiting to be invited, and placed himself, to Joseph's disgust, behind Mrs. Wagner's chair.

"Nobody waits on Mistress at table," he explained, "but me. Sometimes she gives me a bit or a drink over her shoulder. Very little drink—just a sip, and no more. I quite approve of only a sip myself. Oh, I know how to behave. None of your wine-merchant's fire in my head; no Bedlam breaking loose again. Make your minds easy. There are no cooler brains among you than mine." At this, Fritz burst into one of his explosions of laughter. Jack appealed to Fritz's father, with unruffled gravity. "Your son, I believe, sir? Ha! what a blessing it is there's plenty of room for improvement in that young man. I only throw out a remark. If I was afflicted with a son myself, I think I should prefer David."

This specimen of Jack's method of asserting himself, and other similar outbreaks which Fritz and I mischievously encouraged, failed apparently to afford any amusement to Madame Fontaine. Once she roused herself to ask Mr. Keller if his sister had written to him from Munich. Hearing that no reply had been received, she relapsed into silence. The old excuse of a nervous headache was repeated, when Mr. Keller and my aunt politely inquired if anything was amiss.

When the letters were delivered the next morning, two among them were not connected with the customary business of the office. One (with the postmark of Bingen) was for me. And one (with the postmark of Wurzburg) was for Madame Fontaine. I sent it upstairs to her immediately.

When I opened my own letter, I found sad news of poor Mr. Engelman. Time and change had failed to improve his spirits. He complained of a feeling of fullness and oppression in his head, and of hissing noises in his ears, which were an almost constant annoyance to him. On two occasions he had been cupped, and had derived no more than a temporary benefit from the employment of that remedy. His doctor recommended strict attention to diet, and regular exercise. He submitted willingly to the severest rules at table—but there was no rousing him to exert himself in any way. For hours together, he would sit silent in one place, half sleeping, half waking; noticing no one, and caring for nothing but to get to his bed as soon as possible.

This statement of the case seemed to me to suggest very grave considerations. I could no longer hesitate to inform Mr. Keller that I had received intelligence of his absent partner, and to place my letter in his hands.

Whatever little disagreements there had been between them were instantly forgotten. I had never before seen Mr. Keller so distressed and so little master of himself.

"I must go to Engelman directly," he said.

I ventured to submit that there were two serious objections to his doing this: In the first place, his presence in the office was absolutely necessary. In the second place, his sudden appearance at Bingen would prove to be a serious, perhaps a fatal, shock to his old friend.

"What is to be done, then?" he exclaimed.

"I think my aunt may be of some use, sir, in this emergency."

"Your aunt? How can she help us?"

I informed him of my aunt's project; and I added that Madame Fontaine had not positively said No. He listened without conviction, frowning and shaking his head.

"Mrs. Wagner is a very impetuous person," he said. "She doesn't understand a complex nature like Madame Fontaine's."

"At least I may show my aunt the letter from Bingen, sir?"

"Yes. It can do no harm, if it does no good."

On my way to my aunt's room, I encountered Minna on the stairs. She was crying. I naturally asked what was the matter.

"Don't stop me!" was the only answer I received.

"But where are you going, Minna?"

"I am going to Fritz, to be comforted."

"Has anybody behaved harshly to you?"

"Yes, mamma has behaved harshly to me. For the first time in my life," said the spoilt child, with a strong sense of injury, "she has locked the door of her room, and refused to let me in."

"But why?"

"How can I tell? I believe it has something to do with that horrid man I told you of. You sent a letter upstairs this morning. I met Joseph on the landing, and took the letter to her myself. Why shouldn't I look at the postmark? Where was the harm in saying to her, 'A letter, mamma, from Wurzburg'? She looked at me as if I had mortally offended her—and pointed to the door, and locked herself in. I have knocked twice, and asked her to forgive me. Not a word of answer either time! I consider myself insulted. Let me go to Fritz."

I made no attempt to detain her. She had set those every-ready suspicions of mine at work again.

Was the letter which I had sent upstairs a reply to the letter which Minna had seen her mother writing? Was the widow now informed that the senile old admirer who had advanced the money to pay her creditors had been found dead in his bed? and that her promissory note had passed into the possession of the heir-at-law? If this was the right reading of the riddle, no wonder she had sent her daughter out of the room—no wonder she had locked her door!

My aunt wasted no time in expressions of grief and surprise, when she was informed of Mr. Engelman's state of health. "Send the widow here directly," she said. "If there is anything like a true heart under that splendid silk dress of hers, I shall write and relieve poor Engelman by to-night's post."

To confide my private surmises, even to my aunt, would have been an act of inexcusable imprudence, to say the least of it. I could only reply that Madame Fontaine was not very well, and was (as I had heard from Minna) shut up in the retirement of her own room.

The resolute little woman got on her feet instantly. "Show me where she is, David—and leave the rest to me."

I led her to the door, and was dismissed with these words—"Go and wait in my room till I come back to you." As I retired, I heard a smart knock, and my aunt's voice announcing herself outside—"Mrs. Wagner, ma'am, with something serious to say to you." The reply was inaudible. Not so my aunt's rejoinder: "Oh, very well! Just read that letter, will you? I'll push it under the door, and wait for an answer." I lingered for a minute longer—and heard the door opened and closed again.

In little more than half an hour, my aunt returned. She looked serious and thoughtful. I at once anticipated that she had failed. Her first words informed me that I was wrong.

"I've done it," she said. "I am to write to Engelman to-night; and I have the widow's permission to tell him that she regrets her hasty decision. Her own words, mind, when I asked her how I should put it!"

"So there is a true heart under that splendid silk dress of hers?" I said.

My aunt walked up and down the room, silent and frowning—discontented with me, or discontented with herself; it was impossible to tell which. On a sudden, she sat down by me, and hit me a smart slap on the shoulder.

"David!" she said, "I have found out something about myself which I never suspected before. If you want to see a cold-blooded wretch, look at me!"

It was so gravely said, and so perfectly absurd, that I burst out laughing.

She was far too seriously perplexed about herself to take the smallest notice of my merriment.

"Do you know," she resumed, "that I actually hesitate to write to Engelman? David! I ought to be whipped at the cart's tail. I don't believe in Madame Fontaine."

She little knew how that abrupt confession interested me. "Tell me why!" I said eagerly.

"That's the disgraceful part of it," she answered. "I can't tell you why. Madame Fontaine spoke charmingly—with perfect taste and feeling. And all the time some devilish spirit of distrust kept whispering to me, "Don't believe her; she has her motive!" Are you sure, David, it is only a little illness that makes her shut herself up in her room, and look so frightfully pale and haggard? Do you know anything about her affairs? Engelman is rich; Engelman has a position. Has she got into some difficulty since she refused him? and could he, by the barest possibility, be of any use in helping her out of it?"

I declare solemnly that the idea suggested by my aunt never occurred to me until she asked those questions. As a rejected suitor, Mr. Engelman could be of no possible use to the widow. But suppose he was her accepted husband? and suppose the note fell due before Minna was married? In that case, Mr. Engelman might unquestionably be of use—he might lend the money.

My aunt's sharp eyes were on me. "Out with it, David!" she cried. "You don't believe in her, either—and you know why."

"I know absolutely nothing," I rejoined; "I am guessing in the dark; and the event may prove that I am completely at fault. Don't ask me to degrade Madame Fontaine's character in your estimation, without an atom of proof to justify what I say. I have something to propose which I think will meet the difficulty."

With a strong exercise of self-restraint, my aunt resigned herself to listen. "Let's hear your proposal," she said. "Have you any Scotch blood in your veins, David? You are wonderfully prudent and cautious for so young a man."

I went straight on with what I had to say.

"Send the widow's message to Mr. Engelman, by all means," I proceeded; "but not by post. I was with him immediately after his offer of marriage had been refused; and it is my belief that he is far too deeply wounded by the manner in which Madame Fontaine expressed herself when she rejected him, to be either able, or willing, to renew his proposal. I even doubt if he will believe in her expression of regret. This view of mine may turn out, of course, to be quite wrong; but let us at least put it to the test. I can easily get leave of absence for a few days. Let me take your letter to Bingen tomorrow, and see with my own eyes how it is received."

At last I was fortunate enough to deserve my aunt's approval. "An excellent suggestion," she said. "But—I believe I have caught the infection of your prudence, David—don't let us tell Madame Fontaine. Let her suppose that you have gone to Bingen in consequence of the unfavorable news of Engelman's health." She paused, and considered a little. "Or, better still, Bingen is on the way to England. There will be nothing extraordinary in your stopping to visit Engelman, on your journey to London."

This took me completely, and far from agreeably, by surprise. I said piteously, "Must I really leave Frankfort?"

"My good fellow, I have other interests to consider besides Engelman's interests," my aunt explained. "Mr. Hartrey is waiting to hear from me. There is no hope that Engelman will be able to travel to London, in his present state of health, and no possibility of Mr. Keller taking his place until something is settled at Frankfort. I want you to explain all this to Mr. Hartrey, and to help him in the management of the business. There is nobody else here, David, whom I can trust, as I trust you. I see no alternative but to ask you to go to London."

On my side, I had no alternative but to submit—and, what is more (remembering all that I owed to my aunt), to submit with my best grace. We consulted Mr. Keller; and he entirely agreed that I was the fittest person who could be found to reconcile Mr. Hartrey to the commercial responsibilities that burdened him. After a day's delay at Bingen, to study the condition of

Mr. Engelman's health and to write the fullest report to Frankfort, the faster I could travel afterwards, and the sooner I could reach London, the better.

So hard necessity compelled me to leave the stage, before the curtain rose on the final acts of the drama. The mail-post started at six in the morning. I packed up, and took leave of everybody, overnight—excepting Madame Fontaine, who still kept her room, and who was not well enough to see me. The dear kind-hearted Minna offered me her cheek to kiss, and made me promise to return for her marriage. She was strangely depressed at my departure. "You first consoled me," she said; "you have brought me happiness. I don't like your leaving us. Oh, David, I do wish you were not going away!" "Come! come!" my aunt interposed; "no crying, young lady! Always keep a man's spirits up when he leaves you. Give me a good hug, David—and think of the time when you will be a partner in the business." Ah! what a woman she was! Look as you may, my young friends, you will not find the like of her now.

Jack Straw was the one person up and stirring when the coach stopped the next morning at the door. I expected to be amused—but there was no reckoning with Jack. His farewell words literally frightened me.

"I say!" he whispered, as I hurried into the hall, "there's one thing I want to ask you before you go."

"Be quick about it, Jack."

"All right, David. I had a talk with Minna yesterday, about Mr. Keller's illness. Is it true that he was cured out of the blue-glass bottle?"

"Perfectly true.

"Look here, David! I have been thinking of it all night. I was cured out of the blue-glass bottle."

I suddenly stood still, with my eyes riveted on his face. He stepped close up to me, and lowered his voice suddenly.

"And I was poisoned," he said. "What I want to know is—Who poisoned Mr. Keller?"

158

BETWEEN THE PARTS

MR. DAVID GLENNEY PRODUCES HIS CORRESPONDENCE, AND THROWS SOME NEW LIGHTS ON THE STORY

I

Be pleased to read the following letter from Mr. Lawyer's-Clerk-Schmuckle to Mr. Town-Councilor-Hof:

"My honored Sir,—I beg to report that you may make your mind easy on the subject of Madame Fontaine. If she leaves Frankfort, she will not slip away privately as she did at Wurzburg. Wherever she may go now, we need not apply again to her relations in this place to help us to find her. Henceforth I undertake to keep her in view until the promissory note falls due.

"The lady is at present established as housekeeper in the employment of the firm of Wagner, Keller, and Engelman; and there (barring accidents, which I shall carefully look after) she is likely to remain.

"I have made a memorandum of the date at which her promissory note falls due—viz., the 31st December in the present year. The note being made payable at Wurzburg, you must take care (in the event of its not being honored) to have the document protested in that town, and to communicate with me by the same day's post. I will myself see that the law takes its regular course.

"Permit me most gratefully to thank you for the advance on my regular fees which you have so graciously transmitted, and believe me your obedient humble servant to command."

II

I next submit a copy of a letter addressed by the late Chemistry-Professor Fontaine to an honored friend and colleague. This gentleman is still living; and he makes it a condition of supplying the copy that his name shall not appear:—

"Illustrious Friend and Colleague,—You will be surprised at so soon hearing from me again. The truth is, that I have some interesting news for you. An alarming accident has enabled me to test the value of one of my preparations on a living human subject—that subject being a man.

"My last letter informed you that I had resolved on making no further use of the Formula for recomposing some of the Borgia Poisons (erroneously supposed to be destroyed) left to me on the death of my lamented Hungarian friend—my master in chemical science.

"The motives which have led me to this decision are, I hope, beyond the reach of blame.

"You will remember agreeing with me, that the two specimens of these resuscitated poisons which I have succeeded in producing are capable—like the poisons already known to modern medical practice—of rendering the utmost benefit in certain cases of disease, if they are administered in carefully regulated doses. Should I live to devote them to this good purpose, there will still be the danger (common to all poisonous preparations employed in medicine) of their doing fatal mischief, when misused by ignorance or crime.

"Bearing this in mind, I conceive it to be my duty to provide against dangerous results, by devoting myself to the discovery of efficient antidotes, before I adapt the preparations themselves to the capacities of the healing art. I have had some previous experience in this branch of what I call preservative chemistry, and I have already in some degree succeeded in attaining my object.

"The Formula in cipher which I now send to you, on the slip of paper enclosed, is an antidote to that one of the two poisons known to you and to me by the fanciful name which you suggested for it—'Alexander's Wine.'

"With regard to the second of the poisons, which (if you remember) I have entitled—in anticipation of its employment as medicine—'The Looking-Glass Drops,' I regret to say that I have not yet succeeded in discovering the antidote in this case.

"Having now sufficiently explained my present position, I may tell you of the extraordinary accident to which I have alluded at the beginning of my letter.

"About a fortnight since, I was sent for, just as I had finished my lecture to the students, to see one of my servants. He had been suffering from illness for one or two days. I had of course offered him my medical services. He refused, however, to trouble me; sending word that he only wanted rest. Fortunately one of my assistants happened to see him, and at once felt the necessity of calling in my help.

"The man was a poor half-witted friendless creature, whom I had employed out of pure pity to keep my laboratory clean, and to wash and dry my bottles. He had sense enough to perform such small services as these, and no more. Judge of my horror when I went to his bedside, and instantly recognized the symptoms of poisoning by "Alexander's Wine!"

"I ran back to my laboratory, and unlocked the medicine-chest which held the antidote. In the next compartment, the poison itself was always placed. Looking into the compartment now, I found it empty.

"I at once instituted a search, and discovered the bottle left out on a shelf. For the first time in my life, I had been guilty of inexcusable carelessness. I had not looked round me to see that I had left everything safe before quitting the room. The poor imbecile wretch had been attracted by the color of "Alexander's Wine," and had tasted it (in his own phrase) "to see if it was nice." My inquiries informed me that this had happened at least thirty-six hours since! I had but one hope of saving him—derived from experiments on animals, which had shown me the very gradual progress of the deadly action of the poison.

"What I felt when I returned to the suffering man, I shall not attempt to describe. You will understand how completely I was overwhelmed, when I tell you that I meanly concealed my own disgraceful thoughtlessness from my brethren in the University. I was afraid that my experiments might be prohibited as dangerous, and my want of common prudence be made the subject of public reprimand by the authorities. The medical professors were permitted by me to conclude that it was a case of illness entirely new in their experience.

"In administering the antidote, I had no previous experiments to guide me, except my experiments with rabbits and dogs. Whether I miscalculated or whether I was deluded by my anxiety to save the man's life, I cannot say. This at least is certain, I gave the doses too copiously and at too short intervals.

"The patient recovered—but it was after sustaining some incomprehensibly deteriorating change in the blood, which destroyed his complexion, and turned his hair gray. I have since modified the doses; and in dread of losing the memorandum, I have attached a piece of notched paper to the bottle, so as to render any future error of judgment impossible. At the same time, I have facilitated the future administration of the antidote by adding a label to the bottle, stating the exact quantity of the poison taken by my servant, as calculated by myself.

"I ought, by the way, to have mentioned in the cipher that experience has shown me the necessity, if the antidote is to be preserved for any length of time, of protecting it in blue glass from the influence of light.

"Let me also tell you that I found a vegetable diet of use in perfecting the effect of the treatment. That mean dread of discovery, which I have already acknowledged, induced me to avail myself of my wife's help in nursing the man. When he began to talk of what had happened to him, I could trust Madame Fontaine to keep the secret. When he was well enough to get up, the poor harmless creature disappeared. He was probably terrified at the prospect of entering the laboratory again. In any case, I have never seen him or heard of him since.

"If you have had patience to read as far as this, you will understand that I am not sure enough yet of my own discoveries to risk communicating them to any other person than yourself. Favor me with any chemical suggestions which may strike you—and then, in case of accidents, destroy the cipher. For the present farewell."

Note to Doctor Fontaine's Letter

"Alexander's Wine" refers to the infamous Roderic Borgia, historically celebrated as Pope Alexander the Sixth. He was accidentally, and most deservedly, killed by drinking one of the Borgia poisons, in a bowl of wine which he had prepared for another person.

The formula for "The Looking-Glass Drops" is supposed to have been found hidden on removing the wooden lining at the back of a looking-glass, which had been used by Lucrezia Borgia. Hence the name.

III

The third and last letter which I present is written by me, and was addressed to Mrs. Wagner during her stay at Frankfort:—

"I exaggerate nothing, my dear aunt, when I say that I write in great distress. Let me beg you to prepare yourself for very sad news.

"It was late yesterday evening before I arrived at Bingen. A servant was waiting to take my portmanteau, when I got out of the coach. After first asking my name, he communicated to me the melancholy tidings of dear Mr. Engelman's death. He had sunk under a fit of apoplexy, at an early hour that morning.

"Medical help was close at hand, and was (so far as I can hear) carefully and intelligently exercised. But he never rallied in the least. The fit appears to have killed him, as a bullet might have killed him.

"He had been very dull and heavy on the previous day. In the few words that he spoke before retiring to rest, my name was on his lips. He said, "If I get better I should like to have David here, and to go on with him to our house of business in London." He was very much flushed, and complained of feeling giddy; but he would not allow the doctor to be sent for. His brother assisted him to ascend the stairs to his room, and asked him some questions about his affairs. He replied impatiently, 'Keller knows all about it—leave it to Keller.'

"When I think of the good old man's benevolent and happy life, and when I remember that it was accidentally through me that he first met Madame Fontaine, I feel a bitterness of spirit which makes my sense of the loss of him more painful than I can describe. I call to mind a hundred little instances of his kindness to me—and (don't be offended) I wish you had sent some other person than myself to represent you at Frankfort.

"He is to be buried here, in two days' time. I hope you will not consider me negligent of your interest in accepting his brother's invitation to follow him to the grave. I think it will put me in a better frame of mind, if I can pay the last tribute of affection and respect to my old friend. When all is over, I will continue the journey to London, without stopping on the road night or day.

"Write to me at London, dear aunt; and give my love to Minna and Fritz—and ask them to write to me also. I beg my best respects to Mr. Keller. Please assure him of my true sympathy; I know, poor man, how deeply he will be grieved."

PART II

MR. DAVID GLENNEY COLLECTS HIS MATERIALS AND CONTINUES THE STORY HISTORICALLY

CHAPTER I

In the preceding portion of this narrative I spoke as an eye-witness. In the present part of it, my absence from Frankfort leaves me dependent on the documentary evidence of other persons. This evidence consists (first) of letters addressed to myself; (secondly) of statements personally made to me; (thirdly) of extracts from a diary discovered after the lifetime of the writer. In all three cases the materials thus placed at my disposal bear proof of truthfulness on the face of them.

Early in the month of December, Mr. Keller sent a message to Madame Fontaine, requesting to see her on a matter of importance to both of them.

"I hope you feel better to-day, madam," he said, rising to receive the widow when she entered the room.

"You are very good, sir," she answered, in tones barely audible—with her eyes on the ground. "I can't say that I feel much better."

"I have news for you, which ought to act as the best of all restoratives," Mr. Keller proceeded. "At last I have heard from my sister on the subject of the marriage."

He stopped, and, suddenly stepping forward, caught the widow by the arm. At his last words she had started to her feet. Her face suddenly turned from pale to red—and then changed again to a ghastly whiteness. She would have fallen if Mr. Keller had not held her up. He placed her at once in his own easy chair. "You must really have medical advice," he said gravely; "your nerves are seriously out of order. Can I get you anything?"

"A glass of water, sir, if you will be so kind as to ring for it."

"There is no need to ring for it; I have water in the next room."

She laid her hand on his arm, and stopped him as he was about to leave her.

"One word first, sir. You will forgive a woman's curiosity on such an interesting subject as the marriage of her child. Does your sister propose a day for the wedding?"

"My sister suggests," Mr. Keller answered, "the thirtieth of this month."

He left her and opened the door of the next room.

As he disappeared, she rapidly followed out a series of calculations on her fingers. Her eyes brightened, her energies rallied. "No matter what happens so long as my girl is married first," she whispered to herself. "The wedding on the thirtieth, and the money due on the thirty-first. Saved by a day! Saved by a day!"

Mr. Keller returned with a glass of water. He started as he looked at her.

"You seem to have recovered already—you look quite a different woman!" he exclaimed.

She drank the water nevertheless. "My unlucky nerves play me strange tricks, sir," she answered, as she set the empty glass down on a table at her side.

Mr. Keller took a chair and referred to his letter from Munich.

"My sister hopes to be with us some days before the end of the year," he resumed. "But in her uncertain state of health, she suggests the thirtieth so as to leave a margin in case of unexpected delays. I presume this will afford plenty of time (I speak ignorantly of such things) for providing the bride's outfit?"

Madame Fontaine smiled sadly. "Far more time than we want, sir. My poor little purse will leave my girl to rely on her natural attractions—with small help from the jeweler and the milliner, on her wedding day."

Mr. Keller referred to his letter again, and looked up from it with a grim smile.

"My sister will in one respect at least anticipate the assistance of the jeweler," he said. "She proposes to bring with her, as a present to the bride, an heirloom on the female side of our family. It is a pearl necklace (of very great value, I am told) presented to my mother by the Empress Maria Theresa—in recognition of services rendered to that illustrious person early in life. As an expression of my sister's interest in the marriage, I thought an announcement of the proposed gift might prove gratifying to you."

Madame Fontaine clasped her hands, with a fervor of feeling which was in this case, at least, perfectly sincere. A pearl necklace, the gift of an Empress, would represent in money value a little fortune in itself. "I can find no words to express my sense of gratitude," she said; "my daughter must speak for herself and for me."

"And your daughter must hear the good news as soon as possible," Mr. Keller added kindly. "I won't detain you. I know you must be anxious to see Minna. One word before you go. You will, of course, invite any relatives and friends whom you would like to see at the wedding."

Madame Fontaine lifted her sleepy eyes by slow gradations to the ceiling, and devoutly resigned herself to mention her family circumstances.

"My parents cast me off, sir, when I married," she said; "my other relatives here and in Brussels refused to assist me when I stood in need of help. As for friends—you, dear Mr. Keller, are our only friend. Thank you again and again."

She lowered her eyes softly to the floor, and glided out of the room. The back view of her figure was its best view. Even Mr. Keller—constitutionally inaccessible to exhibitions of female grace—followed her with his eyes, and perceived that his housekeeper was beautifully made.

On the stairs she met with the housemaid.

"Where is Miss Minna?" she asked impatiently. "In her room?"

"In your room, madam. I saw Miss Minna go in as I passed the door."

Madame Fontaine hurried up the next flight of stairs, and ran along the corridor as lightly as a young girl. The door of her room was ajar; she saw her daughter through the opening sitting on the sofa, with some work lying idle on her lap. Minna started up when her mother appeared.

"Am I in the way, mamma? I am so stupid, I can't get on with this embroidery——"

Madame Fontaine tossed the embroidery to the other end of the room, threw her arms round Minna, and lifted her joyously from the floor as if she had been a little child.

"The day is fixed, my angel!" she cried; "You are to be married on the thirtieth!"

She shifted one hand to her daughter's head, and clasped it with a fierce fondness to her bosom. "Oh, my darling, you had lovely hair even when you were a baby! We won't have it dressed at your wedding. It shall flow down naturally in all its beauty—and no hand shall brush it but mine." She pressed her lips on Minna's head, and devoured it with kisses; then, driven by some irresistible impulse, pushed the girl away from her, and threw herself on the sofa with a cry of pain.

"Why did you start up, as if you were afraid of me, when I came in?" she said wildly. "Why did you ask if you were in the way? Oh, Minna! Minna! can't you forget the day when I locked you out of my room? My child! I was beside myself—I was mad with my troubles. Do you think I would behave harshly to you? Oh, my own love! when I came to tell you of your marriage, why did you ask me if you were in the way? My God! am I never to know a moment's pleasure again without something to embitter it? People say you take after your father, Minna. Are you as cold-blooded as he was? There! there! I don't mean it; I am a little hysterical, I think—don't notice me. Come and be a child again. Sit on my knee, and let us talk of your marriage."

Minna put her arm round her mother's neck a little nervously. "Dear, sweet mamma, how can you think me so hard-hearted and so ungrateful? I can't tell you how I love you! Let this tell you."

With a tender and charming grace, she kissed her mother—then drew back a little and looked at Madame Fontaine. The subsiding conflict of emotions still showed itself with a fiery brightness in the widow's eyes. "Do you know what I am thinking?" Minna asked, a little timidly.

"What is it, my dear?"

"I think you are almost too fond of me, mamma. I shouldn't like to be the person who stood between me and my marriage—if you knew of it."

Madame Fontaine smiled. "You foolish child, do you take me for a tigress?" she said playfully. "I must have another kiss to reconcile me to my new character."

She bent her head to meet the caress—looked by chance at a cupboard fixed in a recess in the opposite wall of the room—and suddenly checked herself. "This is too selfish of me," she said, rising abruptly. "All this time I am forgetting the bridegroom. His father will leave him to hear the good news from you. Do you think I don't know what you are longing to do?" She led Minna hurriedly to the door. "Go, my dear one—go and tell Fritz!"

The instant her daughter disappeared, she rushed across the room to the cupboard. Her eyes had not deceived her. The key was left in the lock.

CHAPTER II

Madame Fontaine dropped into a chair, overwhelmed by the discovery.

She looked at the key left in the cupboard. It was of an old-fashioned pattern—but evidently also of the best workmanship of the time. On its flat handle it bore engraved the words, "Pink-Room Cupboard"—so called from the color of the curtains and hangings in the bedchamber.

"Is my brain softening?" she said to herself. "What a horrible mistake! What a frightful risk to have run!"

She got on her feet again, and opened the cupboard.

The two lower shelves were occupied by her linen, neatly folded and laid out. On the higher shelf, nearly on a level with her eyes, stood a plain wooden box about two feet in height by one foot in breadth. She examined the position of this box with breathless interest and care—then gently lifted it in both hands and placed it on the floor. On a table near the window lay a half-finished watercolor drawing, with a magnifying glass by the side of it. Providing herself with the glass, she returned to the cupboard, and closely investigated the place on which the box had stood. The slight layer of dust—so slight as to be imperceptible to the unassisted eye—which had surrounded the four sides of the box, presented its four delicate edges in perfectly undisturbed straightness of line. This mute evidence conclusively proved that the box had not been moved during her quarter of an hour's absence in Mr. Keller's room. She put it back again, and heaved a deep breath of relief.

But it was a bad sign (she thought) that her sense of caution had been completely suspended, in the eagerness of her curiosity to know if Mr. Keller's message of invitation referred to the wedding day. "I lose my best treasure," she said to herself sadly, "if I am beginning to lose my steadiness of mind. If this should happen again——"

She left the expression of the idea uncompleted; locked the door of the room; and returned to the place on which she had left the box.

Seating herself, she rested the box on her knee and opened it.

Certain tell-tale indentations, visible where the cover fitted into the lock, showed that it had once been forced open. The lock had been hampered on some former occasion; and the key remained so fast fixed in it that it could neither be turned nor drawn out. In her newly-aroused distrust of her own prudence, she was now considering the serious question of emptying the box, and sending it to be fitted with a lock and key.

"Have I anything by me," she thought to herself, "in which I can keep the bottles?"

She emptied the box, and placed round her on the floor those terrible six bottles which had been the special subjects of her husband's precautionary instructions on his death-bed. Some of them were smaller than others, and were manufactured in glass of different colors—the six compartments in the medicine-chest being carefully graduated in size, so as to hold them all steadily. The labels on three of the bottles were unintelligible to Madame Fontaine; the inscriptions were written in barbarously abridged Latin characters.

The bottle which was the fourth in order, as she took them out one by one, was wrapped in a sheet of thick cartridge-paper, covered on its inner side with characters written in mysterious cipher. But the label pasted on the bottle contained an inscription in good readable German, thus translated:

"The Looking-Glass Drops. Fatal dose, as discovered by experiment on animals, the same as in the case of 'Alexander's Wine.' But the effect, in producing death, more rapid, and more indistinguishable, in respect of presenting traces on post-mortem examination."

The lines thus written were partially erased by strokes of the pen—drawn through them at a later date, judging by the color of the ink. In the last blank space left at the foot of the label, these words were added—also in ink of a fresher color:

"After many patient trials, I can discover no trustworthy antidote to this infernal poison. Under these circumstances, I dare not attempt to modify it for medical use. I would throw it away—but I don't like to be beaten. If I live a little longer I will try once more, with my mind refreshed by other studies."

Madame Fontaine paused before she wrapped the bottle up again in its covering, and looked with longing eyes at the ciphers which filled the inner side of the sheet of paper. There, perhaps, was the announcement of the discovery of the antidote; or possibly, the record of some more recent experiment which placed the terrible power of the poison in a new light! And there also was the cipher defying her to discover its secret!

The fifth bottle that she took from the chest contained "Alexander's Wine." The sixth, and last, was of the well-remembered blue glass, which had played such an important part in the event of Mr. Keller's recovery.

David Glenney had rightly conjectured that the label had been removed

171

from the blue-glass bottle. Madame Fontaine shook it out of the empty compartment. The inscription (also in the German language) ran as follows:—

"Antidote to Alexander's Wine. The fatal dose, in case of accident, is indicated by the notched slip of paper attached to the bottle. Two fluid drachms of the poison (more than enough to produce death) were accidentally taken in my experience. So gradual is the deadly effect that, after a delay of thirty-six hours before my attention was called to the case, the administration of the antidote proved successful. The doses are to be repeated every three or four hours. Any person watching the patient may know that the recovery is certain, and that the doses are therefore to be discontinued, by these signs: the cessation of the trembling in the hands; the appearance of natural perspiration; and the transition from the stillness of apathy to the repose of sleep. For at least a week or ten days afterwards a vegetable diet, with cream, is necessary as a means of completing the cure."

She laid the label aside, and looked at the two bottles—the poison and the antidote—ranged together at her feet.

"Power!" she thought, with a superb smile of triumph. "The power that I have dreamed of all my life is mine at last! Alone among mortal creatures, I have Life and Death for my servants. You were deaf, Mr. Keller, to my reasons, and deaf to my entreaties. What wonderful influence brought you to my feet, and made you the eager benefactor of my child? My servant Death, who threatened you in the night; and my servant Life, who raised you up in the morning. What a position! I stand here, a dweller in a populous city—and every creature in it, from highest to lowest, is a creature in my power!"

She looked through the window of her room over the houses of Frankfort. At last her sleepy eyes opened wide; an infernal beauty irradiated her face. For one moment, she stood—a demon in human form. The next, she suddenly changed into a timid woman, shaken in every limb by the cold grasp of fear.

What influence had wrought the transformation?

Nothing but a knock at the door.

172

"Who's there?" she cried.

The voice that answered her was the voice of Jack Straw.

"Hullo, there, Mrs. Fontaine! Let me in."

She placed a strong constraint on herself; she spoke in friendly tones. "What do you want, Jack?"

"I want to show you my keys."

"What do I care about the crazy wretch's keys?"—was the thought that passed through Madame Fontaine's mind, when Jack answered her from the outer side of the door. But she was still careful, when she spoke to him, to disguise her voice in its friendliest tones.

"Excuse me for keeping you waiting, Jack. I can't let you in yet."

"Why not?"

"Because I am dressing. Come back in half an hour; and I shall be glad to see you."

There was no reply to this. Jack's step was so light that it was impossible to hear, through the door, whether he had gone away or not. After waiting a minute, the widow ventured on peeping out. Jack had taken himself off. Not a sign of him was to be seen, when she bent over the railing of the corridor, and looked down on the stairs.

She locked herself in again. "I hope I haven't offended him!" she thought, as she returned to the empty medicine-chest.

The fear that Jack might talk of what had happened to him in the laboratory at Wurzburg, and that he might allude to his illness in terms which could not fail to recall the symptoms of Mr. Keller's illness, was constantly present to her mind. She decided on agreeably surprising him by a little present, which might help her to win his confidence and to acquire some influence over him. As a madman lately released from Bedlam, it might perhaps not greatly matter what he said. But suspicion was easily excited. Though David Glenney had been sent out of the way, his aunt remained at

Frankfort; and an insolent readiness in distrusting German ladies seemed to run in the family.

Having arrived at these conclusions, she gave her mind again to the still unsettled question of the new lock to the medicine-chest.

Measuring the longest of the bottles (the bottle containing the antidote), she found that her dressing case was not high enough to hold it, while the chest was in the locksmith's workshop. Her trunks, on the other hand, were only protected by very ordinary locks, and were too large to be removed to the safe keeping of the cupboard. She must either leave the six bottles loose on the shelf or abandon the extra security of the new lock.

The one risk of taking the first of these two courses, was the risk of leaving the key again in the cupboard. Was this likely to occur, after the fright she had already suffered? The question was not really worth answering. She had already placed two of the bottles on the shelf—when a fatal objection to trusting the empty box out of her own possession suddenly crossed her mind.

Her husband's colleagues at Wurzburg and some of the elder students, were all acquainted (externally, at least) with the appearance of the Professor's ugly old medicine-chest. It could be easily identified by the initials of his name, inscribed in deeply-burnt letters on the lid. Suppose one of these men happened to be in Frankfort? and suppose he saw the stolen chest in the locksmith's shop? Two such coincidences were in the last degree improbable— but it was enough that they were possible. Who but a fool, in her critical position, would run the risk of even one chance in a hundred turning against her? Instead of trusting the chest in a stranger's hands, the wiser course would be to burn it at the first safe opportunity, and be content with the security of the cupboard, while she remained in Mr. Keller's house. Arriving at this conclusion, she put the chest and its contents back again on the shelf—with the one exception of the label detached from the blue-glass bottle.

In the preternatural distrust that now possessed her, this label assumed the character of a dangerous witness, if, through some unlucky accident, it happened to fall into the hands of any person in the house. She picked it up—advanced to the fireplace to destroy it—paused—and looked at it again.

Nearly two doses of the antidote were still left. Who could say, looking at the future of such a life as hers, that she might not have some need of it yet—after it had already served her so well? Could she be sure, if she destroyed it, of remembering the instructions which specified the intervals at which the doses were to be given, the signs which signified recovery, and the length of time during which the vegetable diet was to be administered?

She read the first sentences again carefully.

"Antidote to Alexander's Wine. The fatal dose, in case of accident, is indicated by the notched slip of paper attached to the bottle. Two fluid drachms of the poison (more than enough to produce death) were accidentally taken in my experience. So gradual is the deadly effect that, after a delay of thirty-six hours before my attention was called to the case, the administration of the antidote proved successful. The doses are to be repeated——"

The remaining instructions, beginning with this last sentence, were not of a nature to excite suspicion. Taken by themselves, they might refer to nothing more remarkable than a remedy in certain cases of illness. First she thought of cutting off the upper part of the label: but the lines of the writing were so close together, that they would infallibly betray the act of mutilation. She opened her dressing-case and took from it a common-looking little paper-box, purchased at the chemist's, bearing the ambitious printed title of "Macula Exstinctor, or Destroyer of Stains"—being an ordinary preparation, in powder, for removing stains from dresses, ink-stains included. The printed directions stated that the powder, partially dissolved in water, might also be used to erase written characters without in any way injuring the paper, otherwise than by leaving a slight shine on the surface. By these means, Madame Fontaine removed the first four sentences on the label, and left the writing on it to begin harmlessly with the instructions for repeating the doses.

"Now I can trust you to refresh my memory without telling tales," she said to herself, when she put the label back in the chest. As for the recorded dose of the poison, she was not likely to forget that. It was her medicine-measuring glass, filled up to the mark of two drachms. Having locked the cupboard, and secured the key in her pocket, she was ready for the reception of Jack. Her watch told her that the half-hour's interval had more than expired. She opened the door of her room. There was no sign of him outside. She looked over the stairs, and called to him softly. There was no reply; the little man's sensitive dignity had evidently taken offense.

The one thing to be done (remembering all that she had to dread from the wanton exercise of Jack's tongue) was to soothe his ruffled vanity without further delay. There would be no difficulty in discovering him, if he had not gone out. Wherever his Mistress might be at the moment, there he was sure to be found.

Trying Mrs. Wagner's room first, without success, the widow descended to the ground floor and made her way to the offices. In the private room, formerly occupied by Mr. Engelman, David Glenney's aunt was working at her desk; and Jack Straw was perched on the old-fashioned window-seat, putting the finishing touches to Minna's new straw hat.

CHAPTER III

In the gloom thrown over the household by Mr. Engelman's death, Mrs. Wagner, with characteristic energy and good sense, had kept her mind closely occupied. During the office hours, she studied those details of the business at Frankfort which differed from the details of the business in London; and soon mastered them sufficiently to be able to fill the vacancy which Mr. Engelman had left. The position that he had held became, with all its privileges and responsibilities, Mrs. Wagner's position—claimed, not in virtue of her rank as directress of the London house, but in recognition of the knowledge that she had specially acquired to fit her for the post.

Out of office-hours, she corresponded with the English writer on the treatment of insane persons, whose work she had discovered in her late husband's library, and assisted him in attracting public attention to the humane system which he advocated. Even the plan for the employment of respectable girls, in suitable departments of the office, was not left neglected by this indefatigable woman. The same friendly consideration which had induced her to spare Mr. Keller any allusion to the subject, while his health was not yet completely restored, still kept her silent until time had reconciled him to the calamity of his partner's death. Privately, however, she had caused inquiries to be made in Frankfort, which would assist her in choosing worthy candidates for employment, when the favorable time came—probably after the celebration of Fritz's marriage—for acting in the interests of the proposed reform.

"Pray send me away, if I interrupt you," said Madame Fontaine, pausing modestly on the threshold before she entered the room. She spoke English admirably, and made a point of ignoring Mrs. Wagner's equally perfect knowledge of German, by addressing her always in the English language.

"Come in by all means," Mrs. Wagner answered. "I am only writing to David Glenney, to tell him (at Minna's request) that the wedding-day is fixed."

"Give your nephew my kind regards, Mrs. Wagner. He will be one of the party at the wedding, of course?"

"Yes—if he can be spared from his duties in London. Is there anything I can do for you, Madame Fontaine?"

"Nothing, thank you—except to excuse my intrusion. I am afraid I have offended our little friend there, with the pretty straw hat in his hand, and I want to make my peace with him."

Jack looked up from his work with an air of lofty disdain. "Oh, dear me, it doesn't matter," he said, in his most magnificent manner.

"I was dressing when he knocked at my door," pursued Madame Fontaine; "and I asked him to come back, and show me his keys in half an hour. Why didn't you return, Jack? Won't you show me the keys now?"

"You see it's a matter of business," Jack replied as loftily as ever. "I am in the business—Keeper of the Keys. Mistress is in the business; Mr. Keller is in the business. You are not in the business. It doesn't matter. Upon my soul, it doesn't matter."

Mrs. Wagner held up her forefinger reprovingly. "Jack! don't forget you are speaking to a lady."

Jack audaciously put his hand to his head, as if this was an effort of memory which was a little too much to expect of him.

"Anything to please you, Mistress," he said. "I'll show her the bag."

He exhibited to Madame Fontaine a leather bag, with a strap fastened round it. "The keys are inside," he explained. "I wore them loose this morning: and they made a fine jingle. Quite musical to my ear. But Mistress thought the noise likely to be a nuisance in the long run. So I strapped them up in a bag to keep them quiet. And when I move about, the bag hangs from my shoulder, like this, by another strap. When the keys are wanted, I open the bag. You don't want them—you're not in the business. Besides, I'm thinking of going out, and showing myself and my bag in the fashionable quarter of the town. On such an occasion, I think I ought to present the appearance of a gentleman—I ought to wear gloves. Oh, it doesn't matter! I needn't detain you any longer. Good morning."

He made one of his fantastic bows, and waved his hand, dismissing Madame Fontaine from further attendance on him. Secretly, he was as eager as ever to show the keys. But the inordinate vanity which was still the mad side of him and the incurable side of him, shrank from opening the leather bag unless the widow first made a special request and a special favor of it. Feeling no sort of interest in the subject, she took the shorter way of making her peace with him. She took out her purse.

"Let me make you a present of the gloves," she said, with her irresistible smile.

Jack lost all his dignity in an instant.

He leapt off the window seat and snatched at the money, like a famished animal snatching at a piece of meat. Mrs. Wagner caught him by the arm, and looked at him. He lifted his eyes to hers, then lowered them again as if he was ashamed of himself.

"Oh, to be sure!" he said, "I have forgotten my manners, I haven't said Thank you. A lapse of memory, I suppose. Thank you, Mrs. Housekeeper." In a moment more, he and his bag were on their way to the fashionable quarter of the town.

"You will make allowances for my poor little Jack, I am sure," said Mrs. Wagner.

"My dear madam, Jack amuses me!"

Mrs. Wagner winced a little at the tone of the widow's reply. "I have cured him of all the worst results of his cruel imprisonment in the mad-house," she went on. "But his harmless vanity seems to be inbred; I can do nothing with him on that side of his character. He is proud of being trusted with anything, especially with keys; and he has been kept waiting for them, while I had far more important matters to occupy me. In a day or two he will be more accustomed to his great responsibility, as he calls it."

"Of course you don't trust him," said Madame Fontaine, "with keys that are of any importance; like the key of your desk there, for instance."

Mrs. Wagner's steady gray eyes began to brighten. "I can trust him with anything," she answered emphatically.

Madame Fontaine arched her handsome brows in a mutely polite expression of extreme surprise.

"In my experience of the world," Mrs. Wagner went on, "I have found that the rarest of all human virtues is the virtue of gratitude. In a hundred little ways my poor friendless Jack has shown me that he is grateful. To my mind that is reason enough for trusting him."

"With money?" the widow inquired.

"Certainly. In London I trusted him with money—with the happiest results. I quieted his mind by an appeal to his sense of trust and self-respect, which he thoroughly appreciated. As yet I have not given him the key of my desk here, because I reserve it as a special reward for good conduct. In a few days more I have no doubt he will add it to the collection in his bag."

"Ah," said Madame Fontaine, with the humility which no living woman knew better when and how to assume, "you understand these difficult questions—you have your grand national common-sense. I am only a poor limited German woman. But, as you say in England, 'Live and learn.' You have indescribably interested me. Good morning."

She left the room. "Hateful woman!" she said in her own language, on the outer side of the door.

"Humbug!" said Mrs. Wagner in her language, on the inner side of the door.

If there had been more sympathy between the two ladies, or if Madame Fontaine had felt a little curiosity on the subject of crazy Jack's keys, she might have taken away with her some valuable materials for future consideration. As it was, Mrs. Wagner had not troubled her with any detailed narrative of the manner in which she had contrived to fill Jack's leather bag.

In London, she had begun cautiously by only giving him some of the useless old keys which accumulate about a house in course of years. When the novelty of merely keeping them had worn off, and when he wanted to see them put to some positive use, she had added one or two keys of her own, and had flattered his pride by asking him to open the box or the desk for her, as the case might be. Proceeding on the same wisely gradual plan at Frankfort, she had asked Mr. Keller to help her, and had been taken by him (while Jack was out of the way) to a lumber-room in the basement of the house, on the floor of which several old keys were lying about. "Take as many as you like," he had said; "they have been here, for all I know, ever since the house was repaired and refurnished in my grandfather's time, and they might be sold for old iron, if there were only enough of them." Mrs. Wagner had picked up the first six keys that presented themselves, and had made Jack Straw the happiest of men. He found no fault with them for being rusty. On the contrary, he looked forward with delight to the enjoyment of cleaning away the rust. "They shall be as bright as diamonds," he had said to his mistress, "before I have done with them."

And what did Madame Fontaine lose, by failing to inform herself of such trifles as these? She never discovered what she had lost. But she had not done with Jack Straw yet.

CHAPTER IV

After leaving Mrs. Wagner, the widow considered with herself, and then turned away from the commercial regions of the house, in search of her daughter.

She opened the dining-room door, and found the bagatelle-board on the table. Fritz and Minna were playing a game of the desultory sort—with the inevitable interruptions appropriate to courtship.

"Are you coming to join us, mamma? Fritz is playing very badly."

"This sort of thing requires mathematical calculation," Fritz remarked; "and Minna distracts my attention."

Madame Fontaine listened with a smile of maternal indulgence. "I am on my way back to my room," she said. "If either of you happen to see Jack Straw——"

"He has gone out," Fritz interposed. "I saw him through the window. He started at a run—and then remembered his dignity, and slackened his pace to a walk. How will he come back, I wonder?"

"He will come back with greater dignity than ever, Fritz. I have given him the money to buy himself a pair of gloves. If you or Minna happen to meet with him before I do, tell him he may come upstairs and show me his new gloves. I like to indulge the poor imbecile creature. You mustn't laugh at him—he is to be pitied."

Expressing these humane sentiments, she left the lovers to their game. While Jack was still pleasurably excited by the new gift, he would be in the right frame of mind to feel her influence. Now or never (if the thing could be done) was the time to provide against the danger of chance-allusions to what had happened at Wurzburg. It was well known in the house that Mrs. Wagner wished to return to London, as soon after the marriage as certain important considerations connected with the management of the office would permit. By Madame Fontaine's calculations, Jack would be happily out of the way of doing mischief (if she could keep him quiet in the meanwhile) in a month or six weeks' time.

The game went on in the dining-room—with the inevitable intervals. Beyond reproach as a lover, Fritz showed no signs of improvement as a bagatelle-player. In a longer pause than usual, during which the persons concerned happened to have their backs turned to the door, a disagreeable interruption occurred. At a moment of absolute silence an intruding voice made itself heard, inviting immediate attention in these words:—

"I say, you two! If you want to see the finest pair of gloves in Frankfort, just look here."

There he stood with outstretched hands, exhibiting a pair of bright green gloves, and standing higher in his own estimation than ever.

"Why do you always come in without knocking?" Fritz asked, with excusable indignation.

"Why have you always got your arm round her waist?" Jack retorted. "I say, Miss Minna (I only offer a remark), the more he kisses you the more you seem to like it."

"Send him away, for Heaven's sake!" Minna whispered.

"Go upstairs!" cried Fritz.

"What! do you want to be at it again?" asked Jack.

"Go and show your new gloves to Madame Fontaine," said Minna.

The girl's quick wit had discovered the right way to get rid of Jack. He accepted the suggestion with enthusiasm. "Ah!" he exclaimed, "that's a good idea! It would never have entered your head, Fritz, would it?"

Before Fritz could reply, Jack was out of his reach.

The widow sat in her room, innocently reading the newspaper. A cake happened to be on the table at her side; and a bottle of sparkling lemonade, by the merest coincidence, was in the near neighborhood of the cake. Jack's eyes brightened, as they turned towards the table when he entered the room.

182

"And those are the gloves!" said Madame Fontaine, with her head held critically a little on one side, as if she was a connoisseur enjoying a fine picture. "How very pretty! And what good taste you have!"

Jack (with his eyes still on the cake) accepted these flattering expressions as no more than his due. "I am pleased with my walk," he remarked. "I have made a successful appearance in public. When the general attention was not occupied with my bag of keys, it was absorbed in my gloves. I showed a becoming modesty—I took no notice of anybody."

"Perhaps your walk has given you a little appetite?" the widow suggested.

"What did you say?" cried Jack. "Appetite! Upon my soul, I could eat—— No, that's not gentleman-like. Mistress gave me one of her looks when I said 'Upon my soul' down in the office. Thank you. Yes; I like cake. Excuse me—I hope it has got plums in it?"

"Plums and other fine things besides. Taste!"

Jack tried hard to preserve his good manners, and only taste as he was told. But the laws of Nature were too much for him. He was as fond of sweet things as a child—he gobbled. "I say, you're uncommonly good to me all of a sudden," he exclaimed between the bites. "You didn't make much of me like this at Wurzburg!"

He had given Madame Fontaine her opportunity. She was not the woman to let it slip. "Oh, Jack!" she said, in tones of gentle reproach, "didn't I nurse you at Wurzburg?"

"Well," Jack admitted, "you did something of the sort."

"What do you mean?"

He had finished his first slice of cake; his politeness began to show signs of wearing out.

"You did what my master the Doctor told you to do," he said. "But I don't believe you cared whether I lived or died. When you had to tuck me up in bed, for instance, you did it with the grossest indifference. Ha! you have

183

improved since that time. Give me some more cake. Never mind cutting it thick. Is that bottle of lemonade for me?"

"You hardly deserve it, Jack, after the way you have spoken of me. Don't you remember," she added, cautiously leading him back to the point, "I used to make your lemonade when you were ill?"

Jack persisted in wandering away from the point. "You are so hungry for compliments," he objected. "Haven't I told you that you have improved? Only go on as you are going on now, and I dare say I shall put you next to Mistress in my estimation, one of these days. Let the cork go out with a pop; I like noises of all kinds. Your good health! Is it manners to smack one's lips after lemonade?—it is such good stuff, and there's such pleasure in feeling it sting one's throat as it goes down. You didn't give me such lemonade as this, when I was ill—Oh! that reminds me."

"Reminds you of something that happened at Wurzburg?" Madame Fontaine inquired.

"Yes. Wait a bit. I'm going to try how the cake tastes dipped in lemonade. Ha! ha! how it fizzes as I stir it round! Yes; something that happened at Wurzburg, as you say. I asked David about it, the morning he went away. But the coach was waiting for him; and he ran off without saying a word. I call that rude."

He was still stirring his lemonade with his bit of cake—or he might have seen something in the widow's face that would have startled him. He did look up, when she spoke to him. His sense of hearing was his quickest sense; and he was struck by the sudden change in her voice.

"What did you ask David?"—was all she ventured to say.

Jack still looked at her. "Anything the matter with you?" he inquired.

"Nothing. What did you ask David?"

"Something I wanted to know."

"Perhaps I can tell you what you want to know?"

"I shouldn't wonder. No: dipping the cake in lemonade doesn't improve it, and it leaves crumbs in the drink."

"Throw away that bit of cake, Jack, and have some more."

"May I help myself?"

"Certainly. But you haven't told me yet what you want to know."

At last he answered directly. "What I want to know is this," he said. "Who poisoned Mr. Keller?"

He was cutting the cake as he spoke, and extracted a piece of candied orange peel with the point of the knife. Once more, the widow's face had escaped observation. She turned away quickly, and occupied herself in mending the fire. In this position, her back was turned towards the table— she could trust herself to speak.

"You are talking nonsense!" she said.

Jack stopped—with the cake half-way to his mouth. Here was a direct attack on his dignity, and he was not disposed to put up with it. "I never talk nonsense," he answered sharply.

"You do," Madame Fontaine rejoined, just as sharply on her side. "Mr. Keller fell ill, as anyone else might fall ill. Nobody poisoned him."

Jack got on his legs. For the moment he actually forgot the cake. "Nobody?" he repeated. "Tell me this, if you please: Wasn't Mr. Keller cured out of the blue-glass bottle—like me?"

(Who had told him this? Joseph might have told him; Minna might have told him. It was no time for inquiry; the one thing needful was to eradicate the idea from his mind. She answered boldly, "Quite right, so far"—and waited to see what came of it.)

"Very well," said Jack, "Mr. Keller was cured out of the blue-glass bottle, like me. And I was poisoned. Now?"

She flatly contradicted him again. "You were not poisoned!"

Jack crossed the room, with a flash of the old Bedlam light in his eyes,

185

and confronted her at the fire place. "The devil is the father of lies," he said, lifting his hand solemnly. "No lies! I heard my master the Doctor say I was poisoned."

She was ready with her answer. "Your master the Doctor said that to frighten you. He didn't want you to taste his medicines in his absence again. You drank double what any person ought to have drunk, you greedy Jack, when you tasted that pretty violet-colored medicine in your master's workshop. And you had yourself to thank—not poison, when you fell ill."

Jack looked hard at her. He could reason so far as that he and Mr. Keller must have taken the same poison, because he and Mr. Keller had been cured out of the same bottle. But to premise that he had been made ill by an overdose of medicine, and that Mr. Keller had been made ill in some other way, and then to ask, how two different illnesses could both have been cured by the same remedy—was an effort utterly beyond him. He hung his head sadly, and went back to the table.

"I wish I hadn't asked you about it," he said. "You puzzle me horribly." But for that unendurable sense of perplexity, he would still have doubted and distrusted her as resolutely as ever. As it was, his bewildered mind unconsciously took its refuge in belief. "If it was medicine," asked the poor creature vacantly, "what is the medicine good for?"

At those words, an idea of the devil's own prompting entered Madame Fontaine's mind. Still standing at the fireplace, she turned her head slowly, and looked at the cupboard.

"It's a better remedy even than the blue-glass bottle," she said; "it cures you so soon when you are tired, or troubled in your mind, that I have brought it away with me from Wurzburg, to use it for myself."

Jack's face brightened with a new interest. "Oh," he said eagerly, "do let me see it again!"

She put her hand in her pocket, took out the key, and hesitated at the last moment.

"Just one look at it," Jack pleaded, "to see if it's the same."

She unlocked the cupboard.

186

CHAPTER V

Jack attempted to follow her, and look in. She waved him back with her hand.

"Wait at the window," she said, "where you can see the medicine in the light." She took the bottle of "Alexander's Wine" from the chest, and having locked the cupboard again, replaced the key in her pocket. "Do you remember it?" she asked, showing him the bottle.

He shuddered as he recognized the color. "Medicine?" he said to himself—troubled anew by doubts which he was not able to realize. "I don't remember how much I took when I tasted it. Do you?"

"I have told you already. You took twice the proper dose."

"Did my master the Doctor say that?"

"Yes."

"And did he tell you what the proper dose was?"

"Yes."

Jack was not able to resist this. "I should like to see it!" he said eagerly. "My master was a wonderful man—my master knew everything."

Madame Fontaine looked at him. He waited to see his request granted, like a child waiting to see a promised toy. "Shall I measure it out, and show you?" she said. "I suppose you don't know what two drachms mean?"

"No, no! Let me see it."

She looked at him again and hesitated. With a certain reluctance of manner, she opened her dressing-case. As she took out a medicine-measuring-glass, her hand began to tremble. A faint perspiration showed itself on her forehead. She put the glass on the table, and spoke to Jack.

"What makes you so curious to see what the dose is?" she said. "Do you think you are likely to want some of it yourself?"

His eyes looked longingly at the poison. "It cures you when you are tired or troubled in your mind," he answered, repeating her own words. "I am but a little fellow—and I'm more easily tired sometimes than you would think."

She passed her handkerchief over her forehead. "The fire makes the room rather warm," she said.

Jack took no notice of the remark; he had not done yet with the confession of his little infirmities. He went on proving his claim to be favored with some of the wonderful remedy.

"And as for being troubled in my mind," he said, "you haven't a notion how bad I am sometimes. If I'm kept away from Mistress for a whole day—when I say or do something wrong, you know—I tell you this, I'm fit to hang myself! If you were to see me, I do think your heart would be touched; I do indeed!"

Instead of answering him, she rose abruptly, and hurried to the door.

"Surely there's somebody outside," she exclaimed—"somebody wanting to speak to me!"

"I don't hear it," said Jack; "and mine are the quickest ears in the house."

"Wait a minute, and let me see."

She opened the door: closed it again behind her; and hurried along the lonely corridor. Throwing up the window at the end, she put her head out into the keen wintry air, with a wild sense of relief. She was almost beside herself, without knowing why. Poor Jack's innocent attempts to persuade her to his destruction had, in their pitiable simplicity, laid a hold on that complex and terrible nature which shook it to its center. The woman stood face to face with her own contemplated crime, and trembled at the diabolical treachery of it. "What's the matter with me?" she wondered inwardly. "I feel as if I could destroy every poison in the chest with my own hands."

Slowly she returned along the corridor, to her room. The refreshing air had strung up her nerves again! she began to recover herself. The strengthened body reacted on the wavering mind. She smiled as she recalled her own weakness, looking at the bottle of poison which she had mechanically kept in her hand. "That feeble little creature might do some serious mischief, between this and the wedding-day," she thought; "and yet——and yet——"

"Well, was there anybody outside?" Jack asked.

"Nothing to matter," she said. The answer was spoken mechanically. Something in him or something in herself, it was impossible to say which, had suddenly set her thinking of the day when her husband had dragged him out of the jaws of death. It seemed strange that the memory of the dead Doctor should come between them in that way, and at that time.

Jack recalled her to the passing moment. He offered her the medicine-measuring-glass left on the table. "It frightens me, when I think of what I did," he said. "And yet it's such a pretty color—I want to see it again."

In silence, she took the glass; in silence, she measured out the fatal two drachms of the poison, and showed it to him.

"Do put it in something," he pleaded, "and let me have it to keep: I know I shall want it."

Still in silence, she turned to the table, and searching again in her dressing-case, found a little empty bottle. She filled it and carefully fitted in the glass stopper. Jack held out his hand. She suddenly drew her own hand back. "No," she said. "On second thoughts, I won't let you have it."

"Why not?"

"Because you can't govern your tongue, and can't keep anything to yourself. You will tell everybody in the house that I have given you my wonderful medicine. They will all be wanting some—and I shall have none left for myself."

"Isn't that rather selfish?" said Jack. "I suppose it's natural, though. Never mind, I'll do anything to please you; I'll keep it in my pocket and not say a word to anybody. Now?"

Once more, he held out his hand. Once more Madame Fontaine checked herself in the act of yielding to him. Her dead husband had got between them again. The wild words he had spoken to her, in the first horror of the discovery that his poor imbecile servant had found and tasted the fatal drug, came back to her memory—"If he dies I shall not survive him. And I firmly believe I shall not rest in my grave." She had never been, like her husband, a believer in ghosts: superstitions of all sorts were to her mind unworthy of a reasonable being. And yet at that moment, she was so completely unnerved that she looked round the old Gothic room, with a nameless fear throbbing at her heart.

It was enough—though nothing appeared: it was enough—though superstitions of all sorts were unworthy of a reasonable being—to shake her fell purpose, for the time. Nothing that Jack could say had the least effect on her. Having arrived at a determination, she was mistress of herself again. "Not yet," she resolved; "there may be consequences that I haven't calculated on. I'll take the night to think of it." Jack tried a last entreaty as she put her hand into her pocket, searching for the cupboard key, and tried it in vain. "No," she said; "I will keep it for you. Come to me when you are really ill, and want it."

Her pocket proved to be entangled for the moment in the skirt of her dress. In irritably trying to disengage it, she threw out the key on the floor. Jack picked the key up and noticed the inscription on the handle. "Pink-Room Cupboard," he read. "Why do they call it by that name?"

In her over-wrought state of mind, she had even felt the small irritating influence of an entangled pocket. She was in no temper to endure simple questions patiently. "Look at the pink curtains, you fool!" she said—and snatched the key out of his hand.

Jack instantly resented the language and the action. "I didn't come here to be insulted," he declared in his loftiest manner.

Madame Fontaine secured the poison in the cupboard without noticing him, and made him more angry than ever.

"Take back your new gloves," he cried, "I don't want them!" He rolled up his gloves, and threw them at her. "I wish I could throw all the cake I've eaten after them!" he burst out fervently.

190

He delivered this aspiration with an emphatic stamp of his foot. The hysterical excitement in Madame Fontaine forced its way outwards under a new form. She burst into a frantic fit of laughter. "You curious little creature," she said; "I didn't mean to offend you. Don't you know that women will lose their patience sometimes? There! Shake hands and make it up. And take away the rest of the cake, if you like it." Jack looked at her in speechless surprise. "Leave me to myself!" she cried, relapsing into irritability. "Do you hear? Go! go! go!"

Jack left the room without a word of protest. The rapid changes in her, the bewildering diversity of looks and tones that accompanied them, completely cowed him. It was only when he was safe outside in the corridor, that he sufficiently recovered himself to put his own interpretation on what had happened. He looked back at the door of Madame Fontaine's room, and shook his little gray head solemnly.

"Now I understand it," he thought to himself "Mrs. Housekeeper is mad. Oh, dear, dear me—Bedlam is the only place for her!"

He descended the first flight of stairs, and stopped again to draw the moral suggested by his own clever discovery. "I must speak to Mistress about this," he concluded. "The sooner we are back in London, the safer I shall feel."

CHAPTER VI

Mrs. Wagner was still hard at work at her desk, when Jack Straw made his appearance again in the private office.

"Where have you been all this time?" she asked. "And what have you done with your new gloves?"

"I threw them at Madame Fontaine," Jack answered. "Don't alarm yourself. I didn't hit her."

Mrs. Wagner laid down her pen, smiling. "Even business must give way to such an extraordinary event as this," she said. "What has gone wrong between you and Madame Fontaine?"

Jack entered into a long rambling narrative of what he had heard on the subject of the wonderful remedy, and of the capricious manner in which a supply of it had been first offered to him, and then taken away again. "Turn it over in your own mind," he said grandly, "and tell me what your opinion is, so far."

"I think you had better let Madame Fontaine keep her medicine in the cupboard," Mrs. Wagner answered; "and when you want anything of that sort, mention it to me." The piece of cake which Jack had brought away with him attracted her attention, as she spoke. Had he bought it himself? or had he carried it off from the housekeeper's room? "Does that belong to you, or to Madame Fontaine?" she asked. "Anything that belongs to Madame Fontaine must be taken back to her."

"Do you think I would condescend to take anything that didn't belong to me?" said Jack indignantly. He entered into another confused narrative, which brought him, in due course of time, to the dropping of the key and the picking of it up. "I happened to read 'Pink-Room Cupboard' on the handle," he proceeded; "and when I asked what it meant she called me a fool, and snatched the key out of my hand. Do you suppose I was going to wear her gloves after that? No! I am as capable of self-sacrifice as any of you—I acted nobly—I threw them at her. Wait a bit! You may laugh at that, but there's something terrible to come. What do you think of a furious person who insults me, suddenly turning into a funny person who shakes hands with me and bursts out laughing? She did that. On the honor of a gentleman, she did that. Follow my wise example; keep out of her way—and let's get back to London as soon as we can. Oh, I have got a reason for what I say. Just let me look through the keyhole before I mention it. All right; there's nobody at the keyhole; I may say it safely. It's a dreadful secret to reveal—Mrs. Housekeeper is mad! No, no; there can be no possible mistake about it. If there's a creature living who thoroughly understands madness when he sees it—by Heaven, I'm that man!"

Watching Jack attentively while he was speaking. Mrs. Wagner beckoned to him to come nearer, and took him by the hand.

"No more now," she said quietly; "you are beginning to get a little excited."

"Who says that?" cried Jack.

"Your eyes say it. Come here to your place."

She rose, and led him to his customary seat in the recess of the old-fashioned window. "Sit down," she said.

"I don't want to sit down."

"Not if I ask you?"

He instantly sat down. Mrs. Wagner produced her pocket-book, and made a mark in it with her pencil. "One good conduct-mark already for Jack," she said. "Now I must go on with my work; and you must occupy yourself quietly, in some way that will amuse you. What will you do?"

Jack, steadily restraining himself under the firm kind eyes that rested on him, was not in the right frame of mind for discovering a suitable employment. "You tell me," he said.

Mrs. Wagner pointed to the bag of keys, hanging over his shoulder. "Have you cleaned them yet?" she asked.

His attention was instantly diverted to the keys; he was astonished at having forgotten them. Mrs. Wagner rang the bell, and supplied him with sandpaper, leather, and whiting. "Now then," she said, pointing to the clock, "for another hour at least—silence and work!"

She returned to her desk; and Jack opened his bag.

He spread out the rusty keys in a row, on the seat at his side. Looking from one to the other before he began the cleansing operations, he started, picked out one key, and held it up to the light. There was something inscribed on the handle, under a layer of rust and dirt. He snatched up his materials, and set to work with such good will that the inscription became visible in a few minutes. He could read it plainly—"Pink-Room Cupboard." A word followed which was not quite so intelligible to him—the word "Duplicate." But he had no need to trouble himself about this. "Pink-Room Cupboard," on a second key, told him all he wanted to know.

His eyes sparkled—he opened his lips—looked at Mrs. Wagner, busily engaged with her pen—and restrained himself within the hard limits of silence. "Aha! I can take Mrs. Housekeeper's medicine whenever I like," he thought slily.

His faith in the remedy was not at all shaken by his conviction that Madame Fontaine was mad. It was the Doctor who had made the remedy—and the Doctor could not commit a mistake. "She's not fit to have the keeping of such a precious thing," he concluded. "I'll take the whole of it under my own charge. Shall I tell Mistress, when we have done work?"

He considered this question, cleaning his keys, and looking furtively from time to time at Mrs. Wagner. The cunning which is almost invariably well developed in a feeble intelligence, decided him on keeping his discovery to himself. "Anything that belongs to Madame Fontaine must be taken back to her"—was what the Mistress had just said to him. He would certainly be ordered to give up the duplicate key (which meant giving up the wonderful remedy) if he took Mrs. Wagner into his confidence. "When I have got what I want," he thought, "I can throw away the key—and there will be an end of it."

The minutes followed each other, the quarters struck—and still the two strangely associated companions went on silently with their strangely dissimilar work. It was close on the time for the striking of the hour, when a third person interrupted the proceedings—that person being no other than Madame Fontaine again.

"A thousand pardons, Mrs. Wagner! At what time can I say two words to you in confidence?"

"You could not have chosen your time better, Madame Fontaine. My work is done for to-day." She paused, and looked at Jack, ostentatiously busy with his keys. The wisest course would be to leave him in the window-seat, harmlessly employed. "Shall we step into the dining-room?" she suggested, leading the way out. "Wait there, Jack, till I return; I may have another good mark to put in my pocket-book."

The two ladies held their conference, with closed doors, in the empty dining-room.

"My only excuse for troubling you, madam," the widow began, "is that I speak in the interest of that poor little Jack, whom we have just left in the office. May I ask if you have lately observed any signs of excitement in him?"

"Certainly!" Mrs. Wagner answered, with her customary frankness of reply; "I found it necessary to compose him, when he came to me about an hour ago—and you have just seen that he is as quiet again as a man can be. I am afraid you have had reason to complain of his conduct yourself?"

Madame Fontaine lifted her hands in gently-expressed protest. "Oh, dear, no—not to complain! To pity our afflicted Jack, and to feel, perhaps, that your irresistible influence over him might be required—no more."

"You are very good," said Mrs. Wagner dryly. "At the same time, I beg you to accept my excuses—not only for Jack, but for myself. I found him so well behaved, and so capable of restraining himself in London, that I thought I was running no risk in bringing him with me to Frankfort."

"Pray say no more, dear madam—you really confuse me. I am the innocent cause of his little outbreak. I most unfortunately reminded him of the time when he lived with us at Wurzburg—and in that way I revived one of his old delusions, which even your admirable treatment has failed to remove from his mind."

"May I ask what the delusion is, Madame Fontaine?"

"One of the commonest delusions among insane persons, Mrs. Wagner—the delusion that he has been poisoned. Has he ever betrayed it in your presence?"

"I heard something of it," Mrs. Wagner answered, "from the superintendent at the madhouse in London."

"Ah, indeed? The superintendent merely repeated, I suppose, what Jack had told him?"

"Exactly. I was careful not to excite him, by referring to it myself, when I took him under my charge. At the same time, it is impossible to look at his hair and his complexion, without seeing that some serious accident must have befallen him."

"Most unquestionably! He is the victim, poor creature—not of poison— but of his own foolish curiosity, in my husband's surgery, and you see the result. Alas! I cannot give you the scientific reasons for it."

"I shouldn't understand them, Madame Fontaine, if you could."

"Ah, dear lady, you kindly say so, because you are unwilling to humiliate me. Is there anything Jack may have said to you about me, which seems to require an explanation—if I can give it?"

She slipped in this question, concealing perfectly the anxiety that suggested it, so far as her voice and her eyes were concerned. But the inner agitation rose to the surface in a momentary trembling of her lips.

Slight as it was, that sign of self-betrayal did not escape Mrs. Wagner's keen observation. She made a cautious reply. "On the contrary," she said, "from what Jack has told me, the conclusion is plain that you have really done him a service. You have succeeded in curing that delusion you spoke of—and I applaud your good sense in refusing to trust him with the medicine."

Madame Fontaine made a low curtsey. "I shall remember those kind words, among the happy events of my life," she said, with her best grace. "Permit me to take your hand." She pressed Mrs. Wagner's hand gratefully— and made an exit which was a triumph of art. Even a French actress might have envied the manner in which she left the room.

But, when she ascended the stairs, with no further necessity for keeping up appearances, her step was as slow and as weary as the step of an old woman. "Oh, my child," she thought sadly, with her mind dwelling again on Minna, "shall I see the end of all these sacrifices, when your wedding-day comes with the end of the year?" She sat down by the fire in her room, and for the first

196

time in her life, the harmless existence of one of those domestic drudges whom she despised began to seem enviable to her. There were merits visible now, in the narrow social horizon that is bounded by gossip, knitting, and tea.

Left by herself in the dining-room, Mrs. Wagner took a turn up and down, with her mind bent on penetrating Madame Fontaine's motives.

There were difficulties in her way. It was easy to arrive at the conclusion that there was something under the surface; but the obstacles to advancing beyond this point of discovery seemed to defy removal. To distrust the graceful widow more resolutely than ever, and to lament that she had not got wise David Glenney to consult with, were the principal results of Mrs. Wagner's reflections when she returned to the office.

There was Jack—in the nursery phrase, as good as gold—still in his place on the window seat, devoted to his keys. His first words related entirely to himself.

"If this isn't good conduct," he said, "I should like to know what is. Give me my other mark."

Mrs. Wagner took out her pocket-book and made the new mark.

"Thank you," said Jack. "Now I want something else. I want to know what Mrs. Housekeeper has been saying. I have been seriously alarmed about you."

"Why, Jack?"

"She hasn't bitten you, has she? Oh, they do it sometimes! What lies has she been telling you of me? Oh, they lie in the most abominable manner! What? She has been talking of me in the kindest terms? Then why did she want to get out of my hearing? Ah, they're so infernally deceitful! I do hate mad people."

Mrs. Wagner produced her pocket-book again. "I shall scratch out your mark," she said sternly, "if I hear any more talk of that sort."

Jack gathered his keys together with a strong sense of injury, and put them back in his leather bag. "You're a little hard on me," he said, "when I'm only warning you for your own good. I don't know why it is, you're not as kind to me here, as you used to be in London. And I feel it, I do!" He laid himself down on the window seat, and began to cry.

Mrs. Wagner was not the woman to resist this expression of the poor little man's feeling. In a moment she was at the window comforting him and drying his eyes, as if he had been a child. And, like a child, Jack took advantage of the impression that he had made. "Look at your desk," he said piteously; "there's another proof how hard you are on me. I used to keep the key of your desk in London. You won't trust it to me here."

Mrs. Wagner went to the desk, locked it, and returned to Jack. Few people know how immensely an act of kindness gains in effect, by being performed in silence. Mrs. Wagner was one of the few. Without a word, she opened the leather bag and dropped the key into it. Jack's gratitude rushed innocently to an extreme which it had never reached yet. "Oh!" he cried, "would you mind letting me kiss you?"

Mrs. Wagner drew back, and held up a warning hand. Before she could express herself in words, Jack's quick ear caught the sound of footsteps approaching the door. "Is she coming back?" he cried, still suspicious of Madame Fontaine. Mrs. Wagner instantly opened the door, and found herself face to face with Joseph the footman.

"Do you know, ma'am, when Mr. Keller will be back?" he asked.

"I didn't even know that he was out, Joseph. Who wants him?"

"A gentleman, ma'am, who says he comes from Munich."

CHAPTER VII

On further inquiry, it turned out that "the gentleman from Munich" had no time to spare. In the absence of Mr. Keller, he had asked if he could see "one of the other partners." This seemed to imply that commercial interests were in some way connected with the stranger's visit—in which case, Mrs. Wagner was perfectly competent to hear what he had to say.

"Where is the gentleman?" she asked.

"In the drawing-room," Joseph answered.

Mrs. Wagner at once left the office. She found herself in the presence of a dignified elderly gentleman, dressed entirely in black, and having the ribbon of some order of merit attached to the buttonhole of his long frock-coat. His eyes opened wide in surprise, behind his gold spectacles, when he found himself face to face with a lady. "I fear there is some mistake," he said, in the smoothest of voices, and with the politest of bows; "I asked to see one of the partners."

Mrs. Wagner added largely to his amazement, by informing him of the position that she held in the firm. "If you come on a matter of business," she proceeded, "you may trust me to understand you, sir, though I am only a woman. If your visit relates to private affairs, I beg to suggest that you should write to Mr. Keller—I will take care that he receives your letter the moment he returns."

"There is not the least necessity for my troubling you," the stranger replied. "I am a physician; and I have been summoned to Frankfort to consult with my colleagues here, on a serious case of illness. Mr. Keller's sister is one of my patients in Munich. I thought I would take the present opportunity of speaking to him about the state of her health."

He had just introduced himself in those words, when Mr. Keller entered the room. The merchant and the physician shook hands like old friends.

"No alarming news of my sister, I hope?" said Mr. Keller.

"Only the old trouble, my good friend. Another attack of asthma."

Mrs. Wagner rose to leave the room. Mr. Keller stopped her. "There is not the least necessity for you to leave us," he said. "Unless my presentiments deceive me, we may even have occasion to ask your advice.—Is there any hope, doctor, of her being well enough to leave Munich, towards the end of the month?"

"I am sorry to say it," answered the physician—"having heard of the interesting occasion on which she had engaged to be one of your guests—but, at her age, I must ask for a little more time."

"In other words, it is impossible for my sister to be with us, on the day of my son's marriage?"

"Quite impossible. She has so few pleasures, poor soul, and she is so bitterly disappointed, that I volunteered to take advantage of my professional errand here, to make a very bold request. Let me first do your excellent sister justice. She will not hear of the young people being disappointed by any postponement of the wedding, on her account. And here is the famous necklace, committed to my care, to prove that she is sincere."

He took his little traveling-bag from the chair on which he had placed it, and produced the case containing the necklace. No woman—not even a head-partner in a great house of business—could have looked at those pearls, and preserved her composure. Mrs. Wagner burst out with a cry of admiration.

Mr. Keller passed the necklace over without notice; his sister was the one object of interest to him. "Would she be fit to travel," he asked, "if we put off the marriage for a month?"

"She shall be fit to travel, barring accidents," said the physician, "if you can put off the marriage for a fortnight. I start this evening on my return to Munich, and not a day shall pass without my seeing her."

Mr. Keller appealed to Mrs. Wagner. "Surely, we might make this trifling sacrifice?" he said. "The pleasure of seeing her nephew married is likely to be the last pleasure of my sister's life."

"In your place," said Mrs. Wagner, "I should not hesitate for an instant to grant the fortnight's delay. But the bride and bridegroom must be consulted, of course."

"And the bride's parents," suggested the discreet physician, "if they are still living."

"There is only her mother living," said Mr. Keller. "She is too high-minded a person to raise any objection, I am sure." He paused, and reflected for awhile. "Fritz counts for nothing," he went on. "I think we ought to put

200

the question, in the first instance, to the bride?" He rang the bell, and then took the necklace out of Mrs. Wagner's hands. "I have a very high opinion of little Minna," he resumed. "We will see what the child's own kind heart says—undisturbed by the influence of the pearls, and without any prompting on the part of her mother."

He closed the jewel case, and put it into a cabinet that stood near him. Joseph was sent upstairs, with the necessary message. "Don't make any mistake," said his master; "I wish to see Miss Minna, alone."

The physician took a pinch of snuff while they were waiting. "The test is hardly conclusive," he remarked slily; "women are always capable of sacrificing themselves. What will the bridegroom say?"

"My good sir," Mr. Keller rejoined a little impatiently, "I have mentioned already that Fritz counts for nothing."

Minna came in. Her color rose when she found herself unexpectedly in the presence of a dignified and decorated stranger. The physician tapped his snuff-box, with the air of a man who thoroughly understood young women. "Charming indeed!" he said confidentially to Mrs. Wagner; "I am young enough (at heart, madam) to wish I was Fritz."

Mr. Keller advanced to meet Minna, and took her hand.

"My dear," he said, "what would you think of me, if I requested you to put off your marriage for two whole weeks—and all on account of an old woman?"

"I should think you had surely some reason, sir, for asking me to do that," Minna replied; "and I confess I should be curious to know who the old woman was."

In the fewest and plainest words, Mr. Keller repeated what the physician had told him. "Take your own time to think of it," he added; "and consult your mother first, if you like."

Minna's sweet face looked lovelier than ever, glowing with the heavenly light of true and generous feeling. "Oh, Mr. Keller!" she exclaimed, "do you really suppose I am cold-hearted enough to want time to think of it? I am sure I may speak for my mother, as well as for myself. Fraulein Keller's time shall be our time. Please tell her so, with my duty—or, may I be bold enough to say already, with my love?"

Mr. Keller kissed her forehead with a fervor of feeling that was rare with him. "You are well worthy of my sister's bridal gift," he said—and took the necklace out of the cabinet, and gave it to her.

For some moments Minna stood looking at the magnificent pearls, in a state of speechless enchantment. When she did speak, her first delightful ardor of admiration had cooled under the chilling perception of a want of proper harmony between her pearls and herself. "They are too grand for me," she said sadly; "I ought to be a great lady, with a wardrobe full of magnificent dresses, to wear such pearls as these!" She looked at them again, with the natural longing of her sex and age. "May I take the necklace upstairs," she asked, with the most charming inconsistency, "and see how it looks when I put it on?"

Mr. Keller smiled and waved his hand. "You can do what you like with your own necklace, my dear," he said. "When I have written a line to my sister, perhaps I may follow you, and admire my daughter-in-law in all her grandeur."

The physician looked at his watch. "If you can write your letter in five minutes," he suggested, "I can take it with me to Munich."

Mrs. Wagner and Minna left the room together. "Come and see how it looks," said Minna; "I should so like to have your opinion."

"I will follow you directly, my dear. There is something I have forgotten in the office."

The events of the day had ended in making Jack drowsy; he was half-asleep on the window-seat. Mrs. Wagner effectually roused him.

"Mr. Keeper of the Keys," she said; "I want my desk opened."

Jack was on his legs in an instant. "Ha, Mistress, it's jolly to hear you say

202

that—it's like being in London again."

The desk was of the spacious commercial sort, with a heavy mahogany lid. Everything inside was in the most perfect order. A row of "pigeon-holes" at the back had their contents specified by printed tickets. "Abstracts of correspondence, A to Z;" "Terms for commission agency;" "Key of the iron safe." "Key of the private ledger"—and so on. The ledger—a stout volume with a brass lock, like a private diary—was placed near the pigeon-holes. On the top of it rested a smaller book, of the pocket—size, entitled "Private Accounts." Mrs. Wagner laid both books open before her, at the pages containing the most recent entries, and compared them. "I felt sure I had forgotten it!" she said to herself—and transferred an entry in the ledger to the private account-book. After replacing the ledger, she locked the desk, and returned the key to Jack.

"Remember," she said, "the rule in London is the rule here. My desk is never to be opened, except when I ask you to do it. And if you allow the key to pass out of your own possession, you cease to be Keeper."

"Did I ever do either of those two things in London?" Jack asked.

"Never."

"Then don't be afraid of my doing them here. I say! you haven't put back the little book." He produced the key again, and put it into the lock—while Mrs. Wagner was occupied in placing her account-book in her pocket.

"Its proper place is not in the desk," she explained; "I usually keep it about me."

Jack's ready suspicion was excited. "Ah," he cried, with an outburst of indignation, "you won't trust it to me!"

"Take care I don't set a bad-conduct mark against you!" said Mrs. Wagner. "You foolish fellow, the little book is a copy of what is in the big book—and I trust you with the big book."

She knew Jack thoroughly well. His irritable dignity was at once appeased when he heard that the biggest of the duplicate books was in his keeping. He took the key out of the lock again. At the same moment, Mr. Keller entered the office. Jack possessed the dog's enviable faculty of distinguishing correctly between the people who are, and the people who are not, their true friends. Mr. Keller privately disliked the idea of having a person about him who had come out of a madhouse. Jack's instincts warned him to leave a room when Mr. Keller entered it. He left the office now.

"Is it possible that you trust that crazy creature with the key of your desk?" said Mr. Keller. "Even your bitterest enemy, Mrs. Wagner, would not believe you could be guilty of such an act of rashness."

"Pardon me, sir, it is you who are guilty of an act of rashness in forming your judgment. 'Fancy a woman in her senses trusting her keys to a man who was once in Bedlam!' Everybody said that of me, when I put Jack to the proof in my own house."

"Aha! there are other people then who agree with me?" said Mr. Keller.

"There are other people, sir (I say it with all needful respect), who know no more of the subject than you do. The most certain curative influence that can be exercised over the poor martyrs of the madhouse, is to appeal to their self-respect. From first to last, Jack has never been unworthy of the trust that I have placed in him. Do you think my friends owned they had been mistaken? No more than you will own it! Make your mind easy. I will be personally answerable for anything that is lost, while I am rash enough to trust my crazy creature with my key."

Mr. Keller's opinion was not in the least shaken; he merely checked any further expression of it, in deference to an angry lady. "I dare say you know best," he remarked politely. "Let me mention the little matter that has brought me here. David Glenney is, no doubt, closely occupied in London. He ought to know at once that the wedding-day is deferred. Will you write to him, or shall I?"

Mrs. Wagner began to recover her temper.

"I will write with pleasure, Mr. Keller. We have half an hour yet before post-time. I have promised Minna to see how the wonderful necklace looks

204

on her. Will you excuse me for a few minutes? Or will you go upstairs with me?—I think you said something about it in the drawing-room."

"Certainly," said Mr. Keller, "if the ladies will let me in."

They ascended the stairs together. On the landing outside the drawing-room, they encountered Fritz and Minna—one out of temper, and the other in tears.

"What's wrong now?" Mr. Keller asked sharply. "Fritz! what does that sulky face mean?"

"I consider myself very badly used," Fritz answered. "I say there's a great want of proper consideration for Me, in putting off our marriage. And Madame Fontaine agrees with me."

"Madame Fontaine?" He looked at Minna, as he repeated the name. "Is this really true?"

Minna trembled at the bare recollection of what had passed. "Oh, don't ask me!" she pleaded piteously; "I can't tell what has come to my mother—she is so changed, she frightens me. And as for Fritz," she said, rousing herself, "if he is to be a selfish tyrant, I can tell him this—I won't marry him at all!"

Mr. Keller turned to Fritz, and pointed contemptuously down the stairs.

"Leave us!" he said. Fritz opened his lips to protest. Mr. Keller interposed, with a protest of his own. "One of these days," he went on, "you may possibly have a son. You will not find his society agreeable to you, when he happens to have made a fool of himself." He pointed down the stairs for the second time. Fritz retired, frowning portentously. His father addressed Minna with marked gentleness of manner. "Rest and recover yourself, my child. I will see your mother, and set things right."

"Don't go away by yourself, my dear," Mrs. Wagner added kindly; "come with me to my room."

Mr. Keller entered the drawing-room, and sent Joseph with another message. "Go up to Madame Fontaine, and say I wish to see her here immediately."

CHAPTER VIII

The widow presented herself, with a dogged resignation singularly unlike her customary manner. Her eyes had a set look of hardness; her lips were fast closed; her usually colorless complexion had faded to a strange grayish pallor. If her dead husband could have risen from the grave, and warned Mr. Keller, he would have said, "Once or twice in my life, I have seen her like that—mind what you are about!"

She puzzled Mr. Keller. He tried to gain time—he bowed and pointed to a chair. Madame Fontaine took the chair in silence. Her hard eyes looked straight at the master of the house, overhung more heavily than usual by their drooping lids. Her thin lips never opened. The whole expression of the woman said plainly, "You speak first!"

Mr. Keller spoke. His kindly instinct warned him not to refer to Minna, in alluding to the persons from whom he had derived his information. "I hear from my son," he said, "that you do not approve of our putting off the wedding-day, though it is only for a fortnight. Are you aware of the circumstances?"

"I am aware of the circumstances."

"Your daughter informed you of my sister's illness, I suppose?"

At that first reference to Minna, some inner agitation faintly stirred the still surface of Madame Fontaine's face.

"Yes," she said. "My thoughtless daughter informed me."

The epithet applied to Minna, aggravated by the deliberate emphasis laid on it, jarred on Mr. Keller's sense of justice. "It appears to me," he said, "that your daughter acted in this matter, not only with the truest kindness, but with the utmost good sense. Mrs. Wagner and my sister's physician were both present at the time, and both agreed with me in admiring her conduct. What has she done to deserve that you should call her thoughtless?"

"She ought to have remembered her duty to her mother. She ought to have consulted me, before she presumed to decide for herself."

"In that case, Madame Fontaine, would you have objected to change the day of the marriage?"

"I am well aware, sir, that your sister has honored my daughter by making her a magnificent present——"

Mr. Keller's face began to harden. "May I beg you to be so good as answer my question plainly?" he said, in tones which were peremptory for the first time. "Would you have objected to grant the fortnight's delay?"

She answered him, on the bare chance that a strong expression of her opinion, as the bride's mother, might, even now, induce him to revert to the date originally chosen for the wedding. "I should certainly have objected," she said firmly.

"What difference could it possibly make to you?" There was suspicion in his manner, as well as surprise, when he put that question. "For what reason would you have objected?"

"Is my objection, as Minna's mother, not worthy of some consideration, sir, without any needless inquiry into motives?"

"Your daughter's objection—as the bride—would have been a final objection, to my mind," Mr. Keller answered. "But your objection is simply unaccountable; and I press you for your motives, having this good reason for doing so on my side. If I am to disappoint my sister—cruelly to disappoint her—it must be for some better cause than a mere caprice."

It was strongly put, and not easily answered. Madame Fontaine made a last effort—she invented the likeliest motives she could think of. "I object, sir, in the first place, to putting off the most important event in my daughter's life, and in my life, as if it was some trifling engagement. Besides, how do I know that some other unlucky circumstance may not cause more delays; and perhaps prevent the marriage from taking place at all?"

Mr. Keller rose from his chair. Whatever her true motives might be, it was now perfectly plain that she was concealing them from him. "If you have any more serious reasons to give me than these," he said quietly and coldly, "let me hear them between this and post-time tomorrow. In the meanwhile, I need not detain you any longer."

Madame Fontaine rose also—but she was not quite defeated yet.

"As things are, then," she resumed, "I am to understand, sir, that the marriage is put off to the thirteenth of January next?"

"Yes, with your daughter's consent."

"Suppose my daughter changes her mind, in the interval?"

"Under your influence?"

"Mr. Keller! you insult me."

"I should insult your daughter, Madame Fontaine—after what she said in this room before me and before other witnesses—if I supposed her to be capable of changing her mind, except under your influence."

"Good evening, sir."

"Good evening, madam."

She went back to her room.

The vacant spaces on the walls were prettily filled up with prints and water-color drawings. Among these last was a little portrait of Mr. Keller, in a glazed frame. She approached it—looked at it—and, suddenly tearing it from the wall, threw it on the floor. It happened to fall with the glass uppermost. She stamped on it, in a perfect frenzy of rage; not only crushing the glass, but even breaking the frame, and completely destroying the portrait as a work of art. "There! that has done me good," she said to herself—and kicked the fragments into a corner of the room.

She was now able to take a chair at the fireside, and shape out for herself the course which it was safest to follow.

Minna was first in her thoughts. She could bend the girl to her will, and send her to Mr. Keller. But he would certainly ask, under what influence she was acting, in terms which would place the alternative between a downright falsehood, or a truthful answer. Minna was truth itself; in her youngest days, she had been one of those rare children who never take their easy refuge in a lie. What influence would be most likely to persuade her to deceive Fritz's father? The widow gave up the idea, in the moment when it occurred to her. Once again, "Jezebel's Daughter" unconsciously touched Jezebel's heart with the light of her purity and her goodness. The mother shrank from deliberately degrading the nature of her own child.

The horrid question of the money followed. On the thirty-first of the month, the promissory note would be presented for payment. Where was the money to be found?

Some little time since, having the prospect of Minna's marriage on the thirtieth of December before her, she had boldly resolved on referring the holder of the note to Mr. Keller. Did it matter to her what the sordid old merchant said or thought, after Minna had become his son's wife? She would coolly say to him, "The general body of the creditors harassed me. I preferred having one creditor to deal with, who had no objection to grant me time. His debt has fallen due; and I have no money to pay it. Choose between paying it yourself, and the disgrace of letting your son's mother-in-law be publicly arrested in Frankfort for debt."

So she might have spoken, if her daughter had been a member of Mr. Keller's family. With floods of tears, with eloquent protestations, with threats even of self-destruction, could she venture on making the confession now?

She remembered how solemnly she had assured Mr. Keller that her debts were really and truly paid. She remembered the inhuman scorn with which he had spoken of persons who failed to meet their pecuniary engagements honestly. Even if he forgave her for deceiving him—which was in the last degree improbable—he was the sort of man who would suspect her of other deceptions. He would inquire if she had been quite disinterested in attending at his bedside, and saving his life. He might take counsel privately with his only surviving partner, Mrs. Wagner. Mrs. Wagner might recall the interview in the drawing-room, and the conversation about Jack; and might see her way to consulting Jack's recollections of his illness at Wurzburg. The risk to herself of encountering these dangers was trifling. But the risk to Minna involved nothing less than the breaking off of the marriage. She decided on keeping up appearances, at any sacrifice, until the marriage released her from the necessities of disguise.

So it came back again to the question of how the money was to be found.

Had she any reasonable hope of success, if she asked for a few days' leave of absence, and went to Wurzburg? Would the holder of the bill allow her to renew it for a fortnight?

She got up, and consulted her glass—and turned away from it again, with a sigh. "If I was only ten years younger!" she thought.

The letter which she received from Wurzburg had informed her that the present holder of the bill was "a middle-aged man." If he had been very young, or very old, she would have trusted in the autumn of her beauty, backed by her ready wit. But experience had taught her that the fascinations of a middle-aged woman are, in the vast majority of cases, fascinations thrown away on a middle-aged man. Even if she could hope to be one of the exceptions that prove the rule, the middle-aged man was an especially inaccessible person, in this case. He had lost money by her already—money either paid, or owing, to the spy whom he had set to watch her. Was this the sort of man who would postpone the payment of his just dues?

She opened one of the drawers in the toilette table, and took out the pearl necklace. "I thought it would come to this," she said quietly. "Instead of paying the promissory note, Mr. Keller will have to take the necklace out of pledge."

The early evening darkness of winter had set in. She dressed herself for going out, and left her room, with the necklace in its case, concealed under her shawl.

Poor puzzled Minna was waiting timidly to speak to her in the corridor. "Oh mamma, do forgive me! I meant it for the best."

The widow put one arm (the other was not at liberty) round her daughter's waist. "You foolish child," she said, "will you never understand that your poor mother is getting old and irritable? I may think you have made a great mistake, in sacrificing yourself to the infirmities of an asthmatic stranger at Munich; but as to being ever really angry with you——! Kiss me, my love; I never was fonder of you than I am now. Lift my veil. Oh, my darling, I don't like giving you to anybody, even to Fritz."

Minna changed the subject—a sure sign that she and Fritz were friends again. "How thick and heavy your veil is!" she said.

"It is cold out of doors, my child, to-night."

"But why are you going out?"

"I don't feel very well, Minna. A brisk walk in the frosty air will do me good."

"Mamma, do let me go with you!"

"No, my dear. You are not a hard old woman like me—and you shall not run the risk of catching cold. Go into my room, and keep the fire up. I shall be back in half an hour.

"Where is my necklace, mamma?"

"My dear, the bride's mother keeps the bride's necklace—and, when we do try it on, we will see how it looks by daylight."

In a minute more, Madame Fontaine was out in the street, on her way to the nearest jeweler.

CHAPTER IX

The widow stopped at a jeweler's window in the famous street called the Zeil. The only person in the shop was a simple-looking old man, sitting behind the counter, reading a newspaper.

She went in. "I have something to show you, sir," she said, in her softest and sweetest tones. The simple old man first looked at her thick veil, and then at the necklace. He lifted his hands in amazement and admiration. "May I examine these glorious pearls?" he asked—and looked at them through a magnifying glass, and weighed them in his hand. "I wonder you are not afraid to walk out alone in the dark, with such a necklace as this," he said. "May I send to my foreman, and let him see it?"

Madame Fontaine granted his request. He rang the bell which communicated with the work-rooms. Being now satisfied that she was speaking to the proprietor of the shop, she risked her first inquiry.

"Have you any necklace of imitation pearls which resembles my necklace?" she asked.

The old gentleman started, and looked harder than ever at the impenetrable veil. "Good heavens—no!" he exclaimed. "There is no such thing in all Frankfort.

"Could an imitation be made, sir?"

The foreman entered the shop—a sullen, self-concentrated man. "Fit for a queen," he remarked, with calm appreciation of the splendid pearls. His master repeated to him Madame Fontaine's last question. "They might do it in Paris," he answered briefly. "What time could you give them, madam?"

"I should want the imitation sent here before the thirteenth of next month."

The master, humanely pitying the lady's ignorance, smiled and said nothing. The foreman's decision was rough and ready. "Nothing like time enough; quite out of the question."

Madame Fontaine had no choice but to resign herself to circumstances. She had entered the shop with the idea of exhibiting the false necklace on the wedding-day, whilst the genuine pearls were pledged for the money of which she stood in need. With the necklace in pawn, and with no substitute to present in its place, what would Minna say, what would Mr. Keller think? It was useless to pursue those questions—some plausible excuse must be found. No matter what suspicions might be excited, the marriage would still take place. The necklace was no essential part of the ceremony which made Fritz and Minna man and wife—and the money must be had.

"I suppose, sir, you grant loans on valuable security—such as this necklace?" she said.

"Certainly, madam."

"Provided you have the lady's name and address," the disagreeable foreman suggested, turning to his master.

The old man cordially agreed. "Quite true! quite true! And a reference besides—some substantial person, madam, well known in this city. The responsibility is serious with such pearls as these."

"Is the reference absolutely necessary?" Madame Fontaine asked.

The foreman privately touched his master behind the counter. Understanding the signal, the simple old gentleman closed the jewel-case, and handed it back. "Absolutely necessary," he answered.

Madame Fontaine went out again into the street. "A substantial reference" meant a person of some wealth and position in Frankfort—a person like Mr. Keller, for example. Where was she to find such a reference? Her relatives in the city had deliberately turned their backs on her. Out of Mr. Keller's house, they were literally the only "substantial" people whom she knew. The one chance left seemed to be to try a pawnbroker.

At this second attempt, she was encountered by a smart young man. The moment he saw the necklace, he uttered a devout ejaculation of surprise and blew a whistle. The pawnbroker himself appeared—looked at the pearls— looked at the veiled lady—and answered as the jeweler had answered, but less civilly. "I'm not going to get myself into a scrape," said the pawnbroker; "I must have a good reference."

Madame Fontaine was not a woman easily discouraged. She turned her steps towards the noble medieval street called the Judengasse—then thickly inhabited; now a spectacle of decrepit architectural old age, to be soon succeeded by a new street.

By twos and threes at a time, the Jews in this quaint quarter of the town clamorously offered their services to the lady who had come among them. When the individual Israelite to whom she applied saw the pearls, he appeared to take leave of his senses. He screamed; he clapped his hands; he called upon his wife, his children, his sisters, his lodgers, to come and feast their eyes on such a necklace as had never been seen since Solomon received the Queen of Sheba.

The first excitement having worn itself out, a perfect volley of questions followed. What was the lady's name? Where did she live? How had she got the necklace? Had it been given to her? and, if so, who had given it? Where had it been made? Why had she brought it to the Judengasse? Did she want to sell it? or to borrow money on it? Aha! To borrow money on it. Very good, very good indeed; but—and then the detestable invitation to produce the reference made itself heard once more.

Madame Fontaine's answer was well conceived. "I will pay you good interest, in place of a reference," she said. Upon this, the Jewish excitability, vibrating between the desire of gain and the terror of consequences, assumed a new form. Some of them groaned; some of them twisted their fingers frantically in their hair; some of them called on the Deity worshipped by their fathers to bear witness how they had suffered, by dispensing with references in other cases of precious deposits; one supremely aged and dirty Jew actually suggested placing an embargo on the lady and her necklace, and sending information to the city authorities at the Town Hall. In the case of a timid woman, this sage's advice might actually have been followed. Madame Fontaine preserved her presence of mind, and left the Judengasse as freely as she had entered it. "I can borrow the money elsewhere," she said haughtily at parting. "Yes," cried a chorus of voices, answering, "you can borrow of a receiver of stolen goods."

It was only too true! The extraordinary value of the pearls demanded, on that account, extraordinary precautions on the part of moneylenders of every degree. Madame Fontaine put back the necklace in the drawer of her toilette-table. The very splendor of Minna's bridal gift made it useless as a means of privately raising money among strangers.

And yet, the money must be found—at any risk, under any circumstances, no matter how degrading or how dangerous they might be.

With that desperate resolution, she went to her bed. Hour after hour she heard the clock strike. The faint cold light of the new day found her still waking and thinking, and still unprepared with a safe plan for meeting the demand on her, when the note became due. As to resources of her own, the value of the few jewels and dresses that she possessed did not represent half the amount of her debt.

It was a busy day at the office. The work went on until far into the evening.

Even when the household assembled at the supper-table, there was an interruption. A messenger called with a pressing letter, which made it immediately necessary to refer to the past correspondence of the firm. Mr. Keller rose from the table. "The Abstracts will rake up less time to examine," he said to Mrs. Wagner; "you have them in your desk, I think?" She at once turned to Jack, and ordered him to produce the key. He took it from his bag, under the watchful eyes of Madame Fontaine, observing him from the opposite side of the table. "I should have preferred opening the desk myself," Jack remarked when Mr. Keller had left the room; "but I suppose I must give way to the master. Besides, he hates me."

The widow was quite startled by this strong assertion. "How can you say so?" she exclaimed. "We all like you, Jack. Come and have a little wine, out of my glass."

Jack refused this proposal. "I don't want wine," he said; "I am sleepy and cold—I want to go to bed."

Madame Fontaine was too hospitably inclined to take No for an answer. "Only a little drop," she pleaded. "You look so cold."

"Surely you forget what I told you?" Mrs. Wagner interposed. "Wine first excites, and then stupefies him. The last time I tried it, he was as dull and heavy as if I had given him laudanum. I thought I mentioned it to you." She turned to Jack. "You look sadly tired, my poor little man. Go to bed at once."

"Without the key?" cried Jack indignantly. "I hope I know my duty better than that."

Mr. Keller returned, perfectly satisfied with the result of his investigation. "I knew it!" he said. "The mistake is on the side of our clients; I have sent them the proof of it."

He handed back the key to Mrs. Wagner. She at once transferred it to Jack. Mr. Keller shook his head in obstinate disapproval. "Would you run such a risk as that?" he said to Madame Fontaine, speaking in French. "I should be afraid," she replied in the same language. Jack secured the key in his bag, kissed his mistress's hand, and approached the door on his way to bed. "Won't you wish me good-night?" said the amiable widow. "I didn't know whether German or English would do for you," Jack answered; "and I can't speak your unknown tongue."

He made one of his fantastic bows, and left the room. "Does he understand French?" Madame Fontaine asked. "No," said Mrs. Wagner; "he only understood that you and Mr. Keller had something to conceal from him."

In due course of time the little party at the supper-table rose, and retired to their rooms. The first part of the night passed as tranquilly as usual. But, between one and two in the morning, Mrs. Wagner was alarmed by a violent beating against her door, and a shrill screaming in Jack's voice. "Let me in! I want a light—I've lost the keys!"

She called out to him to be quiet, while she put on her dressing-gown, and struck a light. They were fortunately on the side of the house occupied by the offices, the other inhabited bedchambers being far enough off to be approached by a different staircase. Still, in the silence of the night, Jack's reiterated cries of terror and beatings at the door might possibly reach the ears of a light sleeper. She pulled him into the room and closed the door again, with an impetuosity that utterly confounded him. "Sit down there, and compose yourself!" she said sternly. "I won't give you the light until you are perfectly quiet. You disgrace me if you disturb the house."

Between cold and terror, Jack shuddered from head to foot. "May I whisper?" he asked, with a look of piteous submission.

Mrs. Wagner pointed to the last living embers in the fireplace. She knew by experience the tranquilizing influence of giving him something to do. "Rake the fire together," she said; "and warm yourself first."

He obeyed, and then laid himself down in his dog-like way on the rug. A quarter of an hour, at least, passed before his mistress considered him to be in a fit state to tell his story. There was little or nothing to relate. He had put his bag under his pillow as usual; and (after a long sleep) he had woke with a horrid fear that something had happened to the keys. He had felt in vain for them under the pillow, and all over the bed, and all over the floor. "After that," he said, "the horrors got hold of me; and I am afraid I went actually mad, for a little while. I'm all right now, if you please. See! I'm as quiet as a bird with its head under its wing."

Mrs. Wagner took the light, and led the way to his little room, close by her own bedchamber. She lifted the pillow—and there lay the leather bag, exactly where he had placed it when he went to bed.

Jack's face, when this discovery revealed itself, would have pleaded for mercy with a far less generous woman than Mrs. Wagner. She took his hand. "Get into bed again," she said kindly; "and the next time you dream, try not to make a noise about it."

No! Jack refused to get into bed again, until he had been heard in his own defense. He dropped on his knees, and held up his clasped hands, as if he was praying.

"When you first taught me to say my prayers," he answered, "you said God would hear me. As God hears me now Mistress, I was wide awake when I put my hand under the pillow—and the bag was not there. Do you believe me?"

Mrs. Wagner was strongly impressed by the simple fervor of this declaration. It was no mere pretense, when she answered that she did believe him. At her suggestion, the bag was unstrapped and examined. Not only the unimportant keys (with another one added to their number) but the smaller key which opened her desk were found safe inside. "We will talk about it to-morrow," she said. Having wished him good-night, she paused in the act of opening the door, and looked at the lock. There was no key in it, but there was another protection in the shape of a bolt underneath. "Did you bolt your door when you went to bed?" she asked.

"No."

The obvious suspicion, suggested by this negative answer, crossed her mind.

"What has become of the key of your door?" she inquired next.

Jack hung his head. "I put it along with the other keys," he confessed, "to make the bag look bigger."

Alone again in her own room, Mrs. Wagner stood by the reanimated fire, thinking.

While Jack was asleep, any person, with a soft step and a delicate hand, might have approached his bedside, when the house was quiet for the night, and have taken his bag. And, again, any person within hearing of the alarm that he had raised, some hours afterwards, might have put the bag back, while he was recovering himself in Mrs. Wagner's room. Who could have been near enough to hear the alarm? Somebody in the empty bedrooms above? Or somebody in the solitary offices below? If a theft had really been committed, the one likely object of it would be the key of the desk. This pointed to the probability that the alarm had reached the ears of the thief in the offices. Was there any person in the house, from the honest servants upwards, whom it would be reasonably possible to suspect of theft? Mrs. Wagner returned to her bed. She was not a woman to be daunted by trifles—but on this occasion her courage failed her when she was confronted by her own question.

CHAPTER X

The office hours, in the winter-time, began at nine o'clock. From the head-clerk to the messenger, not one of the persons employed slept in the house: it was Mr. Keller's wish that they should all be absolutely free to do what they liked with their leisure time in the evening: "I know that I can trust them, from the oldest to the youngest man in my service," he used to say; "and I like to show it."

Under these circumstances, Mrs. Wagner had only to rise earlier than usual, to be sure of having the whole range of the offices entirely to herself. At eight o'clock, with Jack in attendance, she was seated at her desk, carefully examining the different objects that it contained.

Nothing was missing; nothing had been moved out of its customary place. No money was kept in the desk. But her valuable watch, which had stopped on the previous day, had been put there, to remind her that it must be sent to be cleaned. The watch, like everything else, was found in its place. If some person had really opened her desk in the night, no common thief had been concerned, and no common object had been in view.

She took the key of the iron safe from its pigeon-hole, and opened the door. Her knowledge of the contents of this repository was far from being accurate. The partners each possessed a key, but Mr. Keller had many more occasions than Mrs. Wagner for visiting the safe. And to make a trustworthy examination more difficult still, the mist of the early morning was fast turning into a dense white fog.

Of one thing, however, Mrs. Wagner was well aware—a certain sum of money, in notes and securities, was always kept in this safe as a reserve fund. She took the tin box in which the paper money was placed close to the light, and counted its contents. Then, replacing it in the safe, she opened the private ledger next, to compare the result of her counting with the entry relating to the Fund.

Being unwilling to cause surprise, perhaps to excite suspicion, by calling for a candle before the office hours had begun, she carried the ledger also to the window. There was just light enough to see the sum total in figures. To her infinite relief, it exactly corresponded with the result of her counting. She secured everything again in its proper place; and, after finally locking the desk, handed the key to Jack. He shook his head, and refused to take it. More extraordinary still, he placed his bag, with all the other keys in it, on the desk, and said, "Please keep it for me; I'm afraid to keep it myself."

Mrs. Wagner looked at him with a first feeling of alarm, which changed instantly to compassion. The tears were in his eyes; his sensitive vanity was cruelly wounded. "My poor boy," she said gently, "what is it that troubles you?"

The tears rolled down Jack's face. "I'm a wretched creature," he said; "I'm not fit to keep the keys, after letting a thief steal them last night. Take them back, Mistress—I'm quite broken-hearted. Please try me again, in London."

"A thief?" Mrs. Wagner repeated. "Haven't you seen me examine everything? And mind, if there had been any dishonest person about the house last night, the key of my desk is the only key that a thief would have thought worth stealing. I happen to be sure of that. Come! come! don't be down-hearted. You know I never deceive you—and I say you are quite wrong in suspecting that your bag was stolen last night."

Jack solemnly lifted his hand, as his custom was in the great emergencies of his life. "And I say," he reiterated, "there is a thief in the house. And you will find it out before long. When we are back in London again, I will be Keeper of the Keys. Never, never, never more, here!"

It was useless to contend with him; the one wise course was to wait until his humor changed. Mrs. Wagner locked up his bag, and put the key of the desk back in her pocket. She was not very willing to own it even to herself—Jack's intense earnestness had a little shaken her.

After breakfast that morning, Minna lingered at the table, instead of following her mother upstairs as usual. When Mr. Keller also had left the room, she addressed a little request of her own to Mrs. Wagner.

"I have got a very difficult letter to write," she said, "and Fritz thought you might be kind enough to help me."

"With the greatest pleasure, my dear. Does your mother know of this letter?"

"Yes; it was mamma who said I ought to write it. But she is going out this morning; and, when I asked for a word of advice, she shook her head.

220

'They will think it comes from me,' she said, 'and the whole effect of it will be spoilt.' It's a letter, Mrs. Wagner, announcing my marriage to mamma's relations here, who have behaved so badly to her—and she says they may do something for me, if I write to them as if I had done it all out of my own head. I don't know whether I make myself understood?"

"Perfectly, Minna. Come to my writing-room, and we will see what we can do together."

Mrs. Wagner led the way out. As she opened the door, Madame Fontaine passed her in the hall, in walking costume, with a small paper-packet in her hand.

"There is a pen, Minna. Sit down by me, and write what I tell you."

The ink-bottle had been replenished by the person charged with that duty; and he had filled it a little too full. In a hurry to write the first words dictated, Minna dipped her pen too deeply in the bottle. On withdrawing it she not only blotted the paper but scattered some of the superfluous ink over the sleeve of Mrs. Wagner's dress. "Oh, how awkward I am!" she exclaimed. "Excuse me for one minute. Mamma has got something in her dressing-case which will take out the marks directly."

She ran upstairs, and returned with the powder which her mother had used, in erasing the first sentences on the label attached to the blue-glass bottle. Mrs. Wagner looked at the printed instructions on the little paper box, when the stains had been removed from her dress, with some curiosity. "Macula Exstinctor," she read, "or Destroyer of Stains. Partially dissolve the powder in a teaspoonful of water; rub it well over the place, and the stain will disappear, without taking out the color of the dress. This extraordinary specific may also be used for erasing written characters without in any way injuring the paper, otherwise than by leaving a slight shine on the surface."

"Is this to be got in Frankfort?" asked Mrs. Wagner. "I only know lemon-juice as a remedy against ink-marks, when I get them on my dress or my fingers."

"Keep it, dear Mrs. Wagner. I can easily buy another box for mamma where we got this one, at a chemist's in the Zeil. See how easily I can take off the blot that I dropped on the paper! Unless you look very close, you can hardly see the shine—and the ink has completely disappeared."

"Thank you, my dear. But your mother might meet with some little accident, and might want your wonderful powder when I am out of the way. Take it back when we have done our letter. And we will go to the chemist together and buy another box in a day or two."

On the thirtieth of December, after dinner, Mr. Keller proposed a toast—"Success to the adjourned wedding-day!" There was a general effort to be cheerful, which was not rewarded by success. Nobody knew why; but the fact remained that nobody was really merry.

On the thirty-first, there was more hard work at the office. The last day of the old year was the day on which the balance was struck.

Towards noon, Mr. Keller appeared in Mrs. Wagner's office, and opened the safe.

"We must see about the Reserve Fund," he said; "I will count the money, if you will open the ledger and see that the entry is right. I don't know what you think, but my idea is that we keep too much money lying idle in these prosperous times. What do you say to using half of the customary fund for investment? By the by, our day for dividing the profits is not your day in London. When my father founded this business, the sixth of January was the chosen date—being one way, among others, of celebrating his birthday. We have kept to the old custom, out of regard for his memory; and your worthy husband entirely approved of our conduct. I am sure you agree with him?"

"With all my heart," said Mrs. Wagner. "Whatever my good husband thought, I think."

Mr. Keller proceeded to count the Fund. "Fifteen thousand florins," he announced. "I thought it had been more than that. If poor dear Engelman had been here—Never mind! What does the ledger say?"

"Fifteen thousand florins," Mrs. Wagner answered.

"Ah, very well, my memory must have deceived me. This used to be Engelman's business; and you are as careful as he was—I can say no more."

Mr. Keller replaced the money in the safe, and hastened back to his own office.

Mrs. Wagner raised one side of the ledger off the desk to close the book—stopped to think—and laid it back again.

The extraordinary accuracy of Mr. Keller's memory was proverbial in the office. Remembering the compliment which he had paid to her sense of responsibility as Mr. Engelman's successor, Mrs. Wagner was not quite satisfied to take it for granted that he had made a mistake—even on the plain evidence of the ledger. A reference to the duplicate entry, in her private account-book, would at once remove even the shadow of a doubt.

The last day of the old year was bright and frosty; the clear midday light fell on the open page before her. She looked again at the entry, thus recorded in figures—"15,000 florins"—and observed a trifling circumstance which had previously escaped her.

The strokes which represented the figures "15" were unquestionably a little, a very little, thicker than the strokes which represented the three zeros or "noughts" that followed. Had a hair got into the pen of the head-clerk, who had made the entry? or was there some trifling defect in the paper, at that particular part of the page?

She once more raised one side of the ledger so that the light fell at an angle on the writing. There was a difference between that part of the paper on which the figures "15" were written, and the rest of the page—and the difference consisted in a slight shine on the surface.

The side of the ledger dropped from her hand on the desk. She left the office, and ran upstairs to her own room. Her private account-book had not been wanted lately—it was locked up in her dressing-case. She took it out, and referred to it. There was the entry as she had copied it, and compared it with the ledger—"20,000 florins."

"Madame Fontaine!" she said to herself in a whisper.

CHAPTER XI

The New Year had come.

On the morning of the second of January, Mrs. Wagner (on her way to the office at the customary hour) was stopped at the lower flight of stairs by Madame Fontaine—evidently waiting with a purpose.

"Pardon me," said the widow, "I must speak to you."

"These are business hours, madam; I have no time to spare."

Without paying the slightest heed to this reply—impenetrable, in the petrifying despair that possessed her, to all that looks, tones, and words could say—Madame Fontaine stood her ground, and obstinately repeated, "I must speak to you."

Mrs. Wagner once more refused. "All that need be said between us has been said," she answered. "Have you replaced the money?"

"That is what I want to speak about?"

"Have you replaced the money?"

"Don't drive me mad, Mrs. Wagner! As you hope for mercy yourself, at the hour of your death, show mercy to the miserable woman who implores you to listen to her! Return with me as far as the drawing-room. At this time of day, nobody will disturb us there. Give me five minutes!"

Mrs. Wagner looked at her watch.

"I will give you five minutes. And mind, I mean five minutes. Even in trifles, I speak the truth."

They returned up the stairs, Mrs. Wagner leading the way.

There were two doors of entrance to the drawing-room—one, which opened from the landing, and a smaller door, situated at the farther end of the corridor. This second entrance communicated with a sort of alcove, in which a piano was placed, and which was only separated by curtains from the spacious room beyond. Mrs. Wagner entered by the main door, and paused, standing near the fire-place. Madame Fontaine, following her, turned aside to the curtains, and looked through. Having assured herself that no person was in the recess, she approached the fire-place, and said her first words.

"You told me just now, madam, that you spoke the truth. Does that imply a doubt of the voluntary confession——?"

"You made no voluntary confession," Mrs. Wagner interposed. "I had positive proof of the theft that you have committed, when I entered your room. I showed you my private account-book, and when you attempted to defend yourself, I pointed to the means of falsifying the figures in the ledger which lay before me in your own dressing-case. What do you mean by talking of a voluntary confession, after that?"

"You mistake me, madam. I was speaking of the confession of my motives—the motives which, in my dreadful position, forced me to take the money, or to sacrifice the future of my daughter's life. I declare that I have concealed nothing from you. As you are a Christian woman, don't be hard on me!"

Mrs. Wagner drew back, and eyed her with an expression of contemptuous surprise.

"Hard on you?" she repeated. "Do you know what you are saying? Have you forgotten already how I have consented to degrade myself? Must I once more remind you of my position? I am bound to tell Mr. Keller that his money and mine has been stolen; I am bound to tell him that he has taken into his house, and has respected and trusted, a thief. There is my plain duty—and I have consented to trifle with it. Are you lost to all sense of decency? Have you no idea of the shame that an honest woman must feel, when she knows that her unworthy silence makes her—for the time at least—the accomplice of your crime? Do you think it was for your sake—not to be hard on You—that I have consented to this intolerable sacrifice? In the instant when I discovered you I would have sent for Mr. Keller, but for the sweet girl whose misfortune it is to be your child. Once for all, have you anything to say which it is absolutely necessary that I should hear? Have you, or have you not, complied with the conditions on which I consented—God help me!—to be what I am?"

Her voice faltered. She turned away proudly to compose herself. The look that flashed out at her from the widow's eyes, the suppressed fury struggling to force its way in words through the widow's lips, escaped her notice. It was the first, and last, warning of what was to come—and she missed it.

"I wished to speak to you of your conditions," Madame Fontaine resumed, after a pause. "Your conditions are impossibilities. I entreat you, in Minna's interests—oh! not in mine!—to modify them."

The tone in which those words fell from her lips was so unnaturally quiet, that Mrs. Wagner suddenly turned again with a start, and faced her.

"What do you mean by impossibilities? Explain yourself."

"You are an honest woman, and I am a thief," Madame Fontaine answered, with the same ominous composure. "How can explanations pass between you and me? Have I not spoken plainly enough already? In my position, I say again, your conditions are impossibilities—especially the first of them."

There was something in the bitterly ironical manner which accompanied this reply that was almost insolent. Mrs. Wagner's color began to rise for the first time. "Honest conditions are always possible conditions to honest people," she said.

Perfectly unmoved by the reproof implied in those words, Madame Fontaine persisted in pressing her request. "I only ask you to modify your terms," she explained. "Let us understand each other. Do you still insist on my replacing what I have taken, by the morning of the sixth of this month?"

"I still insist."

"Do you still expect me to resign my position here as director of the household, on the day when Fritz and Minna have become man and wife?"

"I still expect that."

"Permit me to set the second condition aside for awhile. Suppose I fail to replace the five thousand florins in your reserve fund?"

"If you fail, I shall do my duty to Mr. Keller, when we divide profits on the sixth of the month."

"And you will expose me in this way, knowing that you make the marriage impossible—knowing that you doom my daughter to shame and misery for the rest of her life?"

"I shall expose you, knowing that I have kept your guilty secret to the last moment—and knowing what I owe to my partner and to myself. You have still four days to spare. Make the most of your time."

"I can do absolutely nothing in the time."

"Have you tried?"

The suppressed fury in Madame Fontaine began to get beyond her control.

"Do you think I should have exposed myself to the insults that you have heaped upon me if I had not tried?" she asked. "Can I get the money back from the man to whom it was paid at Wurzburg, when my note fell due on the last day of the old year? Do I know anybody who will lend me five thousand florins? Will my father do it? His house has been closed to me for twenty years—and my mother, who might have interceded for me, is dead. Can I appeal to the sympathy and compassion (once already refused in the hardest terms) of my merciless relatives in this city? I have appealed! I forced my way to them yesterday—I owned that I owed a sum of money which was more, far more, than I could pay. I drank the bitter cup of humiliation to the dregs—I even offered my daughter's necklace as security for a loan. Do you want to know what reply I received? The master of the house turned his back on me; the mistress told me to my face that she believed I had stolen the necklace. Was the punishment of my offense severe enough, when I heard those words? Surely I have asserted some claim to your pity, at last? I only want more time. With a few months before me—with my salary as housekeeper, and the sale of my little valuables, and the proceeds of my work for the picture-dealers—I can, and will, replace the money. You are rich. What is a loan of five thousand florins to you? Help me to pass through the terrible ordeal of your day of reckoning on the sixth of the month! Help me to see Minna married and happy! And if you still doubt my word, take the pearl necklace as security that you will suffer no loss."

Struck speechless by the outrageous audacity of this proposal, Mrs. Wagner answered by a look, and advanced to the door. Madame Fontaine instantly stopped her.

"Wait!" cried the desperate creature. "Think—before you refuse me!"

Mrs. Wagner's indignation found its way at last into words. "I deserved this," she said, "when I allowed you to speak to me. Let me pass, if you please."

Madame Fontaine made a last effort—she fell on her knees. "Your hard words have roused my pride," she said; "I have forgotten that I am a disgraced woman; I have not spoken humbly enough. See! I am humbled now—I implore your mercy on my knees. This is not only my last chance; it is Minna's last chance. Don't blight my poor girl's life, for my fault!"

"For the second time, Madame Fontaine, I request you to let me pass.

"Without an answer to my entreaties? Am I not even worthy of an answer?"

"Your entreaties are an insult. I forgive you the insult."

Madame Fontaine rose to her feet. Every trace of agitation disappeared from her face and her manner. "Yes," she said, with the unnatural composure that was so strangely out of harmony with the terrible position in which she stood—"Yes, from your point of view, I can't deny that it may seem like an insult. When a thief, who has already robbed a person of money, asks that same person to lend her more money, by way of atoning for the theft, there is something very audacious (on the surface) in such a request. I can't fairly expect you to understand the despair which wears such an insolent look. Accept my apologies, madam; I didn't see it at first in that light. I must do what I can, while your merciful silence still protects me from discovery—I must do what I can between this and the sixth of the month. Permit me to open the door for you." She opened the drawing-room door, and waited.

Mrs. Wagner's heart suddenly quickened its beat.

Under what influence? Could it be fear? She was indignant with herself at the bare suspicion of it. Her face flushed deeply, under the momentary apprehension that some outward change might betray her. She left the room, without even trusting herself to look at the woman who stood by the open door, and bowed to her with an impenetrable assumption of respect as she passed out.

Madame Fontaine remained in the drawing-room.

She violently closed the door with a stroke of her hand—staggered across the room to a sofa—and dropped on it. A hoarse cry of rage and despair burst from her, now that she was alone. In the fear that someone might hear her, she forced her handkerchief into her mouth, and fastened her teeth into it. The paroxysm passed, she sat up on the sofa, and wiped the perspiration from her face, and smiled to herself. "It was well I stopped here," she thought; "I might have met someone on the stairs."

As she rose to leave the drawing-room, Fritz's voice reached her from the far end of the corridor.

"You are out of spirits, Minna. Come in, and let us try what a little music will do for you."

The door leading into the recess was opened. Minna's voice became audible next, on the inner side of the curtains.

"I am afraid I can't sing to-day, Fritz. I am very unhappy about mamma. She looks so anxious and so ill; and when I ask what is troubling her, she puts me off with an excuse."

The melody of those fresh young tones, the faithful love and sympathy which the few simple words expressed, seemed to wring with an unendurable pain the whole being of the mother who heard them. She lifted her hands above her head, and clenched them in the agony which could only venture to seek that silent means of relief. With swift steps, as if the sound of her daughter's voice was unendurable to her, she made for the door. But her movements, on ordinary occasions the perfection of easy grace, felt the disturbing influence of the agitation that possessed her. In avoiding a table on one side, as she passed it, she struck against a chair on the other.

Fritz instantly opened the curtains, and looked through. "Why, here is mamma!" he exclaimed, in his hearty boyish way.

Minna instantly closed the piano, and hastened to her mother. When Madame Fontaine looked at her, she paused, with an expression of alarm. "Oh, how dreadfully pale and ill you look!" She advanced again, and tried to throw her arms round her mother, and kiss her. Gently, very gently, Madame Fontaine signed to her to draw back.

"Mamma! what have I done to offend you?"

"Nothing, my dear."

"Then why won't you let me come to you?"

"No time now, Minna. I have something to do. Wait till I have done it."

"Not even one little kiss, mamma?"

Madame Fontaine hurried out of the room without answering and ran up the stairs without looking back. Minna's eyes filled with tears. Fritz stood at the open door, bewildered.

"I wouldn't have believed it, if anybody had told me," he said; "your mother seems to be afraid to let you touch her."

Fritz had made many mistaken guesses in his time—but, for once, he had guessed right. She was afraid.

CHAPTER XII

As the presiding genius of the household, Madame Fontaine was always first in the room when the table was laid for the early German dinner. A knife with a speck on the blade, a plate with a suspicion of dirt on it, never once succeeded in escaping her observation. If Joseph folded a napkin carelessly, Joseph not only heard of it, but suffered the indignity of seeing his work

230

performed for him to perfection by the housekeeper's dexterous hands.

On the second day of the New Year, she was at her post as usual, and Joseph stood convicted of being wasteful in the matter of wine.

He had put one bottle of Ohligsberger on the table, at the place occupied by Madame Fontaine. The wine had already been used at the dinner and the supper of the previous day. At least two-thirds of it had been drunk. Joseph set down a second bottle on the opposite side of the table, and produced his corkscrew. Madame Fontaine took it out of his hand.

"Why do you open that bottle, before you are sure it will be wanted?" She asked sharply. "You know that Mr. Keller and his son prefer beer."

"There is so little left in the other bottle," Joseph pleaded; "not a full tumbler altogether."

"It may be enough, little as it is, for Mrs. Wagner and for me." With that reply she pointed to the door. Joseph retired, leaving her alone at the table, until the dinner was ready to be brought into the room.

In five minutes more, the family assembled at their meal.

Joseph performed his customary duties sulkily, resenting the housekeeper's reproof. When the time came for filling the glasses, he had the satisfaction of hearing Madame Fontaine herself give him orders to draw the cork of a new bottle, after all.

Mrs. Wagner turned to Jack, standing behind her chair as usual, and asked for some wine. Madame Fontaine instantly took up the nearly empty bottle by her side, and, half-filling a glass, handed it with grave politeness across the table. "If you have no objection," she said, "we will finish one bottle, before we open another."

Mrs. Wagner drank her small portion of wine at a draught. "It doesn't seem to keep well, after it has once been opened," she remarked, as she set down her glass. "The wine has quite lost the good flavor it had yesterday."

"It ought to keep well," said Mr. Keller, speaking from his place at the top of the table. "It's old wine, and good wine. Let me taste what is left."

Joseph advanced to carry the remains of the wine to his master. But Madame Fontaine was beforehand with him. "Open the other bottle directly," she said—and rose so hurriedly to take the wine herself to Mr. Keller, that she caught her foot in her dress. In saving herself from falling, she lost her hold of the bottle. It broke in two pieces, and the little wine left in it ran out on the floor.

"Pray forgive me," she said, smiling faintly. "It is the first thing I have broken since I have been in the house."

The wine from the new bottle was offered to Mrs. Wagner. She declined to take any: and she left her dinner unfinished on her plate.

"My appetite is very easily spoilt," she said. "I dare say there might have been something I didn't notice in the glass—or perhaps my taste may be out of order."

"Very likely," said Mr. Keller. "You didn't find anything wrong with the wine yesterday. And there is certainly nothing to complain of in the new bottle," he added, after tasting it. "Let us have your opinion, Madame Fontaine."

He filled the housekeeper's glass. "I am a poor judge of wine," she remarked humbly. "It seems to me to be delicious."

She put her glass down, and noticed that Jack's eyes were fixed on her, with a solemn and scrutinizing attention. "Do you see anything remarkable in me?" she asked lightly.

"I was thinking," Jack answered.

"Thinking of what?"

"This is the first time I ever saw you in danger of tumbling down. It used to be a remark of mine, at Wurzburg, that you were as sure-footed as a cat. That's all."

"Don't you know that there are exceptions to all rules?" said Madame

Fontaine, as amiably as ever. "I notice an exception in You," she continued, suddenly changing the subject. "What has become of your leather bag? May I ask if you have taken away his keys, Mrs. Wagner?"

She had noticed Jack's pride in his character as "Keeper of the Keys." There would be no fear of his returning to the subject of what he had remarked at Wurzburg, if she stung him in that tender place. The result did not fail to justify her anticipations. In fierce excitement, Jack jumped up on the hind rail of his mistress's chair, eager for the most commanding position that he could obtain, and opened his lips to tell the story of the night alarm. Before he could utter a word, Mrs. Wagner stopped him, with a very unusual irritability of look and manner. "The question was put to me," she said. "I am taking care of the keys, Madame Fontaine, at Jack's own request. He can have them back again, whenever he chooses to ask for them."

"Tell her about the thief," Jack whispered.

"Be quiet!"

Jack was silenced at last. He retired to a corner. When he followed Mrs. Wagner as usual, on her return to her duties in the office he struck his favorite place on the window seat with his clenched fist. "The devil take Frankfort!" he said.

"What do you mean?"

"I hate Frankfort. You were always kind to me in London. You do nothing but lose your temper with me here. It's really too cruel. Why shouldn't I have told Mrs. Housekeeper how I lost my keys in the night? Now I come to think of it, I believe she was the thief."

"Hush! hush! you must not say that. Come and shake hands, Jack, and make it up. I do feel irritable—I don't know what's the matter with me. Remember, Mr. Keller doesn't like your joining in the talk at dinner-time—he thinks it is taking a liberty. That was one reason why I stopped you. And you might have said something to offend Madame Fontaine—that was another. It will not be long before we go back to our dear old London. Now, be a good boy, and leave me to my work."

Jack was not quite satisfied; but he was quiet again.

For awhile he sat watching Mrs. Wagner at her work. His thoughts went back to the subject of the keys. Other people—the younger clerks and the servants, for example—might have observed that he was without his bag, and might have injuriously supposed that the keys had been taken away from him. Little by little, he reached the conclusion that he had been in too great a hurry perhaps to give up the bag. Why not prove himself to be worthier of it than ever, by asking to have it back again, and taking care always to lock the door of his bedroom at night? He looked at Mrs. Wagner, to see if she paused over her work, so as to give him an opportunity of speaking to her.

She was not at work; she was not pausing over it. Her head hung down over her breast; her hands and arms lay helpless on the desk.

He got up and crossed the room on tiptoe, to look at her.

She was not asleep.

Slowly and silently, she turned her head. Her eyes stared at him awfully. Her mouth was a little crooked. There was a horrid gray paleness all over her face.

He dropped terrified on his knees, and clasped her dress in both hands. "Oh, Mistress, Mistress, you are ill! What can I do for you?"

She tried to reassure him by a smile. Her mouth became more crooked still. "I'm not well," she said, speaking thickly and slowly, with an effort. "Help me down. Bed. Bed."

He held out his hands. With another effort, she lifted her arms from the desk, and turned to him on the high office-stool.

"Take hold of me," she said.

"I have got hold of you, Mistress! I have got your hands in my hands. Don't you feel it?"

"Press me harder."

He closed his hands on hers with all his strength. Did she feel it now?

234

Yes; she could just feel it now.

Leaning heavily upon him, she set her feet on the floor. She felt with them as if she was feeling the floor, without quite understanding that she stood on it. The next moment, she reeled against the desk. "Giddy," she said, faintly and thickly. "My head." Her eyes looked at him, cold and big and staring. They maddened the poor affectionate creature with terror. The frightful shrillness of the past days in Bedlam was in his voice, as he screamed for help.

Mr. Keller rushed into the room from his office, followed by the clerks.

"Fetch the doctor, one of you," he cried. "Stop."

He mastered himself directly, and called to mind what he had heard of the two physicians who had attended him, during his own illness. "Not the old man," he said. "Fetch Doctor Dormann. Joseph will show you where he lives." He turned to another of the clerks, supporting Mrs. Wagner in his arms while he spoke. "Ring the bell in the hall—the upstairs bell for Madame Fontaine!"

CHAPTER XIII

Madame Fontaine instantly left her room. Alarmed by the violent ringing of the bell, Minna followed her mother downstairs. The door of the office was open; they both saw what had happened as soon as they reached the hall. In sending for Madame Fontaine, Mr. Keller had placed a natural reliance on the experience and presence of mind of a woman of her age and character. To his surprise, she seemed to be as little able to control herself as her daughter. He was obliged to summon the assistance of the elder of the female servants, in carrying Mrs. Wagner to her room. Jack went with them, holding one of his mistress's helpless hands.

His first paroxysm of terror had passed away with the appearance of Mr. Keller and the clerk, and had left his weak mind stunned by the shock that had fallen on it. He looked about him vacantly. Once or twice, on the slow sad progress up the stairs, they heard him whispering to himself, "She won't die—no, no, no; she won't die." His only consolation seemed to be in that helpless confession of faith. When they laid her on the bed, he was close at the side of the pillow. With an effort, her eyes turned on him. With an effort she whispered, "The Key!"

He understood her—the desk downstairs had been left unlocked.

"I'll take care of the key, Mistress; I'll take care of them all," he said.

As he left the room, he repeated his comforting words, "She won't die—no, no, no; she won't die." He locked the desk and placed the key with the rest in his bag.

Leaving the office with the bag slung over his shoulder, he stopped at the door of the dining-room, on the opposite side of the hall. His head felt strangely dull. A sudden suspicion that the feeling might show itself in his face, made him change his mind and pause before he ascended the stairs. There was a looking-glass in the dining-room. He went straight to the glass, and stood before it, studying the reflection of his face with breathless anxiety. "Do I look stupid-mad?" he asked himself. "They won't let me be with her; they'll send me away, if I look stupid-mad."

He turned from the glass, and dropped on his knees before the nearest chair. "Perhaps God will keep me quiet," he thought, "if I say my prayers."

Repeating his few simple words, the poor creature's memory vaguely recalled to him the happy time when his good mistress had first taught him his prayers. The one best relief that could come to him, came—the relief of tears. Mr. Keller, descending to the hall in his impatience for the arrival of the doctor, found himself unexpectedly confronted by Mrs. Wagner's crazy attendant.

"May I go upstairs to Mistress?" Jack asked humbly. "I've said my prayers, sir, and I've had a good cry—and my head's easier now."

Mr. Keller spoke to him more gently than usual. "You had better not disturb your mistress before the doctor comes."

"May I wait outside her door, sir? I promise to be very quiet."

Mr. Keller consented by a sign. Jack took off his shoes, and noiselessly

236

ascended the stairs. Before he reached the first landing, he turned and looked back into the hall. "Mind this!" he announced very earnestly; "I say she won't die—I say that!"

He went on up the stairs. For the first time Mr. Keller began to pity the harmless little man whom he had hitherto disliked. "Poor wretch!" he said to himself, as he paced up and down the hall, "what will become of him, if she does die?"

In ten minutes more, Doctor Dormann arrived at the house.

His face showed that he thought badly of the case, as soon as he looked at Mrs. Wagner. He examined her, and made all the necessary inquiries, with the unremitting attention to details which was part of his professional character. One of his questions could only be answered generally. Having declared his opinion that the malady was paralysis, and that some of the symptoms were far from being common in his medical experience, he inquired if Mrs. Wagner had suffered from any previous attack of the disease. Mr. Keller could only reply that he had known her from the time of her marriage, and that he had never (in the course of a long and intimate correspondence with her husband) heard of her having suffered from serious illness of any kind. Doctor Dormann looked at his patient narrowly, and looked back again at Mr. Keller with unconcealed surprise.

"At her age," he said, "I have never seen any first attack of paralysis so complicated and so serious as this."

"Is there danger?" Mr. Keller asked in a whisper.

"She is not an old woman," the doctor answered; "there is always hope. The practice in these cases generally is to bleed. In this case, the surface of the body is cold; the heart's action is feeble—I don't like to try bleeding, if I can possibly avoid it."

After some further consideration, he directed a system of treatment which, in some respects, anticipated the practice of a later and wiser time. Having looked at the women assembled round the bed—and especially at Madame Fontaine—he said he would provide a competent nurse, and would return to see the effect of the remedies in two hours.

Looking at Madame Fontaine, after the doctor had gone away, Mr. Keller felt more perplexed than ever. She presented the appearance of a woman who was completely unnerved. "I am afraid you are far from well yourself," he said.

"I have not felt well, sir, for some time past," she answered, without looking at him.

"You had better try what rest and quiet will do for you," he suggested.

"Yes, I think so." With that reply—not even offering, for the sake of appearances, to attend on Mrs. Wagner until the nurse arrived—she took her daughter's arm, and went out.

The woman-servant was fortunately a discreet person. She remembered the medical instructions, and she undertook all needful duties, until the nurse relieved her. Jack (who had followed the doctor into the room, and had watched him attentively) was sent away again for the time. He would go no farther than the outer side of the door. Mr. Keller passed him, crouched up on the mat, biting his nails. He was apparently thinking of the doctor. He said to himself, "That man looked puzzled; that man knows nothing about it."

In the meantime, Madame Fontaine reached her room.

"Where is Fritz?" she asked, dropping her daughter's arm.

"He has gone out, mamma. Don't send me away! You seem to be almost as ill as poor Mrs. Wagner—I want to be with you."

Madame Fontaine hesitated. "Do you love me with all your heart and soul?" she asked suddenly. "Are you worthy of any sacrifice that a mother can make for her child?"

Before the girl could answer, she spoke more strangely still.

"Are you just as fond of Fritz as ever? would it break your heart if you lost him?"

Minna placed her mother's hand on her bosom.

"Feel it, mamma," she said quietly. Madame Fontaine took her chair by the fire-side—seating herself with her back to the light. She beckoned to her daughter to sit by her. After an interval, Minna ventured to break the silence.

"I am very sorry for Mrs. Wagner, mamma; she has always been so kind to me. Do you think she will die?" Resting her elbows on her knees, staring into the fire, the widow lifted her head—looked round—and looked back again at the fire.

"Ask the doctor," she said. "Don't ask me."

There was another long interval of silence. Minna's eyes were fixed anxiously on her mother. Madame Fontaine remained immovable, still looking into the fire.

Afraid to speak again, Minna sought refuge from the oppressive stillness in a little act of attention. She took a fire-screen from the chimney-piece, and tried to place it gently in her mother's hand.

At that light touch, Madame Fontaine sprang to her feet as if she had felt the point of a knife. Had she seen some frightful thing? had she heard some dreadful sound? "I can't bear it!" she cried—"I can't bear it any longer!"

"Are you in pain, mamma? Will you lie down on the bed?" Her mother only looked at her. She drew back trembling, and said no more.

Madame Fontaine crossed the room to the wardrobe. When she spoke next, she was outwardly quite calm again. "I am going out for a walk," she said.

"A walk, mamma? It's getting dark already."

"Dark or light, my nerves are all on edge—I must have air and exercise."

"Let me go with you?"

She paced backwards and forwards restlessly, before she answered. "The room isn't half large enough!" she burst out. "I feel suffocated in these four walls. Space! space! I must have space to breathe in! Did you say you wished to go out with me? I want a companion, Minna. Don't you mind the cold?"

"I don't even feel it, in my fur cloak."

"Get ready, then, directly."

In ten minutes more, the mother and daughter were out of the house.

CHAPTER XIV

Doctor Dormann was punctual to his appointment. He was accompanied by a stranger, whom he introduced as a surgeon. As before, Jack slipped into the room, and waited in a corner, listening and watching attentively.

Instead of improving under the administration of the remedies, the state of the patient had sensibly deteriorated. On the rare occasions when she attempted to speak, it was almost impossible to understand her. The sense of touch seemed to be completely lost—the poor woman could no longer feel the pressure of a friendly hand. And more ominous still, a new symptom had appeared; it was with evident difficulty that she performed the act of swallowing. Doctor Dormann turned resignedly to the surgeon.

"There is no other alternative," he said; "you must bleed her."

At the sight of the lancet and the bandage, Jack started out of his corner. His teeth were fast set; his eyes glared with rage. Before he could approach the surgeon Mr. Keller took him sternly by the arm and pointed to the door. He shook himself free—he saw the point of the lancet touch the vein. As the blood followed the incision, a cry of horror burst from him: he ran out of the room.

"Wretches! Tigers! How dare they take her blood from her! Oh, why am I only a little man? why am I not strong enough to fling the brutes out of the window? Mistress! Mistress! is there nothing I can do to help you?"

These wild words poured from his lips in the solitude of his little bedchamber. In the agony that he suffered, as the sense of Mrs. Wagner's danger now forced itself on him, he rolled on the floor, and struck himself with his clenched fists. And, again and again, he cried out to her, "Mistress! Mistress! is there nothing I can do to help you?"

The strap that secured his keys became loosened, as his frantic movements beat the leather bag, now on one side, and now on the other, upon the floor. The jingling of the keys rang in his ears. For a moment, he lay quite still. Then, he sat up on the floor. He tried to think calmly. There was no candle in the room. The nearest light came from a lamp on the landing below. He got up, and went softly down the stairs. Alone on the landing, he held up the bag and looked at it. "There's something in my mind, trying to speak to me," he said to himself. "Perhaps, I shall find it in here?"

He knelt down under the light, and shook out the keys on the landing.

One by one he ranged them in a row, with a single exception. The key of the desk happened to be the first that he took up. He kissed it—it was her key—and put it back in the bag. Placing the others before him, the duplicate key was the last in the line. The inscription caught his eye. He held it to the light and read "Pink-Room Cupboard."

The lost recollection now came back to him in intelligible form. The "remedy" that Madame Fontaine had locked up—the precious "remedy" made by the wonderful master who knew everything—was at his disposal. He had only to open the cupboard, and to have it in his own possession.

He threw the other keys back into the bag. They rattled as he ran down the lower flight of stairs. Opposite to the offices, he stopped and buckled them tight with the strap. No noise! Nothing to alarm Mrs. Housekeeper! He ascended the stairs in the other wing of the house, and paused again when he approached Madame Fontaine's room. By this time, he was in the perilous fever of excitement, which was still well remembered among the authorities of Bedlam. Suppose the widow happened to be in her room? Suppose she refused to let him have the "remedy"?

He looked at the outstretched fingers of his right hand. "I am strong enough to throttle a woman," he said, "and I'll do it."

He opened the door without knocking, without stopping to listen outside. Not a creature was in the room.

In another moment the fatal dose of "Alexander's Wine," which he innocently believed to be a beneficent remedy, was in his possession.

As he put it into the breast-pocket of his coat, the wooden chest caught his eye. He reached it down and tried the lid. The lid opened in his hand, and disclosed the compartments and the bottles placed in them. One of the bottles rose higher by an inch or two than any of the others. He drew that one out first to look at it, and discovered—the "blue-glass bottle."

From that moment all idea of trying the effect on Mrs. Wagner of the treacherous "remedy" in his pocket vanished from his mind. He had secured the inestimable treasure, known to him by his own experience. Here was the heavenly bottle that had poured life down his throat, when he lay dying at Wurzburg! This was the true and only doctor who had saved Mr. Keller's life, when the poor helpless fools about his bed had given him up for lost! The Mistress, the dear Mistress, was as good as cured already. Not a drop more of her precious blood should be shed by the miscreant, who had opened his knife and wounded her. Oh, of all the colors in the world, there's no color like blue! Of all the friends in the world, there never was such a good friend as this! He kissed and hugged the bottle as if it had been a living thing. He jumped up and danced about the room with it in his arms. Ha! what music there was in the inner gurgling and splashing of the shaken liquid, which told him that there was still some left for the Mistress! The striking of the clock on the mantelpiece sobered him at the height of his ecstasy. It told him that time was passing. Minute by minute, Death might be getting nearer and nearer to her; and there he was, with Life in his possession, wasting the time, far from her bedside.

On his way to the door, he stopped. His eyes turned slowly towards the inner part of the room. They rested on the open cupboard—and then they looked at the wooden chest, left on the floor.

Suppose the housekeeper should return, and see the key in the cupboard, and the chest with one of the bottles missing?

His only counselor at that critical moment was his cunning; stimulated into action by the closely related motive powers of his inbred vanity, and his devotion to the benefactress whom he loved.

The chance of being discovered by Madame Fontaine never entered into his calculations. He cared nothing whether she discovered him or not—he had got the bottle, and woe to her if she tried to take it away from him! What he really dreaded was, that the housekeeper might deprive him of the glory of saving Mrs. Wagner's life, if she found out what had happened. She might follow him to the bedside; she might claim the blue-glass bottle as her property; she might say, "I saved Mr. Keller; and now I have saved Mrs. Wagner. This little man is only the servant who gave the dose, which any other hand might have poured out in his place."

Until these considerations occurred to him, his purpose had been to announce his wonderful discovery publicly at Mrs. Wagner's bedside. This intention he now abandoned, without hesitation. He saw a far more inviting prospect before him. What a glorious position for him it would be, if he watched his opportunity of administering the life-giving liquid privately—if he waited till everybody was astonished at the speedy recovery of the suffering woman—and then stood up before them all, and proclaimed himself as the man who had restored her to health!

He replaced the chest, and locked the cupboard; taking the key away with him. Returning to the door, he listened intently to make sure that nobody was outside, and kept the blue-glass bottle hidden under his coat when he ventured at last to leave the room. He reached the other wing of the house, and ascended the second flight of stairs, without interruption of any kind. Safe again in his own room, he watched through the half-opened door.

Before long, Doctor Dormann and the surgeon appeared, followed by Mr. Keller. The three went downstairs together. On the way, the Doctor mentioned that he had secured a nurse for the night.

Still keeping the bottle concealed, Jack knocked softly at the door, and entered Mrs. Wagner's room.

He first looked at the bed. She lay still and helpless, noticing nothing; to all appearance, poor soul, a dying woman. The servant was engaged in warming something over the fire. She shook her head gloomily, when Jack inquired if any favorable change had place in his absence. He sat down, vainly trying to discover how he might find the safe opportunity of which he was in search.

The slow minutes followed each other. After a little while the woman-servant looked at the clock. "It's time Mrs. Wagner had her medicine," she remarked, still occupied with her employment at the fire. Jack saw his opportunity in those words. "Please let me give the medicine," he said.

"Bring it here," she answered; "I mustn't trust anybody to measure it out."

"Surely I can give it to her, now it's ready?" Jack persisted.

The woman handed the glass to him. "I can't very well leave what I am about," she said. "Mind you are careful not to spill any of it. She's as patient as a lamb, poor creature. If she can only swallow it, she won't give you any trouble."

Jack carried the glass round to the farther side of the bed, so as to keep the curtains as a screen between himself and the fire-place. He softly dropped out the contents of the glass on the carpet, and filled it again from the bottle concealed under his coat. Waiting a moment after that, he looked towards the door. What if the housekeeper came in, and saw the blue-glass bottle? He snatched it up—an empty bottle now—and put it in the side-pocket of his coat, and arranged his handkerchief so as to hide that part of it which the pocket was not deep enough to conceal. "Now!" he thought to himself, "now I may venture!" He gently put his arm round Mrs. Wagner, and raised her on the pillow.

"Your medicine, dear Mistress," he whispered. "You will take it from poor Jack, won't you?"

The sense of hearing still remained. Her vacant eyes turned towards him by slow degrees. No outward expression answered to her thought; she could show him that she submitted, and she could do no more.

He dashed away the tears that blinded him. Supported by the firm belief that he was saving her life, he took the glass from the bedside-table and put it to her lips.

244

With painful efforts, with many intervals of struggling breath, she swallowed the contents of the glass, by a few drops at a time. He held it up under the shadowed lamplight, and saw that it was empty.

As he laid her head back on the pillows, he ventured to touch her cold cheek with his lips. "Has she taken it?" the woman asked. He was just able to answer "Yes"—just able to look once more at the dear face on the pillow. The tumult of contending emotions, against which he had struggled thus far, overpowered his utmost resistance. He ran to hide the hysterical passion in him, forcing its way to relief in sobs and cries, on the landing outside.

In the calmer moments that followed, the fear still haunted him that Madame Fontaine might discover the empty compartment in the medicine-chest—might search every room in the house for the lost bottle—and might find it empty. Even if he broke it, and threw the fragments into the dusthole, the fragments might be remarked for their beautiful blue color, and the discovery might follow. Where could he hide it?

While he was still trying to answer that question, the hours of business came to an end, and the clerks were leaving the offices below. He heard them talking about the hard frost as they went out. One of them said there were blocks of ice floating down the river already. The river! It was within a few minutes' walk of the house. Why not throw the bottle into the river?

He waited until there was perfect silence below, and then stole downstairs. As he opened the door, a strange man met him, ascending the house-steps, with a little traveling bag in his hand.

"Is this Mr. Keller's?" asked the strange man.

He was a jolly-looking old fellow with twinkling black eyes and a big red nose. His breath was redolent of the smell of wine, and his thick lips expanded into a broad grin, when he looked at Jack.

"My name's Schwartz," he said; "and here in this bag are my sister's things for the night."

"Who is your sister?" Jack inquired.

Schwartz laughed. "Quite right, little man, how should you know who she is? My sister's the nurse. She's hired by Doctor Dormann, and she'll be here in an hour's time. I say! that's a pretty bottle you're hiding there under your coat. Is there any wine in it?"

Jack began to tremble. He had been discovered by a stranger. Even the river might not be deep enough to keep his secret now!

"The cold has got into my inside," proceeded the jolly old man. "Be a good little fellow—and give us a drop!"

"I haven't got any wine in it," Jack answered.

Schwartz laid his forefinger confidentially along the side of his big red nose. "I understand," he said, "you were just going out to get some." He put his sister's bag on one of the chairs in the hall, and took Jack's arm in the friendliest manner. "Suppose you come along with me?" he suggested. "I am the man to help you to the best tap of wine in Frankfort. Bless your heart! you needn't feel ashamed of being in my company. My sister's a most respectable woman. And what do you think I am? I'm one of the city officers. Ho! ho! just think of that! I'm not joking, mind. The regular Night Watchman at the Deadhouse is ill in bed, and they're obliged to find somebody to take his place till he gets well again. I'm the Somebody. They tried two other men—but the Deadhouse gave them the horrors. My respectable sister spoke for me, you know. "The regular watchman will be well in a week," she says; "try him for a week." And they tried me. I'm not proud, though I am a city officer. Come along—and let me carry the bottle."

"The bottle" again! And, just as this intrusive person spoke of it, Joseph's voice was audible below, and Joseph's footsteps gave notice that he was ascending the kitchen stairs. In the utter bewilderment of the moment, Jack ran out, with the one idea of escaping the terrible possibilities of discovery in the hall. He heard the door closed behind him—then heavy boots thumping the pavement at a quick trot. Before he had got twenty yards from the house, the vinous breath of Schwartz puffed over his shoulder, and the arm of the deputy-night-watchman took possession of him again.

"Not too fast—I'm nimble on my legs for a man of my age—but not too fast," said his new friend. "You're just the sort of little man I like. My sister will tell you I take sudden fancies to people of your complexion. My sister's a most respectable woman. What's your name?—Jack? A capital name! Short, with a smack in it like the crack of a whip. Do give me the bottle!" He took it this time, without waiting to have it given to him. "There! might drop it, you know," he said. "It's safe in my friendly hands. Where are you going to? You don't deal, I hope, at the public-house up that way? A word in your ear— the infernal scoundrel waters his wine. Here's the turning where the honest publican lives. I have the truest affection for him. I have the truest affection for you. Would you like to see the Deadhouse, some night? It's against the rules; but that don't matter. The cemetery overseer is a deal too fond of his bed to turn out these cold nights and look after the watchman. It's just the right place for me. There's nothing to do but to drink, when you have got the liquor; and to sleep, when you haven't. The Dead who come our way, my little friend, have one great merit. We are supposed to help them, if they're perverse enough to come to life again before they're buried. There they lie in our house, with one end of the line tied to their fingers, and the other end at the spring of the alarm-bell. And they have never rung the bell yet—never once, bless their hearts, since the Deadhouse was built! Come and see me in the course of the week, and we'll drink a health to our quiet neighbors."

They arrived at the door of the public-house.

"You've got some money about you, I suppose?" said Schwartz.

Madame Fontaine's generosity, when she gave Jack the money to buy a pair of gloves, had left a small surplus in his pocket. He made a last effort to escape from the deputy-watchman. "There's the money," he said. "Give me back the bottle, and go and drink by yourself."

Schwartz took him by the shoulder, and surveyed him from head to foot by the light of the public-house lamp. "Drink by myself?" he repeated. "Am I a jolly fellow, or am I not? Yes, or No?"

"Yes," said Jack, trying hard to release himself.

Schwartz tightened his hold. "Did you ever hear of a jolly fellow, who left his friend at the public-house door?" he asked.

"If you please, sir, I don't drink," Jack pleaded.

Schwartz burst into a great roar of laughter, and kicked open the door of the public-house. "That's the best joke I ever heard in my life," he said. "We've got money enough to fill the bottle, and to have a glass a-piece besides. Come along!"

He dragged Jack into the house. The bottle was filled; the glasses were filled. "My sister's health! Long life and prosperity to my respectable sister! You can't refuse to drink the toast." With those words, he put the fatal glass into his companion's hand.

Jack tasted the wine. It was cool; it was good. Perhaps it was not so strong as Mr. Keller's wine? He tried it again—and emptied the glass.

An hour later, there was a ring at the door of Mr. Keller's house.

Joseph opened the door, and discovered a red-nosed old man, holding up another man who seemed to be three parts asleep, and who was quite unable to stand on his legs without assistance. The light of the hall lamp fell on this helpless creature's face, and revealed—Jack.

"Put him to bed," said the red-nosed stranger. "And, look here, take charge of the bottle for him, or he'll break it. Somehow, the wine has all leaked out. Where's my sister's bag?"

"Do you mean the nurse?"

"Of course I do! I defy the world to produce the nurse's equal. Has she come?"

Joseph held up his hand with a gesture of grave reproof.

"Not so loud," he said. "The nurse has come too late."

"Has the lady got well again?"

"The lady is dead."

CHAPTER XV

Doctor Dormann had behaved very strangely.

He was the first person who made the terrible discovery of the death. When he came to the house, on his evening visit to his patient, Mr. Keller was in the room. Half an hour before, Mrs. Wagner had spoken to him. Seeing a slight movement of her lips, he had bent over her, and had just succeeded in hearing her few last words, "Be kind to Jack." Her eyelids dropped wearily, after the struggle to speak. Mr. Keller and the servant in attendance both supposed that she had fallen asleep. The doctor's examination was not only prolonged beyond all customary limits of time in such cases—it was the examination (judging by certain expressions which escaped him) of a man who seemed to be unwilling to trust his own experience. The new nurse arrived, before he had definitely expressed his opinion; and the servant was instructed to keep her waiting downstairs. In expectation of the doctor's report, Mr. Keller remained in the bedroom. Doctor Dormann might not have noticed this circumstance, or might not have cared to conceal what was passing in his mind. In either case, when he spoke at last, he expressed himself in these extraordinary terms:—

"The second suspicious illness in this house! And the second incomprehensible end to it!"

Mr. Keller at once stepped forward, and showed himself.

"Did you mean me to hear what you have just said?" he asked.

The doctor looked at him gravely and sadly. "I must speak to you privately, Mr. Keller. Before we leave the room, permit me to send for the nurse. You may safely trust her to perform the last sad duties."

Mr. Keller started. "Good God!" he exclaimed, "is Mrs. Wagner dead?"

"To my astonishment, she is dead." He laid a strong emphasis on the first part of his reply.

The nurse having received her instructions, Mr. Keller led the way to his private room. "In my responsible position," he said, "I may not unreasonably expect that you will explain yourself without reserve."

"On such a serious matter as this," Doctor Dormann answered, "it is my duty to speak without reserve. The person whom you employ to direct the funeral will ask you for the customary certificate. I refuse to give it."

This startling declaration roused a feeling of anger, rather than of alarm, in a man of Mr. Keller's resolute character. "For what reason do you refuse?" he asked sternly.

"I am not satisfied, sir, that Mrs. Wagner has died a natural death. My experience entirely fails to account for the suddenly fatal termination of the disease, in the case of a patient of her healthy constitution, and at her comparatively early age."

"Doctor Dormann, do you suspect there is a poisoner in my house?"

"In plain words, I do."

"In plain words on my side, I ask why?"

"I have already given you my reason."

"Is your experience infallible? Have you never made a mistake?"

"I made a mistake, Mr. Keller (as it appeared at the time), in regard to your own illness."

"What! you suspected foul play in my case too?"

"Yes; and, by way of giving you another reason, I will own that the suspicion is still in my mind. After what I have seen this evening—and only after that, observe—I say the circumstances of your recovery are suspicious circumstances in themselves. Remember, if you please, that neither I nor my colleague really understood what was the matter with you; and that you were cured by a remedy, not prescribed by either of us. You were rapidly sinking; and your regular physician had left you. I had to choose between the certainty of your death, and the risk of letting you try a remedy, with the nature of which (though I did my best to analyze it) I was imperfectly acquainted. I ran the risk. The result has justified me—and up to this day, I have kept my misgivings to myself. I now find them renewed by Mrs. Wagner's death—and

I speak."

Mr. Keller's manner began to change. His tone was sensibly subdued. He understood the respect which was due to the doctor's motives at last.

"May I ask if the symptoms of my illness resembled the symptoms of Mrs. Wagner's illness?" he said.

"Far from it. Excepting the nervous derangement, in both cases, there was no other resemblance in the symptoms. The conclusion, to my mind, is not altered by this circumstance. It simply leads me to the inference that more than one poison may have been used. I don't attempt to solve the mystery. I have no idea why your life has been saved, and Mrs. Wagner's life sacrificed— or what motives have been at work in the dark. Ask yourself—don't ask me— in what direction suspicion points. I refuse to sign the certificate of death; and I have told you why."

"Give me a moment," said Mr. Keller, "I don't shrink from my responsibility; I only ask for time to compose myself."

It was the pride of his life to lean on nobody for help. He walked to the window; hiding all outward betrayal of the consternation that shook him to the soul. When he returned to his chair, he scrupulously avoided even the appearance of asking Doctor Dormann for advice.

"My course is plain," he said quietly. "I must communicate your decision to the authorities; and I must afford every assistance in my power to the investigation that will follow. It shall be done, when the magistrates meet to-morrow morning."

"We will go together to the town-hall, Mr. Keller. It is my duty to inform the burgomaster that this is a case for the special safeguards, sanctioned by the city regulations. I must also guarantee that there is no danger to the public health, in the removal of the body from your house."

"The immediate removal?" Mr. Keller asked.

"No! The removal twenty-four hours after death."

"To what place?"

"To the Deadhouse."

CHAPTER XVI

Acting on the doctor's information, the burgomaster issued his order. At eight o'clock in the evening, on the third of January, the remains of Mrs. Wagner were to be removed to the cemetery-building, outside the Friedberg Gate of Frankfort.

Long before the present century, the dread of premature interment—excited by traditions of persons accidentally buried alive—was a widely-spread feeling among the people of Germany. In other cities besides Frankfort, the municipal authorities devised laws, the object of which was to make this frightful catastrophe impossible. In the early part of the present century, these laws were re-enacted and revised by the City of Frankfort. The Deadhouse was attached to the cemetery, with a double purpose. First, to afford a decent resting-place for the corpse, when death occurred among the crowded residences of the poorer class of the population. Secondly, to provide as perfect a safeguard as possible against the chances of premature burial. The use of the Deadhouse (strictly confined to the Christian portion of the inhabitants) was left to the free choice of surviving relatives or representatives—excepting only those cases in which a doctor's certificate justified the magistrate in pronouncing an absolute decision. Even in the event of valid objections to the Deadhouse as a last resting-place on the way to the grave, the doctor in attendance on the deceased person was subjected to certain restrictions in issuing his certificate. He was allowed to certify the death informally, for the purpose of facilitating the funeral arrangements. But he was absolutely forbidden to give his written authority for the burial, before the expiration of three nights from the time of the death; and he was further bound to certify that the signs of decomposition had actually begun to show themselves. Have these multiplied precautions, patiently applied in many German cities, through a long lapse of years, ever yet detected a case in which Death has failed to complete its unintelligible work? Let the answer be found in the cells of the dead. Pass, with the mourners, through the iron gates—hear and see!

On the evening of the third, as the time approached for the arrival of the hearse, the melancholy stillness in the house was only broken by Mr.

Keller's servants, below-stairs. Collecting together in one room, they talked confidentially, in low voices. An instinctive horror of silence, in moments of domestic distress, is, in all civilized nations, one of the marked characteristics of their class.

"In ten minutes," said Joseph, "the men from the cemetery will be here to take her away. It will be no easy matter to carry her downstairs on the couch."

"Why is she not put in her coffin, like other dead people?" the housemaid asked.

"Because the crazy creature she brought with her from London is allowed to have his own way in the house," Joseph answered irritably. "If I had been brought to the door drunk last night, I should have been sent away this morning. If I had been mad enough to screech out, 'She isn't dead; not one of you shall put her in a coffin!'—I should have richly deserved a place in the town asylum, and I should have got my deserts. Nothing of the sort for Master Jack. Mr. Keller only tells him to be quiet, and looks distressed. The doctor takes him away, and speaks to him in another room—and actually comes back converted to Jack's opinion!"

"You don't mean to tell us," exclaimed the cook, "that the doctor said she wasn't dead?"

"Of course not. It was he who first found out that she was dead—I only mean that he let Jack have his own way. He asked me for a foot rule, and he measured the little couch in the bedroom. 'It's no longer than the coffin' (he says); 'and I see no objection to the body being laid on it, till the time comes for the burial.' Those were his own words; and when the nurse objected to it, what do you think he said?—'Hold your tongue! A couch is a pleasanter thing all the world over than a coffin.'"

"Blasphemous!" said the cook—"that's what I call it."

"Ah, well, well!" the housemaid remarked, "couch or coffin, she looks beautiful, poor soul, in her black velvet robe, with the winter flowers in her pretty white hands. Who got the flowers? Madame Fontaine, do you think?"

"Bah! Madame Fontaine, indeed! Little Crazybrains went out (instead of eating the good dinner I cooked for him), and got the flowers. He wouldn't let anybody put them into her hands but himself—at least, so the nurse said. Has anybody seen Madame Housekeeper? Was she downstairs at dinner to-day, Joseph?"

"Not she! You mark my words," said Joseph, "there's some very serious reason for her keeping her room, on pretense of being ill."

"Can you give any guess what it is?"

"You shall judge for yourself," Joseph answered. "Did I tell you what happened yesterday evening, before Jack was brought home by the nurse's brother? I answered a ring at the door-bell—and there was Mr. Fritz in a towering passion, with Miss Minna on his arm looking ready to drop with fatigue. They rang for some wine; and I heard what he said to his father. It seems that Madame Fontaine had gone out walking in the dark and the cold (and her daughter with her), without rhyme or reason. Mr. Fritz met them, and insisted on taking Miss Minna home. Her mother didn't seem to care what he said or did. She went on walking by herself, as hard as she could lay her feet to the ground. And what do you suppose her excuse was? Her nerves were out of order! Mr. Fritz's notion is that there is something weighing on her mind. An hour afterwards she came back to the house—and I found reason to agree with Mr. Fritz."

"Tell us all about it, Joseph! What did she do?"

"You shall hear. It happened, just after I had seen crazy Jack safe in his bed. When I heard the bell, I was on my way downstairs, with a certain bottle in my hand. One of you saw the nurse's brother give it to me, I think? How he and Crazybrains came into possession of it, mind you, is more than I know."

"It looked just like the big medicine-bottle that cured Mr. Keller," said the cook.

"It was the bottle; and, what is more, it smelt of wine, instead of medicine, and it was empty. Well, I opened the door to Madame Housekeeper, with the bottle in my hand. The instant she set eyes on it, she snatched it away from me. She looked—I give you my word of honor, she looked as if she could have cut my throat. "You wretch!"—nice language to use to a respectable servant, eh?—"You wretch" (she says), "how did you come by this?" I made her a low bow. I said, "Civility costs nothing, ma'am; and sometimes buys a great deal" (severe, eh?). I told her exactly what had happened, and exactly what Schwartz had said. And then I ended with another hard hit. "The next time anything of yours is put into my hands," I said, "I shall leave it to take care of itself." I don't know whether she heard me; she was holding the bottle up to the light. When she saw it was empty—well! I can't tell you, of course, what was passing in her mind. But this I can swear; she shivered and shuddered as if she had got a fit of the ague; and pale as she was when I let her into the house, I do assure you she turned paler still. I thought I should have to take her upstairs next. My good creatures, she's made of iron! Upstairs she went. I followed her as far as the first landing, and saw Mr. Keller waiting—to tell her the news of Mrs. Wagner's death, I suppose. What passed between them I can't say. Mr. Fritz tells me she has never left her room since; and his father has not even sent a message to know how she is. What do you think of that?"

"I think Mr. Fritz was mistaken, when he told you she had never left her room," said the housemaid. "I am next to certain I heard her whispering, early this morning, with crazy Jack. Do you think she will follow the hearse to the Deadhouse, with Mr. Keller and the doctor?"

"Hush!" said Joseph. As he spoke, the heavy wheels of the hearse were heard in the street. He led the way to the top of the kitchen stairs. "Wait here," he whispered, "while I answer the door—and you will see."

Upstairs, in the drawing-room, Fritz and Minna were alone. Madame Fontaine's door, closed to everyone, was a closed door even to her daughter.

Fritz had refused to let Minna ask a second time to be let in. "It will soon be your husband's privilege, my darling, to take care of you and comfort you," he said. "At this dreadful time, there must be no separation between you and me."

His arm was round her; her head rested on his shoulder. She looked up at him timidly.

"Are you not going with them to the cemetery?" she asked.

"I am going to stay with you, Minna."

"You were angry yesterday, Fritz, when you met me with my mother. Don't think the worse of her, because she is ill and troubled in her mind. You will make allowances for her as I do—won't you?"

"My sweet girl, there is nothing I won't do to please you! Kiss me, Minna. Again! again!"

On the higher floor of the house, Mr. Keller and the doctor were waiting in the chamber of death.

Jack kept his silent watch by the side of the couch, on which the one human creature who had befriended him lay hushed in the last earthly repose. Still, from time to time, he whispered to himself the sad senseless words, "No, no, no—not dead, Mistress! Not dead yet!"

There was a soft knock at the door. The doctor opened it. Madame Fontaine stood before him. She spoke in dull monotonous tones—standing in the doorway; refusing, when she was invited by a gesture, to enter the room.

"The hearse has stopped at the door," she said. "The men wish to ask you if they can come in."

It was Joseph's duty to make this announcement. Her motive for forestalling him showed itself dimly in her eyes. They were not on Mr. Keller; not on the doctor; not on the couch. From the moment when the door had been opened to her, she fixed her steady look on Jack. It never moved until the bearers of the dead hid him from her when they entered the room.

The procession passed out. Jack, at Mr. Keller's command, followed last. Standing back at the doorway, Madame Fontaine caught him by the arm as he came out.

"You were half asleep this morning," she whispered. "You are not half asleep now. How did you get the blue-glass bottle? I insist on knowing."

256

"I won't tell you!"

Madame Fontaine altered her tone.

"Will you tell me who emptied the bottle? I have always been kind to you—it isn't much to ask. Who emptied it?"

His variable temper changed; he lifted his head proudly. Absolutely sure of his mistress's recovery, he now claimed the merit that was his due.

"I emptied it!"

"How did you empty it?" she asked faintly. "Did you throw away what was in it? Did you give it to anybody?"

He seized her in his turn—and dragged her to the railing of the corridor. "Look there!" he cried, pointing to the bearers, slowly carrying their burden down the stairs. "Do you see her, resting on her little sofa till she recovers? I gave it to her!"

He left her, and descended the stairs. She staggered back against the wall of the corridor. Her sight seemed to be affected. She groped for the stair-rail, and held by it. The air was wafted up through the open street-door. It helped her to rally her energies. She went down steadily, step by step, to the first landing—paused, and went down again. Arrived in the hall, she advanced to Mr. Keller, and spoke to him.

"Are you going to see the body laid in the Deadhouse?"

"Yes."

"Is there any objection to my seeing it too?"

"The authorities have no objection to admitting friends of the deceased person," Mr. Keller answered. He looked at her searchingly, and added, "Do you go as a friend?"

It was rashly said; and he knew it. The magistrates had decided that the first inquiries should be conducted with the greatest secrecy. For that day, at least, the inmates of the house were to enjoy their usual liberty of action (under private superintendence), so that no suspicion might be excited in the mind of the guilty person. Conscious of having trifled with the serious necessity of keeping a guard over his tongue, Mr. Keller waited anxiously for Madame Fontaine's reply.

Not a word fell from her lips. There was a slight hardening of her face, and no more. In ominous silence, she turned about and ascended the stairs again.

CHAPTER XVII

The departure from the house was interrupted by an unforeseen cause of delay.

Jack refused to follow the hearse with Doctor Dormann and Mr. Keller. "I won't lose sight of her!" he cried—"no! not for a moment! Of all living creatures, I must be the first to see her when she wakes."

Mr. Keller turned to the doctor. "What does he mean?"

The doctor, standing back in the shadow of the house, seemed to have some reason for not answering otherwise than by gesture. He touched his forehead significantly; and, stepping out into the road, took Jack by the hand. The canopy of the hearse, closed at the sides, was open at either end. From the driver's seat, the couch became easily visible on looking round. With inexhaustible patience the doctor quieted the rising excitement in Jack, and gained him permission to take his place by the driver's side. Always grateful for kindness, he thanked Doctor Dormann, with the tears falling fast over his cheeks. "I'm not crying for her," said the poor little man; "she will soon be herself again. But it's so dreadful, sir, to go out driving with her in such a carriage as this!"

The hearse moved away.

Doctor Dormann, walking with Mr. Keller, felt his arm touched, and, looking round, saw the dimly-outlined figure of a woman beckoning to him. He drew back, after a word of apology to his companion, who continued to follow the hearse. The woman met him half way. He recognized Madame Fontaine.

258

"You are a learned man," she began abruptly. "Do you understand writing in cipher?"

"Sometimes."

"If you have half an hour to spare this evening, look at that—and do me the favor of telling me what it means."

She offered something to him, which appeared in the dim light to be only a sheet of paper. He hesitated to take it from her. She tried to press it on him.

"I found it among my husband's papers," she said. "He was a great chemist, as you know. It might be interesting to you."

He still hesitated.

"Are you acquainted with chemical science?" he asked.

"I am perfectly ignorant of chemical science."

"Then what interest can you have in interpreting the cipher?"

"I have a very serious interest. There may be something dangerous in it, if it fell into unscrupulous hands. I want to know if I ought to destroy it."

He suddenly took the paper from her. It felt stiff, like a sheet of cartridge-paper.

"You shall hear," he said. "In case of necessity, I will destroy it myself. Anything more?"

"One thing more. Does Jack go to the cemetery with you and Mr. Keller?"

"Yes."

Walking away rapidly to overtake Mr. Keller, he looked behind him once or twice. The street was dimly lit, in those days, by a few oil lamps. He might be mistaken—but he thought that Madame Fontaine was following him.

On leaving the city, the lanterns were lit to guide the hearse along the road that led to the cemetery. The overseer met the bearers at the gates.

They passed, under a Doric portico, into a central hall. At its right-hand extremity, an open door revealed a room for the accommodation of mourners. Beyond this there was a courtyard; and, farther still, the range of apartments devoted to the residence of the cemetery-overseer. Turning from the right-hand division of the building, the bearers led the way to the opposite extremity of the hall; passed through a second room for mourners; crossed a second courtyard beyond it; and, turning into a narrow passage, knocked at a closed door.

The door was opened by a watchman. He admitted them into a long room, situated between the courtyard at one end, and the cemetery at the other, and having ten side recesses which opened out of it. The long room was the Watchman's Chamber. The recesses were the cells which held the dead.

The couch was set down in the Watchman's Chamber. It was a novelty in the Deadhouse; and the overseer asked for an explanation. Doctor Dormann informed him that the change had been made, with his full approval, to satisfy a surviving friend, and that the coffin would be provided before the certificate was granted for the burial.

While the persons present were all gathered round the doctor and the overseer, Madame Fontaine softly pushed open the door from the courtyard. After a look at the recesses—situated, five on either side of the length of the room, and closed by black curtains—she parted the curtains of the nearest recess to her, on her left hand; and stepped in without being noticed by anyone.

"You take the responsibility of the couch, doctor, if the authorities raise any objection?" said the overseer.

This condition being complied with, he addressed himself to the watchman. "The cells are all empty to-night, Duntzer, are they not?"

"Yes, sir."

"Are you off duty, early or late this evening?"

"I am off duty in half an hour, sir."

The overseer pointed to the couch. "You can attend to this," he said. "Take the cell that is the nearest to you, where the watchman's chair is placed—Number Five."

He referred to the fifth recess, at the upper end of the room on the right, counting from the courtyard door. The watchman looped up the black curtains, while the bearers placed the couch in the cell. This done, the bearers were dismissed.

Doctor Dormann pointed through the parted curtains to the lofty cell, ventilated from the top, and warmed (like the Watchman's Chamber) by an apparatus under the flooring. In the middle of the cell was a stand, placed there to support the coffin. Above the stand a horizontal bar projected, which was fixed over the doorway. It was furnished with a pulley, through which passed a long thin string hanging loosely downward at one end, and attached at the other to a small alarm-bell, placed over the door on the outer side— that is to say, on the side of the Watchman's Chamber.

"All the cells are equal in size," said the doctor to Mr. Keller, "and are equally clean, and well warmed. The hot bath, in another room, is always ready; and a cabinet, filled with restorative applications, is close by. Now look at the watchman, and mark the care that is taken—in the event, for instance, of a cataleptic trance, and of a revival following it."

Duntzer led the way into the cell. He took the loose end of the string, hanging from above, and attached to it two shorter and lighter strings, each of which terminated in five loose ends.

From these ten ends hung ten little thimble-shaped objects, made of brass.

First slightly altering the position of the couch on the stand, Duntzer lifted the dead hands—fitted the ten brass thimbles to the fingers and the thumbs—and gently laid the hands back on the breast of the corpse. When he had looked up, and had satisfied himself of the exact connection between the hands and the line communicating with the alarm-bell outside, his duty was done. He left the cell; and, seating himself in his chair, waited the arrival of the night-watchman who was to relieve him.

Mr. Keller came out into the chamber, and spoke to the overseer.

"Is all done now?"

"All is done."

"I should like, while I am here, to speak to you about the grave."

The overseer bowed. "You can see the plan of the cemetery," he said, "in my office on the other side of the building."

Mr. Keller looked back into the cell. Jack had taken his place in it, when the couch had been carried in; and Doctor Dormann was quietly observing him. Mr. Keller beckoned to Jack. "I am waiting for you," he said. "Come!"

"And leave Mistress?" Jack answered. "Never!"

Mr. Keller was on the point of stepping into the cell, when Doctor Dormann took his arm, and led him away out of hearing.

"I want to ask you a question," said the doctor. "Was that poor creature's madness violent madness, when Mrs. Wagner took him out of the London asylum?"

"I have heard her say so."

"Be careful what you do with him. Mrs. Wagner's death has tried his weak brain seriously. I am afraid of a relapse into that violent madness—leave him to me."

Mr. Keller left the room with the overseer. Doctor Dormann returned to the cell.

"Listen to me, Jack," he said. "If your mistress revives (as you think), I want you to see for yourself how she will tell it to the man who is on the watch." He turned, and spoke to Duntzer. "Is the alarm-bell set?"

"Yes, sir."

The doctor addressed himself once more to Jack.

"Now look, and listen!" he said.

He delicately touched one of the brass thimbles, fitted to the fingers of the corpse. The bell rang instantly in the Watchman's Chamber.

"The moment the man hears that," he resumed, "he will make the signal, which calls the overseer and the nurses to help your mistress back to life. At the same time, a messenger will be sent to Mr. Keller's house to tell you what has happened. You see how well she is taken care of—and you will behave sensibly, I am sure? I am going away. Come with me."

Jack answered as he had answered Mr. Keller.

"Never!" he said.

He flung himself on the floor, and clasped his arms round one of the pillars supporting the stand on which the couch was placed. "Tear my arms out of their sockets," he cried—"you won't get me away till you've done that!"

Before the doctor could answer, footsteps were heard in the Watchman's Chamber. A jolly voice asked a question. "Any report for the night, Duntzer?"

Jack seemed to recognize the voice. He looked round eagerly.

"A corpse in Number Five," Duntzer answered. "And strangers in the cell. Contrary to the order for the night, as you know. I have reported them; it's your duty to send them away. Good night."

A red-nosed old man looked in at the doorway of the cell. Jack started to his feet. "Here's Schwartz!" he cried—"leave me with Schwartz!"

CHAPTER XVIII

The discovery of Jack agreeably surprised Schwartz, without in the least perplexing him.

His little friend (as he reasoned) had, no doubt, remembered the invitation to the Deadhouse, and had obtained admission through the interference of the strange gentleman who was with him. But who was the gentleman? The deputy night-watchman (though he might carry messages for his relative the nurse) was not personally acquainted with his sister's medical patrons in Frankfort. He looked at the doctor with an expression of considerable doubt.

"I beg your pardon, sir," he ventured to say, "you're not a member of the city council, are you?"

"I have nothing to do with the city council."

"And nothing to do with managing the Deadhouse?"

"Nothing. I am Doctor Dormann."

Schwartz snapped his clumsy fingers, as an appropriate expression of relief. "All right, sir! Leave the little man with me—I'll take care of him."

"Do you know this person?" asked the doctor, turning to Jack.

"Yes! yes! leave me here with him," Jack answered eagerly. "Good-night, sir—good-night!"

Doctor Dormann looked again at Jack's friend.

"I thought strangers were not allowed here at night," he said.

"It's against the rules," Schwartz admitted. "But, Lord love you, sir, think of the dullness of this place! Besides, I'm only a deputy. In three nights more, the regular man will come on duty again. It's an awful job, doctor, watching alone here, all night. One of the men actually went mad, and hanged himself. To be sure he was a poet in his way, which makes it less remarkable. I'm not a poet myself—I'm only a sociable creature. Leave little Jack with me! I'll send him home safe and sound—I feel like a father to him."

The doctor hesitated. What was he to do? Jack had already returned to the cell in which his mistress lay. To remove him by the brutal exercise of main force was a proceeding from which Doctor Dormann's delicacy of feeling naturally recoiled—to say nothing of the danger of provoking that outbreak of madness against which the doctor had himself warned Mr. Keller. Persuasion he had already tried in vain. Delegated authority to control Jack had not been conferred on him. There seemed to be no other course than to yield.

"If you persist in your obstinacy," he said to Jack, "I must return alone to Mr. Keller's house, and tell him that I have left you here with your friend."

Jack was already absorbed in his own thoughts. He only repeated vacantly, "Good-night."

Doctor Dormann left the room. Schwartz looked in at his guest. "Wait there for the present," he said. "The porter will be here directly: I don't want him to see you."

The porter came in after an interval. "All right for the night?" he asked.

"All right," Schwartz answered.

The porter withdrew in silence. The night-watchman's reply was his authority for closing the gates of the Deadhouse until the next morning.

Schwartz returned to Jack—still watching patiently by the side of the couch. "Was she a relation of yours?" he asked.

"All the relations in the world to me!" Jack burst out passionately. "Father and mother—and brother and sister and wife."

"Aye, aye? Five relations in one is what I call an economical family," said Schwartz. "Come out here, to the table. You stood treat last time—my turn now. I've got the wine handy. Yes, yes—she was a fine woman in her time, I dare say. Why haven't you put her into a coffin like other people?"

"Why?" Jack repeated indignantly. "I couldn't prevent them from bringing her here; but I could have burnt the house down over their heads, if they had dared to put her into a coffin! Are you stupid enough to suppose that Mistress is dead? Don't you know that I'm watching and waiting here till she wakes? Ah! I beg your pardon—you don't know. The rest of them would have let her die. I saved her life. Come here, and I'll tell you how."

He dragged Schwartz into the cell. As the watchman disappeared from view, the wild white face of Madame Fontaine appeared between the

265

curtains of her hiding-place, listening to Jack's narrative of the opening of the cupboard, and the discovery that had followed.

Schwartz humored his little friend (evidently, as he now concluded, his crazy little friend), by listening in respectful silence. Instead of making any remark at the end, he mentioned once more that the wine was handy. "Come!" he reiterated; "come to the table!"

Madame Fontaine drew back again behind the curtains. Jack remained obstinately in the cell. "I mean to see it," he said, "the moment she moves."

"Do you think your eyes will tell you?" Schwartz remonstrated. "You look dead-beat already; your eyes will get tired. Trust the bell here, over the door. Brass and steel don't get tired; brass and steel don't fall asleep; brass and steel will ring, and call you to her. Take a rest and a drink."

These words reminded Jack of the doctor's experiment with the alarm-bell. He could not disguise from himself the stealthily-growing sense of fatigue in his head and his limbs. "I'm afraid you're right," he said sadly. "I wish I was a stronger man." He joined Schwartz at the table, and dropped wearily into the watchman's chair.

His head sank on his breast, his eyes closed. He started up again. "She may want help when she wakes!" he cried, with a look of terror. "What must we do? Can we carry her home between us? Oh! Schwartz, I was so confident in myself a little while since—and it seems all to have left me now!"

"Don't worry that weary little head of yours about nothing," Schwartz answered, with rough good-nature. "Come along with me, and I'll show you where help's to be got when help's wanted. No! no! you won't be out of hearing of the bell—if it rings. We'll leave the door open. It's only on the other side of the passage here."

He lighted a lantern, and led Jack out.

Leaving the courtyard and the waiting-room on their left hand, he advanced along the right-hand side of the passage, and opened the door of a bed-chamber, always kept ready for use. A second door in the bed-chamber led to a bath-room. Here, opposite the bath, stood the cabinet in which the restorative applications were kept, under the care of the overseer.

When the two men had gone out, Madame Fontaine ventured into the Watchman's Chamber. Her eyes turned towards the one terrible cell, at the farther end of the row of black curtains. She advanced towards it; and stopped, lifting her hands to her head in the desperate effort to compose herself.

The terror of impending discovery had never left her, since Jack had owned the use to which he had put the contents of the blue-glass bottle.

Animated by that all-mastering dread, she had thrown away every poison in the medicine-chest—had broken the bottles into fragments—and had taken those fragments out with her, when she left the house to follow Doctor Dormann. On the way to the cemetery, she had scattered the morsels of broken glass and torn paper on the dark road outside the city gate. Nothing now remained but the empty medicine-chest, and the writing in cipher, once rolled round the poison called the "Looking-Glass Drops."

Under these altered circumstances, she had risked asking Doctor Dormann to interpret the mysterious characters, on the bare chance of their containing some warning by which she might profit, in her present ignorance of the results which Jack's ignorant interference might produce.

Acting under the same vague terror of that possible revival, to which Jack looked forward with such certain hope, she had followed him to the Deadhouse, and had waited, hidden in the cells, to hear what dangerous confidences he might repose in the doctor or in Mr. Keller, and to combat on the spot the suspicion which he might ignorantly rouse in their minds. Still in the same agony of doubt, she now stood, with her eyes on the cell, trying to summon the resolution to judge for herself. One look at the dead woman, while the solitude in the room gave her the chance—one look might assure her of the livid pallor of death, or warn her of the terrible possibilities of awakening life. She hurried headlong over the intervening space, and looked in.

There, grand and still, lay her murderous work! There, ghostly white on the ground of the black robe, were the rigid hands, topped by the hideous machinery which was to betray them, if they trembled under the mysterious return of life!

In the instant when she saw it, the sight overwhelmed her with horror. She turned distractedly, and fled through the open door. She crossed the courtyard, like a deeper shadow creeping swiftly through the darkness of the winter night. On the threshold of the solitary waiting-room, exhausted nature claimed its rest. She wavered—groped with her hands at the empty air—and sank insensible on the floor.

In the meantime, Schwartz revealed the purpose of his visit to the bath-room.

The glass doors which protected the upper division of the cabinet were locked; the key being in the possession of the overseer. The cupboard in the lower division, containing towels and flannel wrappers, was left unsecured. Opening the door, the watchman drew out a bottle and an old traveling flask, concealed behind the bath-linen. "I call this my cellar," he explained. "Cheer up, Jacky; we'll have a jolly night of it yet."

"I don't want to see your cellar!" said Jack impatiently. "I want to be of use to Mistress—show me the place where we call for help."

"Call?" repeated Schwartz, with a roar of laughter. "Do you think they can hear us at the overseer's, through a courtyard, and a waiting-room, and a grand hall, and another courtyard, and another waiting-room beyond? Not if we were twenty men all bawling together till we were hoarse! I'll show you how we can make the master hear us—if that miraculous revival of yours happens," he added facetiously in a whisper to himself.

He led the way back into the passage, and held up his lantern so as to show the cornice. A row of fire-buckets was suspended there by books. Midway between them, a stout rope hung through a metal-lined hole in the roof.

"Do you see that?" said Schwartz. "You have only to pull, and there's an iron tongue in the belfry above that will speak loud enough to be heard at the city gate. The overseer will come tumbling in, with his bunch of keys, as if the devil was at his heels, and the two women-servants after him—old and ugly, Jack!—they attend to the bath, you know, when a woman wants it. Wait a bit! Take the light into the bedroom, and get a chair for yourself—we haven't much accommodation for evening visitors. Got it? that's right. Would you like to see where the mad watchman hung himself? On the last hook at the end of the row there. We've got a song he made about the Deadhouse. I think it's in the drawer of the table. A gentleman had it printed and sold, for the benefit of the widow and children. Wait till we are well warmed with our liquor, and I'll tell you what I'll do—I'll sing you the mad watchman's song; and Jacky, my man, you shall sing the chorus! Tow-row-rub-a-dub-boom—that's the tune. Pretty, isn't it? Come along back to our snuggery." He led the way to the Watchman's Chamber.

CHAPTER XIX

Jack looked eagerly into the cell again. There was no change—not a sign of that happy waking in which he so firmly believed.

Schwartz opened the drawer of the table. Tobacco and pipes; two or three small drinking-glasses; a dirty pack of playing-cards; the mad watchman's song, with a woodcut illustration of the suicide—all lay huddled together. He took from the drawer the song, and two of the drinking-glasses, and called to his little guest to come out of the cell.

"There;" he said, filling the glasses, "you never tasted such wine as that in all your life. Off with it!"

Jack turned away with a look of disgust. "What did you say of wine, when I drank with you the other night?" he asked reproachfully. "You said it would warm my heart, and make a man of me. And what did it do? I couldn't stand on my legs. I couldn't hold up my head—I was so sleepy and stupid that Joseph had to take me upstairs to bed. I hate your wine! Your wine's a liar, who promises and doesn't perform! I'm weary enough, and wretched enough in my mind, as it is. No more wine for me!"

"Wrong!" remarked Schwartz, emptying his glass, and smacking his lips after it.

"You made a serious mistake the other night—you didn't drink half enough. Give the good liquor a fair chance, my son. No, you won't? Must I try a little gentle persuasion before you will come back to your chair?" Suiting the action to the word, he put his arm round Jack. "What's this I feel under my hand?" he asked. "A bottle?" He took it out of Jack's breast-pocket. "Lord help us!" he exclaimed; "it looks like physic!"

Jack snatched it away from him, with a cry of delight. "The very thing for me—and I never thought of it!"

It was the phial which Madame Fontaine had repentantly kept to herself, after having expressly filled it for him with the fatal dose of "Alexander's Wine"—the phial which he had found, when he first opened the "Pink-Room Cupboard." In the astonishment and delight of finding the blue-glass bottle immediately afterwards, he had entirely forgotten it. Nothing had since happened to remind him that it was in his pocket, until Schwartz had stumbled on the discovery.

"It cures you when you are tired or troubled in your mind," Jack announced in his grandest manner, repeating Madame Fontaine's own words. "Is there any water here?"

"Not a drop, thank Heaven!" said Schwartz, devoutly.

"Give me my glass, then. I once tried the remedy by itself, and it stung me as it went down. The wine won't hurt me, with this splendid stuff in it. I'll take it in the wine."

"Who told you to take it?" Schwartz asked, holding back the glass.

"Mrs. Housekeeper told me."

"A woman!" growled Schwartz, in a tone of sovereign contempt. "How dare you let a woman physic you, when you've got me for a doctor? Jack! I'm ashamed of you."

Jack defended his manhood. "Oh, I don't care what she says! I despise her—she's mad. You don't suppose she made this? I wouldn't touch it, if she had. No, no; her husband made it—a wonderful man! the greatest man in

270

Germany!"

He reached across the table and secured his glass of wine. Before it was possible to interfere, he had emptied the contents of the phial into it, and had raised it to his lips. At that moment, Schwartz's restraining hand found its way to his wrist. The deputy watchman had far too sincere a regard for good wine to permit it to be drunk, in combination with physic, at his own table.

"Put it down!" he said gruffly. "You're my visitor, ain't you? Do you think I'm going to let housekeeper's cat-lap be drunk at my table? Look here!"

He held up his traveling-flask, with the metal drinking-cup taken off, so as to show the liquor through the glass. The rich amber color of it fascinated Jack. He put his wine-glass back on the table. "What is it?" he asked eagerly.

"Drinkable gold, Jack! My physic. Brandy!"

He poured out a dram into the metal cup. "Try that," he said, "and don't let me hear any more about the housekeeper's physic."

Jack tasted it. The water came into his eyes—he put his hands on his throat. "Fire!" he gasped faintly.

"Wait!" said Schwartz.

Jack waited. The fiery grip of the brandy relaxed; the genial warmth of it was wafted through him persuasively from head to foot. He took another sip. His eyes began to glitter. "What divine being made this?" he asked. Without waiting to be answered, he tried it again, and emptied the cup. "More!" he cried. "I never felt so big, I never felt so strong, I never felt so clever, as I feel now!"

Schwartz, drinking freely from his own bottle, recovered, and more than recovered, his Bacchanalian good humor. He clapped Jack on the shoulder. "Who's the right doctor now?" he asked cheerfully. "A drab of a housekeeper? or Father Schwartz? Your health, my jolly boy! When the bottle's empty, I'll help you to finish the flask. Drink away! and the devil take all heel-taps!"

The next dose of brandy fired Jack's excitable brain with a new idea.

271

He fell on his knees at the table, and clasped his hands in a sudden fervor of devotion. "Silence!" he commanded sternly. "Your wine's only a poor devil. Your drinkable gold is a god. Take your cap off, Schwartz—I'm worshipping drinkable gold!"

Schwartz, highly diverted, threw his cap up to the ceiling. "Drinkable gold, ora pro nobis!" he shouted, profanely adapting himself to Jack's humor. "You shall be Pope, my boy—and I'll be the Pope's butler. Allow me to help your sacred majesty back to your chair."

Jack's answer betrayed another change in him. His tones were lofty; his manner was distant. "I prefer the floor," he said; "hand me down my mug." As he reached up to take it, the alarm-bell over the door caught his eye. Debased as he was by the fiery strength of the drink, his ineradicable love for his mistress made its noble influence felt through the coarse fumes that were mounting to his brain. "Stop!" he cried. "I must be where I can see the bell—I must be ready for her, the instant it rings."

He crawled across the floor, and seated himself with his back against the wall of one of the empty cells, on the left-hand side of the room. Schwartz, shaking his fat sides with laughter, handed down the cup to his guest. Jack took no notice of it. His eyes, reddened already by the brandy, were fixed on the bell opposite to him. "I want to know about it," he said. "What's that steel thing there, under the brass cover?"

"What's the use of asking?" Schwartz replied, returning to his bottle.

"I want to know!"

"Patience, Jack—patience. Follow my fore-finger. My hand seems to shake a little; but it's as honest a hand as ever was. That steel thing there, is the bell hammer, you know. And, bless your heart, the hammer's everything. Cost, Lord knows how much. Another toast, my son. Good luck to the bell!"

Jack changed again; he began to cry. "She's sleeping too long on that sofa, in there," he said sadly. "I want her to speak to me; I want to hear her scold me for drinking in this horrid place. My heart's all cold again. Where's the mug?" He found it, as he spoke; the fire of the brandy went down his throat

272

once more, and lashed him into frantic high spirits. "I'm up in the clouds!" he shouted; "I'm riding on a whirlwind. Sing, Schwartz! Ha! there are the stars twinkling through the skylight! Sing the stars down from heaven!"

Schwartz emptied his bottle, without the ceremony of using the glass. "Now we are primed!" he said—"now for the mad watchman's song!" He snatched up the paper from the table, and roared out hoarsely the first verse:

> The moon was shining, cold and bright,
>
> In the Frankfort Deadhouse, on New Year's night
>
> And I was the watchman, left alone,
>
> While the rest to feast and dance were gone;
>
> I envied their lot, and cursed my own—
>
> Poor me!

"Chorus, Jack! 'I envied their lot and cursed my own'——"

The last words of the verse were lost in a yell of drunken terror. Schwartz started out of his chair, and pointed, panic-stricken, to the lower end of the room. "A ghost!" he screamed. "A ghost in black, at the door!"

Jack looked round, and burst out laughing. "Sit down again, you old fool," he said. "It's only Mrs. Housekeeper. We are singing, Mrs. Housekeeper! You haven't heard my voice yet—I'm the finest singer in Germany."

Madame Fontaine approached him humbly. "You have a kind heart, Jack—I am sure you will help me," she said. "Show me how to get out of this frightful place."

"The devil take you!" growled Schwartz, recovering himself. "How did you get in?"

"She's a witch!" shouted Jack. "She rode in on a broomstick—she crept in through the keyhole. Where's the fire? Let's take her downstairs, and burn her!"

Schwartz applied himself to the brandy-flask, and began to laugh again.

"There never was such good company as Jack," he said, in his oiliest tones. "You can't get out to-night, Mrs. Witch. The gates are locked—and they don't trust me with the key. Walk in, ma'am. Plenty of accommodation for you, on that side of the room where Jack sits. We are slack of guests for the grave, to-night. Walk in."

She renewed her entreaties. "I'll give you all the money I have about me! Who can I go to for the key? Jack! Jack! speak for me!"

"Go on with the song!" cried Jack.

She appealed again in her despair to Schwartz. "Oh, sir, have mercy on me! I fainted, out there—and, when I came to myself, I tried to open the gates—and I called, and called, and nobody heard me."

Schwartz's sense of humor was tickled by this. "If you could bellow like a bull," he said, "nobody would hear you. Take a seat, ma'am."

"Go on with the song!" Jack reiterated. "I'm tired of waiting."

Madame Fontaine looked wildly from one to the other of them. "Oh, God, I'm locked in with an idiot and a drunkard!" The thought of it maddened her as it crossed her mind. Once more, she fled from the room. Again, and again, in the outer darkness, she shrieked for help.

Schwartz advanced staggering towards the door, with Jack's empty chair in his hand. "Perhaps you'll be able to pipe a little higher, ma'am, if you come back, and sit down? Now for the song, Jack!"

He burst out with the second verse:

> Backwards and forwards, with silent tread,
>
> I walked on my watch by the doors of the dead.
>
> And I said, It's hard, on this New Year,
>
> While the rest are dancing to leave me here,
>
> Alone with death and cold and fear—
>
> Poor me!

"Chorus, Jack! Chorus, Mrs. Housekeeper! Ho! ho! look at her! She can't resist the music—she has come back to us already. What can we do for you, ma'am? The flask's not quite drained yet. Come and have a drink."

She had returned, recoiling from the outer darkness and silence, giddy with the sickening sense of faintness which was creeping over her again. When Schwartz spoke she advanced with tottering steps. "Water!" she exclaimed, gasping for breath. "I'm faint—water! water!"

"Not a drop in the place, ma'am! Brandy, if you like?"

"I forbid it!" cried Jack, with a peremptory sign of the hand. "Drinkable gold is for us—not for her!"

The glass of wine which Schwartz had prevented him from drinking caught his notice. To give Madame Fontaine her own "remedy," stolen from her own room, was just the sort of trick to please Jack in his present humor. He pointed to the glass, and winked at the watchman. After a momentary hesitation, Schwartz's muddled brain absorbed the new idea. "Here's a drop of wine left, ma'am," he said. "Suppose you try it?"

She leaned one hand on the table to support herself. Her heart sank lower and lower; a cold perspiration bedewed her face. "Quick! quick!" she murmured faintly. She seized the glass, and emptied it eagerly to the last drop.

Schwartz and Jack eyed her with malicious curiosity. The idea of getting away was still in her mind. "I think I can walk now," she said. "For God's sake, let me out!"

"Haven't I told you already? I can't get out myself."

At that brutal answer, she shrank back. Slowly and feebly she made her way to the chair, and dropped on it.

"Cheer up, ma'am!" said Schwartz. "You shall have more music to help you—you shall hear how the mad watchman lost his wits. Another drop of the drinkable gold, Jack. A dram for you and a dram for me—and here goes!" He roared out the last verses of the song:—

Any company's better than none, I said:

If I can't have the living, I'd like the dead.

In one terrific moment more,

The corpse-bell rang at each cell door,

The moonlight shivered on the floor—

Poor me!

The curtains gaped; there stood a ghost,

On every threshold, as white as frost,

You called us, they shrieked, and we gathered soon;

Dance with your guests by the New Year's moon!

I danced till I dropped in a deadly swoon—

Poor me!

And since that night I've lost my wits,

And I shake with ceaseless ague-fits:

For the ghosts they turned me cold as stone,

On that New Year's night when the white moon shone,

And I walked on my watch, all, all alone—

Poor me!

And, oh, when I lie in my coffin-bed,

Heap thick the earth above my head!

Or I shall come back, and dance once more,

With frantic feet on the Deadhouse floor,

And a ghost for a partner at every door—

Poor me!

The night had cleared. While Schwartz was singing, the moon shone in at the skylight. At the last verse of the song, a ray of the cold yellow light streamed across Jack's face. The fire of the brandy leapt into flame—the madness broke out in him, with a burst of its by-gone fury. He sprang, screaming, to his feet.

"The moon!" he shouted—"the mad watchman's moon! The mad watchman himself is coming back. There he is, sliding down on the slanting light! Do you see the brown earth of the grave dropping from him, and the rope round his neck? Ha! how he skips, and twists, and twirls! He's dancing again with the dead ones. Make way there! I mean to dance with them too. Come on, mad watchman—come on! I'm as mad as you are!"

He whirled round and round with the fancied ghost for a partner in the dance. The coarse laughter of Schwartz burst out again at the terrible sight. He called, with drunken triumph, to Madame Fontaine. "Look at Jacky, ma'am. There's a dancer for you! There's good company for a dull winter night!" She neither looked nor moved—she sat crouched on the chair, spellbound with terror. Jack threw up his arms, turned giddily once or twice, and sank exhausted on the floor. "The cold of him creeps up my hands," he said, still possessed by the vision of the watchman. "He cools my eyes, he calms my heart, he stuns my head. I'm dying, dying, dying—going back with him to the grave. Poor me! poor me!"

He lay hushed in a strange repose; his eyes wide open, staring up at the moon. Schwartz drained the last drop of brandy out of the flask. "Jack's name ought to be Solomon," he pronounced with drowsy solemnity; "Solomon was wise; and Jack's wise. Jack goes to sleep, when the liquor's done. Take away the bottle, before the overseer comes in. If any man says I am not sober, that man lies. The Rhine wine has a way of humming in one's head. That's all, Mr. Overseer—that's all. Do I see the sun rising, up there in the skylight? I wish you good-night; I wish—you—good—night."

He laid his heavy arms on the table; his head dropped on them—he slept.

The time passed. No sound broke the silence but the lumpish snoring of Schwartz. No change appeared in Jack; there he lay, staring up at the moon.

Somewhere in the building (unheard thus far in the uproar) a clock struck the first hour of the morning.

Madame Fontaine started. The sound shook her with a new fear—a fear that expressed itself in a furtive look at the cell in which the dead woman lay. If the corpse-bell rang, would the stroke of it be like the single stroke of the clock?

"Jack!" she whispered. "Do you hear the clock? Oh, Jack, the stillness is dreadful—speak to me."

He slowly raised himself. Perhaps the striking of the clock—perhaps some inner prompting—had roused him. He neither answered Madame Fontaine, nor looked at her. With his arms clasped round his knees, he sat on the floor in the attitude of a savage. His eyes, which had stared at the moon, now stared with the same rigid, glassy look at the alarm-bell over the cell-door.

The time went on. Again the oppression of silence became more than Madame Fontaine could endure. Again she tried to make Jack speak to her.

"What are you looking at?" she asked. "What are you waiting for? Is it——?" The rest of the sentence died away on her lips: the words that would finish it were words too terrible to be spoken.

The sound of her voice produced no visible impression on Jack. Had it influenced him, in some unseen way? Something did certainly disturb the strange torpor that held him. He spoke. The tones were slow and mechanical—the tones of a man searching his memory with pain and difficulty; repeating his recollections, one by one, as he recovered them, to himself.

"When she moves," he muttered, "her hands pull the string. Her hands send a message up: up and up to the bell." He paused, and pointed to the cell-door.

The action had a horrible suggestiveness to the guilty wretch who was watching him.

"Don't do that!" she cried. "Don't point there!"

His hand never moved; he pursued his newly-found recollections of what the doctor had shown to him.

"Up and up to the bell," he repeated. "And the bell feels it. The steel thing moves. The bell speaks. Good bell! Faithful bell!"

The clock struck the half-hour past one. Madame Fontaine shrieked at the sound—her senses knew no distinction between the clock and the bell.

She saw his pointing hand drop back, and clasp itself with the other hand, round his knees. He spoke—softly and tenderly now—he was speaking to the dead. "Rise Mistress, rise! Dear soul, the time is long; and poor Jack is waiting for you!"

She thought the closed curtains moved: the delusion was reality to her. She tried to rouse Schwartz.

"Watchman! watchman! Wake up!"

He slept on as heavily as ever.

She half rose from her chair. She was almost on her feet—when she sank back again. Jack had moved. He got up on his knees. "Mistress hears me!" he said. The light of vivid expression showed itself in his eyes. Their vacancy was gone: they looked longingly at the door of the cell. He got on his feet—he pressed both hands over his bosom. "Come!" he said. "Oh, Mistress, come!"

There was a sound—a faint premonitory rustling sound—over the door.

The steel hammer moved—rose—struck the metal globe. The bell rang.

He stood rooted to the floor, sobbing hysterically. The iron grasp of suspense held him.

Not a cry, not a movement escaped Madame Fontaine. The life seemed to have been struck out of her by the stroke of the bell. It woke Schwartz. Except that he looked up, he too never moved: he too was like a living creature turned to stone.

A minute passed.

The curtains swayed gently. Tremulous fingers crept out, parting them. Slowly, over the black surface of the curtain, a fair naked arm showed itself, widening the gap.

The figure appeared, in its velvet pall. On the pale face the stillness of repose was barely ruffled yet. The eyes alone were conscious of returning life. They looked out on the room, softly surprised and perplexed—no more. They looked downwards: the lips trembled sweetly into a smile. She saw Jack, kneeling in ecstasy at her feet.

And now again, there was stillness in the room. Unutterable happiness rejoiced, unutterable dread suffered, in the same silence.

The first sound heard came suddenly from the lonely outer hall. Hurrying footsteps swept over the courtyard. The flash of lights flew along the dark passage. Voices of men and women, mingled together, poured into the Watchman's Chamber.

POSTSCRIPT

MR. DAVID GLENNEY RETURNS TO FRANKFORT, AND CLOSES THE STORY

I

On the twelfth of December, I received a letter from Mrs. Wagner, informing me that the marriage of Fritz and Minna had been deferred until the thirteenth of January. Shortly afterwards I left London, on my way to Frankfort.

My departure was hurried, to afford me time to transact business with some of our correspondents in France and in Northern Germany. Our head-clerk, Mr. Hartrey (directing the London house in Mrs. Wagner's absence), had his own old-fashioned notions of doing nothing in a hurry. He insisted on allowing me a far larger margin of time, for treating with our correspondents, than I was likely to require. The good man little suspected to what motive my ready submission to him was due. I was eager to see my aunt and the charming Minna once more. Without neglecting any of my duties (and with the occasional sacrifice of traveling by night), I contrived to reach Frankfort a week before I was expected—that is to say, in the forenoon of the fourth of January.

II

Joseph's face, when he opened the door, at once informed me that something extraordinary was going on in the house.

"Anything wrong?" I asked.

Joseph looked at me in a state of bewilderment. "You had better speak to the doctor," he said.

"The doctor! Who is ill? My aunt? Mr. Keller? Who is it?" In my impatience, I took him by the collar of his coat, and shook him. I shook out nothing but the former answer, a little abridged:—

"Speak to the doctor."

The office-door was close by me. I asked one of the clerks if Mr. Keller was in his room. The clerk informed me that Mr. Keller was upstairs with the doctor. In the extremity of my suspense, I inquired again if my aunt was ill. The man opened his eyes. "Is it possible you haven't heard?" he said.

"Is she dead or alive?" I burst out, losing all patience.

"Both," answered the clerk.

I began—not unnaturally, I think—to wonder whether I was in Mr. Keller's house, or in an asylum for idiots. Returning to the hall, I collared Joseph for the second time. "Take me up to the doctor instantly!" I said.

Joseph led the way upstairs—not on my aunt's side of the house, to my infinite relief. On the first landing, he made a mysterious communication. "Mr. David, I have given notice to leave," he said. "There are some things that no servant can put up with. While a person lives, I expect a person to live. When a person dies, I expect a person to die. There must be no confusion on such a serious subject as life and death. I blame nobody—I understand nothing—I merely go. Follow me, if you please, sir."

Had he been drinking? He led the way up the next flight of stairs, steadily and quietly. He knocked discreetly at Madame Fontaine's door. "Mr. David Glenney," he announced, "to see Doctor Dormann."

Mr. Keller came out first, closing the door behind him. He embraced me, with a demonstrative affection far from characteristic of him at other times. His face was disturbed; his voice faltered, as he spoke his first words to me.

"Welcome back, David—more welcome than ever!"

"My aunt is well, I hope?"

He clasped his hands fervently. "God is merciful," he said. "Thank God!"

"Is Madame Fontaine ill?"

Before he could answer, the door was opened again. Doctor Dormann

282

came out.

"The very man I want!" he exclaimed. "You could not possibly have arrived at a better time." He turned to Mr. Keller. "Where can I find writing-materials? In the drawing-room? Come down, Mr. Glenney. Come down, Mr. Keller."

In the drawing-room, he wrote a few lines rapidly. "See us sign our names," he said. He handed the pen to Mr. Keller after he had signed himself—and then gave me the paper to read.

To my unspeakable amazement, the writing certified that, "the suspended vital forces in Mrs. Wagner had recovered their action, in the Deadhouse of Frankfort, at half-past one o'clock on the morning of the fourth of January; that he had professionally superintended the restoration to life; and that he thereby relieved the magistrates from any further necessity for pursuing a private inquiry, the motive for which no longer existed." To this statement there was a line added, declaring that Mr. Keller withdrew his application to the magistrates; authenticated by Mr. Keller's signature.

I stood with the paper in my hand, looking from one to the other of them, as completely bewildered as Joseph himself.

"I can't leave Madame Fontaine," said the doctor; "I am professionally interested in watching the case. Otherwise, I would have made my statement in person. Mr. Keller has been terribly shaken, and stands in urgent need of rest and quiet. You will do us both a service if you will take that paper to the town-hall, and declare before the magistrates that you know us personally, and have seen us sign our names. On your return, you shall have every explanation that I can give; and you shall see for yourself that you need feel no uneasiness on the subject of your aunt."

Having arrived at the town-hall, I made the personal statement to which the doctor had referred. Among the questions put to me, I was asked if I had any direct interest in the matter—either as regarded Mrs. Wagner or any other person. Having answered that I was Mrs. Wagner's nephew, I was instructed to declare in writing, that I approved (as Mrs. Wagner's representative) of the doctor's statement and of Mr. Keller's withdrawal of his application.

With this, the formal proceedings terminated, and I was free to return to the house.

III

Joseph had his orders, this time. He spoke like a reasonable being—he said the doctor was waiting for me, in Madame Fontaine's room. The place of the appointment rather surprised me.

The doctor opened the door—but paused before he admitted me.

"I think you were the first person," he said, "who saw Mr. Keller, on the morning when he was taken ill?"

"After the late Mr. Engelman," I answered, "I was the first person."

"Come in, then. I want you to look at Madame Fontaine."

He led me to the bedside. The instant I looked at her, I saw Mr. Keller's illness reproduced, in every symptom. There she lay, in the same apathy; with the same wan look on her face, and the same intermittent trembling of her hands. When I recovered the first shock of the discovery, I was able to notice poor Minna, kneeling at the opposite side of the bed, weeping bitterly. "Oh, my dear one!" she cried, in a passion of grief, "look at me! speak to me!"

The mother opened her eyes for a moment—looked at Minna—and closed them again wearily. "Leave me quiet," she said, in tones of fretful entreaty. Minna rose and bent over the pillow tenderly. "Your poor lips look so parched," she said; "let me give you some lemonade?" Madame Fontaine only repeated the words, "Leave me quiet." The same reluctance to raise her heavy eyelids, the same entreaty to be left undisturbed, which had alarmed me on the memorable morning when I had entered Mr. Keller's room!

Doctor Dormann signed to me to follow him out. As he opened the door, the nurse inquired if he had any further instructions for her. "Send for me, the moment you see a change," he answered; "I shall be in the drawing-room, with Mr. Glenney." I silently pressed poor Minna's hand, before I left her. Who could have presumed, at that moment, to express sympathy in words?

The doctor and I descended the stairs together. "Does her illness remind you of anything?" he asked.

"Of Mr. Keller's illness," I answered, "exactly as I remember it."

He made no further remark. We entered the drawing-room. I inquired if I could see my aunt.

"You must wait a little," he said. "Mrs. Wagner is asleep. The longer she sleeps the more complete her recovery will be. My main anxiety is about Jack. He is quiet enough now, keeping watch outside her door; but he has given me some trouble. I wish I knew more of his early history. From all I can learn, he was only what is called "half-witted," when they received him at the asylum in London. The cruel repressive treatment in that place aggravated his imbecility into violent madness—and such madness has a tendency to recur. Mrs. Wagner's influence, which has already done so much, is my main hope for the future. Sit down, and let me explain the strange position in which you find us here, as well as I can."

IV

"Do you remember how Mr. Keller's illness was cured?" the doctor began.

Those words instantly reminded me, not only of Doctor Dormann's mysterious suspicions at the time of the illness, but of Jack's extraordinary question to me, on the morning when I left Frankfort. The doctor saw that I answered him with some little embarrassment.

"Let us open our minds to each other, without reserve," he said. "I have set you thinking of something. What is it?"

I replied, concealing nothing. Doctor Dormann was equally candid on his side. He spoke to me, exactly as he is reported to have spoken to Mr. Keller, in the Second Part of this narrative.

"You now know," he proceeded, "what I thought of Mr. Keller's extraordinary recovery, and what I feared when I found Mrs. Wagner (as

I then firmly believed) dead. My suspicions of poisoning pointed to the poisoner. Madame Fontaine's wonderful cure of Mr. Keller, by means of her own mysterious remedy, made me suspect Madame Fontaine. My motive, in refusing to give the burial certificate, was to provoke the legal inquiry, which I knew that Mr. Keller would institute, on the mere expression of a doubt, on my part, whether your aunt had died a natural death. At that time, I had not the slightest anticipation of the event that has actually occurred. Before, however, we had removed the remains to the Deadhouse, I must own I was a little startled—prepare yourself for a surprise—by a private communication, addressed to me by Jack."

He repeated Jack's narrative of the opening of the Pink-Room cupboard, and the administration of the antidote to Mrs. Wagner.

"You will understand," he went on, "that I was too well aware of the marked difference between Mr. Keller's illness and Mrs. Wagner's illness to suppose for a moment that the same poison had been given to both of them. I was, therefore, far from sharing Jack's blind confidence in the efficacy of the blue-glass bottle, in the case of his mistress. But I tell you, honestly, my mind was disturbed about it. Towards night, my thoughts were again directed to the subject, under mysterious circumstances. Mr. Keller and I accompanied the hearse to the Deadhouse. On our way through the streets, I was followed and stopped by Madame Fontaine. She had something to give me. Here it is."

He laid on the table a sheet of thick paper, closely covered with writing in cipher.

V

"Whose writing is this?" I asked.

"The writing of Madame Fontaine's late husband."

"And she put it into your hands!"

"Yes—and asked me to interpret the cipher for her."

"It's simply incomprehensible."

"Not in the least. She knew the use to which Jack had put her antidote, and (in her ignorance of chemistry) she was eager to be prepared for any consequences which might follow. Can you guess on what chance I calculated, when I consented to interpret the cipher?"

"On the chance that it might tell you what poison she had given to Mrs. Wagner?"

"Well guessed, Mr. Glenney!"

"And you have actually discovered the meaning of these hieroglyphics?"

He laid a second sheet of paper on the table.

"There is but one cipher that defies interpretation," he said. "If you and your correspondent privately arrange to consult the same edition of the same book, and if your cipher, or his, refers to a given page and to certain lines on that page, no ingenuity can discover you, unaided by a previous discovery of the book. All other ciphers, so far as I know, are at the mercy of skill and patience. In this case I began (to save time and trouble) by trying the rule for interpreting the most simple, and most elementary, of all ciphers—that is to say, the use of the ordinary language of correspondence, concealed under arbitrary signs. The right way to read these signs can be described in two words. On examination of the cipher, you will find that some signs will be more often repeated than others. Count the separate signs, and ascertain, by simple addition, which especial sign occurs oftenest—which follows next in point of number—and so on. These comparisons established, ask yourself what vowel occurs oftenest, and what consonant occurs oftenest, in the language in which you suppose the cipher to be written. The result is merely a question of time and patience."

"And this is the result?" I said, pointing to the second sheet of paper.

"Read it," he answered; "and judge for yourself."

The opening sentence of the interpreted cipher appeared to be intended by Doctor Fontaine to serve the purpose of a memorandum; repeating privately the instructions already attached by labels to the poison called "Alexander's Wine," and to its antidote.

The paragraphs that followed were of a far more interesting kind. They alluded to the second poison, called "The Looking-Glass Drops;" and they related the result of one of the Professor's most remarkable experiments in the following words:—

VI

"The Looking-Glass Drops. Fatal Dose, as discovered by experiments on animals, the same as in the case of Alexander's Wine. But the effect, in producing death, more rapid, and more indistinguishable, in respect of presenting traces on post-mortem examination.

"After many patient trials, I can discover no trustworthy antidote to this infernal poison. Under these circumstances, I dare not attempt to modify it for medical use. I would throw it away—but I don't like to be beaten. If I live a little longer, I will try once more, with my mind refreshed by other studies.

"A month after writing these lines (which I have repeated in plain characters, on the bottle, for fear of accidents), I tried again—and failed again. Annoyed by this new disappointment, I did something unworthy of me as a scientific man.

"After first poisoning an animal with the Looking-Glass Drops, I administered a dose from the blue bottle, containing the antidote to Alexander's Wine—knowing perfectly well the different nature of the two poisons; expecting nothing of any scientific importance to follow; and yet trusting stupidly to chance to help me.

"The result was startling in the last degree. It was nothing less than the complete suspension of all the signs of life (as we know them) for a day, and a night, and part of another day. I only knew that the animal was not really dead, by observing, on the morning of the second day, that no signs of decomposition had set in—the season being summer, and the laboratory badly ventilated.

"An hour after the first symptoms of revival had astonished me, the creature was as lively again as usual, and ate with a good appetite. After a lapse of ten days, it is still in perfect health. This extraordinary example of the action and reaction of the ingredients of the poison and the ingredients of the antidote on each other, and on the sources of life, deserves, and shall have, the most careful investigation. May I live to carry the inquiry through to some good use, and to record it on another page!"

There was no other page, and no further record. The Professor's last scientific aspiration had not been fulfilled.

VII

"It was past midnight," said the doctor, "when I made the discovery, with which you are now acquainted. I went at once to Mr. Keller. He had fortunately not gone to bed; and he accompanied me to the Deadhouse. Knowing the overseer's private door, at the side of the building, I was able to rouse him with very little delay. In the excitement that possessed me, I spoke of the revival as a possible thing in the hearing of the servants. The whole household accompanied us to the Deadhouse, at the opposite extremity of the building. What we saw there, I am utterly incapable of describing to you. I was in time to take the necessary measures for keeping Mrs. Wagner composed, and for removing her without injury to Mr. Keller's house. Having successfully accomplished this, I presumed that my anxieties were at an end. I was completely mistaken."

"You refer to Madame Fontaine, I suppose?"

"No; I refer to Jack. The poor wretch's ignorant faith had unquestionably saved his mistress's life. I should never have ventured (even if I had been acquainted with the result of the Professor's experiment, at an earlier hour) to run the desperate risk, which Jack confronted without hesitation. The events of the night (aggravated by the brandy that Schwartz had given to him) had completely overthrown the balance of his feeble brain. He was as mad, for the time being, as ever he could have been in Bedlam. With some difficulty, I prevailed on him to take a composing mixture. He objected irritably to trust me; and, even when the mixture had begun to quiet him, he was ungrateful enough to speak contemptuously of what I had done for him. 'I had a much better remedy than yours,' he said, 'made by a man who was worth a hundred of you. Schwartz and I were fools enough to give it to Mrs. Housekeeper, last night.' I thought nothing of this—it was one of the eccentricities which were to be expected from him, in his condition. I left him quietly asleep; and I was about to go home, and get a little rest myself—when Mr. Keller's son stopped me in the hall. 'Do go and see Madame Fontaine,' he said; 'Minna is alarmed about her mother.' I went upstairs again directly."

"Had you noticed anything remarkable in Madame Fontaine," I asked, "before Fritz spoke to you?"

"I noticed, at the Deadhouse, that she looked frightened out of her senses; and I was a little surprised—holding the opinion I did of her—that such a woman should show so much sensibility. Mr. Keller took charge of her, on our way back to the house. I was quite unprepared for what I saw afterwards, when I went to her room at Fritz's request."

"Did you discover the resemblance to Mr. Keller's illness?"

"No—not till afterwards. She sent her daughter out of the room; and I thought she looked at me strangely, when we were alone. 'I want the paper that I gave you in the street, last night,' she said. I asked her why she wanted it. She seemed not to know how to reply; she became excited and confused. 'To destroy it, to be sure!' she burst out suddenly. 'Every bottle my husband left is destroyed—strewed here, there, and everywhere, from the Gate to the Deadhouse. Oh, I know what you think of me—I defy you!' She seemed to forget what she had said, the moment she had said it—she turned away, and opened a drawer, and took out a book closed by metal clasps. My presence in the room appeared to be a lost perception in her mind. The clasps of the book, as well as I could make it out, opened by touching some spring. I noticed that her hands trembled as they tried to find the spring. I attributed the trembling to the terrors of the night, and offered to help her. 'Let my secrets alone,' she said—and pushed the book under the pillow of her bed. It was my professional duty to assist her, if I could. Though I attached no sort of importance to what Jack had said, I thought it desirable, before I prescribed for her, to discover whether she had really taken some medicine of her own or not. She staggered back from me, on my repeating what I had heard from Jack, as if I had terrified her. 'What remedy does he mean? I drank nothing but a glass of wine. Send for him directly—I must, and will speak to him!' I told her this was impossible; I could not permit his sleep to be disturbed. 'The watchman!' she cried; 'the drunken brute! send for him.' By this time I began to conclude that there was really something wrong. I called in her daughter to look after her while I was away, and then left the room to consult with Fritz. The only hope of finding Schwartz (the night-watch at the Deadhouse being over by that time) was to apply to his sister the nurse. I knew where she lived; and Fritz most kindly offered to go to her. By the time Schwartz was found, and brought to the house, Madame Fontaine was just able to understand what he said, and no more. I began to recognize the symptoms of Mr. Keller's illness. The apathy which you remember was showing itself already. 'Leave me to die,' she said quietly; 'I deserve it.' The last effort of the distracted mind, rousing for a moment the sinking body, was made almost immediately afterwards. She raised herself on the pillow, and seized my arm. 'Mind!' she said, 'Minna is to be married on the thirteenth!' Her eyes rested steadily on me, while she spoke. At the last word, she sank back, and relapsed into the condition in which you have just seen her."

"Can you do nothing for her?"

"Nothing. Our modern science is absolutely ignorant of the poisons which Professor Fontaine's fatal ingenuity revived. Slow poisoning by reiterated doses, in small quantities, we understand. But slow poisoning by one dose is so entirely beyond our experience, that medical men in general refuse to believe in it."

"Are you sure that she is poisoned?" I asked.

"After what Jack told me this morning when he woke, I have no doubt she is poisoned by 'Alexander's Wine.' She appears to have treacherously offered it to him as a remedy—and to have hesitated, at the last moment, to let him have it. As a remedy, Jack's ignorant faith gave it to her by the hands of Schwartz. When we have more time before us, you shall hear the details. In the meanwhile, I can only tell you that the retribution is complete. Madame Fontaine might even now be saved, if Jack had not given all that remained of the antidote to Mrs. Wagner.

"Is there any objection to my asking Jack for the particulars?"

"The strongest possible objection. It is of the utmost importance to discourage him from touching on the subject, in the future. He has already told Mrs. Wagner that he has saved her life; and, just before you came in, I found him comforting Minna. 'Your mamma has taken her own good medicine, Missy; she will soon get well.' I have been obliged—God forgive me!—to tell your aunt and Minna that he is misled by insane delusions, and that they are not to believe one word of what he has said to them."

"No doubt your motive justifies you," I said—not penetrating his motive at the moment.

"You will understand me directly," he answered. "I trust to your honor under any circumstances. Why have I taken you into my confidence, under these circumstances? For a very serious reason, Mr. David. You are likely to be closely associated, in the time to come, with your aunt and Minna—and I look to you to help the good work which I have begun. Mrs. Wagner's future life must not be darkened by a horrible recollection. That sweet girl must enjoy the happy years that are in store for her, unembittered by the knowledge of her mother's guilt. Do you understand, now, why I am compelled to speak unjustly of poor Jack?"

As a proof that I understood him, I promised the secrecy which he had every right to expect from me.

The entrance of the nurse closed our conference. She reported Madame Fontaine's malady to be already altering for the worse.

The doctor watched the case. At intervals, I too saw her again.

Although it happened long ago, I cannot prevail upon myself to dwell on the deliberate progress of the hellish Borgia poison, in undermining the forces of life. The nervous shudderings reached their climax, and then declined as gradually as they had arisen. For hours afterwards, she lay in a state of complete prostration. Not a last word, not a last look, rewarded the devoted girl, watching faithfully at the bedside. No more of it—no more! Late in the afternoon of the next day, Doctor Dormann, gently, most gently, removed Minna from the room. Mr. Keller and I looked at each other in silence. We knew that Madame Fontaine was dead.

VIII

I had not forgotten the clasped book that she had tried vainly to open, in Doctor Dormann's presence. Taking it myself from under the pillow, I left Mr. Keller and the doctor to say if I should give it, unopened, to Minna.

"Certainly not!" said the doctor.

"Why not?"

"Because it will tell her what she must never know. I believe that book to be a Diary. Open it, and see."

I found the spring and opened the clasps. It was a Diary.

"You judged, I suppose, from the appearance of the book?" I said.

"Not at all. I judged from my own experience, at the time when I was Medical Officer at the prison here. An educated criminal is almost invariably an inveterate egotist. We are all interesting to ourselves—but the more vile we are, the more intensely we are absorbed in ourselves. The very people who have, logically speaking, the most indisputable interest in concealing their crimes, are also the very people who, almost without exception, yield to the temptation of looking at themselves in the pages of a Diary."

"I don't doubt your experience, doctor. But your results puzzle me."

"Think a little, Mr. David, and you will not find the riddle so very hard to read. The better we are, the more unselfishly we are interested in others. The worse we are, the more inveterately our interest is concentrated on ourselves. Look at your aunt as an example of what I say. This morning there were some letters waiting for her, on the subject of those reforms in the treatment of mad people, which she is as resolute as ever to promote—in this country as well as in England. It was with the greatest difficulty that I prevailed on her not to answer those letters just yet: in other words, not to excite her brain and nervous system, after such an ordeal as she has just passed through. Do you think a wicked woman—with letters relating merely to the interests of other people waiting for her—would have stood in any need of my interference? Not she! The wicked woman would have thought only of herself, and would have been far too much interested in her own recovery to run the risk of a relapse. Open that book of Madame Fontaine's at any of the later entries. You will find the miserable woman self-betrayed in every page."

It was true! Every record of Madame Fontaine's most secret moments, presented in this narrative, was first found in her Diary.

As an example:—Her Diary records, in the fullest detail, the infernal ingenuity of the stratagem by which she usurped her title to Mr. Keller's confidence, as the preserver of his life. "I have only to give him the Alexander's Wine," she writes, "to make sure, by means of the antidote, of curing the illness which I have myself produced. After that, Minna's mother becomes Mr. Keller's guardian angel, and Minna's marriage is a certainty."

On a later page, she is similarly self described—in Mrs. Wagner's case—as acting from an exactly opposite motive, in choosing the Looking-Glass Drops. "They not only kill soonest, and most surely defy detection," she proceeds, "but I have it on the authority of the label, that my husband has tried to find the antidote to these Drops, and has tried in vain. If my heart fails me, when the deed is done, there can be no reprieve for the woman whose tongue I must silence for ever—or, after all I have sacrificed, my child's future is ruined."

There is little doubt that she intended to destroy these compromising pages, on her return to Mr. Keller's house—and that she would have carried out her intention, but for those first symptoms of the poison, which showed themselves in the wandering of her mind, and the helpless trembling of her hands.

The final entry in the Diary has an interest of its own, which I think justifies the presentation of it in this place. It shows the purifying influence of the maternal instinct in a wicked nature, surviving to the last. Even Madame Fontaine's nature preserved, in this way, a softer side. On the memorable occasion of her meeting with Mr. Keller in the hall, she had acted as imprudently as if she had been the most foolish woman living, in her eagerness to plead Minna's cause with the man on whom Minna's marriage depended. She had shrunk from poisoning harmless Jack, even for her own protection. She would not even seduce Minna into telling a lie, when a lie would have served them both at the most critical moment of their lives.

Are such redeeming features unnatural in an otherwise wicked woman? Think of your own "inconsistencies." Read these last words of a sinner—and thank God that you were not tempted as she was:

"... Sent Minna out of my room, and hurt my sensitive girl cruelly. I am afraid of her! This last crime seems to separate me from that pure creature—all the more, because it has been committed in her dearest interests, and for her sweet sake. Every time she looks at me, I am afraid she may see what I have done for her, in my face. Oh, how I long to take her in my arms, and devour her with kisses! I daren't do it—I daren't do it."

Lord, have mercy on her—miserable sinner!

IX

The night is getting on; and the lamp I am writing by grows dim.

My mind wanders away from Frankfort, and from all that once happened there. The picture now in my memory presents an English scene.

I am at the house of business in London. Two friends are waiting for me. One of them is Fritz. The other is the most popular person in the neighborhood; a happy, harmless creature, known to everyone by the undignified nickname of Jack Straw. Thanks to my aunt's influence, and to the change of scene, no return of the relapse at Frankfort has shown itself. We are easy about the future of our little friend.

As to the past, we have made no romantic discoveries, relating to the earlier years of Jack's life. Who were his parents; whether they died or whether they deserted him; how he lived, and what he suffered, before he drifted into the service of the chemistry-professor at Wurzburg—these, and other questions like them, remain unanswered. Jack himself feels no sort of interest in our inquiries. He either will not or cannot rouse his feeble memory to help us. "What does it matter now?" he says. "I began to live when Mistress first came to see me. I don't remember, and won't remember, anything before that."

So the memoirs of Jack remain unwritten, for want of materials—like the memoirs of many another foundling, in real life.

While I am speaking of Jack, I am keeping my two friends waiting in the reception-room. I dress myself in my best clothes and join them. Fritz is silent and nervous; unreasonably impatient for the arrival of the carriage at the door. Jack promenades the room, with a superb nosegay in the button-hole of a glorious blue coat. He has a watch; he carries a cane; he wears white gloves, and tight nankeen pantaloons. He struts out before us, when the carriage comes at last. "I don't deny that Fritz is a figure in the festival," he says, when we drive away; "but I positively assert that the thing is not complete without Me. If my dress fails in any respect to do me justice, for Heaven's sake mention it, one of you, before we pass the tailor's door!" I answer Jack, by telling him that he is in all respects perfect. And Jack answers me, "David, you have your faults; but your taste is invariably correct. Give me a little more room; I can't face Mistress with crumpled coat-tails."

We reach a little village in the neighborhood of London, and stop at the gate of the old church.

We walk up to the altar-rails, and wait there. All the women in the place are waiting also. They merely glance at Fritz and at me—their whole attention is concentrated on Jack. They take him for the bridegroom. Jack discovers it; and is better pleased with himself than ever.

The organist plays a wedding-march. The bride, simply and unpretendingly dressed, just fluttered enough to make her eyes irresistible, and her complexion lovely, enters the church, leaning on Mr. Keller's arm.

Our good partner looks younger than usual. At his own earnest request, the business in Frankfort has been sold; the head-partner first stipulating for the employment of a given number of reputable young women in the office. Removed from associations which are inexpressibly repellent to him, Mr. Keller is building a house, near Mrs. Wagner's pretty cottage, on the hill above the village. Here he proposes to pass the rest of his days peacefully, with his two married children.

On their way to the altar, Mr. Keller and Minna are followed by Doctor Dormann (taking his annual holiday, this year, in England). The doctor gives his arm to the woman of all women whom Jack worships and loves. My kind and dear aunt—with the old bright charm in her face; the firm friend of all friendless creatures—why does my calmness desert me, when I try to draw my little portrait of her; Minna's second mother, standing by Minna's side, on the greatest day of her life?

I can't even see the paper. Nearly fifty years have passed, since that wedding-day. Oh, my coevals, who have outlived your dearest friends, like me, you know what is the matter with my eyes! I must take out my handkerchief, and put down my pen—and leave some of you younger ones to finish the story of the marriage for yourself.

THE GUILTY RIVER

CHAPTER I. ON THE WAY TO THE RIVER

FOR reasons of my own, I excused myself from accompanying my stepmother to a dinner-party given in our neighborhood. In my present humor, I preferred being alone—and, as a means of getting through my idle time, I was quite content to be occupied in catching insects.

Provided with a brush and a mixture of rum and treacle, I went into Fordwitch Wood to set the snare, familiar to hunters of moths, which we call sugaring the trees.

The summer evening was hot and still; the time was between dusk and dark. After ten years of absence in foreign parts, I perceived changes in the outskirts of the wood, which warned me not to enter it too confidently when I might find a difficulty in seeing my way. Remaining among the outermost trees, I painted the trunks with my treacherous mixture—which allured the insects of the night, and stupefied them when they settled on its rank surface. The snare being set, I waited to see the intoxication of the moths.

A time passed, dull and dreary. The mysterious assemblage of trees was blacker than the blackening sky. Of millions of leaves over my head, none pleased my ear, in the airless calm, with their rustling summer song.

The first flying creatures, dimly visible by moments under the gloomy sky, were enemies whom I well knew by experience. Many a fine insect specimen have I lost, when the bats were near me in search of their evening meal.

What had happened before, in other woods, happened now. The first moth that I had snared was a large one, and a specimen well worth securing. As I stretched out my hand to take it, the apparition of a flying shadow passed, swift and noiseless, between me and the tree. In less than an instant the insect was snatched away, when my fingers were within an inch of it. The bat had begun his supper, and the man and the mixture had provided it for him.

Out of five moths caught, I became the victim of clever theft in the case of three. The other two, of no great value as specimens, I was just quick enough to secure. Under other circumstances, my patience as a collector would still have been a match for the dexterity of the bats. But on that evening—a memorable evening when I look back at it now—my spirits were depressed, and I was easily discouraged. My favorite studies of the insect-world seemed to have lost their value in my estimation. In the silence and the darkness I lay down under a tree, and let my mind dwell on myself and on my new life to come.

I am Gerard Roylake, son and only child of the late Gerard Roylake of Trimley Deen.

At twenty-two years of age, my father's death had placed me in possession of his large landed property. On my arrival from Germany, only a few hours since, the servants innocently vexed me. When I drove up to the door, I heard them say to each other: "Here is the young Squire." My father used to be called "the old Squire." I shrank from being reminded of him—not as other sons in my position might have said, because it renewed my sorrow for his death. There was no sorrow in me to be renewed. It is a shocking confession to make: my heart remained unmoved when I thought of the father whom I had lost.

Our mothers have the most sacred of all claims on our gratitude and our love. They have nourished us with their blood; they have risked their lives in bringing us into the world; they have preserved and guided our helpless infancy with divine patience and love. What claim equally strong and equally tender does the other parent establish on his offspring? What motive does the instinct of his young children find for preferring their father before any other person who may be a familiar object in their daily lives? They love him—naturally and rightly love him—because he lives in their remembrance (if he is a good man) as the first, the best, the dearest of their friends.

My father was a bad man. He was my mother's worst enemy; and he was never my friend.

The little that I know of the world tells me that it is not the common lot in life of women to marry the object of their first love. A sense of duty had compelled my mother to part with the man who had won her heart, in the first days of her maidenhood; and my father had discovered it, after his marriage. His insane jealousy foully wronged the truest wife, the most long-suffering woman that ever lived. I have no patience to write of it. For ten miserable years she suffered her martyrdom; she lived through it, dear angel, sweet suffering soul, for my sake. At her death, my father was able to gratify his hatred of the son whom he had never believed to be his own child. Under pretence of preferring the foreign system of teaching, he sent me to a school in France. My education having been so far completed, I was next transferred to a German University. Never again did I see the place of my birth, never did I get a letter from home, until the family lawyer wrote from Trimley Deen, requesting me to assume possession of my house and lands, under the entail.

I should not even have known that my father had taken a second wife but for some friend (or enemy)—I never discovered the person—who sent me a newspaper containing an announcement of the marriage.

When we saw each other for the first time, my stepmother and I met necessarily as strangers. We were elaborately polite, and we each made a meritorious effort to appear at our ease. On her side, she found herself confronted by a young man, the new master of the house, who looked more like a foreigner than an Englishman—who, when he was congratulated (in view of the approaching season) on the admirable preservation of his partridges and pheasants, betrayed an utter want of interest in the subject; and who showed no sense of shame in acknowledging that his principal amusements were derived from reading books, and collecting insects. How I must have disappointed Mrs. Roylake! and how considerately she hid from me the effect that I had produced!

Turning next to my own impressions, I discovered in my newly-found relative, a little light-eyed, light-haired, elegant woman; trim, and bright, and smiling; dressed to perfection, clever to her fingers' ends, skilled in making herself agreeable—and yet, in spite of these undeniable fascinations, perfectly incomprehensible to me. After my experience of foreign society, I was incapable of understanding the extraordinary importance which my stepmother seemed to attach to rank and riches, entirely for their own sakes. When she described my unknown neighbors, from one end of the county to the other, she took it for granted that I must be interested in them on account of their titles and their fortunes. She held me up to my own face, as a kind of idol to myself, without producing any better reason than might be found in my inheritance of an income of sixteen thousand pounds. And when I expressed (in excusing myself for not accompanying her, uninvited, to the dinner-party) a perfectly rational doubt whether I might prove to be a welcome guest, Mrs. Roylake held up her delicate little hands in unutterable astonishment. "My dear Gerard, in your position!" She appeared to think that this settled the question. I submitted in silence; the truth is, I was beginning already to despair of my prospects. Kind as my stepmother was, and agreeable as she was, what chance could I see of establishing any true sympathy between us? And, if my neighbors resembled her in their ways of thinking, what hope could I feel of finding new friends in England to replace the friends in Germany whom I had lost? A stranger among my own country people, with the every-day habits and every-day pleasures of my youthful life left behind me—without plans or hopes to interest me in looking at the future—it is surely not wonderful that my spirits had sunk to their lowest ebb, and that I even failed to appreciate with sufficient gratitude the fortunate accident of my birth.

Perhaps the journey to England had fatigued me, or perhaps the controlling influences of the dark and silent night proved irresistible. This only is certain: my solitary meditations under the tree ended in sleep.

I was awakened by a light falling on my face.

The moon had risen. In the outward part of the wood, beyond which I had not advanced, the pure and welcome light penetrated easily through the scattered trees. I got up and looked about me. A path into the wood now showed itself, broader and better kept than any path that I could remember in the days of my boyhood. The moon showed it to me plainly, and my curiosity was aroused.

Following the new track, I found that it led to a little glade which I at once recognized. The place was changed in one respect only. A neglected water-spring had been cleared of brambles and stones, and had been provided with a drinking cup, a rustic seat, and a Latin motto on a marble slab. The spring at once reminded me of a greater body of water—a river, at some little distance farther on, which ran between the trees on one side, and the desolate open country on the other. Ascending from the glade, I found myself in one of the narrow woodland paths, familiar to me in the by-gone time.

Unless my memory was at fault, this was the way which led to an old water-mill on the river-bank. The image of the great turning wheel, which half-frightened half-fascinated me when I was a child, now presented itself to my memory for the first time after an interval of many years. In my present frame of mind, the old scene appealed to me with the irresistible influence of an old friend. I said to myself: "Shall I walk on, and try if I can find the river and the mill again?" This perfectly trifling question to decide presented to me, nevertheless, fantastic difficulties so absurd that they might have been difficulties encountered in a dream. To my own astonishment, I hesitated— walked back again along the path by which I had advanced—reconsidered my decision, without knowing why—and turning in the opposite direction, set my face towards the river once more. I wonder how my life would have ended, if I had gone the other way?

CHAPTER II. THE RIVER INTRODUCES US

I stood alone on the bank of the ugliest stream in England.

The moonlight, pouring its unclouded radiance over open space, failed to throw a beauty not their own on those sluggish waters. Broad and muddy, their stealthy current flowed onward to the sea, without a rock to diversify, without a bubble to break, the sullen surface. On the side from which I was looking at the river, the neglected trees grew so close together that they were undermining their own lives, and poisoning each other. On the opposite bank, a rank growth of gigantic bulrushes hid the ground beyond, except where it rose in hillocks, and showed its surface of desert sand spotted here and there by mean patches of health. A repellent river in itself, a repellent river in its surroundings, a repellent river even in its name. It was called The Loke. Neither popular tradition nor antiquarian research could explain what the name meant, or could tell when the name had been given. "We call it The Loke; they do say no fish can live in it; and it dirties the clean salt water when it runs into the sea." Such was the character of the river in the estimation of the people who knew it best. But I was pleased to see The Loke again. The ugly river, like the woodland glade, looked at me with the face of an old friend.

On my right hand side rose the venerable timbers of the water-mill.

The wheel was motionless, at that time of night; and the whole structure looked—as remembered objects will look, when we see them again after a long interval—smaller than I had supposed it to be. Otherwise, I could discover no change in the mill. But the wooden cottage attached to it had felt the devastating march of time. A portion of the decrepit building still stood revealed in its wretched old age; propped, partly by beams which reached from the thatched roof to the ground, and partly by the wall of a new cottage attached, presenting in yellow brick-work a hideous modern contrast to all that was left of its ancient neighbor.

Had the miller whom I remembered, died; and were these changes the work of his successor? I thought of asking the question, and tried the door: it was fastened. The windows were all dark excepting one, which I discovered in the upper storey, at the farther side of the new building. Here, there was a dim light burning. It was impossible to disturb a person, who, for all I knew to the contrary, might be going to bed. I turned back to The Loke, proposing to extend my walk, by a mile or a little more, to a village that I remembered on the bank of the river.

I had not advanced far, when the stillness around me was disturbed by an intermittent sound of splashing in the water. Pausing to listen, I heard next the working of oars in their rowlocks. After another interval a boat appeared, turning a projection in the bank, and rowed by a woman pulling steadily against the stream.

As the boat approached me in the moonlight, this person corrected my first impression, and revealed herself as a young girl. So far as I could perceive she was a stranger to me. Who could the girl be, alone on the river at that time of night? Idly curious I followed the boat, instead of pursuing my way to the village, to see whether she would stop at the mill, or pass it.

She stopped at the mill, secured the boat, and stepped on shore.

Taking a key from her pocket, she was about to open the door of the cottage, when I advanced and spoke to her. As far from recognizing her as ever, I found myself nevertheless thinking of an odd outspoken child, living at the mill in past years, who had been one of my poor mother's favorites at our village school. I ran the risk of offending her, by bluntly expressing the thought which was then in my mind.

"Is it possible that you are Cristel Toller?" I said.

The question seemed to amuse her. "Why shouldn't I be Cristel Toller?" she asked.

"You were a little girl," I explained, "when I saw you last. You are so altered now—and so improved—that I should never have guessed you might be the daughter of Giles Toller of the mill, if I had not seen you opening the cottage door."

She acknowledged my compliment by a curtsey, which reminded me again of the village school. "Thank you, young man," she said smartly; "I wonder who you are?"

"Try if you can recollect me," I suggested.

"May I take a long look at you?"

"As long as you like."

She studied my face, with a mental effort to remember me, which gathered her pretty eyebrows together quaintly in a frown.

"There's something in his eyes," she remarked, not speaking to me but to herself, "which doesn't seem to be quite strange. But I don't know his voice, and I don't know his beard." She considered a little, and addressed herself directly to me once more. "Now I look at you again, you seem to be a gentleman. Are you one?"

"I hope so."

"Then you're not making game of me?"

"My dear, I am only trying if you can remember Gerard Roylake."

While in charge of the boat, the miller's daughter had been rowing with bared arms; beautiful dusky arms, at once delicate and strong. Thus far, she had forgotten to cover them up. The moment mentioned my name, she started back as if I had frightened her—pulled her sleeves down in a hurry—and hid the objects of my admiration as an act of homage to myself! Her verbal apologies followed.

"You used to be such a sweet-spoken pretty little boy," she said, "how should I know you again, with a big voice and all that hair on your face?" It seemed to strike her on a sudden that she had been too familiar. "Oh, Lord," I heard her say to herself, "half the county belongs to him!" She tried another apology, and hit this time on the conventional form. "I beg your pardon, sir. Welcome back to your own country, sir. I wish you good-night, sir."

She attempted to escape into the cottage; I followed her to the threshold of the door. "Surely it's not time to go to bed yet," I ventured to say.

She was still on her good behavior to her landlord. "Not if you object to it, sir," she answered.

This recognition of my authority was irresistible. Cristel had laid me under an obligation to her good influence for which I felt sincerely grateful—she had made me laugh, for the first time since my return to England.

"We needn't say good-night just yet," I suggested; "I want to hear a little more about you. Shall I come in?"

She stepped out of the doorway even more rapidly than she had stepped into it. I might have been mistaken, but I thought Cristel seemed to be actually alarmed by my proposal. We walked up and down the river-bank. On every occasion when we approached the cottage, I detected her in stealing a look at the ugly modern part of it. There could be no mistake this time; I saw doubt, I saw anxiety in her face. What was going on at the mill? I made some domestic inquiries, beginning with her father. Was the miller alive and well?

"Oh yes, sir. Father gets thinner as he gets older—that's all."

"Did he send you out by yourself, at this late hour, in the boat?"

"They were waiting for a sack of flour down there," she replied, pointing in the direction of the river-side village. "Father isn't as quick as he used to be. He's often late over his work now."

Was there no one to give Giles Toller the help that he must need at his age? "Do you and your father really live alone in this solitary place?" I said.

A change of expression appeared in her bright brown eyes which roused my curiosity. I also observed that she evaded a direct reply. "What makes you doubt, sir, if father and I live alone?" she asked.

I pointed to the new cottage. "That ugly building," I answered, "seems to give you more room than you want—unless there is somebody else living at the mill."

I had no intention of trying to force the reply from her which she had hitherto withheld; but she appeared to put that interpretation on what I had said. "If you will have it," she burst out, "there is somebody else living with us."

"A man who helps your father?"

"No. A man who pays my father's rent."

I was quite unprepared for such a reply as this: Cristel had surprised me. To begin with, her father was "well-connected," as we say in England. His younger brother had made a fortune in commerce, and had vainly offered him the means of retiring from the mill with a sufficient income. Then again, Giles Toller was known to have saved money. His domestic expenses made no heavy demand on his purse; his German wife (whose Christian name was now borne by his daughter) had died long since; his sons were no burden on him; they had never lived at the mill in my remembrance. With all these reasons against his taking a stranger into his house, he had nevertheless, if my interpretation of Cristel's answer was the right one, let his spare rooms to a lodger. "Mr. Toller can't possibly be in want of money," I said.

"The more money father has, the more he wants. That's the reason," she added bitterly, "why he asked for plenty of room when the cottage was built, and why we have got a lodger."

"Is the lodger a gentleman?"

"I don't know. Is a man a gentleman, if he keeps a servant? Oh, don't trouble to think about it, sir! It isn't worth thinking about."

This was plain speaking at last. "You don't seem to like the lodger," I said.

"I hate him!"

"Why?"

She turned on me with a look of angry amazement—not undeserved, I must own, on my part—which showed her dark beauty in the perfection of its luster and its power. To my eyes she was at the moment irresistibly charming. I daresay I was blind to the defects in her face. My good German tutor used to lament that there was too much of my boyhood still left in me. Honestly admiring her, I let my favorable opinion express itself a little too plainly. "What a splendid creature you are!" I burst out. Cristel did her duty to herself and to me; she passed over my little explosion of nonsense without taking the smallest notice of it.

"Master Gerard," she began—and checked herself. "Please to excuse me, sir; you have set my head running on old times. What I want to say is: you were not so inquisitive when you were a young gentleman in short jackets. Please behave as you used to behave then, and don't say anything more about our lodger. I hate him because I hate him. There!"

Ignorant as I was of the natures of women, I understood her at last. Cristel's opinion of the lodger was evidently the exact opposite of the lodger's opinion of Cristel. When I add that this discovery did decidedly operate as a relief to my mind, the impression produced on me by the miller's daughter is stated without exaggeration and without reserve.

"Good-night," she repeated, "for the last time." I held out my hand. "Is it quite right, sir," she modestly objected, "for such as me to shake hands with such as you?"

She did it nevertheless; and dropping my hand, cast a farewell look at the mysterious object of her interest—the new cottage. Her variable humor changed on the instant. Apparently in a state of unendurable irritation, she stamped on the ground. "Just what I didn't want to happen!" she said to herself.

CHAPTER III. HE SHOWS HIMSELF

I too, looked at the cottage, and made a discovery that surprised me at one of the upper windows.

If I could be sure that the moon had not deceived me, the most beautiful face that I had ever seen was looking down on us—and it was the face of a man! By the uncertain light I could discern the perfection of form in the features, and the expression of power which made it impossible to mistake the stranger for a woman, although his hair grew long and he was without either moustache or beard. He was watching us intently; he neither moved nor spoke when we looked up at him.

"Evidently the lodger," I whispered to Cristel. "What a handsome man!"

She tossed her head contemptuously: my expression of admiration seemed to have irritated her.

"I didn't want him to see you!" she said. "The lodger persecutes me with his attentions; he's impudent enough to be jealous of me."

She spoke without even attempting to lower her voice. I endeavored to warn her. "He's at the window still," I said, in tones discreetly lowered; "he can hear everything you are saying."

"Not one word of it, Mr. Gerard."

"What do you mean?"

"The man is deaf. Don't look at him again. Don't speak to me again. Go home—pray go home!"

Without further explanation, she abruptly entered the cottage, and shut the door.

As I turned into the path which led through the wood I heard a voice behind me. It said: "Stop, sir." I stopped directly, standing in the shadow cast by the outermost line of trees, which I had that moment reached. In the moonlight that I had left behind me, I saw again the man whom I had discovered at the window. His figure, tall and slim; his movements, graceful and easy, were in harmony with his beautiful face. He lifted his long finely-shaped hands, and clasped them with a frantic gesture of entreaty.

"For God's sake," he said, "don't be offended with me!"

His voice startled me even more than his words; I had never heard anything like it before. Low, dull, and muffled, it neither rose nor fell; it spoke slowly and deliberately, without laying the slightest emphasis on any one of the words that it uttered. In the astonishment of the moment, I forgot what Cristel had told me. I answered him as I should have answered any other unknown person who had spoken to me.

"What do you want?"

His hands dropped; his head sunk on his breast. "You are speaking, sir, to a miserable creature who can't hear you. I am deaf."

I stepped nearer to him, intending to raise my voice in pity for his infirmity. He shuddered, and signed to me to keep back.

"Don't come close to my ear; don't shout." As he spoke, strong excitement flashed at me in his eyes, without producing the slightest change in his voice. "I don't deny," he resumed, "that I can hear sometimes when people take that way with me. They hurt when they do it. Their voices go through my nerves as a knife might go through my flesh. I live at the mill, sir; I have a great favour to ask. Will you come and speak to me in my room—for five minutes only?"

I hesitated. Any other man in my place, would, I think, have done the same; receiving such an invitation as this from a stranger, whose pitiable infirmity seemed to place him beyond the pale of social intercourse.

He must have guessed what was passing in my mind; he tried me again in words which might have proved persuasive, had they been uttered in the customary variety of tone.

"I can't help being a stranger to you; I can't help being deaf. You're a young man. You look more merciful and more patient than young men in general. Won't you hear what I have to say? Won't you tell me what I want to know?"

How were we to communicate? Did he by any chance suppose that I had learnt the finger alphabet? I touched my fingers and shook my head, as a means of dissipating his delusion, if it existed.

He instantly understood me.

"Even if you knew the finger alphabet," he said, "it would be of no use. I have been too miserable to learn it—my deafness only came on me a little more than a year since. Pardon me if I am obliged to give you trouble—I ask persons who pity me to write their answers when I speak to them. Come to my room, and you will find what you want—a candle to write by."

Was his will, as compared with mine, the stronger will of the two? And was it helped (insensibly to myself) by his advantages of personal appearance? I can only confess that his apology presented a picture of misery to my mind, which shook my resolution to refuse him. His ready penetration discovered this change in his favour: he at once took advantage of it. "Five minutes of your time is all I ask for," he said. "Won't you indulge a man who sees his fellow-creatures all talking happily round him, and feels dead and buried among them?"

The very exaggeration of his language had its effect on my mind. It revealed to me the horrible isolation among humanity of the deaf, as I had never understood it yet. Discretion is, I am sorry to say, not one of the strong points in my character. I committed one more among the many foolish actions of my life; I signed to the stranger to lead the way back to the mill.

CHAPTER IV. HE EXPLAINS HIMSELF

Giles Toller's miserly nature had offered to his lodger shelter from wind and rain, and the furniture absolutely necessary to make a bedroom habitable—and nothing more. There was no carpet on the floor, no paper on the walls, no ceiling to hide the rafters of the roof. The chair that I sat on was the one chair in the room; the man whose guest I had rashly consented to be found a seat on his bed. Upon his table I saw pens and pencils, paper and ink, and a battered brass candlestick with a common tallow candle in it. His changes of clothing were flung on the bed; his money was left on the unpainted wooden chimney-piece; his wretched little morsel of looking-glass (propped up near the money) had been turned with its face to the wall. He perceived that the odd position of this last object had attracted my notice.

"Vanity and I have parted company," he explained; "I shrink from myself when I look at myself now. The ugliest man living—if he has got his hearing—is a more agreeable man in society than I am. Does this wretched place disgust you?"

He pushed a pencil and some sheets of writing-paper across the table to me. I wrote my reply: "The place makes me sorry for you."

He shook his head. "Your sympathy is thrown away on me. A man who has lost his social relations with his fellow-creatures doesn't care how he lodges or where he lives. When he has found solitude, he has found all he wants for the rest of his days. Shall we introduce ourselves? It won't be easy for me to set the example."

I used the pencil again: "Why not?"

"Because you will expect me to give you my name. I can't do it. I have ceased to bear my family name; and, being out of society, what need have I for an assumed name? As for my Christian name, it's so detestably ugly that I hate the sight and sound of it. Here, they know me as The Lodger. Will you have that? or will you have an appropriate nick-name? I come of a mixed breed; and I'm likely, after what has happened to me, to turn out a worthless fellow. Call me The Cur. Oh, you needn't start! that's as accurate a description of me as any other. What's your name?"

I wrote it for him. His face darkened when he found out who I was.

"Young, personally attractive, and a great landowner," he said. "I saw you just now talking familiarly with Cristel Toller. I didn't like that at the time; I like it less than ever now."

My pencil asked him, without ceremony, what he meant.

He was ready with his reply. "I mean this: you owe something to the good luck which has placed you where you are. Keep your familiarity for ladies in your own rank of life."

This (to a young man like me) was unendurable insolence. I had hitherto refrained from taking him at his own bitter word in the matter of nick-name. In the irritation of the moment, I now first resolved to adopt his suggestion seriously. The next slip of paper that I handed to him administered the smartest rebuff that my dull brains could discover on the spur of the moment: "The Cur is requested to keep his advice till he is asked for it."

For the first time, something like a smile showed itself faintly on his lips—and represented the only effect which my severity had produced. He still followed his own train of thought, as resolutely and as impertinently as ever.

"I haven't seen you talking to Cristel before to-night. Have you been meeting her in secret?"

In justice to the girl, I felt that I ought to set him right, so far. Taking up the pencil again, I told this strange man that I had just returned to England, after an absence of many years in foreign countries—that I had known Cristel when we were both children—and that I had met her purely by accident, when he had detected us talking outside the cottage. Seeing me pause, after advancing to that point in the writing of my reply, he held out his hand impatiently for the paper. I signed him to wait, and added a last sentence:

"Understand this; I will answer no more questions—I have done with the subject."

He read what I had written with the closest attention. But his inveterate suspicion of me was not set at rest, even yet.

"Are you likely to come this way again?" he asked.

I pointed to the final lines of my writing, and got up to go.

This assertion of my will against his roused him. He stopped me at the door—not by a motion of his hand but by the mastery of his look. The dim candlelight afforded me no help in determining the color of his eyes. Dark, large, and finely set in his head, there was a sinister passion in them, at that moment, which held me in spite of myself. Still as monotonous as ever, his voice in some degree expressed the frenzy that was in him, by suddenly rising in its pitch when he spoke to me next.

"Mr. Roylake, I love her. Mr. Roylake, I am determined to marry her. Any man who comes between me and that cruel girl—ah, she's as hard as one of her father's millstones; it's the misery of my life, it's the joy of my life, to love her—I tell you, young sir, any man who comes between Cristel and me does it at his peril. Remember that."

I had no wish to give offence—but his threatening me in this manner was so absurd that I gave way to the impression of the moment, and laughed. He stepped up to me, with such an expression of demoniacal rage and hatred in his face that he became absolutely ugly in an instant.

"I amuse you, do I?" he said. "You don't know the man you're trifling with. You had better know me. You shall know me." He turned away, and walked up and down the wretched little room, deep in thought. "I don't want this matter between us to end badly," he said, interrupting his meditations—then returning to them again—and then once more addressing me. "You're young, you're thoughtless; but you don't look like a bad fellow. I wonder whether I can trust you? Not one man in a thousand would do it. Never mind. I'm the one man in ten thousand who does it. Mr. Gerard Roylake, I'm going to trust you."

With this incoherent expression of a resolution unknown to me, he unlocked a shabby trunk hidden in a corner, and took from it a small portfolio.

"Men of your age," he resumed, "seldom look below the surface. Learn that valuable habit, sir—and begin by looking below the surface of Me." He forced the portfolio into my hand. Once more, his beautiful eyes held me with their irresistible influence; they looked at me with an expression of sad and solemn warning. "Discover for yourself," he said, "what devils my deafness has set loose in me; and let no eyes but yours see that horrid sight. You will find me here tomorrow, and you will decide by that time whether you make an enemy of me or not."

He threw open the door, and bowed as graciously as if he had been a sovereign dismissing a subject.

Was he mad?

I hesitated to adopt that conclusion. There is no denying it, the deaf man had found his own strange and tortuous way to my interest, in spite of myself. I might even have been in some danger of allowing him to make a friend of me, if I had not been restrained by the fears for Cristel which his language and his manner amply justified, to my mind. Although I was far from foreseeing the catastrophe that really did happen, I felt that I had returned to my own country at a critical time in the life of the miller's daughter. My friendly interference might be of serious importance to Cristel's peace of mind—perhaps even to her personal safety as well.

Eager to discover what the contents of the portfolio might tell me, I hurried back to Trimley Deen. My stepmother had not yet returned from the dinner-party. As one of the results of my ten years' banishment from home, I was obliged to ask the servant to show me the way to my own room, in my own house! The windows looked out on a view of Fordwitch Wood. As I opened the leaves which were to reveal to me the secret soul of the man whom I had so strangely met, the fading moonlight vanished, and the distant trees were lost in the gloom of a starless night.

CHAPTER V. HE BETRAYS HIMSELF

The confession was entitled, "Memoirs of a Miserable Man." It began abruptly in these words:

I

"I acknowledge, at the outset, that misfortune has had an effect on me which frail humanity is for the most part anxious to conceal. Under the influence of suffering, I have become of enormous importance to myself. In this frame of mind, I naturally enjoy painting my own portrait in words. Let me add that they must be written words because it is a painful effort to me (since I lost my hearing) to speak to anyone continuously, for any length of time.

"I have also to confess that my brains are not so completely under my own command as I could wish.

"For instance, I possess considerable skill (for an amateur) as a painter in water colors. But I can only produce a work of art, when irresistible impulse urges me to express my thoughts in form and color. The same obstacle to regular exertion stands in my way, if I am using my pen. I can only write when the fit takes me—sometimes at night when I ought to be asleep; sometimes at meals when I ought to be handling my knife and fork; sometimes out of doors when I meet with inquisitive strangers who stare at me. As for paper, the first stray morsel of anything that I can write upon will do, provided I snatch it up in time to catch my ideas as they fly.

"My method being now explained, I proceed to the deliberate act of self-betrayal which I contemplate in producing this picture of myself."

II

"I divide my life into two Epochs—respectively entitled: Before my Deafness, and After my Deafness. Or, suppose I define the melancholy change in my fortunes more sharply still, by contrasting with each other my days of prosperity and my days of disaster? Of these alternatives, I hardly know which to choose. It doesn't matter; the one thing needful is to go on.

"In any case, then, I have to record that I passed a happy childhood—thanks to my good mother. Her generous nature had known adversity, and had not been deteriorated by undeserved trials. Born of slave-parents, she had not reached her eighteenth year, when she was sold by auction in the Southern States of America. The person who bought her (she never would tell me who he was) freed her by a codicil, added to his will on his deathbed. My father met with her, a few years afterwards, in American society—fell (as I have heard) madly in love with her—and married her in defiance of the wishes of his family. He was quite right: no better wife and mother ever lived. The one vestige of good feeling that I still possess, lives in my empty heart when I dwell at times on the memory of my mother.

"My good fortune followed me when I was sent to school.

"Our head master was more nearly a perfect human being than any other man that I have ever met with. Even the worst-tempered boys among us ended in loving him. Under his encouragement, and especially to please him, I won every prize that industry, intelligence, and good conduct could obtain; and I rose, at an unusually early age, to be the head boy in the first class. When I was old enough to be removed to the University, and when the dreadful day of parting arrived, I fainted under the agony of leaving the teacher—no! the dear friend—whom I devotedly loved. There must surely have been some good in me at that time. What has become of it now?

"The years followed each other—and I was Fortune's spoilt child still.

"Under adverse circumstances, my sociable disposition, my delight in the society of young people of my own age, might have exposed me to serious dangers in my new sphere of action. Happily for me, my father consulted a wise friend, before he sent me to Cambridge. I was entered at one of the smaller colleges; and I fell, at starting, among the right set of men. Good examples were all round me. We formed a little club of steady students; our pleasures were innocent; we were too proud and too poor to get into debt. I look back on my career at Cambridge, as I look back on my career at school, and wonder what has become of my better self."

III

"During my last year at Cambridge, my father died.

"The profession which he had intended that I should follow was the Bar. I believed myself to be quite unfit for the sort of training imperatively required by the Law; and my mother agreed with me. When I left the University, my own choice of a profession pointed to the medical art, and to that particular branch of it called surgery. After three years of unremitting study at one of the great London hospitals, I started in practice for myself. Once more, my persistent luck was faithful to me at the outset of my new career.

"The winter of that year was remarkable for alternate extremes of frost and thaw. Accidents to passengers in the streets were numerous; and one of them happened close to my own door. A gentleman slipped on the icy pavement, and broke his leg. On sending news of the accident to his house, I found that my chance-patient was a nobleman.

"My lord was so well satisfied with my services that he refused to be attended by any of my elders and betters in the profession. Little did I think at the time, that I had received the last of the favours which Fortune was to bestow on me. I enjoyed the confidence and goodwill of a man possessing boundless social influence; and I was received most kindly by the ladies of his family. In one word, at the time when my professional prospects justified the brightest hopes that I could form, sudden death deprived me of the dearest and truest of all friends—I suffered the one dreadful loss which it is impossible to replace, the loss of my mother. We had parted at night when she was, to all appearance, in the enjoyment of her customary health. The next morning, she was found dead in her bed."

IV

"Keen observers, who read these lines, will remark that I have said nothing about the male members of my family, and that I have even passed over my father with the briefest possible allusion to his death.

"This curious reticence on my part, is simply attributable to pure ignorance. Until affliction lay heavy on me, my father, my uncle, and my grandfather were hardly better known to me, in their true characters, than if they had been strangers passing in the street. How I contrived to become more intimately acquainted with my ancestors, I am now to reveal.

"In the absence of any instructions to guide me, after my mother's death, I was left to use my own discretion in examining the papers which she had left behind her. Reading her letters carefully, before I decided what to keep and what to destroy, I discovered a packet, protected by an unbroken seal, and bearing an inscription, addressed abruptly to my mother in these words:

'For fear of accidents, my dear, we will mention no names in this place. The sight of my handwriting will remind you of my devotion to your interests in the past, and will satisfy you that I am to be trusted in the service that I now offer to my good sister-friend. In the fewest words, let me tell you that I have heard of the circumstances under which your marriage has taken place. Your origin has unfortunately become known to the members of your husband's family; their pride has been deeply wounded; and the women especially regard you with feelings of malignant hatred. I have good reason for fearing that they may try to excuse their inhuman way of speaking of you, by making public the calamity of your slave-birth. What deplorable influence might be exercised on your husband's mind, by such an exposure as this, I will not stop to inquire. It will be more to the purpose to say that I am able to offer you a sure means of protecting yourself—through information which I have unexpectedly obtained, and the source of which I am obliged to keep secret. If you are ever threatened by your enemies, open the packet which I have now sealed up, and you will command the silence of the bitterest man or woman who longs to injure you. I may add that absolute proof accompanies every assertion which my packet contains. Keep it carefully, as long as you live—and God grant you may never have occasion to break the seal.'

"Such was the inscription; copied exactly, word for word.

"I cannot even guess who my mother's devoted friend may have been. Neither can I doubt that she would have destroyed the packet, but for the circumstance of her sudden death.

"After hesitating a little—I hardly know why—I summoned my

resolution, and broke the seal. Of the horror with which I read the contents of the packet I shall say nothing. Who ever yet sympathized with the sorrows and sufferings of strangers? Let me merely announce that I knew my ancestors at last, and that I am now able to present them in their true characters, as follows:

V

"My grandfather was tried on a charge of committing willful murder—was found guilty on the clearest evidence—and died on the scaffold by the hangman's hands.

"His two sons abandoned the family name, and left the family residence. They were, nevertheless, not unworthy representatives of their atrocious father, as will presently appear.

"My uncle (a captain in the Army) was discovered at the hazard table, playing with loaded dice. Before this abject scoundrel could be turned out of his regiment, he was killed in a duel by one of his brother officers whom he had cheated.

"My father, when he was little more than a lad, deserted a poor girl who had trusted him under a promise of marriage. Friendless and hopeless, she drowned herself and her child. His was the most infamous in the list of the family crimes—and he escaped, without answering to a court of law or a court of honor for what he had done.

"Some of us come of one breed, and some of another. There is the breed from which I drew the breath of life. What do you think of me now?"

VI

"I looked back over the past years of my existence, from the time of my earliest recollections to the miserable day when I opened the sealed packet.

"What wholesome influences had preserved me, so far, from moral contamination by the vile blood that ran in my veins? There were two answers to that question which, in some degree, quieted my mind. In the first place, resembling my good mother physically, I might hope to have resembled her morally. In the second place, the happy accidents of my career had preserved me from temptation, at more than one critical period of my life. On the other hand, in the ordinary course of nature, not one half of that life had yet elapsed. What trials might the future have in store for me? and what protection against them would the better part of my nature be powerful enough to afford?

"While I was still troubled by these doubts, the measure of my disasters was filled by an attack of illness which threatened me with death. My medical advisers succeeded in saving my life—and left me to pay the penalty of their triumph by the loss of one of my senses.

"At an early period of my convalescence, I noticed one day, with languid surprise, that the voices of the doctors, when they asked me how I had slept and if I felt better, sounded singularly dull and distant. A few hours later, I observed that they stooped close over me when they had something important to say. On the same evening, my day nurse and my night nurse happened to be in the room together. To my surprise, they had become so wonderfully quiet in their movements, that they opened the door or stirred the fire, without making the slightest noise. I intended to ask them what it meant; I had even begun to put the question, when I was startled by another discovery relating this time to myself. I was certain that I had spoken—and yet, I had not heard myself speak! As well as my weakness would let me, I called to the nurses in my loudest tones. "Has anything happened to my voice?" I asked. The two women consulted together, looking at me with pity in their eyes. One of them took the responsibility on herself. She put her lips close to my ear; the horrid words struck me with a sense of physical pain: 'Your illness has left you in a sad state, sir. You are deaf.'"

VII

"As soon as I was able to leave my bed, well-meaning people, in and out of the medical profession, combined to torment me with the best intentions.

"One famous aural surgeon after another came to me, and quoted his experience of cases, in which the disease that had struck me down had affected the sense of hearing in other unhappy persons: they had submitted to surgical treatment, generally with cheering results. I submitted in my turn. All that skill could do for me was done, and without effect. My deafness steadily increased; my case was pronounced to be hopeless; the great authorities retired.

"Judicious friends, who had been waiting for their opportunity, undertook the moral management of me next.

"I was advised to cultivate cheerfulness, to go into society, to encourage kind people who tried to make me hear what was going on, to be on my guard against morbid depression, to check myself when the sense of my own horrible isolation drove me away to my room, and, last but by no means least, to beware of letting my vanity disincline me to use an ear-trumpet.

"I did my best, honestly did my best, to profit by the suggestions that were offered to me—not because I believed in the wisdom of my friends, but because I dreaded the effect of self-imposed solitude on my nature. Since the fatal day when I had opened the sealed packet, I was on my guard against the inherited evil lying dormant, for all I knew to the contrary, in my father's son. Impelled by that horrid dread, I suffered my daily martyrdom with a courage that astonishes me when I think of it now.

"What the self-inflicted torture of the deaf is, none but the deaf can understand.

"When benevolent persons did their best to communicate to me what was clever or amusing, while conversation was going on in my presence, I was secretly angry with them for making my infirmity conspicuous, and directing the general attention to me. When other friends saw in my face that I was not grateful to them, and gave up the attempt to help me, I suspected them of talking of me contemptuously, and amusing themselves by making my misfortune the subject of coarse jokes.

"Even when I deserved encouragement by honestly trying to atone for my bad behavior, I committed mistakes (arising out of my helpless position) which prejudiced people against me. Sometimes, I asked questions which appeared to be so trivial, to ladies and gentlemen happy in the possession of a sense of hearing, that they evidently thought me imbecile as well as deaf. Sometimes, seeing the company enjoying an interesting story or a good joke, I ignorantly appealed to the most incompetent person present to tell me what had been said—with this result, that he lost the thread of the story or missed the point of the joke, and blamed my unlucky interference as the cause of it.

"These mortifications, and many more, I suffered patiently until, little by little, my last reserves of endurance felt the cruel strain on them, and failed me. My friends detected a change in my manner which alarmed them. They took me away from London, to try the renovating purity of country air.

"So far as any curative influence over the state of my mind was concerned, the experiment proved to be a failure.

"I had secretly arrived at the conclusion that my deafness was increasing, and that my friends knew it and were concealing it from me. Determined to put my suspicions to the test, I took long solitary walks in the neighborhood of my country home, and tried to hear the new sounds about me. I was deaf to everything—with the one exception of the music of the birds.

"How long did I hear the little cheering songsters who comforted me?

"I am unable to measure the interval that elapsed: my memory fails me. I only know that the time came, when I could see the skylark in the heavens, but could no longer hear its joyous notes. In a few weeks more the nightingale, and even the loud thrush, became silent birds to my doomed ears. My last effort to resist my own deafness was made at my bedroom window. For some time I still heard, faintly and more faintly, the shrill twittering just above me, under the eaves of the house. When this last poor enjoyment came to an end—when I listened eagerly, desperately, and heard nothing (think of it, nothing!)—I gave up the struggle. Persuasions, arguments, entreaties were entirely without effect on me. Reckless what came of it, I retired to the one fit place for me—to the solitude in which I have buried myself ever since."

VIII

"With some difficulty, I discovered the lonely habitation of which was in search.

324

"No language can describe the heavenly composure of mind that came to me, when I first found myself alone; living the death-in-life of deafness, apart from creatures—no longer my fellow-creatures—who could hear: apart also from those privileged victims of hysterical impulse, who wrote me love-letters, and offered to console the 'poor beautiful deaf man' by marrying him. Through the distorting medium of such sufferings as I have described, women and men—even young women—were repellent to me alike. Ungratefully impatient of the admiration excited by my personal advantages, savagely irritated by tender looks and flattering compliments, I only consented take lodgings, on condition that there should be no young women living under the same roof with me. If this confession of morbid feeling looks like vanity, I can only say that appearances lie. I write in sober sadness; determined to present my character, with photographic accuracy, as a true likeness.

"What were my habits in solitude? How did I get through the weary and wakeful hours of the day?

"Living by myself, I became (as I have already acknowledged) important to myself—and, as a necessary consequence, I enjoyed registering my own daily doings. Let passages copied from my journal reveal how I got through the day."

IX

EXTRACTS FROM A DEAF MAN'S DIARY

"Monday.—Six weeks today since I first occupied my present retreat.

"My landlord and landlady are two hideous old people. They look as if they disliked me, on the rare occasions when we meet. So much the better; they don't remind me of my deafness by trying to talk, and they keep as much as possible out of my way. This morning, after breakfast, I altered the arrangement of my books—and then I made my fourth attempt, in the last ten days, to read some of my favorite authors. No: my taste has apparently changed since the time when I could hear. I closed one volume after another; caring nothing for what used to be deeply interesting to me.

"Reckless and savage—with a burning head and a cold heart—I went

325

out to look about me.

"After two hours of walking and thinking, I found that I had wandered to our county town. The rain began to fall heavily just as I happened to be passing a bookseller's shop. After some hesitation—for I hate exposing my deafness to strangers—I asked leave to take shelter, and looked at the books.

"Among them was a collection of celebrated Trials. I thought of my grandfather; consulted the index; and, finding his name there, bought the work. The shopman (as I could guess from his actions and looks) proposed sending the parcel to me. I insisted on taking it away. The sky had cleared; and I was eager to read the details of my grandfather's crime.

"Tuesday—Sat up late last night, reading my new book. My favorite poets, novelists, and historians have failed to interest me. I devoured the Trials with breathless delight; beginning of course with the murder in which I felt a family interest. Prepared to find my grandfather a ruffian, I confess I was surprised by the discovery that he was also a fool. The officers of justice had no merit in tracing the crime to him; his own stupidity delivered him into their hands. I read the evidence twice over, and put myself in his position, and saw the means plainly by which he might have set discovery at defiance.

"In the Preface to the Trials I found an allusion, in terms of praise, to a work of the same kind, published in the French language. I wrote to London at once, and ordered the book."

"Wednesday.—Is there some mysterious influence, in the silent solitude of my life, that is hardening my nature? Is there something unnatural in the existence of a man who never hears a sound? Is there a moral sense that suffers when a bodily sense is lost?

"These questions have been suggested to me by an incident that happened this morning.

"Looking out of window, I saw a brutal carter, on the road before the house, beating an over-loaded horse. A year since I should have interfered to protect the horse, without a moment's hesitation. If the wretch had been insolent, I should have seized his whip, and applied the heavy handle of it to his own shoulders. In past days, I have been more than once fined by a magistrate (privately in sympathy with my offence) for assaults committed by me in the interests of helpless animals. What did I feel now? Nothing but a selfish sense of uneasiness, at having been accidentally witness of an act which disturbed my composure. I turned away, regretting that I had gone to the window and looked out.

"This was not an agreeable train of thought to follow. What could I do? I was answered by the impulse which commands me to paint.

"I sharpened my pencils, and opened my box of colors, and determined to produce a work of art. To my astonishment, the brutal figure of the carter forced its way into my memory again and again. It (without in the least knowing why) as if the one chance of getting rid of this curious incubus, was to put the persistent image of the man on paper. It was done mechanically, and yet done so well, that I was encouraged to add to the picture. I put in next the poor beaten horse (another good likeness!); and then I introduced a life-like portrait of myself, giving the man the sound thrashing that he had deserved. Strange to say, this representation of what I ought to have done, relieved my mind as if I had actually done it. I looked at the pre-eminent figure of myself, and felt good, and turned to my Trials, and read them over again, and liked them better than ever."

"Thursday.—The bookseller has found a second-hand copy of the French Trials, and has sent them to me (as he expresses it) 'on approval'.

"I more than approve—I admire; and I more than admire—I imitate. These criminal stories are told with a dramatic power, which has impelled me to try if I can rival the clever French narrative. I found a promising subject by putting myself in my grandfather's place, and tracing the means by which it had occurred to me that he might have escaped the discovery of his crime.

"I cannot remember having read any novel with a tenth part of the interest that absorbed me, in constructing my imaginary train of circumstances. So completely did the reality of the narrative impress itself on my mind, that I felt as if the murder that I was relating had been a crime committed by myself. It was my own ingenuity that hid the dead body, and removed the traces of blood—and my own self-control that presented me as an innocent person, when the victim was missing, and I was asked (among other respectable people) to say whether I thought he was living or dead."

"A whole week has passed—and has been occupied by my new literary pursuit.

"My inexhaustible imagination invents plots and conspiracies of which I am the happy hero. I set traps which invariably catch my enemies. I place myself in positions which are entirely new to me. Yesterday, for instance, I invented a method of spiriting away a young person, whose disappearance was of considerable importance under the circumstances, and succeeded in completely bewildering her father, her friends, and the police: not a trace of her could they find. If I ever have occasion to do, in reality, what I only suppose myself to do in these exercises of ingenuity, what a dangerous man I may yet prove to be!

"This morning, I rose, planning to amuse myself with a new narrative, when the ideal world in which I am now living, became a world annihilated by collision with the sordid interests of real life.

"In plainer words, I received a written message from my landlord which has annoyed me—and not without good cause. This tiresome person finds himself unexpectedly obliged to give up possession of his house. The circumstances are not worth relating. The result is important—I am compelled to find new lodgings. Where am I to go?

"I left it to chance. That is to say, I looked at the railway time-table, and took a ticket for the first place, of which the name happened to catch my eye. Arrived at my destination, I found myself in a dirty manufacturing town, with an ugly river running through it.

"After a little reflection, I turned my back on the town, and followed the course of the river, in search of shelter and solitude on one or the other of its banks. An hour of walking brought me to an odd-looking cottage, half old and half new, attached to a water-mill. A bill in one of the windows announced that rooms were to be let; and a look round revealed a thick wood on my left hand, and a wilderness of sand and heath on my right. So far as appearances went, here was the very place for me.

"I knocked at the door, and was admitted by a little lean sly-looking old man. He showed me the rooms—one for myself, and one for my servant. Wretched as they were, the loneliness of the situation recommended them to me. I made no objections; and I consented to pay the rent that was asked. The one thing that remained to be done, in the interests of my tranquillity, was to ascertain if any other persons lived the cottage besides my new landlord. He wrote his answer to the question: 'Nobody but my daughter.' With serious misgivings, I inquired if his daughter was young. He wrote two fatal figures: '18'.

"Here was a discovery which disarranged all my plans, just as I had formed them! The prospect of having a girl in the house, at the age associated with my late disagreeable experience of the sensitive sex, was more than my irritable temper could endure. I saw the old man going to the window to take down the bill. Turning in a rage to stop him, I was suddenly brought to a standstill by the appearance of a person who had just entered the room.

"Was this the formidable obstacle to my tranquillity, which had prevented me from taking the rooms that I had chosen? Yes! I knew the miller's daughter intuitively. Delirium possessed me; my eyes devoured her; my heart beat as if it would burst out of my bosom. The old man approached me; he nodded, and grinned, and pointed to her. Did he claim his parental interest in her? Did he mean that she belonged to him? No! she belonged to me. She might be his daughter. She was My Fate.

"I don't know what it was in the girl that took me by storm. Nothing in her look or her manner expressed the slightest interest in me. That famous "beauty" of mine which had worked such ravages in the hearts of other young women, seemed not even to attract her notice. When her father put his hand to his ear, and told her (as I guessed) that I was deaf, there was no pity in her splendid brown eyes; they expressed a momentary curiosity, and nothing more. Possibly she had a hard heart? or perhaps she took a dislike to me, at first sight? It made no difference to my mind, either way. Was she the most beautiful creature I had ever seen? Not even that excuse was to be made for me. I have met with women of her dark complexion who were, beyond dispute, her superiors in beauty, and have looked at them with indifference. Add to this, that I am one of the men whom women offend if they are not perfectly well-dressed. The miller's daughter was badly dressed; her magnificent figure was profaned by the wretchedly-made gown that she wore. I forgave the profanation. In spite of the protest of my own better taste, I resigned myself to her gown. Is it possible adequately to describe such infatuation as this? Quite possible! I have only to acknowledge that I took the rooms at the cottage—and there is the state of my mind, exposed without mercy!

"How will it end?"

CHAPTER VI. THE RETURN OF THE PORTFOLIO

With that serious question the last of the leaves entrusted to me by the Lodger at the Mill came to an end.

I betray no confidence in presenting this copy of his confession. Time has passed since I first read it, and changes have occurred in the interval, which leave me free to exercise my own discretion, and to let the autobiography speak for itself.

If I am asked what impression of the writer those extraordinary pages produced on me, I feel at a loss how to reply.

Not one impression, but many impressions, troubled and confused my mind. Certain passages in the confession inclined me to believe that the writer was mad. But I altered my opinion at the next leaf, and set him down as a man with a bitter humor, disposed to make merry over his own bad qualities. At one time, his tone in writing of his early life, and his allusions to his mother, won my sympathy and respect. At another time, the picture of himself in his later years, and the defiant manner in which he presented it, almost made me regret that he had not died of the illness which had struck him deaf. In this state of uncertainty I may claim the merit of having arrived, so far as my own future conduct was concerned, at one positive conclusion. As strangers he and I had first met. As strangers I was determined we should remain.

Having made up my mind, so far, the next thing to do (with the clock on the mantel-piece striking midnight) was to go to bed.

I slept badly. The events that had happened, since my arrival in England, had excited me I suppose. Now and then, in the wakeful hours of the night, I thought of Cristel with some anxiety. Taking the Loger's exaggerated language for what it was really worth, the poor girl (as I was still inclined to fear) might have serious reason to regret that he had ever entered her father's cottage.

At the breakfast table, my stepmother and I met again.

Mrs. Roylake—in an exquisite morning dress; with her smile in perfect order—informed me that she was dying with curiosity. She had heard, from the servants, that I had not returned to the house until past ten o'clock on the previous night; and she was absolutely bewildered by the discovery. What could her dear Gerard have been doing, out in the dark by himself, for all that time?

"For some part of the time," I answered, "I was catching moths in Fordwitch Wood."

"What an extraordinary occupation for a young man! Well? And what did you do after that?"

"I walked on through the wood, and renewed my old associations with the river and the mill."

Mrs. Roylake's fascinating smile disappeared when I mentioned the mill. She suddenly became a cold lady—I might even say a stiff lady.

"I can't congratulate you on the first visit you have paid in our neighborhood," she said. "Of course that bold girl contrived to attract your notice?"

I replied that I had met with the "bold girl" purely by accident, on her side as well as on mine; and then I started a new topic. "Was it a pleasant dinner-party last night?" I asked—as if the subject really interested me. I had not been quite four and twenty hours in England yet, and I was becoming a humbug already.

My stepmother was her charming self again the moment my question had passed my lips. Society—provided it was not society at the mill—was always attractive as a topic of conversation. "Your absence was the only drawback," she answered. "I have asked the two ladies (my lord has an engagement) to dine here to-day, without ceremony. They are most anxious to meet you. My dear Gerard! you look surprised. Surely you know who the ladies are?"

I was obliged to acknowledge my ignorance.

Mrs. Roylake was shocked. "At any rate," she resumed, "you have heard of their father, Lord Uppercliff?"

I made another shameful confession. Either I had forgotten Lord Uppercliff, during my long absence abroad, or I had never heard of him.

Mrs. Roylake was disgusted. "And this is a foreign education!" she exclaimed. "Thank Heaven, you have returned to your own country! We will drive out after luncheon, and pay a round of visits." When this prospect was placed before me, I remembered having read in books of sensitive persons receiving impressions which made their blood run cold; I now found myself one of those persons, for the first time in my life. "In the meanwhile," Mrs. Roylake continued, "I must tell you—excuse me for laughing; it seems so very absurd that you should not know who Lord Uppercliff's daughters are—I must tell you that Lady Rachel is the eldest. She is married to the Honorable Captain Millbay, of the Navy, now away in his ship. A person of extraordinary strength of mind (I don't mean the Captain; I mean Lady Rachel); I admire her intellect, but her political and social opinions I must always view with regret. Her younger sister, Lady Lena—not married, Gerard; remember that!—is simply the most charming girl in England. If you don't fall in love with her, you will be the only young man in the county who has resisted Lady Lena. Poor Sir George—she refused him last week; you really must have heard of Sir George; our member of parliament; conservative of course; quite broken-hearted about Lady Lena; gone away to America to shoot bears. You seem to be restless. What are you fidgeting about? Ah, I know! You want to smoke after breakfast. Well, I won't be in your way. Go out on the terrace; your poor father always took his cigar on the terrace. They say smoking leads to meditation; I leave you to meditate on Lady Lena. Don't forget—luncheon at one o'clock, and the carriage at two."

She smiled, and kissed her hand, and fluttered out of the room. Charming; perfectly charming. And yet I was ungrateful enough to wish myself back in Germany again.

I lit my cigar, but not on the terrace. Leaving the house, I took the way once more that led to Fordwitch Wood. What would Mrs. Roylake have said, if she had discovered that I was going back to the mill? There was no other alternative. The portfolio was a trust confided to me; the sooner I returned it to the writer of the confession—the sooner I told him plainly the conclusion at which I had arrived—the more at ease my mind would be.

The sluggish river looked muddier than ever, the new cottage looked uglier than ever, exposed to the searching ordeal of sunlight. I knocked at the door on the ancient side of the building.

Cristel's father—shall I confess I had hoped that it might be Cristel herself?—let me in. In by-gone days, I dimly remembered him as old and small and withered. Advancing years had wasted him away, in the interval, until his white miller's clothes hung about him in empty folds. His fleshless face would have looked like the face of a mummy, but for the restless brightness of his little watchful black eyes. He stared at me in momentary perplexity, and, suddenly recovering himself, asked me to walk in.

"Are you the young master, sir? Ah, yes, yes; I thought so. My girl Cristy said she saw the young master last night. Thank you kindly, sir; I'm pretty well, considering how I've fallen away in my flesh. I have got a fine appetite, but somehow or other, my meals don't show on me. You will excuse my receiving you in the kitchen, sir; it's the best room we have. Did Cristy tell you how badly we are off here for repairs? You being our landlord, we look to you to help us. We are falling to pieces, as it were, on this old side of the house. There's first drains——"

He proceeded to reckon up the repairs, counting with his fleshless thumb on his skinny fingers, when he was interrupted by a curious succession of sounds which began with whining, and ended with scratching at the cottage door.

In a minute after, the door was opened from without. A brown dog, of the companionable retriever breed, ran in and fawned upon old Toller. Cristel followed (from the kitchen garden), with a basket of vegetables on her arm. Unlike the river and the cottage, she gained by being revealed in the brilliant sunlight. I now saw, in their full beauty, the luster of her brown eyes, the warm rosiness of her dark complexion, the delightful vivacity of expression which was the crowning charm of her face. She paused confusedly in the

334

doorway, and tried to resist me when I insisted on relieving her of the basket.

"Mr. Gerard," she protested, "you are treating me as if I was a young lady. What would they say at the great house, if they knew you had done that?"

My answer would no doubt have assumed the form of a foolish compliment, if her father had not spared her that infliction. He returned to the all-important question, the question of repairs.

"You see, sir, it's no use speaking to the bailiff. Saving your presence, he's a miser with his master's money. He says, 'All right,' and he does nothing. There's first, as I told you just now, the truly dreadful state of the drains——"

I tried to stop him by promising to speak to the bailiff myself. On hearing this good news, Mr. Toller's gratitude became ungovernable: he was more eager than ever, and more eloquent than ever, in returning to the repairs.

"And then, sir, there's the oven. They do call bread the staff of life. It's a burnt staff at one time, and a clammy staff at another, in our domestic experience. Satisfy yourself, sir; do please cross the kitchen and look with your own eyes at the state, the scandalous state, of the oven."

His daughter interfered, and stopped him at the critical moment when he was actually offering his arm to conduct me in state across the kitchen. Cristel had just put her pretty brown hand over his mouth, and said, "Oh, father, do pray be quiet!" when we were all three disturbed by another interruption.

A second door communicating, as I concluded from its position, with the new cottage, was suddenly opened. In the instant before the person behind it appeared, the dog looked that way—started up, frightened—and took refuge under the table. At the next moment, the deaf Lodger walked into the room. It was he beyond all doubt who had frightened the dog, forewarned by instinct of his appearance.

What I had read of his writing disposed me, now that I saw the man by daylight, to find something devilish in the expression of his face. No! strong as it was, my prejudice failed to make any discoveries that presented him at a disadvantage. His personal attractions triumphed in the clear searching light. I now perceived that his eyes were of that deeply dark blue, which is commonly and falsely described as resembling the color of the violet. To my thinking, they were so entirely beautiful that they had no right to be in a man's face. I might have felt the same objection to the pale delicacy of his complexion, to the soft profusion of his reddish-brown hair, to his finely shaped sensitive lips, but for two marked peculiarities in him which would have shown me to be wrong—that is to say: the expression of power about his head, and the signs of masculine resolution presented by his mouth and chin.

On entering the room, the first person, and the only person, who attracted his attention was Cristel.

He bowed, smiled, possessed himself abruptly of her hand, and kissed it. She tried to withdraw it from his grasp, and met with an obstinate resistance. His gallantry addressed her in sweet words; and his voice destroyed their charm by the dreary monotony of the tone in which he spoke. "On this lovely day, Cristel, Nature pleads for me. Your heart feels the sunshine and softens towards the poor deaf man who worships you. Ah, my dear, it's useless to say No. My affliction is my happiness, when you say cruel things to me. I live in my fool's paradise; I don't hear you." He tried to draw her nearer to him. "Come, my angel; let me kiss you."

She made a second attempt to release herself; and this time, she wrenched her hand out of his grasp with a strength for which he was not prepared.

That fiercest anger which turns the face pale, was the anger that had possession of Cristel as she took refuge with her father. "You asked me to bear with that man," she said, "because he paid you a good rent. I tell you this, father; my patience is coming to an end. Either he must go, or I must go. Make up your mind to choose between your money and me."

Old Toller astonished me. He seemed to have caught the infection of his daughter's anger. Placed between Cristel and his money, he really acted as if he preferred Cristel. He hobbled up to his lodger, and shook his infirm fists, and screamed at the highest pitch of his old cracked voice: "Let her be, or I won't have you here no longer! You deaf adder, let her be!"

The sensitive nerves of the deaf man shrank as those shrill tones pierced them. "If you want to speak to me, write it!" he said, with rage and suffering in every line of his face. He tore from his pocket his little book, filled with blank leaves, and threw it at Toller's head. "Write," he repeated. "If you murder me with your screeching again, look out for your skinny throat—I'll throttle you."

Cristel picked up the book. She was gratefully sensible of her father's interference. "He shall know what you said to him," she promised the old man. "I'll write it myself."

She took the pencil from its sheath in the leather binding of the book. Controlling himself, the lover whom she hated advanced towards her with a persuasive smile.

"Have you forgiven me?" he asked. "Have you been speaking kindly of me? I think I see it in your face. There are some deaf people who can tell what is said by looking at the speaker's lips. I am too stupid, or too impatient, or too wicked to be able to do that. Write it for me, dear, and make me happy for the day."

Cristel was not attending to him, she was speaking to me. "I hope, sir, you don't think that father and I are to blame for what has happened this morning," she said. He looked where she was looking—and discovered, for the first time, that I was in the room.

He had alluded to his wickedness a moment since. When his face turned my way, I thought it bore witness to his knowledge of his own character.

"Why didn't you come to my side of the house?" he said to me. "What am I to understand, sir, by seeing you here?"

Cristel dropped his book on the table, and hurried to me in breathless surprise. "He speaks as if he knew you!" she cried. "What does it mean?"

"Only that I met him last night," I explained, "after leaving you."

"Did you know him before that?"

"No. He was a perfect stranger to me."

He picked up his book from the table, and took his pencil out of Cristel's hand, while we were speaking. "I want my answer," he said, handing me the book and the pencil. I gave him his answer.

"You find me here, because I don't wish to return to your side of the house."

"Is that the impression," he asked, "produced by what I allowed you to read?"

I replied by a sign in the affirmative. He inquired next if I had brought his portfolio with me. I put it at once into his hand.

In some way unknown to me, I had apparently roused his suspicions. He opened the portfolio, and counted the loose leaves of writing in it carefully. While he was absorbed in this occupation, old Toller's eccentricity assumed a new form. His little restless black eyes followed the movements of his lodger's fingers, as they turned over leaf after leaf of the manuscript, with such eager curiosity and interest that I looked at him in surprise. Finding that he had attracted my notice, he showed no signs of embarrassment—he seized the opportunity of asking for information.

"Did my gentleman trust you, sir, with all that writing?" he began.

"Yes."

"Did he want you to read it?"

"He did."

"What's it all about, sir?"

Confronted by this cool inquiry, I informed Mr. Toller that the demands of curiosity had their limits, and that he had reached them. On this ground, I declined to answer any more questions. Mr. Toller went on with his questions immediately.

"Do you notice, sir, that he seems to set a deal of store by his writings?

338

Perhaps you can say what the value of them may be?"

I shook my head. "It won't do, Mr. Toller!"

He tried again—I declare it positively, he tried again. "You'll excuse me, sir? I've never seen his portfolio before. Am I right if I think you know where he keeps it?"

"Spare your breath, Mr. Toller. Once more, it won't do!"

Cristel joined us, amazed at his pertinacity. "Why are you so anxious, father, to know about that portfolio?" she asked.

Her father seemed to have reasons of his own for following my example and declining to answer questions. More polite, however, than I had been, he left his resolution to be inferred. His daughter was answered by a few general remarks, setting forth the advantage to the landlord of having a lodger who had lost one of senses.

"You see there's something convenient, my dear, in the circumstance of that nice-looking gentleman over there being deaf. We can talk about him before his face, just as comfortably as if it was behind his back. Isn't that so, Mr. Gerard? Don't you see it yourself, Cristy? For instance, I say it without fear in his presence: 'tis the act of a fool to be fumbling over writings, when there's nothing in them that's not well known to himself already—unless indeed they are worth money, which I don't doubt is no secret to you, Mr. Gerard? Eh? I beg your pardon, sir, did you speak? No? I beg your pardon again. Yes, yes, Cristy, I'm noticing him; he's done with his writings. Suppose I offer to put them away for him? You can see in his face he finds the tale of them correct. He's coming this way. What's he going to do next?"

He was going to establish a claim on my gratitude, by relieving me of Giles Toller.

"I have something to say to Mr. Roylake," he announced, with a haughty look at his landlord. "Mind! I don't forget your screaming at me just now, and I intend to know what you meant by it. That will do. Get out of the way."

The old fellow received his dismissal with a low bow, and left the kitchen with a look at the Lodger which revealed (unless I was entirely mistaken) a sly sense of triumph. What did it mean?

The deaf man addressed me with a cold and distant manner. "We must understand each other," he said. "Will you follow me to my side of the cottage?" I shook my head. "Very well," he resumed; "we will have it out, here. When I trusted you with my confession last night, I left you to decide (after reading it) whether you would make an enemy of me or not. You remember that?" I nodded my head. "Then I now ask you, Mr. Roylake: Which are we—enemies or friends?"

I took the pencil, and wrote my reply:

"Neither enemies nor friends. We are strangers from this time forth."

Some internal struggle produced a change in his face—visible for one moment, hidden from me in a moment more. "I think you will regret the decision at which you have arrived." He said that, and saluted me with his grandly gracious bow. As he turned away, he perceived Cristel at the other end of the room, and eagerly joined her.

"The only happy moments I have are my moments passed in your presence," he said. "I shall trouble you no more for to-day. Give me a little comfort to take back with me to my solitude. I didn't notice that there were other persons present when I asked leave to kiss you. May I hope that you forgive me?"

He held out his hand; it was not taken. He waited a little, in the vain hope that she would relent: she turned away from him.

A spasm of pain distorted his handsome face. He opened the door that led to his side of the cottage—paused—and looked back at Cristel. She took no notice of him. As he moved again to the door and left us, the hysterical passion in him forced its way outward—he burst into tears.

The dog sprang up from his refuge under the table, and shook himself joyfully. Cristel breathed again freely, and joined me at my end of the room. Shall I make another acknowledgment of weakness? I began to fear that we

340

might all of us (even including the dog!) have been a little hard on the poor deaf wretch who had gone away in such bitter distress. I communicated this view of the matter to Cristel. She failed to see it as I did.

The dog laid his head on her lap, asking to be caressed. She patted him while she answered me.

"I agree with this old friend, Mr. Gerard. We were both of us frightened, on the very first day, when the person you are pitying came to lodge with us. I have got to hate him, since that time—perhaps to despise him. But the dog has never changed; he feels and knows there is something dreadful in that man. One of these days, poor Ponto may turn out to be right.—May I ask you something, sir?"

"Of course!"

"You won't think I am presuming on your kindness?"

"You ought to know me better than that, Cristel!"

"The truth is, sir, I have been a little startled by what I saw in our lodger's face, when he asked if you were his enemy or his friend. I know he is thought to be handsome—but, Mr. Gerard, those beautiful eyes of his sometimes tell tales; and I have seen his pretty complexion change to a color that turned him into an ugly man. Will you tell me what you wrote when you answered him?"

I repeated what I had written, word for word. It failed to satisfy her.

"He is very vain," she said, "and you may have wounded his vanity by treating him like a stranger, after he had given you his writings to read, and invited you to his room. But I thought I saw something much worse than mortification in his face. Shall I be taking a liberty, if I ask how it was you got acquainted with him last night?"

She was evidently in earnest. I saw that I must answer her without reserve; and I was a little afraid of being myself open to a suspicion of vanity, if I mentioned the distrust which I had innocently excited in the mind of my new acquaintance. In this state of embarrassment I took a young man's way out of the difficulty, and spoke lightly of a serious thing.

"I became acquainted with your deaf Lodger, Cristel, under ridiculous circumstances. He saw us talking last night, and did me the honor to be jealous of me."

I had expected to see her blush. To my surprise she turned pale, and vehemently remonstrated.

"Don't laugh, sir! There's nothing to be amused at in what you have just told me. You didn't go into his room last night? Oh, what made you do that!"

I described his successful appeal to my compassion—not very willingly, for it made me look (as I thought) like a weak person. Little by little, she extracted from me the rest: how he objected to find a young man, especially in my social position, talking to Cristel; how he insisted on my respecting his claims, and engaging not to see her again; how, when I refused to do this, he gave me his confession to read, so that I might find out what a formidable man I was setting at defiance; how I had not been in the least alarmed, and had treated him (as Cristel had just heard) on the footing of a perfect stranger.

"There's the whole story," I concluded. "Like a scene in a play, isn't it?"

She protested once more against the light tone that I persisted in assuming.

"I tell you again, sir, this is no laughing matter. You have roused his jealousy. You had better have roused the fury of a wild beast. Knowing what you know of him, why did you stay here, when he came in? And, oh, why did I humiliate him in your presence? Leave us, Mr. Gerard—pray, pray leave us, and don't come near this place again till father has got rid of him."

Did she think I was to be so easily frightened as that? My sense of my own importance was up in arms at the bare suspicion of it!

"My dear child," I said grandly, "do you really suppose I am afraid of that poor wretch? Am I to give up the pleasure of seeing you, because a mad fellow is simple enough to think you will marry him? Absurd, Cristel—absurd!"

The poor girl wrung her hands in despair.

"Oh, sir, don't distress me by talking in that way! Do please remember who you are, and who I am. If I was the miserable means of your coming to any harm—I can't bear even to speak of it! Pray don't think me bold; I don't know how to express myself. You ought never to have come here; you ought to go; you must go!"

Driven by strong impulse, she ran to the place in which I had left my hat, and brought it to me, and opened the door with a look of entreaty which it was impossible to resist. It would have been an act of downright cruelty to persist in opposing her. "I wouldn't distress you, Cristel, for the whole world," I said—and left her to conclude that I had felt the influence of her entreaties in the right way. She tried to thank me; the tears rose in her eyes—she signed to me to leave her, poor soul, as if she felt ashamed of herself. I was shocked; I was grieved; I was more than ever secretly resolved to go back to her. When we said good-bye—I have been told that I did wrong; I meant no harm—I kissed her.

Having traversed the short distance between the cottage and the wood, I remembered that I had left my walking-stick behind me, and returned to get it.

Cristel was leaving the kitchen; I saw her at the door which communicated with the Lodger's side of the cottage. Her back was turned towards me; astonishment held me silent. She opened the door, passed through it, and closed it behind her.

Going to that man, after she had repelled his advances, in my presence! Going to the enemy against whom she had warned me, after I had first been persuaded to leave her! Angry thoughts these—and surely thoughts unworthy of me? If it had been the case of another man I should have said he was jealous. Jealous of the miller's daughter—in my position? Absurd! contemptible! But I was still in such a vile temper that I determined to let Cristel know she had been discovered. Taking one of my visiting cards, I wrote on it: "I came back for my stick, and saw you go to him." After I had pinned this spiteful little message to the door, so that she might see it when she returned, I suffered a disappointment. I was not half so well satisfied with myself as I had anticipated.

343

CHAPTER VII. THE BEST SOCIETY

Leaving the cottage for the second time, I was met at the door by a fat man of solemn appearance dressed in black, who respectfully touched his hat. My angry humor acknowledged the harmless stranger's salute by a rude inquiry: "What the devil do you want?" Instead of resenting this uncivil language, he indirectly reproved me by becoming more respectful than ever.

"My mistress desires me to tell you, sir, that luncheon is waiting." I was in the presence of a thoroughbred English servant—and I had failed to discover it until he spoke of his mistress! I had also, by keeping luncheon waiting, treated an English institution with contempt. And, worse even than this, as a misfortune which personally affected me, my stepmother evidently knew that I had paid another visit to the mill.

I hurried along the woodland path, followed by the fat domestic in black. Not used apparently to force his legs into rapid motion, he articulated with the greatest difficulty in answering my next question: "How did you know where to find me?"

"Mrs. Roylake ordered inquiries to be made, sir. The head gardener—" There his small reserves of breath failed him.

"The head gardener saw me?"

"Yes, sir."

"When?"

"Hours ago, sir—when you went into Toller's cottage."

I troubled my fat friend with no more questions.

Returning to the house, and making polite apologies, I discovered one more among Mrs. Roylake's many accomplishments. She possessed two smiles—a sugary smile (with which I was already acquainted), and an acid smile which she apparently reserved for special occasions. It made its appearance when I led her to the luncheon table.

"Don't let me detain you," my stepmother began.

"Won't you give me some luncheon?" I inquired.

"Dear me! hav'n't you lunched already?"

"Where should I lunch, my dear lady?" I thought this would induce the sugary smile to show itself. I was wrong.

"Where?" Mrs. Roylake repeated. "With your friends at the mill of course. Very inhospitable not to offer you lunch. When are we to have flour cheaper?"

I began to get sulky. All I said was: "I don't know."

"Curious!" Mrs. Roylake observed. "You not only don't get luncheon among your friends: you don't even get information. To know a miller, and not to know the price of flour, is ignorance presented in one of its most pitiable aspects. And how is Miss Toller looking? Perfectly charming?"

I was angry by this time. "You have exactly described her," I said. Mrs. Roylake began to get angry, on her side.

"Surely a little coarse and vulgar?" she suggested, reverting to poor Cristel.

"Would you like to judge for yourself?" I asked. "I shall be happy, Mrs. Roylake, to take you to the mill."

My stepmother's knowledge of the world implied considerable acquaintance—how obtained I do not pretend to know—with the characters of men. Discovering that she was in danger of overstepping the limits of my patience, she drew back with a skill which performed the retrograde movement without permitting it to betray itself.

"We have carried our little joke, my dear Gerard, far enough," she said.

"I fancy your residence in Germany has rather blunted your native English sense of humor. You don't suppose, I hope and trust, that I am so insensible to our relative positions as to think of interfering in your choice of friends or associates. If you are not aware of it already, let me remind you that this house is now yours; not mine. I live here—gladly live here, my dear boy—by your indulgence; fortified (I am sure) by your regard for your excellent father's wishes as expressed in his will—"

I stopped her there. She had got the better of me with a dexterity which I see now, but which I was not clever enough to appreciate at time. In a burst of generosity, I entreated her to consider Trimley Deen as her house, and never to mention such a shocking subject as my authority again.

After this, need I say that the most amiable of women took me out in her carriage, and introduced me to some of the best society in England?

If I could only remember all the new friends to whom I made my bow, as well as the conversation in which we indulged, I might write a few pages here, interesting in a high degree to persons with well-balanced minds. Unhappily, so far as my own impressions were concerned, the best society proved to be always the same society. Every house that we entered was in the same beautiful order; every mistress of the house was dressed in the best taste; every master of the house had the same sensible remarks to make on conservative prospects at the coming election; every young gentleman wanted to know how my game preserves had been looked after in my absence; every young lady said: "How nice it must have been, Mr. Roylake, to find yourself again at Trimley Deen." Has anybody ever suffered as I suffered, during that round of visits, under the desire to yawn and the effort to suppress it? Is there any sympathetic soul who can understand me, when I say that I would have given a hundred pounds for a gag, and for the privilege of using it to stop my stepmother's pleasant chat in the carriage, following on our friends' pleasant chat in the drawing-room? Finally, when we got home, and when Mrs. Roylake kindly promised me another round of visits, and more charming people in the neighborhood to see, will any good Christian forgive me, if I own that I took advantage of being alone to damn the neighborhood, and to feel relieved by it?

Now that I was no longer obliged to listen to polite strangers, my thoughts reverted to Cristel, and to the suspicions that she had roused in me.

Recovering its influence, in the interval that had passed, my better nature sharply reproached me. I had presumed to blame Cristel, with nothing to justify me but my own perverted view of her motives. How did I know that she had not opened that door, and gone to that side of the cottage, with a perfectly harmless object in view? I was really anxious, if I could find the right way to do it, to make amends for an act of injustice of which I felt ashamed. If I am asked why I was as eager to set myself right with a miller's daughter, as if she had been a young lady in the higher ranks of life, I can only reply that no such view of our relative positions as this ever occurred to me. A strange state of mind, no doubt. What was the right explanation of it?

The right explanation presented itself at a later time, when troubles had quickened my intellect, and when I could estimate the powerful influence of circumstances at its true value.

I had returned to England, to fill a prominent place in my own little world, without relations whom I loved, without friends whose society I could enjoy. Hopeful, ardent, eager for the enjoyment of life, I had brought with me to my own country the social habits and the free range of thought of a foreign University; and, as a matter of course, I failed to feel any sympathy with the society—new to me—in which my lot had been cast. Beset by these disadvantages, I had met with a girl, possessed of remarkable personal attractions, and associated with my earliest remembrances of my own happy life and of my mother's kindness—a girl, at once simple and spirited; unspoilt by the world and the world's ways, and placed in a position of peril due to the power of her own beauty, which added to the interest that she naturally inspired. Estimating these circumstances at their true value, did a state of mind which rendered me insensible to the distinctions that separate the classes in England, stand in any need of explanation? As I thought—and think still—it explained itself.

My stepmother and I parted on the garden terrace, which ran along the pleasant southern side of the house.

The habits that I had contracted, among my student friends in Germany, made tobacco and beer necessary accompaniments to the process of thinking.

I had nearly exhausted my cigar, my jug, and my thoughts, when I saw two men approaching me from the end of the terrace.

As they came nearer, I recognized in one of the men my fat domestic in black. He stopped the person who was accompanying him and came on to me by himself.

"Will you see that man, sir, waiting behind me?"

"Who is he?"

"I don't know, sir. He says he has got a letter to give you, and he must put it in your own hands. I think myself he's a beggar. He's excessively insolent—he insists on seeing you. Shall I tell him to go?"

The servant evidently expected me to say Yes. He was disappointed; my curiosity was roused; I said I would see the insolent stranger.

As he approached me, the man certainly did not look like a beggar. Poor he might be, judging by his dress. The upper part of him was clothed in an old shooting jacket of velveteen; his legs presented a pair of trousers, once black, now turning brown with age. Both garments were too long for him, and both were kept scrupulously clean. He was a short man, thickly and strongly made. Impenetrable composure appeared on his ugly face. His eyes were sunk deep in his head; his nose had evidently been broken and not successfully mended; his grey hair, when he took off his hat on addressing me, was cut short, and showed his low forehead and his bull neck. An Englishman of the last generation would, as I have since been informed, have set him down as a retired prize-fighter. Thanks to my ignorance of the pugilistic glories of my native country, I was totally at a loss what to make of him.

"Have I the honor of speaking to Mr. Roylake?" he asked. His quiet steady manner prepossessed me in his favour; it showed no servile reverence for the accident of birth, on the one hand, and no insolent assertion of independence, on the other. When I had told him that my name was Roylake, he searched one of the large pockets of his shooting jacket, produced a letter, and silently offered it to me.

Before I took the letter—seeing that he was a stranger, and that he mentioned no name known to me—I thought it desirable to make some inquiry.

"Is it a letter of your own writing?" I asked.

"No, sir."

"Who sends you with it?"

He was apparently a man of few words. "My master," was the guarded answer that this odd servant returned.

I became as inquisitive as old Toller himself.

"Who is your master?" I went on.

The reply staggered me. Speaking as quietly and respectfully as ever, he said: "I can't tell you, sir."

"Do you mean that you are forbidden to tell me?"

"No, sir."

"Then what do you mean?"

"I mean that I don't know my master's name."

I instantly took the letter from him, and looked at the address. For once in a way, I had jumped at a conclusion and I had proved to be right. The handwriting on the letter, and the handwriting of the confession which I had read overnight, were one and the same.

"Are you to wait for an answer?" I asked, as I opened the envelope.

"I am to wait, sir, if you tell me to do so."

The letter was a long one. After running my eye over the first sentences, I surprised myself by acting discreetly. "You needn't wait," I said; "I will send a reply." The man of few words raised his shabby hat, turned about in silence, and left me.

CHAPTER VIII. THE DEAF LODGER

The letter was superscribed: "Private and Confidential." It was written in these words:

"Sir,—You will do me grievous wrong if you suppose that I am trying to force myself on your acquaintance. My object in writing is to prevent you (if I can) from misinterpreting my language and my conduct, on the only two occasions when we happen to have met.

"I am conscious that you must have thought me rude and ungrateful— perhaps even a little mad—when I returned your kindness last night, in honoring me with a visit, by using language which has justified you in treating me as a stranger.

"Fortunately for myself, I gave you my autobiography to read. After what you now know of me, I may hope that your sense of justice will make some allowance for a man, tried (I had almost written, cursed) by such suffering as mine.

"There are other deaf persons, as I have heard, who set me a good example.

"They feel the consolations of religion. Their sweet tempers find relief even under the loss of the most precious of all the senses. They mix with society; submitting to their dreadful isolation, and preserving unimpaired sympathy with their happier fellow-creatures who can hear. I am not one of those persons. With sorrow I say it—I never have submitted, I never can submit, to my hard fate.

"Let me not omit to ask your indulgence for my behavior, when we met at the cottage this morning.

"What unfavorable impression I may have produced on you, I dare not inquire. So little capable am I of concealing the vile feelings which sometimes get the better of me, that Miss Cristel (observe that I mention her with respect) appears to have felt positive alarm, on your account, when she looked at me.

"I may tell you, in confidence, that this charming person came to my side of the cottage, as soon as you had taken your departure, to intercede with me in your favour. 'If your wicked mind is planning to do evil to Mr. Roylake,' she wrote in my book, 'either you will promise me to give it up, or I will never allow you to see me again; I will even leave home secretly, to be out of your way.' In that strong language she expressed—how shall I refer to it?—shall I say the sisterly interest that she felt in your welfare?"

I laid down the letter for a moment. If I had not already reproached myself for having misjudged Cristel—and if I had not, in that way, done her some little justice in my own better thoughts—I should never have recovered my self-respect after reading the deaf man's letter. The good girl! The dear good girl! Yes: that was how I thought of her, under the windows of my stepmother's boudoir—while Mrs. Roylake, for all I knew to the contrary, might be looking down at me, and when Lady Lena, the noble and beautiful, was coming to dinner!

The letter concluded as follows:

"To return to myself. I gave Miss Cristel the promise on which she had insisted; and then, naturally enough, I inquired into her motive for interfering in your favour.

"She frankly admitted that she was interested in you. First: in grateful remembrance of old times, when you and your mother had been always good to her. Secondly: because she had found you as kind and as friendly as ever, now that you were a man and had become the greatest landowner in the county. There was the explanation I had asked for, at my service. And, on that, she left me.

"Did I believe her when I was meditating on our interview, alone in my room? Or did I suspect you of having robbed me of the only consolation that makes my life endurable?

"No such unworthy suspicion as this was admitted to my mind. With all my heart, I believe her. And with perfect sincerity, I trust You.

"If your knowledge of me has failed to convince you that there is any such thing as a better side to my nature, you will no doubt conclude that this letter is a trick of mine to throw you off your guard; and you will continue to distrust me as obstinately as ever. In that case, I will merely remind you that my letter is private and confidential, and I will not ask you to send me a reply.

"I remain, Sir, yours as you may receive me,   "THE DEAF LODGER

I wonder what another man, in my position, would have done when he had read this letter? Would he have seen in it nothing to justify some respect and some kindly feeling towards the writer? Could he have reconciled it to his conscience to leave the afflicted man who had trusted him without a word of reply?

For my part (do not forget what a young man I was in those days), I made up my mind to reply in the friendliest manner—that is to say, in person.

After consulting my watch, I satisfied myself that I could go to the mill, and get back again, before the hour fixed for our late dinner—supper we should have called it in Germany. For the second time that day, and without any hesitation, I took the road that led to Fordwitch Wood.

Crossing the glade, I encountered a stout young woman, filling a can with water from the spring. She curtseyed on seeing me. I asked if she belonged to the village.

The reply informed me that I had taken another of my servants for a stranger. The stout nymph of the spring was my kitchen-maid; and she was fetching the water which we drank at the house; "and there's no water, sir, like yours for all the country round." Furnished with these stores of information, I went my way, and the kitchen-maid went hers. She spoke, of course, of having seen her new master, on returning to the servants' hall. In this manner, as I afterwards heard, the discovery of me at the spring, and my departure by the path that led to the mill, reached Mrs. Roylake's ears—the medium of information being the lady's own maid. So far, Fordwitch Wood seemed to be a place to avoid, in the interests of my domestic tranquillity.

Arriving at the cottage, I found the Lodger standing by the open window at which I had first seen him.

But on this occasion, his personal appearance had undergone a singular process of transformation. The lower part of his face, from his nostrils to his chin, was hidden by a white handkerchief tied round it. He had removed the stopper from a strangely shaped bottle, and was absorbed in watching some interesting condition in a dusky liquid that it contained. To attract his attention by speaking was of course out of the question; I could only wait until he happened to look my way.

My patience was not severely tried: he soon replaced the stopper in the bottle, and, looking up from it, saw me. With his free hand, he quickly removed the handkerchief, and spoke.

"Let me ask you to wait in the boat-house," he said; "I will come to you directly." He pointed round the corner of the new cottage; indicating of course the side of it that was farthest from the old building.

Following his directions, I first passed the door that he used in leaving or returning to his room, and then gained the bank of the river. On my right hand rose the mill building, with its big waterwheel—and, above it, a little higher up the stream, I recognized the boat-house; built out in the water on piles, and approached by a wooden pier.

No structure of this elaborate and expensive sort would have been set up by my father, for the miller's convenience. The boat-house had been built, many years since, by a rich retired tradesman with a mania for aquatic pursuits. Our ugly river had not answered his expectations, and our neighborhood had abstained from returning his visits. When he left us, with his wherries and canoes and outriggers, the miller took possession of the abandoned boat-house. "It's the sort of fixture that don't pay nohow," old Toller remarked. "Suppose you remove it—there's a waste of money. Suppose you knock it to pieces—is it worth a rich gentleman's while to sell a cartload of firewood?" Neither of these alternatives having been adopted, and nobody wanting an empty boat-house, the clumsy mill boat, hitherto tied to a stake, and exposed to the worst that the weather could do to injure it, was now snugly sheltered under a roof, with empty lockers (once occupied by aquatic luxuries) gaping on either side of it.

I was looking out on the river, and thinking of all that had happened since my first meeting with Cristel by moonlight, when the voice of the deaf man made itself discordantly heard, behind me.

"Let me apologize for receiving you here," he said; "and let me trouble you with one more of my confessions. Like other unfortunate deaf people, I suffer from nervous irritability. Sometimes, we restlessly change our places of abode. And sometimes, as in my case, we take refuge in variety of occupation. You remember the ideal narratives of crime which I was so fond of writing at one time?"

I gave the affirmative answer, in the usual way.

"Well," he went on, "my literary inventions have ceased to interest me. I have latterly resumed the chemical studies, associated with that happy time in my life when I was entering on the medical profession. Unluckily for you, I have been trying an experiment to-day, which makes such an abominable smell in my room that I dare not ask you to enter it. The fumes are not only disagreeable, but in some degree dangerous. You saw me at the window, perhaps, with my nose and mouth protected before I opened the bottle?"

I repeated the affirmative sign. He produced his little book of blank leaves, and opened it ready for use.

"May I hope," he said, "that your visit is intended as a favorable reply to my letter?"

I took the pencil, and answered him in these terms:

"Your letter has satisfied me that I was mistaken in treating you like a stranger. I have come here to express my regret at having failed to do you justice. Pray be assured that I believe in your better nature, and that I accept your letter in the spirit in which you have written it."

He read my reply, and suddenly looked at me.

Never had I seen his beautiful eyes so brightly soft, so irresistibly tender, as they appeared now. He held out his hand to me. It is one of my small merits to be (in the popular phrase) as good as my word. I took his hand; well knowing that the action committed me to accepting his friendship.

In relating the events which form this narrative, I look back at the chain, as I add to it link by link—sometimes with surprise, sometimes with interest, and sometimes with the discovery that I have omitted a circumstance which it is necessary to replace. But I search my memory in vain, while I dwell on the lines that I have just written, for a recollection of some attendant event which might have warned me of the peril towards which I was advancing blindfold. My remembrance presents us as standing together with clasped hands; but nothing in the slightest degree ominous is associated with the picture. There was no sinister chill communicated from his hand to mine; no shocking accident happened close by us in the river; not even a passing cloud obscured the sunlight, shining in its gayest glory over our heads.

After having shaken hands, neither he nor I had apparently anything more to say. A little embarrassed, I turned to the boat-house window, and looked out. Trifling as the action was, my companion noticed it.

"Do you like that muddy river?" he asked.

I took the pencil again: "Old associations make even the ugly Loke interesting to me."

He sighed as he read those words. "I wish, Mr. Roylake, I could say the same. Your interesting river frightens me."

It was needless to ask for the pencil again. My puzzled face begged for an explanation.

"When you were in my room," he said, "you may have noticed a second window which looks out on The Loke. I have got into a bad habit of sitting by that window on moonlight nights. I watch the flow of the stream, and it seems to associate itself with the flow of my thoughts. Nothing remarkable, so far—while I am awake. But, later, when I get to sleep, dreams come to me. All of them, sir, without exception connect Cristel with the river. Look at the stealthy current that makes no sound. In my last night's sleep, it made itself heard; it was flowing in my ears with a water-music of its own. No longer my deaf ears; I heard, in my dream, as well as you can hear. Yes; the same water-music, singing over and over again the same horrid song: "Fool, fool, no Cristel for you; bid her good-bye, bid her good-bye." I saw her floating away from me on those hideous waters. The cruel current held me back when I tried to follow her. I struggled and screamed and shivered and cried. I woke up with a start that shook me to pieces, and cursed your interesting river. Don't write to me about it again. Don't look at it again. Why did you bring up the subject? I beg your pardon; I had no right to say that. Let me be polite; let me be hospitable. I beg to invite you to come and see me, when my room is purified from its pestilent smell. I can only offer you a cup of tea. Oh, that river, that river, what devil set me talking about it? I'm not mad, Mr. Roylake; only wretched. When may I expect you? Choose your own evening next week."

Who could help pitying him? Compared with my sound sweet dreamless sleep, what dreadful nights were his!

I accepted his invitation as a matter of course. When we had completed our arrangements, it was time for me to think of returning to Trimley Deen. Moving towards the door, I accidentally directed his attention to the pier by which the boat-house was approached.

His face instantly reminded me of Cristel's description of him, when he was strongly and evilly moved. I too saw "his beautiful eyes tell tales, and his pretty complexion change to a color which turned him into an ugly man." He seized my arm, and pointed to the pier, at the end of it which joined the river-bank. "Pray accept my excuses; I can't answer for my temper if that wretch comes near me." With this apology he hurried away; and sly Giles Toller, having patiently waited until the coast was clear, accosted me with his best bow, and said: "Beautiful weather, isn't it, sir?"

I had no remarks to make on the weather; but I was interested in discovering what had happened at the cottage.

"You have mortally offended the gentleman who has just left me," I said. "What have you done?"

Mr. Toller had purposes of his own to serve, and kept those purposes (as usual) exclusively in view: he presented deaf ears to me now!

"I don't think I ever remember such wonderful weather, sir, in my time; and I'm an old fellow, as I needn't tell you. Being at the mill just now, I saw you in the boat-house, and came to pay my respects. Would you be so good as to look at this slip of paper, Mr. Gerard? If you will kindly ask what it is, you will in a manner help me."

I knew but too well what it was. "The repairs again!" I said resignedly. "Hand it over, you obstinate old man."

Mr. Toller was so tickled by my discovery, and by the cheering prospect consequent on seeing his list of repairs safe in my pocket, that he laughed until I really thought he would shake his lean little body to pieces. By way of bringing his merriment to an end, I assumed a look of severity, and insisted on knowing how he had offended the Lodger. My venerable tenant, trembling for his repairs, drifted into a question of personal experience, and seemed to anticipate that it might improve my temper.

"When you have a woman about the house, Mr. Gerard, you may have noticed that she's an everlasting expense to you—especially when she's a young one. Isn't that so?"

I inquired if he applied this remark to his daughter.

"That's it, sir; I'm talking of Cristy. When her back's up, there isn't her equal in England for strong language. My gentleman has misbehaved himself in some way (since you were with us this morning, sir); how, I don't quite understand. All I can tell you is, I've given him notice to quit. A clear loss of money to me every week, and Cristy's responsible for it. Yes, sir! I've been worked up to it by my girl. If Cristy's mother had asked me to get rid of a paying lodger, I should have told her to go to—— we won't say where, sir; you'll know where when you're married yourself. The upshot of it is that I have offended my gentleman, for the sake of my girl: which last is a luxury I can't afford, unless I let the rooms again. If you hear of a tenant, say what a good landlord I am, and what sweet pretty rooms I've got to let."

I led the way to the bank of the river, before Mr. Toller could make any more requests.

We passed the side of the old cottage. The door was open; and I saw Cristel employed in the kitchen.

My watch told me that I had still two or three minutes to spare; and my guilty remembrance of the message that I had pinned to the door suggested an immediate expression of regret. I approached Cristel with a petition for pardon on my lips. She looked distrustfully at the door of communication with the new cottage, as if she expected to see it opened from the other side.

"Not now!" she said—and went on sadly with her household work.

"May I see you to-morrow?" I asked.

"It had better not be here, sir," was the only reply she made.

I offered to meet her at any other place which she might appoint. Cristel persisted in leaving it to me; she spoke absently, as if she was thinking all the time of something else. I could propose no better place, at the moment, than the spring in Fordwitch Wood. She consented to meet me there, on the next day, if seven o'clock in the morning would not be too early for me. My German habits had accustomed me to early rising. She heard me tell her this—and looked again at the Lodger's door—and abruptly wished me good evening.

Her polite father was shocked at this unceremonious method of dismissing the great man, who had only to say the word and stop the repairs. "Where are your manners, Cristy?" he asked indignantly. Before he could say another word, I was out of the cottage.

As I passed the spring on my way home, I thought of my two

appointments. On that evening, my meeting with the daughter of the lord. On the next morning, my meeting with the daughter of the miller. Lady Lena at dinner; Cristel before breakfast. If Mrs. Roylake found out that social contrast, what would she say? I was a merry young fool; I burst out laughing.

CHAPTER IX. MRS ROYLAKE'S GAME: FIRST MOVE

The dinner at Trimley Deen has left in my memory little that I can distinctly recall. Only a faintly-marked vision of Lady Lena rewards me for doing my best to remember her. A tall slim graceful person, dressed in white with a simplicity which is the perfection of art, presents to my admiration gentle blue eyes, a pale complexion delicately touched with color, a well-carried head crowned by lovely light brown hair. So far, time helps the reviving past to come to life again—and permits nothing more. I cannot say that I now remember the voice once so musical in my ears, or that I am able to repeat the easy unaffected talk which once interested me, or that I see again (in my thoughts) the perfect charm of manner which delighted everybody, not forgetting myself. My unworthy self, I might say; for I was the only young man, honored by an introduction to Lady Lena, who stopped at admiration, and never made use of opportunity to approach love.

On the other hand, I distinctly recollect what my stepmother and I said to each other when our guests had wished us good-night.

If I am asked to account for this, I can only reply that the conspiracy to lead me into proposing marriage to Lady Lena first showed itself on the occasion to which I have referred. In her eagerness to reach her ends, Mrs. Roylake failed to handle the fine weapons of deception as cleverly as usual. Even I, with my small experience of worldly women, discovered the object that she had in view.

I had retired to the seclusion of the smoking-room, and was already encircled by the clouds which float on the heaven of tobacco, when I heard a rustling of silk outside, and saw the smile of Mrs. Roylake beginning to captivate me through the open door.

"If you throw away your cigar," cried this amiable person, "you will drive me out of the room. Dear Gerard, I like your smoke."

My fat man in black, coming in at the moment to bring me some soda water, looked at his mistress with an expression of amazement and horror, which told me that he now saw Mrs. Roylake in the smoking-room for the first time. I involved myself in new clouds. If I suffocated my stepmother, her own polite equivocation would justify the act. She settled herself opposite to me in an armchair. The agonies that she must have suffered, in preventing her face from expressing emotions of disgust, I dare not attempt to imagine, even at this distance of time.

"Now, Gerard, let us talk about the two ladies. What do you think of my friend, Lady Rachel?"

"I don't like your friend, Lady Rachel."

"You astonish me. Why?"

"I think she's a false woman."

"Heavens, what a thing to say of a lady—and that lady my friend! Her politics may very reasonably have surprised you. But surely her vigorous intellect ought to have challenged your admiration; you can't deny that?"

I was not clever enough to be able to deny it. But I was bold enough to say that Lady Rachel seemed to me to be a woman who talked for the sake of producing effect. She expressed opinions, as I ventured to declare, which (in her position) I did not believe she could honestly entertain.

Mrs. Roylake entered a vigorous protest. She assured me that I was completely mistaken. "Lady Rachel," she said, "is the most perfectly candid person in the whole circle of my acquaintance."

With the best intentions on my part, this was more than I could patiently endure.

"Isn't she the daughter of a nobleman?" I asked. "Doesn't she owe her rank and her splendor, and the respect that people show to her, to the fortunate circumstance of her birth? And yet she talks as if she was a red republican. You yourself heard her say that she was a thorough Radical, and hoped she might live to see the House of Lords abolished. Oh, I heard her! And what is more, I listened so attentively to such sentiments as these, from a lady with a title, that I can repeat, word for word, what she said next. "We hav'n't deserved our own titles; we hav'n't earned our own incomes; and we legislate for the country, without having been trusted by the country. In short, we are a set of impostors, and the time is coming when we shall be found out." Do you believe she really meant that? All as false as false can be—that's what I say of it."

There I stopped, privately admiring my own eloquence.

Quite a mistake on my part; my eloquence had done just what Mrs. Roylake wished me to do. She wanted an opportunity of dropping Lady Rachel, and taking up Lady Lena, with a producible reason which forbade the imputation of a personal motive on her part. I had furnished her with the reason. Thus far, I cannot deny it, my stepmother was equal to herself.

"Really, Gerard, you are so violent in your opinions that I am sorry I spoke of Lady Rachel. Shall I find you equally prejudiced, and equally severe, if I change the subject to dear Lady Lena? Oh, don't say you think She is false, too!"

Here Mrs. Roylake made her first mistake. She over-acted her part; and, when it was too late, she arrived, I suspect, at that conclusion herself.

"If you hav'n't seen that I sincerely admire Lady Lena," I said, as smartly as I could, "the sooner you disfigure yourself with a pair of spectacles, my dear lady, the better. She is very pretty, perfectly unaffected, and, if I may presume to judge, delightfully well-bred and well-dressed."

My stepmother's face actually brightened with pleasure. Reflecting on it now, I am strongly disposed to think that she had not allowed her feelings to express themselves so unreservedly, since the time when she was a girl. After all, Mrs. Roylake was paying her step-son a compliment in trying to entrap him into a splendid marriage. It was my duty to think kindly of my ambitious relative. I did my duty.

"You really like my sweet Lena?" she said. "I am so glad. What were you talking about, with her? She made you exert all your powers of conversation, and she seemed to be deeply interested."

More over-acting! Another mistake! And I could see through it! With no English subject which we could discuss in common, Lady Lena's ready tact alluded to my past life. Mrs. Roylake had told her that I was educated at a German University. She had heard vaguely of students with long hair, who wore Hessian boots, and fought duels; and she appealed to my experience to tell her something more. I did my best to interest her, with very indifferent success, and was undeservedly rewarded by a patient attention, which presented the unselfish refinements of courtesy under their most perfect form.

But let me do my step-mother justice. She contrived to bend me to her will, before she left the smoking-room—I am sure I don't know how.

"You have entertained the charming daughters at dinner," she reminded me; "and the least you can do, after that, is to pay your respects to their noble father. In your position, my dear boy, you cannot neglect our English customs without producing the worst possible impression."

In two words, I found myself pledged, under pretence of visiting my lord, to improve my acquaintance with Lady Lena on the next day.

"And pray be careful," Mrs. Roylake proceeded, still braving the atmosphere of the smoking-room, "not to look surprised if you find Lord Uppercliff's house presenting rather a poor appearance just now."

I was dying for another cigar, and I entirely misunderstood the words of warning which had just been addressed to me. I tried to bring our interview to a close by making a generous proposal.

"Does he want money?" I asked. "I'll lend him some with the greatest pleasure."

Mrs. Roylake's horror expressed itself in a little thin wiry scream.

"Oh, Gerard, what people you must have lived among! What shocking ignorance of my lord's enormous fortune! He and his family have only just returned to their country seat, after a long absence—parliament you know, and foreign baths, and so on—and their English establishment is not yet complete. I don't know what mistake you may not make next. Do listen to what I want to say to you."

Listening, I must acknowledge, with an absent mind, my attention was suddenly seized by Mrs. Roylake—without the slightest conscious effort towards that end, on the part of the lady herself.

The first words that startled me, in her flow of speech, were these:

"And I must not forget to tell you of poor Lord Uppercliff's misfortune. He had a fall, some time since, and broke his leg. As I think, he was so unwise as to let a plausible young surgeon set the broken bone. Anyway, the end of it is that my lord slightly limps when he walks; and pray remember that he hates to see it noticed. Lady Rachel doesn't agree with me in attributing her father's lameness to his surgeon's want of experience. Between ourselves, the man seems to have interested her. Very handsome, very clever, very agreeable, and the manners of a gentleman. When his medical services came to an end, he was quite an acquisition at their parties in London—with one drawback: he mysteriously disappeared, and has never been heard of since. Ask Lady Lena about it. She will give you all the details, without her elder sister's bias in favour of the handsome young man. What a pretty compliment you are paying me! You really look as if I had interested you."

Knowing what I knew, I was unquestionably interested.

Although the recent return of Lord Uppercliff and his daughter to their country home had, as yet, allowed no opportunity of a meeting, out of doors, between the deaf Lodger and the friends whom he had lost sight of—no doubt at the time of his serious illness—still, the inevitable discovery might happen on any day. What result would follow? And what would be the effect on Lady Rachel, when she met with the fascinating young surgeon, and discovered the terrible change in him?

CHAPTER X. WARNED!

We were alone in the glade, by the side of the spring. At that early hour there were no interruptions to dread; but Cristel was ill at ease. She seemed to be eager to get back to the cottage as soon as possible.

"Father tells me," she began abruptly, "he saw you at the boathouse. And it seemed to him, that you were behaving yourself like a friend to that terrible man."

I reminded her of my having expressed the fear that we had been needlessly hard on him; and, I added that he had written a letter which confirmed me in that opinion. She looked, not only disappointed, but even alarmed.

"I had hoped," she said sadly, "that father was mistaken."

"So little mistaken," I assured her, "that I am going to drink tea with the man who seems to frighten you. I hope he will ask you to meet—"

She recoiled from the bare idea of an invitation.

"Will you hear what I want to tell you?" she said earnestly. "You may alter your opinion if you know what I have been foolish enough to do, when you saw me go to the other side of the cottage."

"Dear Cristel, I know what I owe to your kind interest in me on that occasion!" Before I could say a word of apology for having wronged her by my suspicions, she insisted on an explanation of what I had just said.

"Did he mention it in his letter?" she asked.

I owned that I had obtained my information in this way. And I declared that he had expressed his admiration of her, and his belief in her, in terms which made it a subject of regret to me not to be able to show what he had written.

Cristel forgot her fear of our being interrupted. Her dismay expressed itself in a cry that rang through the wood.

"You even believe in his letter?" she exclaimed. "Mr. Gerard! His writing in that way to You about Me is a proof that he lies; and I'll make you see it. If you were anybody else but yourself, I would leave you to your fate. Yes, your fate," she passionately repeated. "Oh, forgive me, sir! I'm behaving disrespectfully; I beg your pardon. No, no; let me go on. When I spoke to him in your best interests (as I did most truly believe) I never suspected what mischief I had done, till I looked in his face. Then, I saw how he hated you, and how vilely he was thinking in secret of me—"

Pure delusion! How could I allow it to go on? I interrupted her.

"My dear, you have quite mistaken him. As I have already said, he sincerely respects you—and he owns that he misjudged me when he and I first met."

"What! Is that in his letter too? It's worse even than I feared. Again, and again, and again, I say it"—she stamped on the ground in the fervor of her conviction—"he hates you with the hatred that never forgives and never forgets. You think him a good man. Do you suppose I would have begged and prayed of my father to send him away, without having reasons that justified me? Mr. Gerard, you force me to tell you what my unlucky visit did put into his head. Yes, he does believe—believes firmly—that you have forgotten what is due to your rank; that I have been wicked enough to forget it too; and that you are going to take me away from him. Say what he may, and write what he may, he is deceiving you for his own wicked ends. If you go to drink tea with him, God only knows what cause you may have to regret it. Forgive me for being so violent, sir; I have done now. You have made me very wretched, but you are too good and kind to mean it. Good-bye."

I took her hand, I pressed it tenderly; I was touched, deeply touched.

No! let me write honestly. Her eyes betrayed her, her voice betrayed her, while she said her parting words. What I saw, what I heard, was no longer within the limits of doubt. The sweet girl's interest in my welfare was not the merely friendly interest which she herself believed it to be. And I said just now that I was "touched." Cant! Lies! I loved her more dearly than I had ever loved her yet. There is the truth—stripped of poor prudery, and the mean fear of being called Vain!

What I might have said to her, if the opportunity had offered itself, may be easily imagined. Before I could open my lips, a man appeared on the path which led from the mill to the spring—the man whom Cristel had secretly suspected of a design to follow her.

I felt her hand trembling in my hand, and gave it a little encouraging squeeze. "Let us judge him," I suggested, "by what he says and does, on finding us together."

Without an attempt at concealment on his part, he advanced towards us briskly, smiling and waving his hand.

"What, Mr. Roylake, you have already found out the virtues of your wonderful spring, and you are drinking the water before breakfast! I have often done it myself when I was not too lazy to get up. And this charming girl," he went on, turning to Cristel, "has she been trying the virtues of the spring by your advice? She won't listen to me, or I should have recommended it long since. See me set the example."

He took a silver mug from his pocket, and descended the few steps that led to the spring. Allowing for the dreadful deaf monotony in his voice, no man could have been more innocently joyous and agreeable. While he was taking his morning draught, I appealed to Cristel's better sense.

"Is this the hypocrite, who is deceiving me for his own wicked ends?" I asked. "Does he look like the jealous monster who is plotting my destruction, and who will succeed if I am fool enough to accept his invitation?"

Poor dear, she was as obstinate as ever! "Think over what I have said to you—think, for your own sake," was her only reply.

"And a little for your sake?" I ventured to add.

She ran away from me, taking the path which would lead her home again. The deaf man and I were left together. He looked after her until she was out of sight. Then he produced his book of blank leaves. But, instead of handing it to me as usual, he began to write in it himself.

"I have something to say to you," he explained.

It was only possible, while the book was in his possession, to remind him that I could hear, and that he could speak, by using the language of signs. I touched my lips, and pointed to him; I touched my ear, and pointed to myself.

"Yes," he said, understanding me with his customary quickness; "but I want you to remember as well as to hear. When I have filled this leaf, I shall beg you to keep it about you, and to refer to it from time to time."

He wrote on steadily, until he had filled both sides of the slip of paper.

"Quite a little letter," he said. "Pray read it."

This is what I read:

"You must have seen for yourself that I was incapable of insulting you and Miss Cristel by an outbreak of jealousy, when I found you together just now. Only remember that we all have our weaknesses, and that it is my hard lot to be in a state of contest with the inherited evil which is the calamity of my life. With your encouragement, I may resist temptation in the future, and keep the better part of me in authority over my thoughts and actions. But, be on your guard, and advise Miss Cristel to be on her guard, against false appearances. As we all know, they lie like truth. Consider me. Pity me. I ask no more."

Straightforward and manly and modest—I appeal to any unprejudiced mind whether I should not have committed a mean action, if I had placed an evil construction on this?

"Am I understood?" he asked.

I signed to him to give me his book, and relieved him of anxiety in these words:

"If I had failed to understand you, I should have felt ashamed of myself.

368

May I show what you have written to Cristel?"

He smiled, more sweetly and pleasantly than I had seen him smile yet.

"If you wish it," he answered. "I leave it entirely to you. Thank you—and good morning."

Having advanced a few steps on his way to the cottage, he paused, and reminded me of the tea-drinking: "Don't forget to-morrow evening, at seven o'clock."

CHAPTER XI. WARNED AGAIN!

The breakfast hour had not yet arrived when I got home. I went into the garden to refresh my eyes—a little weary of the solemn uniformity of color in Fordwitch Wood—by looking at the flowers.

Reaching the terrace, in the first place, I heard below me a man's voice, speaking in tones of angry authority, and using language which expressed an intention of turning somebody out of the garden. I at once descended the steps which led to the flower-beds. The man in authority proved to be one of my gardeners; and the man threatened with instant expulsion was the oddly-dressed servant of the friend whom I had just left.

The poor fellow's ugly face presented a picture of shame and contrition, the moment I showed myself. He piteously entreated me to look over it, and to forgive him.

"Wait a little," I said. "Let me see if I have anything to forgive." I turned to the gardener. "What is your complaint of this man?"

"He's a trespasser on your grounds, sir. And, his impudence, to say the least of it, is such as I never met with before."

"What harm has he done?"

"Harm, sir?"

"Yes—harm. Has he been picking the flowers?"

The gardener looked round him, longing to refer me to the necessary evidence, and failing to discover it anywhere. The wretched trespasser took heart of grace, and said a word in his own defence.

"Nobody ever knew me to misbehave myself in a gentleman's garden," he said; "I own, sir, to having taken a peep at the flowers, over the wall."

"And they tempted you to look a little closer at them?"

"That's the truth, sir."

"So you are fond of flowers?"

"Yes, sir. I once failed in business as a nurseryman—but I don't blame the flowers."

The delightful simplicity of this was lost on the gardener. I heard the brute mutter to himself: "Gammon!" For once I asserted my authority over my servant.

"Understand this," I said to him: "I don't confine the enjoyment of my garden to myself and my friends. Any well-behaved persons are welcome to come here and look at the flowers. Remember that. Now you may go."

Having issued these instructions, I next addressed myself to my friend in the shabby shooting jacket; telling him to roam wherever he liked, and to stay as long as he pleased. Instead of thanking me and using his liberty, he hesitated, and looked thoroughly ill at ease.

"What's the matter now?" I asked.

"I'm afraid you don't know, sir, who it is you are so kind to. I've been something else in my time, besides a nurseryman."

"What have you been?"

"A prize-fighter."

If he expected me to exhibit indignation or contempt, he was disappointed. My ignorance treated him as civilly as ever.

"What is a prize-fighter?" I inquired.

The unfortunate pugilist looked at me in speechless bewilderment. I told him that I had been brought up among foreigners, and that I had never even seen an English newspaper for the last ten years. This explanation seemed to encourage the man of few words: it set him talking freely at last. He delivered a treatise on the art of prizefighting, and he did something else which I found more amusing—he told me his name. To my small sense of humor his name, so to speak, completed this delightfully odd man: it was Gloody. As to the list of his misfortunes, the endless length of it became so unendurably droll, that we both indulged in unfeeling fits of laughter over the sorrows of Gloody. The first lucky accident of the poor fellow's life had been, literally, the discovery of him by his present master.

This event interested me. I said I should like to hear how it had happened.

Gloody modestly described himself as "one of the starving lot, sir, that looks out for small errands. I got my first dinner for three days, by carrying a gentleman's portmanteau for him. And he, if you please, was afterwards my master. He lived alone. Bless you, he was as deaf then as he is now. He says to me, 'If you bawl in my ears, I'll knock you down.' I thought to myself, you wouldn't say that, master, if you knew how I was employed twenty years ago. He took me into his service, sir, because I was ugly. 'I'm so handsome myself,' he says, 'I want a contrast of something ugly about me.' You may have noticed that he's a bitter one—and bitterly enough he sometimes behaved to me. But there's a good side to him. He gives me his old clothes, and sometimes he speaks almost as kindly to me as you do. But for him, I believe I should have perished of starvation—"

He suddenly checked himself. Whether he was afraid of wearying me, or whether some painful recollection had occurred to him, it was of course impossible to say.

The ugly face, to which he owed his first poor little morsel of prosperity, became overclouded by care and doubt. Bursting into expressions of gratitude which I had certainly not deserved—expressions, so evidently sincere, that they bore witness to constant ill-usage suffered in the course of his hard life— he left me with a headlong haste of movement, driven away as I fancied by an unquiet mind.

I watched him retreating along the path, and saw him stop abruptly, still with his back to me. His deep strong voice travelled farther than he supposed. I heard him say to himself: "What an infernal rascal I am!" He waited a little, and turned my way again. Slowly and reluctantly, he came back to me. As he approached I saw the man, who had lived by the public exhibition of his courage, looking at me with fear plainly visible in the change of his color, and the expression of his face.

"Anything wrong?" I inquired.

"Nothing wrong, sir. Might I be so bold as to ask—"

We waited a little; I gave him time to collect his thoughts. Perhaps the silence confused him. Anyhow, I was obliged to help him to get on.

"What do you wish to ask of me?" I said.

"I wished to speak, sir—"

He stopped again.

"About what?" I asked.

"About to-morrow evening."

"Well?"

He burst out with it, at last. "Are you coming to drink tea with my master?"

"Of course, I am coming! Mr. Gloody, do you know that you rather surprise me?"

"I hope no offence, sir."

"Nonsense! It seems odd, my good fellow, that your master shouldn't have told you I was coming to drink tea with him. Isn't it your business to get the things ready?"

He shifted from one foot to another, and looked as if he wished himself out of my way. At a later time of my life, I have observed that these are signs by which an honest man is apt to confess that he has told, or is going to tell, a lie. As it was, I only noticed that he answered confusedly.

"I can't quite say, Mr. Roylake, that my master didn't mention the thing to me."

"But you failed to understand him—is that it?"

"Well, sir, if I want to ask him anything I have to write it. I'm slow at writing, and bad at writing, and he isn't always patient. However, as you reminded me just now, I have got to get the things ready. To cut it short, perhaps I might say that I didn't quite expect the tea-party would come off."

"Why shouldn't it come off?"

"Well, sir, you might have some other engagement."

Was this a hint? or only an excuse? In either case it was high time, if he still refused to speak out, that I should set him the example.

"You have given me some curious information," I said, "on the subject of fighting with the fists; and you have made me understand the difference between 'fair hitting' and 'foul hitting'. Are you hitting fair now? Very likely I am mistaken—but you seem to me to be trying to prevent my accepting your master's invitation."

He pulled off his hat in a hurry.

"I beg your pardon, sir; I won't detain you any longer. If you will allow me, I'll take my leave."

"Don't go, Mr. Gloody, without telling me whether I am right or wrong. Is there really some objection to my coming to tea tomorrow?"

"Quite a mistake, sir," he said, still in a hurry. "I've led you wrong without meaning it—being an ignorant man, and not knowing how to express myself. Don't think me ungrateful, Mr. Roylake! After your kindness to me, I'd go through fire and water for you—I would!"

His sunken eyes moistened, his big voice faltered. I let him leave me, in mercy to the strong feeling which I had innocently roused. But I shook hands with him first. Yielding to one of my headlong impulses? Yes. And doing a very indiscreet thing? Wait a little—and we shall see.

CHAPTER XII. WARNED FOR THE LAST TIME!

My loyalty towards the afflicted man, whose friendly advances I had seen good reason to return, was in no sense shaken. His undeserved misfortunes, his manly appeal to me at the spring, his hopeless attachment to the beautiful girl whose aversion towards him I had unhappily encouraged, all pleaded with me in his favour. I had accepted his invitation; and I had no other engagement to claim me: it would have been an act of meanness amounting to a confession of fear, if I had sent an excuse. Still, while Cristel's entreaties and Cristel's influence had failed to shake me, Gloody's strange language and Gloody's incomprehensible conduct had troubled my mind. I felt vaguely uneasy; irritated by my own depression of spirits. If I had been a philosopher, I should have recognized the symptoms of a very common attack of a very widely-spread moral malady. The meanest of all human infirmities is also the most universal; and the name of it is Self-esteem.

It is perhaps only right to add that my patience had been tried by the progress of domestic events, which affected Lady Lena and myself—viewed as victims.

Calling, with my stepmother, at Lord Uppercliff's house later in the day, I perceived that Lady Rachel and Mrs. Roylake found (or made) an opportunity of talking together confidentially in a corner; and, once or twice, I caught them looking at Lady Lena and at me. Even Lord Uppercliff (perhaps not yet taken into their confidence) noticed the proceedings of the two ladies, and seemed to be at a loss to understand them.

When Mrs. Roylake and I were together again, on our way home, I was prepared to hear the praise of Lady Lena, followed by a delicate examination into the state of my heart. Neither of these anticipations was realized. Once more, my clever stepmother had puzzled me.

Mrs. Roylake talked as fluently as ever; exhausting one common-place subject after another, without the slightest allusion to my lord's daughter, to my matrimonial prospects, or to my visits at the mill. I was secretly annoyed, feeling that my stepmother's singular indifference to domestic interests of paramount importance, at other times, must have some object in view, entirely beyond the reach of my penetration. If I had dared to commit such an act of rudeness, I should have jumped out of the carriage, and have told Mrs. Roylake that I meant to walk home.

The day was Sunday. I loitered about the garden, listening to the distant church-bell ringing for the afternoon service. Without any cause that I knew of to account for it, I was so restless that nothing I could do attracted me or quieted me.

Returning to the house, I tried to occupy myself with my collection of insects, sadly neglected of late. Useless! My own moths failed to interest me.

I went back to the garden. Passing the open window of one of the lower rooms which looked out on the terrace, I saw Mrs. Roylake reading a book in sad-colored binding. She was yawning over it fearfully, when she discovered that I was looking at her. Equal to any emergency, this remarkable woman instantly handed to me a second and similar volume. "The most precious sermons, Gerard, that have been written in our time." I looked at the book; I opened the book; I recovered my presence of mind, and handed it back. If a female humbug was on one side of the window, a male humbug was on the other. "Please keep it for me till the evening," I said; "I am going for a walk."

Which way did I turn my steps?

Men will wonder what possessed me—women will think it a proceeding that did me credit—I took the familiar road which led to the gloomy wood and the guilty river. The longing in me to see Cristel again, was more than I could resist. Not because I was in love with her; only because I had left her in distress.

Beyond the spring, and within a short distance of the river, I saw a lady advancing towards me on the path which led from the mill.

Brisk, smiling, tripping along like a young girl, behold the mock-republican, known in our neighborhood as Lady Rachel! She held out both

376

hands to me. But for her petticoats, I should have thought I had met with a jolly young man.

"I have been wandering in your glorious wood, Mr. Roylake. Anything to escape the respectable classes on Sunday, patronizing piety on the way to afternoon church. I must positively make a sketch of the cottage by the mill—I mean, of course, the picturesque side of it. That fine girl of Toller's was standing at the door. She is really handsomer than ever. Are you going to see her, you wicked man? Which do you admire—that gypsy complexion, or Lena's lovely skin? Both, I have no doubt, at your age. Good-bye."

When we had left each other, I thought of the absent Captain in the Navy who was Lady Rachel's husband. He was a perfect stranger—but I put myself in his place, and felt that I too should have gone to sea.

Old Toller was alone in his kitchen, evidently annoyed and angry.

"We are all at sixes and sevens, Mr. Gerard. I've had another row with that deaf-devil—my new name for him, and I think it's rather clever. He swears, sir, that he won't go at the end of his week's notice. Says, if I think I'm likely to get rid of him before he has married Cristy, I'm mistaken. Threatens, if any man attempts to take her away, he'll shoot her, and shoot the man, and shoot himself. Aha! old as I am, if he believes he's going to have it all his own way, he's mistaken. I'll be even with him. You mark my words: I'll be even with him."

That old Toller—the most exasperating of men, judged by a quick temper—had irritated my friend into speaking rashly was plain enough. Nevertheless, I felt some anxiety (jealous anxiety, I am afraid) about Cristel. After looking round the kitchen again, I asked where she was.

"Sitting forlorn in her bedroom, crying," her father told me. "I went out for a walk by the river, and I sat down, and (being Sunday) I fell asleep. When I woke, and got home again just now, that was how I found her. I don't like to hear my girl crying; she's as good as gold and better. No, sir; our deaf-devil is not to blame for this. He has given Cristy no reason to complain of him. She says so herself—and she never told a lie yet."

"But, Mr. Toller," I objected, "something must have happened to distress her. Has she not told you what it is?"

"Not she! Obstinate about it. Leaves me to guess. It's clear to my mind, Mr. Gerard, that somebody has got at her in my absence, and said something to upset her. You will ask me who the person is. I can't say I have found that out yet."

"But you mean to try?"

"Yes; I mean to try."

He answered me with little of the energy which generally distinguished him. Perhaps he was fatigued, or perhaps he had something else to think of. I offered a suggestion.

"When we are in want of help," I said, "we sometimes find it, nearer than we had ventured to expect—at our own doors."

The ancient miller rose at that hint like a fish at a fly.

"Gloody!" he cried.

"Find him at once, Mr. Toller."

He hobbled to the door—and looked round at me. "I've got burdens on my mind," he explained, "or I should have thought of it too." Having done justice to his own abilities, he bustled out. In less than a minute, he was back again in a state of breathless triumph. "Gloody has seen the person," he announced; "and (what do you think, sir?) it's a woman!"

I beckoned to Gloody, waiting modestly at the door, to come in, and tell me what he had discovered.

"I saw her outside, sir—rapping at the door here, with her parasol." That was the servant's report.

Her parasol? Not being acquainted with the development of dress among female servants in England, I asked if she was a lady. There seemed to be no doubt of it in the man's mind. She was also, as Gloody supposed, a person whom he had never seen before.

"How is it you are not sure of that?" I said.

"Well, sir, she was waiting to be let in; and I was behind her, coming out of the wood."

"Who let her in?"

"Miss Cristel." His face brightened with an expression of interest when he mentioned the miller's daughter. He went on with his story without wanting questions to help him. "Miss Cristel looked like a person surprised at seeing a stranger—what I should call a free and easy stranger. She walked in, sir, as if the place belonged to her."

I am not suspicious by nature, as I hope and believe. But I began to be reminded of Lady Rachel already.

"Did you notice the lady's dress?" I asked.

A woman who had seen her would have been able to describe every morsel of her dress from head to foot. The man had only observed her hat; and all he could say was that he thought it "a smartish one."

"Any particular color?" I went on.

"Not that I know of. Dark green, I think."

"Any ornament in it?"

"Yes! A purple feather."

The hat I had seen on the head of that hateful woman was now sufficiently described—for a man. Sly old Toller, leaving Gloody unnoticed, and keeping his eye on me, saw the signs of conviction in my face, and said with his customary audacity: "Who is she?"

I followed, at my humble distance, the example of Sir Walter Scott, when inquisitive people asked him if he was the author of the Waverley Novels. In plain English, I denied all knowledge of the stranger wearing the green hat. But, I was naturally desirous of discovering next what Lady Rachel had said;

and I asked to speak with Cristel. Her far-seeing father might or might not have perceived a chance of listening to our conversation. He led me to the door of his daughter's room; and stood close by, when I knocked softly, and begged that she would come out.

The tone of the poor girl's voice—answering, "Forgive me, sir; I can't do it"—convicted the she-socialist (as I thought) of merciless conduct of some sort. Assuming this conclusion to be the right one, I determined, then and there, that Lady Rachel should not pass the doors of Trimley Deen again. If her bosom-friend resented that wise act of severity by leaving the house, I should submit with resignation, and should remember the circumstance with pleasure.

"I am afraid you are ill, Cristel?" was all I could find to say, under the double disadvantage of speaking through a door, and having a father listening at my side.

"Oh no, Mr. Gerard, not ill. A little low in my mind, that's all. I don't mean to be rude, sir—pray be kinder to me than ever! pray let me be!"

I said I would return on the next day; and left the room with a sore heart.

Old Toller highly approved of my conduct. He rubbed his fleshless hands, and whispered: "You'll get it out of Cristy to-morrow, and I'll help you."

I found Gloody waiting for me outside the cottage. He was anxious about Miss Cristel; his only excuse, he told me, being the fear that she might be ill. Having set him at ease, in that particular, I said: "You seem to be interested in Miss Cristel."

His answer raised him a step higher in my estimation.

"How can I help it, sir?"

An odd man, with a personal appearance that might excite a prejudice against him, in some minds. I failed to see it myself in that light. It struck me, as I walked home, that Cristel might have made many a worse friend than the retired prize-fighter.

A change in my manner was of course remarked by Mrs. Roylake's ready observation. I told her that I had been annoyed, and offered no other explanation. Wonderful to relate, she showed no curiosity and no surprise. More wonderful still, at every fair opportunity that offered, she kept out of my way.

My next day's engagement being for seven o'clock in the evening, I put Mrs. Roylake's self-control to a new test. With prefatory excuses, I informed her that I should not be able to dine at home as usual. Impossible as it was that she could have been prepared to hear this, her presence of mind was equal to the occasion. I left the house, followed by my stepmother's best wishes for a pleasant evening.

Hoping to speak with Cristel alone, I had arranged to reach the cottage before seven o'clock.

On the river-margin of the wood, I was confronted by a wild gleam of beauty in the familiar view, for which previous experience had not prepared me. Am I wrong in believing that all scenery, no matter how magnificent or how homely it may be, derives a splendor not its own from favouring conditions of light and shade? Our gloomy trees and our repellent river presented an aspect superbly transfigured, under the shadows of the towering clouds, the fantastic wreaths of the mist, and the lurid reddening of the sun as it stooped to its setting. Lovely interfusions of sobered color rested, faded, returned again, on the upper leaves of the foliage as they lightly moved. The mist, rolling capriciously over the waters, revealed the grandly deliberate course of the flowing current, while it dimmed the turbid earthy yellow that discolored and degraded the stream under the full glare of day. While my eyes followed the successive transformations of the view, as the hour advanced, tender and solemn influences breathed their balm over my mind. Days, happy days that were past, revived. Again, I walked hand in hand with my mother, among the scenes that were round me, and learnt from her to be grateful for the beauty of the earth, with a heart that felt it. We were tracing our way along our favorite woodland path; and we found a companion of tender years, hiding from us. She showed herself; blushing, hesitating, offering a nosegay of wild flowers. My mother whispered to me—I thanked the little mill-girl, and gave her a kiss. Did I feel the child's breath, in my day-dream, still fluttering on my cheek? Was I conscious of her touch? I started, trembled, returned reluctantly to my present self. A visible hand touched my arm. As I turned suddenly, a living breath played on my face. The child had faded into a vanishing shade: the perfected woman who had grown from her had stolen on me unawares, and was asking me to pardon her. "Mr. Gerard, you were lost in your thoughts; I spoke, and you never heard me."

I looked at her in silence.

Was this the dear Cristel so well known to me? Or was it a mockery of her that had taken her place?

"I hope I have not offended you?" she said.

"You have surprised me," I answered. "Something must have happened, since I saw you last. What is it?"

"Nothing."

I advanced a step, and drew her closer to me. A dark flush discolored her face. An overpowering brilliancy flashed from her eyes; there was an hysterical defiance in her manner. "Are you excited? are you angry? are you trying to startle me by acting a part?" I urged those questions on her, one after another; and I was loudly and confidently answered.

"I dare say I am excited, Mr. Gerard, by the honor that has been done me. You are going to keep your engagement, of course? Well, your friend, your favorite friend, has invited me to meet you. No! that's not quite true. I invited myself—the deaf gentleman submitted."

"Why did you invite yourself?"

"Because a tea-party is not complete without a woman."

Her manner was as strangely altered as her looks. That she was beside herself for the moment, I clearly saw. That she had answered me unreservedly, it was impossible to believe. I began to feel angry, when I ought to have made allowances for her.

"Is this Lady Rachel's doing?" I said.

"What do you know of Lady Rachel, sir?"

"I know that she has visited you, and spoken to you."

"Do you know what she has said?"

"I can guess."

"Mr. Gerard, don't abuse that good and kind lady. She deserves your gratitude as well as mine."

Her manner had become quieter; her face was more composed; her expression almost recovered its natural charm while she spoke of Lady Rachel. I was stupefied.

"Try, sir, to forget it and forgive it," she resumed gently, "if I have misbehaved myself. I don't rightly know what I am saying or doing."

I pointed to the new side of the cottage, behind us.

"Is the cause there?" I asked.

"No! no indeed! I have not seen him; I have not heard from him. His servant often brings me messages. Not one message to-day."

"Have you seen Gloody to-day?"

"Oh, yes! There's one thing, if I may make so bold, I should like to know. Mr. Gloody is as good to me as good can be; we see each other continually, living in the same place. But you are different; and he tells me himself he has only seen you twice. What have you done, Mr. Gerard, to make him like you so well, in that short time?"

I told her that he had been found in my garden, looking at the flowers. "As he had done no harm," I said, "I wouldn't allow the servant to turn him out; and I walked round the flower-beds with him. Little enough to deserve such gratitude as the poor fellow expressed—and felt, I don't doubt it."

I had intended to say no more than this. But the remembrance of Gloody's mysterious prevarication, and of the uneasiness which I had undoubtedly felt when I thought of it afterwards, led me (I cannot pretend to say how) into associating Cristel's agitation with something which this man might have said to her. I was on the point of putting the question, when she held up her hand, and said, "Hush!"

The wind was blowing towards us from the river-side village, to which I have already alluded. I am not sure whether I have mentioned that the name of the place was Kylam. It was situated behind a promontory of the river-bank, clothed thickly with trees, and was not visible from the mill. In the present direction of the wind, we could hear the striking of the church clock. Cristel counted the strokes.

"Seven," she said. "Are you determined to keep your engagement?"

She had repeated—in an unsteady voice, and with a sudden change in her color to paleness—the strange question put to me by Gloody. In his case I had failed to trace the motive. I tried to discover it now.

"Tell me why I ought to break my engagement," I said.

"Remember what I told you at the spring," she answered. "You are deceived by a false friend who lies to you and hates you."

The man she was speaking of turned the corner of the new cottage. He waved his hand gaily, and approached us along the road.

"Go!" she said. "Your guardian angel has forgotten you. It's too late now."

Instead of letting me precede her, as I had anticipated, she ran on before me—made a sign to the deaf man, as she passed him, not to stop her—and disappeared through the open door of her father's side of the cottage.

I was left to decide for myself. What should I have done, if I had been twenty years older?

Say that my moral courage would have risen superior to the poorest of all fears, the fear of appearing to be afraid, and that I should have made my excuses to my host of the evening—how would my moral courage have answered him, if he had asked for an explanation? Useless to speculate on it! Had I possessed the wisdom of middle life, his book of leaves would not have told him, in my own handwriting, that I believed in his better nature, and accepted his friendly letter in the spirit in which he had written.

Explain it who can—I knew that I was going to drink tea with him, and yet I was unwilling to advance a few steps, and meet him on the road!

"I find a new bond of union between us," he said, as he joined me. "We both feel that." He pointed to the grandly darkening view. "The two men who could have painted the mystery of those growing shadows and fading lights, lie in the graves of Rembrandt and Turner. Shall we go to tea?"

On our way to his room we stopped at the miller's door.

"Will you inquire," he said, "if Miss Cristel is ready?"

I went in. Old Toller was in the kitchen, smoking his pipe without appearing to enjoy it.

"What's come to my girl?" he asked, the moment he saw me. "Yesterday she was in her room, crying. To-day she's in her room, praying."

The warnings which I had neglected rose in judgment against me. I was silent; I was awed. Before I recovered myself, Cristel entered the kitchen. Her father whispered, "Look at her!"

Of the excitement which had disturbed—I had almost said, profaned—her beautiful face, not a vestige remained. Pale, composed, resolute, she said, "I am ready," and led the way out.

The man whom she hated offered his arm. She took it!

CHAPTER XIII. THE CLARET JUG

I perceived but one change in the Lodger's miserable room, since I had seen it last.

A second table was set against one of the walls. Our boiling water for the tea was kept there, in a silver kettle heated by a spirit-lamp. I next observed a delicate little china vase which held the tea, and a finely-designed glass claret jug, with a silver cover. Other men, possessing that beautiful object, would have thought it worthy of the purest Bordeaux wine which the arts of modern adulteration permit us to drink. This man had filled the claret jug with water.

"All my valuable property, ostentatiously exposed to view," he said, in his bitterly facetious manner. "My landlord's property matches it on the big table."

The big table presented a coarse earthenware teapot; cups and saucers with pieces chipped out of them; a cracked milk jug; a tumbler which served as a sugar basin; and an old vegetable dish, honored by holding delicate French sweet-meats for the first time since it had left the shop.

My deaf friend, in boisterously good spirits, pointed backwards and forwards between the precious and the worthless objects on the two tables, as if he saw a prospect that delighted him.

"I don't believe the man lives," he said, "who enjoys Contrast as I do.— What do you want now?"

This question was addressed to Gloody, who had just entered the room. He touched the earthenware teapot. His master answered: "Let it alone."

"I make the tea at other times," the man persisted, looking at me.

"What does he say? Write it down for me, Mr. Roylake. I beg you will write it down."

There was anger in his eyes as he made that request. I took his book, and wrote the words—harmless words, surely? He read them, and turned savagely to his unfortunate servant.

"In the days when you were a ruffian in the prize-ring, did the other men's fists beat all the brains out of your head? Do you think you can make tea that is fit for Mr. Roylake to drink?"

He pointed to an open door, communicating with another bedroom. Gloody's eyes rested steadily on Cristel: she failed to notice him, being occupied at the moment in replacing the pin of a brooch which had slipped out of her dress. The man withdrew into the second bedroom, and softly closed the door.

Our host recovered his good humor. He took a wooden stool, and seated himself by Cristel.

"Borrowed furniture," he said, "as well as borrowed tea-things. What a debt of obligation I owe to your excellent father. How quiet you are, dear girl. Do you regret having followed the impulse which made you kindly offer to drink tea with us?" He suddenly turned to me. "Another proof, Mr. Roylake, of the sisterly interest that she feels in you; she can't hear of your coming to my room, without wanting to be with you. Ah, you possess the mysterious attractions which fascinate the sex. One of these days, some woman will love you as never man was loved yet." He addressed himself again to Cristel. "Still out of spirits? I dare say you are tired of waiting for your tea. No? You have had tea already? It's Gloody's fault; he ought to have told me that seven o'clock was too late for you. The poor devil deserved that you should take no notice of him when he looked at you just now. Are you one of the few women who dislike an ugly man? Women in general, I can tell you, prefer ugly men. A handsome man matches them on their own ground, and they don't like that. 'We are so fond of our ugly husbands; they set us off to such advantage.' Oh, I don't report what they say; I speak the language in which they think.—Mr. Roylake, does it strike you that the Cur is a sad cynic? By-the-by, do you call me 'the Cur' (as I suggested) when you speak of me to other people—to Miss Cristel, for instance? My charming young friends, you both look shocked; you both shake your heads. Perhaps I am in one of my tolerant humors to-day; I see nothing disgraceful in being a Cur. He is a dog who represents different breeds. Very well, the English are a people who represent different breeds: Saxons, Normans, Danes. The consequence, in one case, is a great nation. The consequence, in the other case, is the cleverest member of the whole dog family—as you may find out for yourself if you will only teach him. Ha—how I am running on. My guests try to slip in a word or two, and can't find their opportunity. Enjoyment, Miss Cristel. Excitement, Mr. Roylake. For more than a year past, I have not luxuriated in the pleasures of society. I feel the social glow; I love the human family; I never, never, never was such a good man as I am now. Let vile slang express my emotions: isn't it jolly?"

Cristel and I stopped him, at the same moment. We instinctively lifted our hands to our ears.

In his delirium of high spirits, he had burst through the invariable monotony of his articulation. Without the slightest gradation of sound, his voice broke suddenly into a screech, prolonged in its own discord until it became perfectly unendurable to hear. The effect that he had produced upon us was not lost on him. His head sank on his breast; horrid shudderings shook him without mercy; he said to himself not to us:

"I had forgotten I was deaf."

There was a whole world of misery in those simple words. Cristel kept her place, unmoved. I rose, and put my hand kindly on his shoulder. It was the best way I could devise of assuring him of my sympathy.

He looked up at me, in silence.

His book of leaves was on the table; he did once more, what he had already done at the spring. Instead of using the book as usual, he wrote in it himself, and then handed it to me.

"Let me spare your nerves a repetition of my deaf discord. Sight, smell, touch, taste—I would give them all to be able to hear. In reminding me of that vain aspiration, my infirmity revenges itself: my deafness is not accustomed to be forgotten. Well! I can be silently useful; I can make the tea."

He rose, and, taking the teapot with him, went to the table that had been placed against the wall. In that position, his back was turned towards us.

At the same time, I felt his book gently taken out of my hand. Cristel had been reading, while I read, over my shoulder. She wrote on the next blank leaf: "Shall I make the tea?"

"Now," she said to me, "notice what happens."

Following him, she touched his arm, and presented her request. He shook his head in token of refusal. She came back to her place by me.

"You expected that?" I said.

"Yes."

"Why did you ask me to notice his refusal?"

"Because I may want to remind you that he wouldn't let me make the tea."

"Mysteries, my dear?"

"Yes: mysteries."

"Not to be mentioned more particularly?"

"I will mention one of them more particularly. After the tea has been made, you may possibly feel me touch your knee under the table."

I was fool enough to smile at this, and wise enough afterwards to see in her face that I had made a mistake.

"What is your touch intended to mean?" I asked.

"It means, 'Wait,' she said."

My sense of humor was, by this time, completely held in check. That some surprise was in store for me, and that Cristel was resolved not to take me into her confidence, were conclusions at which I naturally arrived. I felt, and surely not without good cause, a little annoyed. The Lodger came back to us with the tea made. As he put the teapot on the table, he apologized to Cristel.

"Don't think me rude, in refusing your kind offer. If there is one thing I know I can do better than anybody else, that thing is making tea. Do you take sugar and milk, Mr. Roylake?"

I made the affirmative sign. He poured out the tea. When he had filled two cups, the supply was exhausted. Cristel and I noticed this. He saw it, and at once gratified our curiosity.

"It is a rule," he said, "with masters in the art of making tea, that one infusion ought never to be used twice. If we want any more, we will make more; and if you feel inclined to join us, Miss Cristel, we will fill the third cup."

What was there in this (I wondered) to make her turn pale? And why, after what he had just said, did I see her eyes willingly rest on him, for the first time in my experience? Entirely at a loss to understand her, I resignedly stirred my tea. On the point of tasting it next, felt her hand on my knee, under the table.

Bewildered as I was, I obeyed my instructions, and went on stirring my tea. Our host smiled.

"Your sugar takes a long time to melt," he said—and drank his tea. As he emptied the cup, the touch was taken off me. I followed his example.

In spite of his boasting, the tea was the worst I ever tasted. I should have thrown it out of the window, if they had offered us such nasty stuff at Trimley Deen. When I set down my cup, he asked facetiously if I wished him to brew any more. My negative answer was a masterpiece of strong expression, in the language of signs.

Instead of sending for Gloody to clear the table, he moved away the objects near him, so as to leave an empty space at his disposal.

"I ought perhaps to have hesitated, before I asked you to spend the evening with me," he said, speaking with a gentleness and amiability of manner, strongly in contrast with his behavior up to this time. "It is my misfortune, as you both well know, to be a check on conversation. I dare say you have asked yourselves: How is he going to amuse us, after tea? If you will allow me, I propose to amuse you by exhibiting the dexterity of my fingers and thumbs. Before I was deaf, I should have preferred the piano for this purpose. As it is, an inferior accomplishment must serve my turn."

He opened a cupboard in the wall, close by the second table, and returned with a pack of cards.

Cristel imitated the action of dealing cards for a game. "No," he said, "that is not the amusement which I have in view. Allow me to present myself in a new character. I am no longer the Lodger, and no longer the Cur. My new name is more honorable still—I am the Conjurer."

He shuffled the pack by pouring it backwards and forwards from one hand to the other, in a cascade of cards. The wonderful ease with which he did it prepared me for something worth seeing. Cristel's admiration of his dexterity expressed itself by a prolonged clapping of hands, and a strange uneasy laugh. As his excitement subsided, her agitation broke out. I saw the flush again on her face, and the fiery brightness in her eyes. Once, when his attention was engaged, she stole a look at the door by which Gloody had left the room. Did this indicate another of the mysteries which, by her own confession, she had in preparation for me? My late experience had not inclined me favorably towards mysteries. I devoted my whole attention to the Conjurer.

Whether he chose the easiest examples of skill in sleight of hand is more than I know. I can only say that I never was more completely mystified by any professor of legerdemain on the public platform. After the performance of each trick, he asked leave to time himself by looking at his watch; being anxious to discover if he had lost his customary quickness of execution through recent neglect of the necessary practice.

Of Cristel's conduct, while he was amusing us, I can only say that it justified Mrs. Roylake's spiteful description of her as a bold girl. The more cleverly the tricks were performed, the more they seemed to annoy and provoke her.

"I hate being puzzled!" she said, addressing herself of course to me.

"Yes, yes; his fingers are quicker than my eyes—I have heard that explanation before. When he has done one of his tricks, I want to know how he does it. Conjurers are people who ask riddles, and, when one can't guess them, refuse to say what the answer is. It's as bad as calling me a fool, to suppose that I like being deceived. Ah," she cried, with a shocking insolence of look and manner, "if our friend could only hear what I am saying!"

He had paused while she was speaking, observing her attentively. "Your face doesn't encourage me," he said, with a patience and courtesy of manner which it was impossible not to admire. "I am coming gradually to my greatest triumph; and I think I can surprise and please you."

He timed his last trick, and returned to the table placed against the wall.

"Excuse me for a moment," he resumed; "I am suffering as usual, after drinking tea. I so delight in it that the temptation to-night was more than I could resist. Tea disagrees with my weak stomach. It always produces thirst."

"What nonsense he talks!" Cristel exclaimed. "All mere fancy! He reminds me of the old song called 'The Nervous Man.' Do you know it, Mr. Roylake?"

In spite of my efforts to prevent her, she burst out with the first verse of a stupid comic song. Spared by his deafness from this infliction of vulgarity, our host filled a tumbler from the water in the claret jug, and drank it.

As he set the tumbler down, we were startled by an accident in the next room. The floor was suddenly shaken by the sound of a heavy fall. The fall was followed by a groan which instantly brought me to my feet.

Although his infirmity made him unconscious of the groan, my friend felt the vibration of the floor, and saw me start up from my chair. He looked even more alarmed than I was, judging by the ghastly change that I saw in his color; and he reached the door of the second room as soon as I did. It is needless to say that I allowed him to enter first.

On the point of following him, I felt myself roughly pulled back. When I turned round, and saw Cristel, I did really and truly believe that she was mad. The furious impatience in her eyes, the frenzied strength of her grasp on my arm, would have led most other men to form the same conclusion.

"Come!" she cried. "No! not a word. There isn't a moment to lose." She dragged me across the room to the table on which the claret jug stood. She filled the tumbler from it, as he had filled the tumbler. The material of which the jug had been made was so solid (crystal, not glass as I had supposed) that the filling of the two tumblers emptied it. Cristel held the water out to me, gasping for breath, trembling as if she saw some frightful reptile before her instead of myself.

"Drink it," she said, "if you value your life!"

I should of course have found it perfectly easy to obey her, strange as her language was, if I had been in full possession of myself. Between distress and alarm, my mind (I suppose) had lost its balance. With or without a cause, I hesitated.

She crossed the room, and threw open the window which looked out on the river.

"You shan't die alone," she said. "If you don't drink it, I'll throw myself out!"

I drank from the tumbler to the last drop.

It was not water.

It had a taste which I can compare to no drink, and to no medicine, known to me. I thought of the other strange taste peculiar to the tea. At last, the tremendous truth forced itself on my mind. The man in whom my boyish generosity had so faithfully believed had attempted my life.

Cristel took the tumbler from me. My poor angel clasped her free arm round my neck, and pressed her lips, in an ecstasy of joy, on my cheek. The next instant, she seized the claret jug, and dashed it into pieces on the floor. "Get the jug from his washhand-stand," she said. When I gave it to her, she poured some of the water upon the broken fragments of crystal scattered on the floor. I had put the jug back in its place, and was returning to Cristel, when the poisoner showed himself, entering from the servant's room.

"Don't be alarmed," he said. "Gloody's name ought to be Glutton. An attack of giddiness, thoroughly well deserved. I have relieved him. You remember, Mr. Roylake, that I was once a surgeon—"

The broken claret jug caught his eye.

We have all read of men who were petrified by terror. Of the few persons who have really witnessed that spectacle, I am one. The utter stillness of him was really terrible to see. Cristel wrote in his book an excuse, no doubt prepared beforehand: "That fall in the next room frightened me, and I felt faint. I went to get some water from the jug you drank out of, and it slipped from my hand."

She placed those words under his eyes—she might just as well have shown them to the dog. A dead man, erect on his feet—so he looked to our eyes. So he still looked, when I took Cristel's arm, and led her out of that dreadful presence.

"Take me into the air!" she whispered.

A burst of tears relieved her, after the unutterable suspense that she had so bravely endured. When she was in some degree composed again, we walked gently up and down for a minute or two in the cool night air. "Don't speak to me," she said, as we stopped before her father's door. "I am not fit for it yet; I know what you feel." I pressed her to my heart, and let the embrace speak for me. She yielded to it, faintly sighing. "To-morrow?" I whispered. She bent her head, and left me.

Walking home through the wood, I became aware, little by little, that my thoughts were not under the customary control. Over and over again, I tried to review the events of that terrible evening, and failed. Fragments of other memories presented themselves—and then deserted me. Nonsense, absolute nonsense, found its way into my mind next, and rose in idiotic words to my lips. I grew too lazy even to talk to myself. I strayed from the path. The mossy earth began to rise and sink under my feet, like the waters in a ground-swell at sea. I stood still, in a state of idiot-wonder. The ground suddenly rose right up to my face. I remember no more.

My first conscious exercise of my senses, when I revived, came to me by way of my ears. Leaden weights seemed to close my eyes, to fetter my movements, to silence my tongue, to paralyze my touch. But I heard a wailing voice, speaking close to me, so close that it might have been my own voice: I distinguished the words; I knew the tones.

"Oh, my master, my lord, who am I that I should live—and you die! and you die!"

Was it her warm young breath that quickened me with its vigorous life? I only know that the revival of my sense of touch did certainly spring from the contact of her lips, pressed to mine in the reckless abandonment of grief without hope. Her cry of joy, when my first sigh told her that I was still a living creature, ran through me like an electric shock. I opened my eyes; I held out my hand; I tried to help her when she raised my head, and set me against the tree under which I had been stretched helpless. With an effort I could call her by her name. Even that exhausted me. My mind was so weak that I should have believed her, if she had declared herself to be a spirit seen in a dream, keeping watch over me in the wood.

Wiser than I was, she snatched up my hat, ran on before me, and was lost in the darkness.

An interval, an unendurable interval, passed. She returned, having filled my hat from the spring. But for the exquisite coolness of the water falling on my face, trickling down my throat, I should have lost my senses again. In a few minutes more, I could take that dear hand, and hold it to me as if I was holding to my life. We could only see each other obscurely, and in that very circumstance (as we confessed to each other afterwards) we found the needful composure before we could speak.

"Cristel! what does it mean?"

"Poison," she answered. "And he has suffered too."

To my astonishment, there was no anger in her tone: she spoke of him as quietly as if she had been alluding to an innocent man.

"Do you mean that he has been at death's door, like me?"

"Yes, thank God—or I should never have found you here. Poor old Gloody came to us, in search of help. 'My master's in a swoon, and I can't bring him to.' Directly I heard that, I remembered that you had drunk what he had drunk. What had happened to him, must have happened to you. Don't ask me how long it was before I found you, and what I felt when I did find you. I do so want to enjoy my happiness! Only let me see you safely home, and I ask no more."

She helped me to rise, with the encouraging words which she might have used to a child. She put my arm in hers, and led me carefully along through the wood, as if I had been an old man.

Cristel had saved my life—but she would hear of no allusion to it. She knew how the poisoner had plotted to get rid of me—but nothing that I could say induced her to tell me how she had made the discovery. In view of Trimley Deen, my guardian angel dropped my arm.

"Go on," she said, "and let me see the servant let you in, before I run home."

If she had not been once more wiser than I was, I should have taken her with me to the house; I should have positively refused to let her go back by herself. Nothing that I could say or do had the slightest effect on her resolution. Does the man live who could have taken leave of her calmly, in my place? She tore herself away from me, with a sigh of bitterness that was dreadful to hear.

"Oh, my darling," I said, "do I distress you?"

"Horribly," she answered; "but you are not to blame."

Those were her farewell words. I called after her. I tried to follow her. She was lost to me in the darkness.

CHAPTER XIV. GLOODY SETTLES THE ACCOUNT

A night of fever; a night, when I did slumber for a few minutes, of horrid dreams—this was what I might have expected, and this is what really happened. The fresh morning air, flowing through my open window, cooled and composed me; the mercy of sleep found me. When I woke, and looked at my watch, I was a new man. The hour was noon.

I rang my bell. The servant announced that a man was waiting to see me. "The same man, sir, who was found in the garden, looking at your flowers." I at once gave directions to have him shown up into my bedroom. The delay of dressing was more than I had patience to encounter. Unless I was completely mistaken, here was the very person whom I wanted to enlighten me.

Gloody showed himself at the door, with a face ominously wretched, as well as ugly. I instantly thought of Cristel.

"If you bring me bad news," I said, "don't keep me waiting for it."

"It's nothing that need trouble You, sir. I'm dismissed from my master's service—that's all."

It was plainly not "all." Relieved even by that guarded reply, I pointed to a chair by the bedside.

"Do you believe that I mean well by you?" I asked.

"I do, sir, with all my heart."

"Then sit down, Gloody, and make a clean breast of it."

He lifted his enormous fist, by way of emphasizing his answer.

"I was within a hair's breadth, sir, of striking him. If I hadn't kept my temper, I might have killed him."

"What did he do?"

"Flew into a furious rage. I don't complain of that; I daresay I deserved it. Please to excuse my getting up again. I can't look you in the face, and tell you of it." He walked away to the window. "Even a poor devil, like me, does sometimes feel it when he is insulted. Mr. Roylake, he kicked me. Say no more about it, sir! I would never have mentioned it, if I hadn't had something else to tell you; only I don't know how." In this difficulty, he came back to my bedside. "Look here, sir! What I say is—that kick has wiped out the debt of thanks I owe him. Yes. I say the account between us two is settled now, on both sides. In two words, sir, if you mean to charge him before the magistrates with attempting your life, I'll take my Bible oath he did attempt it, and you may call me as your witness. There! Now it's out."

What his master had no doubt inferred, was what I saw plainly too. Cristel had saved my life, and had been directed how to do it by the poor fellow who had suffered in my cause.

"We will wait a little before we talk of setting the law in force," I said. "In the meantime, Gloody, I want you to tell me what you would tell the magistrate if I called you as a witness."

He considered a little. "The magistrate would put questions to me—wouldn't he, sir? Very good. You put questions to me, and I'll answer them to the best of my ability."

The investigation that followed was far too long and too wearisome to be related here. If I give the substance of it, I shall have done enough.

Sometimes when he was awake, and supposed that he was alone—sometimes when he was asleep and dreaming—the Cur had betrayed himself. (It was a paltry vengeance, I own, to gratify a malicious pleasure—as I did now—in thinking of him and speaking of him by the degrading name which his morbid humility had suggested. But are the demands of a man's dignity always paid in the ready money of prompt submission?) Anyway, it appeared that Gloody had heard enough, in the sleeping moments and the solitary moments of his master, to give him some idea of the jealous hatred with which the Cur regarded me. He had done his best to warn me, without actually betraying the man who had rescued him from starvation or the workhouse—and he had failed.

But his resolution to do me good service, in return for my kindness to him, far from being shaken, was confirmed by circumstances.

When his master returned to the chemical studies which have been already mentioned, Gloody was employed as assistant, to the extent of his limited capacity for making himself useful. He had no reason to suppose that I was the object of any of the experiments, until the day before the tea-party. Then, he saw the dog enticed into the new cottage, and apparently killed by the administration of poison of some sort. After an interval, a dose of another kind was poured down the poor creature's throat, and he began to revive. A lapse of a quarter of an hour followed; the last dose was repeated; and the dog soon sprang to his feet again, as lively as ever. Gloody was thereupon told to set the animal free; and was informed at the same time that he would be instantly dismissed, if he mentioned to any living creature what he had just seen.

By what process he arrived at the suspicion that my safety might be threatened, by the experiment on the dog, he was entirely unable to explain.

"It was borne in on my mind, sir; and that's all I can tell you," he said. "I didn't dare speak to you about it; you wouldn't have believed me. Or, if you did believe me, you might have sent for the police. The one way of putting a stop to murdering mischief (if murdering mischief it might be) was to trust Miss Cristel. That she was fond of you—I don't mean any offence, sir—I pretty well guessed. That she was true as steel, and not easily frightened, I didn't need to guess; I knew it."

Gloody had done his best to prepare Cristel for the terrible confidence which he had determined to repose in her, and had not succeeded. What the poor girl must have suffered, I could but too readily understand, on recalling the startling changes in her look and manner when we met at the river-margin of the wood. She was pledged to secrecy, under penalty of ruining the man who was trying to save me; and to her presence of mind was trusted the whole responsibility of preserving my life. What a situation for a girl of eighteen!

"We made it out between us, sir, in two ways," Gloody proceeded. "First and foremost, she was to invite herself to tea. And, being at the table, she was to watch my master. Whatever she saw him drink, she was to insist on your drinking it too. You heard me ask leave to make the tea?"

"Yes."

"Well, that was one of the signals agreed on between us. When he sent me away, we were certain of what he had it in his mind to do."

"And when you looked at Miss Cristel, and she was too busy with her brooch to notice you, was that another signal?"

"It was, sir. When she handled her silver ornament, she told me that I might depend on her to forget nothing, and to be afraid of nothing."

I remembered the quiet firmness in her face, after the prayer that she had said in her own room. Her steady resolution no longer surprised me.

"Did you wonder, sir, what possessed her," Gloody went on, "when she burst out singing? That was a signal to me. We wanted him out of our way, while you were made to drink what he had drunk out of the jug."

"How did you know that he would not drink the whole contents of the jug?"

"You forget, sir, that I had seen the dog revived by two doses, given with a space of time between them."

I ought to have remembered this, after what he had already told me. My intelligence brightened a little as I went on.

"And your accident in the next room was planned, of course?" I said. "Do you think he saw through it? I should say, No; judging by his looks. He turned pale when he felt the floor shaken by your fall. For once in a way, he was honest—honestly frightened."

"I noticed the same thing, sir, when he picked me up, off the floor. A man who can change his complexion, at will, is a man we hav'n't heard of yet, Mr. Roylake."

I had been dressing for some time past; longing to see Cristel, it is needless to say.

"Is there anything more," I asked, "that I ought to know?"

"Only one thing, Mr. Roylake, that I can think of," Gloody replied. "I'm afraid it's Miss Cristel's turn next."

"What do you mean?"

"While the deaf man lodges at the cottage, he means mischief, and his eye is on Miss Cristel. Early this morning, sir, I happened to be at the boat-house. Somebody (I leave you to guess who it is) has stolen the oars."

I was dressed by this time, and so eager to get to the cottage, that I had already opened my door. What I had just heard brought me back into the room. As a matter of course, we both suspected the same person of stealing the oars. Had we any proof to justify us?

Gloody at once acknowledged that we had no proof. "I happened to look at the boat," he said, "and I missed the oars. Oh, yes; I searched the boat-house. No oars! no oars!"

"And nothing more that you have forgotten, and ought to tell me?"

"Nothing, sir."

I left Gloody to wait my return; being careful to place him under the protection of the upper servants—who would see that he was treated with respect by the household generally.

CHAPTER XV. THE MILLER'S HOSPITALITY

On the way to Toller's cottage, my fears for Cristel weighed heavily on my mind.

That the man who had tried to poison me was capable of committing any other outrage, provided he saw a prospect of escaping with impunity, no sane person could hesitate to conclude. But the cause of my alarm was not to be traced to this conviction. It was a doubt that made me tremble.

After what I had myself seen, and what Gloody had told me, could I hope to match my penetration, or the penetration of any person about me whom I could trust, against the fathomless cunning, the Satanic wickedness, of the villain who was still an inmate with Cristel, under her father's roof?

I have spoken of his fathomless cunning, and his Satanic wickedness. The manner in which the crime had been prepared and carried out would justify stronger expressions still. Such was the deliberate opinion of the lawyer whom I privately consulted, under circumstances still to be related.

"Let us arrive at a just appreciation of the dangerous scoundrel whom we have to deal with," this gentleman said. "His preliminary experiment with the dog; his resolution to make suspicion an impossibility, by drinking from the same tea which he had made ready for you; his skilled preparation of an antidote, the color of which might court appearances by imitating water— are there many poisoners clever enough to provide themselves beforehand with such a defence as this? How are you to set the circumstances in their true light, on your side? You may say that you threw out the calculations, on which he had relied for securing his own safety, by drinking his second dose of the antidote while he was out of the room; and you can appeal to the fainting-fits from which you and he suffered on the same evening, as a proof that the action of the poison was partially successful; in your case and in his, because you and he were insufficiently protected by half doses only of the antidote. A bench of Jesuits would understand these refinements. A bench of

British magistrates would look at each other, and say: Where is the medical evidence? No, Mr. Roylake, we must wait. You can't even turn him out of the cottage before he has had the customary notice to quit. The one thing to take care of—in case some other suspicions of ours turn out to be well founded—is that our man shall not give us the slip. One of my clerks, and one of your gamekeepers shall keep watch on his lodgings, turn and turn about, till his time is up. Go where he may after that, he shall not escape us."

I may now take up the chain of events again.

On reaching Toller's cottage, I was distressed (but hardly surprised) to hear that Cristel, exhausted after a wakeful night, still kept her bed, in the hope of getting some sleep. I was so anxious to know if she was at rest, that her father went upstairs to look at her.

I followed him—and saw Ponto watching on the mat outside her door. Did this indicate a wise distrust of the Cur? "A guardian I can trust, sir," the old man whispered, "while I'm at the mill."

He looked into Cristel's room, and permitted me to look over his shoulder. My poor darling was peacefully asleep. Judging by the miller's manner, which was as cool and composed as usual, I gathered that Cristel had wisely kept him in ignorance of what had happened on the previous evening.

The inquiry which I had next in my mind was forestalled by old Toller.

"Our deaf-devil, Mr. Gerard, has done a thing this morning which puzzles me," he began; "and I should like to hear what you think of it. For the first time since we have had him here, he has opened his door to a visitor. And—what a surprise for you!—it's the other devil with the hat and feather who got at my Cristy, and made her cry."

That this meeting would be only too likely to happen, in due course of time, I had never doubted. That it had happened, now, confirmed me in my resolution to keep guard over Cristel at the cottage, till the Cur left it.

I asked, of course, how those two enemies of mine had first seen each other.

"She was just going to knock at our door, Mr. Gerard, when she happened to look up. There he was, airing himself at his window as usual. Do you think she was too much staggered at the sight of him to speak? At any rate, he got the start of her. 'Wait till I come down,' says he—and there he was, almost as soon as he said it. They went into his place together; and for best part of an hour they were in each other's company. Every man has his failings; I don't deny that I'm a little inquisitive by nature. Between ourselves, I got under the open window and listened. At a great disadvantage, I needn't tell you; for she was obliged to write what she had to say. But he talked. I was too late for the cream of it; I only heard him wish her good-bye. 'If your ladyship telegraphs this morning,' says he, 'when will the man come to me?' Now what do you say to that?"

"More than I have time to say now, Mr. Toller. Can you find me a messenger to take a note to Trimley Deen?"

"We have no messengers in this lonesome place, sir."

"Very well. Then I must take my own message. You will see me again, as soon as I can get back."

Mr. Toller's ready curiosity was roused in a moment.

"Perhaps, you wish to have a look at the repairs?" he suggested in his most insinuating manner.

"I wish to see what her ladyship's telegram brings forth," I said; "and mean to be here when 'the man' arrives."

My venerable tenant was delighted. "Turn him inside out, sir, and get at his secrets. I'll help you."

Returning to Trimley Deen, I ordered the pony-chaise to be got ready, and a small portmanteau to be packed—speaking in the hall. The sound of my voice brought Mrs. Roylake out of the morning-room. She was followed by Lady Rachel. If I could only have heard their private conference, I should have seen the dangerous side of the Cur's character under a new aspect.

"Gerard!" cried my stepmother, "what did I hear just now? You can't be going back to Germany!"

"Certainly not," I answered.

"Going to stay with some friends perhaps?" Lady Rachel suggested. "I wonder whether I know them?"

It was spitefully done—but, in respect of tone and manner, done to perfection.

The pony-chaise drew up at the door. This was another of the rare occasions in my life on which I acted discreetly. It was necessary for me to say something. I said, "Good morning."

Nothing had happened at the cottage, during the interval of my absence. Clever as he was, old Toller had never suspected that I should return to him (with luggage!) in the character of a self-invited guest. His jaw dropped, and his wicked little eyes appealed to the sky. Merciful Providence! what have I done to deserve this? There, as I read him, was the thought in the miller's mind, expressed in my best English.

"Have you got a spare bed in the house?" I asked.

Mr. Toller forgot the respect due to the person who could stop the repairs at a moment's notice. He answered in the tone of a man who had been grossly insulted: "No!"

But for the anxieties that oppressed me, I should have only perceived the humorous side of old Toller's outbreak of temper. He had chosen his time badly, and he got a serious reply.

"Understand this," I said: "either you receive me civilly—or you make up your mind to find a flour-mill on some other property than mine."

This had its effect. The miller's servility more than equalled his insolence. With profuse apologies, he offered me his own bedroom. I preferred a large old-fashioned armchair which stood in a corner of the kitchen. Listening in a state of profound bewilderment—longing to put inquisitive questions, and afraid to do so—Toller silently appealed to my compassion. I had nothing to conceal; I mentioned my motive. Without intending it, I had wounded him in one of his most tender places; the place occupied by his good opinion of himself. He said with sulky submission:

"Much obliged, Mr. Gerard. My girl is safe under my protection. Leave it to me, sir—leave it to me."

I had just reminded old Toller of his age, and of the infirmities which age brings with it, when his daughter—pale and languid, with signs of recent tears in her eyes—entered the kitchen. When I approached her, she trembled and drew back; apparently designing to leave the room. Her father stopped her. "Mr. Gerard has something to tell you," he said. "I'm off to the mill." He took up his hat, and left us.

Submitting sadly, she let me take her in my arms, and try to cheer her. But when I alluded to what I owed to her admirable devotion and courage, she entreated me to be silent. "Don't bring it all back!" she cried, shuddering at the remembrances which I had awakened, "Father said you had something to tell me. What is it?"

I repeated (in language more gentle and more considerate) what I had already said to her father. She took my hand, and kissed it gratefully. "You have your mother's face, and your mother's heart," she said; "you are always good, you are never selfish. But it mustn't be. How can I let you suffer the discomfort of staying here? Indeed, I am in no danger; you are alarming yourself without a cause."

"How can you be sure of that?" I asked.

She looked reluctantly at the door of communication.

"Must I speak of him?"

"Only to tell me," I pleaded, "whether you have seen him since last night."

She had both seen him and heard from him, on reaching home. "He opened that door," she told me, "and threw on the floor one of the leaves out of his book. After doing that, he relieved me from the sight of him."

406

"Show me the leaf, Cristel."

"Father has got it. I thought he was asleep in the armchair. He snatched it out of my hand. It isn't worth reading."

She turned pale, nevertheless, when she replied in those terms. I could see that I was disturbing her, when I asked if she remembered what the Cur had written. But our position was far too serious to be trifled with. "I suppose he threatened you?" I said, trying to lead her on. "What did he say?"

"He said, if any attempt was made to remove me out of his reach, after what had happened that evening, my father would find him on the watch day and night, and would regret it to the end of his life. The wretch thinks me cruel enough to have told my father of the horrors we went through! You know that he has dismissed his poor old servant? Was I wrong in advising Gloody to go to you?"

"You were quite right. He is at my house—and I should like to keep him at Trimley Deen; but I am afraid he and the other servants might not get on well together?"

"Will you let him come here?"

She spoke earnestly; reminding me that I had thought it wrong to leave her father, at his age, without someone to help him.

"If an accident separated me from him," she went on, "he would be left alone in this wretched place."

"What accident are you thinking of?" I asked. "Is there something going on, Cristel, that I don't know of?"

Had I startled her? or had I offended her?

"Can we tell what may or may not happen to us, in the time to come?" she asked abruptly. "I don't like to think of my father being left without a creature to take care of him. Gloody is so good and so true; and they always get on well together. If you have nothing better in view for him—?"

"My dear, I have nothing half so good in view; and Gloody, I am sure, will think so too." I privately resolved to insure a favorable reception for the poor fellow, by making him the miller's partner. Bank notes in Toller's pocket! What a place reserved for Gloody in Toller's estimation!

But I confess that Cristel's allusion to a possible accident rather oppressed my mind, situated as we were at that time. What we talked of next has slipped from my memory. I only recollect that she made an excuse to go back to her room, and that nothing I could say or do availed to restore her customary cheerfulness.

As the twilight was beginning to fade, we heard the sound of a carriage. The new man had arrived in a fly from the station. Before bedtime, he made his appearance in the kitchen, to receive the domestic instructions of which a stranger stood in need. A quiet man and a civil man: even my prejudiced examination could discover nothing in him that looked suspicious. I saw a well-trained servant—and I saw nothing more.

Old Toller made a last attempt to persuade me that it was not worth a gentleman's while to accept his hospitality, and found me immovable. I was equally obstinate when Cristel asked leave to make up a bed for me in the counting-house at the mill.

With the purpose that I had in view, if I accepted her proposal I might as well have been at Trimley Deen.

Left alone, I placed the armchair and another chair for my feet, across the door of communication. That done, I examined a little door behind the stairs (used I believe for domestic purposes) which opened on a narrow pathway, running along the river-side of the house. It was properly locked. I have only to add that nothing happened during the night.

The next day showed no alteration for the better, in Cristel. She made an excuse when I proposed to take her out with me for a walk. Her father's business kept him away from the cottage, and thus gave me many opportunities of speaking to her in private. I was so uneasy, or so reckless—I hardly know which—that I no longer left it to be merely inferred that I had resolved to propose marriage to her.

"My sweet girl, you are so wretched, and so unlike yourself, in this place, that I entreat you to leave it. Come with me to London, and let me make you safe and happy as my wife."

"Oh, Mr. Roylake!"

"Why do you call me, 'Mr Roylake'? Have I done anything to offend you? There seems to be some estrangement between us. Do you believe that I love you?"

"I wish I could doubt it!" she answered.

"Why?"

"You know why."

"Cristel! Have I made some dreadful mistake? The truth! I want the truth! Do you love me?"

A low cry of misery burst from her. Was she mastered by love, or by despair? She threw herself on my breast. I kissed her. She murmured, "Oh don't tempt me! Don't tempt me!" Again and again, I kissed her. "Ah," I broke out, in the ecstasy of my sense of relief, "I know that you love me, now!"

"Yes," she said, simply and sadly, "I do love you."

My selfish passion asked for more even than this.

"Prove it by being my wife," I answered.

She put me back from her, firmly and gently.

"I will prove it, Gerard, by not letting you disgrace yourself."

With those horrible words—put into her mouth, beyond all doubt by the woman who had interfered between us—she left me. The long hours of the day passed: I saw her no more.

People who are unable to imagine what I suffered, are not the people to whom I now address myself. After all the years that have passed—after age and contact with the world have hardened me—it is still a trial to my self-control to look back to that day. Events I can remember with composure. To events, therefore, let me return.

No communication of any sort reached us from the Cur. Towards evening, I saw him pacing up and down on the road before the cottage, and speaking to his new servant. The man (listening attentively) had the master's book of leaves in his hand, and wrote in it from time to time as replies were wanted from him. He was probably receiving instructions. The Cur's discretion was a bad sign. I should have felt more at ease, if he had tried to annoy Cristel, or to insult me.

Towards bedtime, old Toller's sense of hospitality exhibited marked improvement. He was honored and happy to have me under his poor roof—a roof, by the way, which was also in need of repairs—but he protested against my encountering the needless hardship of sleeping in a chair, when a bed could be set up for me in the counting-house. "Not what you're used to, Mr. Gerard. Empty barrels, and samples of flour, and account-books smelling strong of leather, instead of velvet curtains and painted ceilings; but better than a chair, sir—better than a chair!"

I was as obstinate as ever. With thanks, I insisted on the chair.

Feverish, anxious, oppressed in my breathing—with nerves unstrung, as a doctor would have put it—I disturbed the order of the household towards twelve o'clock by interfering with old Toller in the act of locking up the house-door.

"Let me get a breath of fresh air," I said to him, "or there will be no sleep for me to-night."

He opened the door with a resignation to circumstances, so exemplary that it claimed some return. I promised to be back in a quarter of an hour. Old Toller stifled a yawn. "I call that truly considerate," he said—and stifled another yawn. Dear old man!

Stepping into the road, I first examined the Cur's part of the cottage. Not a sound was audible inside; not a creature was visible outside. The usual dim light was burning behind the window that looked out on the road.

Nothing, absolutely nothing, that was suspicious could I either hear or see.

I walked on, by what we called the upper bank of the river; leading from the village of Kylam. The night was cloudy and close. Now the moonlight reached the earth at intervals; now again it was veiled in darkness. The trees, at this part of the wood, so encroached on the bank of the stream as considerably to narrow and darken the path. Seeing a possibility of walking into the river if I went on much farther, I turned back again in the more open direction of Kylam, and kept on briskly (as I reckon) for about five minutes more.

I had just stopped to look at my watch, when I saw something dark floating towards me, urged by the slow current of the river. As it came nearer, I thought I recognized the mill-boat.

It was one of the dark intervals when the moon was overcast. I was sufficiently interested to follow the boat, on the chance that a return of the moonlight might show me who could possibly be in it. After no very long interval, the yellow light for which I was waiting poured through the lifting clouds.

The mill-boat, beyond all doubt—and nobody in it! The empty inside of the boat was perfectly visible to me. Even if I had felt inclined to do so, it would have been useless to jump into the water and swim to the boat. There were no oars in it, and therefore no means of taking it back to the mill. The one thing I could do was to run to old Toller and tell him that his boat was adrift.

On my way to the cottage, I thought I heard a sound like the shutting of a door. I was probably mistaken. In expectation of my return, the door was secured by the latch only; and the miller, looking out of his bedroom window, said: "Don't forget to lock it, sir; the key's inside."

I followed my instructions, and ascended the stairs. Surprised to hear me in that part of the house, he came out on the landing in his nightgown.

"What is it?" he asked.

"Nothing very serious," I said. "The boat's adrift. I suppose it will run

411

on shore somewhere."

"It will do that, Mr. Gerard; everybody along the river knows the boat." He held up his lean trembling hand. "Old fingers don't always tie fast knots."

He went back into his bed. It was opposite the window; and the window, being at the side of the old cottage, looked out on the great open space above the river. When the moonlight appeared, it shone straight into his eyes. I offered to pull down the blind.

"Thank you kindly, sir; please to let it be. I wake often in the night, and I like to see the heavens when I open my eyes."

Something touched me behind: it was the dog. Like his noble and beautiful race, Ponto knew his friends. He licked my hand, and then he walked out through the bedroom door. Instead of taking his usual place, on the mat before Cristel's room, he smelt for a moment under the door—whined softly—and walked up and down the landing.

"What's the matter with the dog?" I asked.

"Restless to-night," said old Toller. "Dogs are restless sometimes. Lie down!" he called through the doorway.

The dog obeyed, but only for a moment. He whined at the door again—and then, once more, he walked up and down the landing.

I went to the bedside. The old man was just going to sleep. I shook him by the shoulder.

"There's something wrong," I said. "Come out and look at Ponto."

He grumbled—but he came out. "Better get the whip," he said.

"Before you do that," I answered, "knock at your daughter's door."

"And wake her?" he asked in amazement.

I knocked at the door myself. There was no reply. I knocked again, with the same result.

"Open the door," I said, "or I will do it myself."

412

He obeyed me. The room was empty; and the bed had not been slept in.

Standing helpless on the threshold of the door, I looked into the empty room; hearing nothing but my heart thumping heavily, seeing nothing but the bed with the clothes on it undisturbed.

The sudden growling of the dog shook me back (if I may say so) into the possession of myself. He was looking through the balusters that guarded the landing. The head of a man appeared, slowly ascending the stairs. Acting mechanically, I held the dog back. Thinking mechanically, I waited for the man. The face of the new servant showed itself. The dog frightened him: he spoke in tones that trembled, standing still on the stairs.

"My master has sent me, sir—"

A voice below interrupted him. "Come back," I heard the Cur say; "I'll do it myself. Toller! where is Toller?"

The enraged dog, barking furiously, struggled to get away from me. I dragged him—the good honest creature who was incapable of concealments and treacheries!—into his master's room. In the moment before I closed the door again, I saw Toller down on his knees with his arms laid helplessly on the window-sill, staring up at the sky as if he had gone mad. There was no time for questions; I drove poor Ponto back into the room, and shut the door.

On the landing, I found myself face to face with the Cur.

"You!" he said.

I lifted my hand. The servant ran between us. "For God's sake, control yourself, sir! We mean no harm. It's only to tell Mr. Toller that his boat is missing."

"Mr. Toller knows it already," I said. "No honest man would touch your master if he could help it. I warn him to go; and I make him understand me by a sign." I pointed down the stairs, and turned my head to look at him.

He was no longer before me. His face, hideously distorted by rage and terror, showed itself at the door of Cristel's empty room. He rushed out on

413

me; his voice rose to the detestable screech which I had heard once already.

"Where have you hidden her? Give her back to me—or you die." He drew a pistol out of the breast-pocket of his coat. I seized the weapon by the barrel, and snatched it away from him. As the charge exploded harmlessly between us, I struck him on the head with the butt-end of the pistol. He dropped on the landing.

The door of Toller's room opened behind me. He stood speechless; the report of the pistol had terrified him. In the instant when I looked at the old man, I saw, through the window of his room, a rocket soar into the sky, from behind the promontory between us and Kylam.

Some cry of surprise must, I suppose, have escaped me. Toller suddenly looked round towards the window, just as the last fiery particles of the rocket were floating slowly downwards against the black clouds.

I had barely time enough to see this, before a trembling hand was laid on my shoulder, from behind. The servant, white with terror, pointed to his master.

"Have you killed him?" the man said.

The same question must have been in the mind of the dog. He was quiet now. Doubtfully, reluctantly, he was smelling at the prostrate human creature. I knelt down, and put my hand on the wretch's heart. Ponto, finding us both on a level together, gave me the dog's kiss; I returned the caress with my free hand. The servant saw me, with my attention divided in this way between the animal and the man.

"Damn it, sir," he burst out indignantly, "isn't a Christian of more importance than a dog?"

A Christian!—but I was in no humor to waste words. "Are you strong enough to carry him to his own side of the house?" I asked.

"I won't touch him, if he's dead!"

"He is not dead. Take him away!"

All this time my mind was pre-occupied by the extraordinary appearance of the rocket, rising from the neighborhood of a lonely little village between midnight and one in the morning. How I connected that mysterious signal with a possibility of tracing Cristel, it is useless to inquire. That was the thought in me, when I led my lost darling's father back to his room. Without stopping to explain myself, I reminded him that the cottage was quiet again, and told him to wait my return.

In the kitchen, I overtook the servant and his burden. The door of communication (by which they had entered) was still open.

"Lock that door," I said.

"Lock it yourself," he answered; "I'll have nothing to do with this business." He passed through the doorway, and along the passage, and ascended his master's stairs.

It struck me directly that the man had suggested a sure way of protecting Toller, during my absence. The miller's own door was already secured; I took the key, so as to be able to let myself in again—then passed through the door of communication—fastened it—and put the key in my pocket. The third door, by which the Cur entered his lodgings, was of course at my disposal. I had just closed it, when I discovered that I had a companion. Ponto had followed me.

I felt at once that the dog's superior powers of divination might be of use, on such an errand as mine was. We set out together for Kylam.

Wildly hurried—without any fixed idea in my mind—I ran to Kylam, for the greater part of the way. It was now very dark. On a sandy creek, below the village, I came in contact with something solid enough to hurt me for the moment. It was the stranded boat.

A smoker generally has matches about him. Helped by my little short-lived lights, I examined the interior of the boat. There was absolutely nothing in it but a strip of old tarpaulin—used, as I guessed, to protect the boat, or something that it carried, in rainy weather.

The village population had long since been in bed. Silence and darkness mercilessly defied me to discover anything. For a while I waited, encouraging the dog to circle round me and exercise his sense of smell. Any suspicious person or object he would have certainly discovered. Nothing—not even the fallen stick of the rocket—rewarded our patience. Determined to leave nothing untried, I groped, rather than found, my way to the village ale house, and succeeded at last in rousing the landlord. He hailed me from the window (naturally enough) in no friendly voice. I called out my name. Within my own little limits, it was the name of a celebrated person. The landlord opened his door directly; eager to answer my questions if he could do it. Nothing in the least out of the common way had happened at Kylam. No strangers had been seen in, or near, the place. The stranded boat had not been discovered; and the crashing flight of the rocket into the air had failed to disturb the soundly-sleeping villagers.

On my melancholy way back, fatigue of body—and, far worse, fatigue of mind—forced me to take a few minutes' rest.

The dimly-flowing river was at my feet; the river on which I had seen Cristel again, for the first time since we were children. Thus far, the dreadful loss of her had been a calamity, held away from me in some degree by events which had imperatively taken possession of my mind. In the darkness and the stillness, the misery of having lost her was free to crush me. My head dropped on the neck of the dog, nestling close at my side. "Oh, Ponto!" I said to him, "she's gone!" Nobody could see me; nobody could despise me—I burst out crying.

CHAPTER XVI. BRIBERY AND CORRUPTION

Twice, I looked into Toller's room during the remainder of the night, and found him sleeping. When the sun rose, I could endure the delay no longer. I woke him.

"What is it?" he asked peevishly.

"You must be the last person who saw Cristel," I answered. "I want to know all that you can tell me."

His anger completely mastered him; he burst out with a furious reply.

"It's you two—you my landlord, and him my lodger—who have driven Cristy away from her home. She said she would go, and she has gone. Get out of my place, sir! You ought to be ashamed to look at me."

It was useless to reason with him, and it was of vital importance to lose no time in instituting a search. After the reception I had met with, I took care to restore the key of the door leading into the new cottage, before I left him. It was his key; and the poor distracted old man might charge me with taking away his property next.

As I set forth on my way home, I found the new man-servant on the look-out.

His first words showed that he was acting under orders. He asked if I had found the young lady; and he next informed me that his master had revived some hours since, and "bore no malice." This outrageous assertion suddenly fired me with suspicion. I believed that the Cur had been acting a part when he threatened me with his pistol, and that he was answerable for the disappearance of Cristel. My first impulse now was to get the help of a lawyer.

The men at my stables were just stirring when I got home. In ten minutes more, I was driving to our town.

The substance of the professional opinion which I received has been already stated in these pages.

One among my answers to the many questions which my legal adviser put to me led him to a conclusion that made my heart ache. He was of opinion that my brief absence, while I was taking that fatal "breath of air" on the banks of the river, had offered to Cristel her opportunity of getting away without discovery. "Her old father," the lawyer said, "was no doubt in his bed, and you yourself found nobody watching, in the neighborhood of the cottage."

"Employ me in some way!" I burst out. "I can't endure my life, if I'm not helping to trace Cristel."

He was most kind. "I understand," he said. "Try what you can get those two ladies to tell you—and you may help us materially."

Mrs. Roylake was nearest to me. I appealed to her womanly sympathies, and was answered by tears. I made another attempt; I said I was willing to believe that she meant well, and that I should be sorry to offend her. She got up, and indignantly left the room.

I went to Lady Rachel next.

She was at home, but the servant returned to me with an excuse: her ladyship was particularly engaged. I sent a message upstairs, asking when I might hope to be received. The servant was charged with the delivery of another excuse: her ladyship would write. After waiting at home for hours I was foolish enough to write, on my side; and (how could I help it?) to express myself strongly. The she-socialist's reply is easy to remember: "Dear Mr. Roylake, when you have recovered your temper, you will hear from me again."

Even my stepmother gained by comparison with this.

To rest, and do nothing, was to exercise a control over myself of which I was perfectly incapable. I went back to the cottage. Having no hopeful prospect in any other quarter, I persisted in believing that Toller must have

418

seen something or heard something that might either help me, or suggest an idea to my legal adviser.

On entering the kitchen, I found the door of communication wide open, and the new servant established in the large armchair.

"I'm waiting for my master, sir."

He had got over his fright, and had recovered his temper. The respectful side of him was turned to me again.

"Your master is with Mr. Toller?"

"Yes, sir."

What I felt, amply justified the lawyer in having exacted a promise from me to keep carefully out of the Cur's presence. "You might knock him on the head again, Mr. Roylake, and might hit a little too hard next time."

But I had an idea of my own. I said, as if speaking to myself: "I would give a five pound note to know what is going on upstairs."

"I shall be glad to earn it, sir," the fellow said. "If I make a clean breast of what I know already, and if I tell you to-morrow what I can find out—will it be worth the money?"

I began to feel degraded in my own estimation. But I nodded to him, for all that.

"I am the innocent cause, sir, of what happened last night," he coolly resumed. "We kept a look-out on the road and saw you, though you didn't see us. But my master never suspected you (for reasons which he kept to himself) of making use of the boat. I reminded him that one of us had better have an eye on the slip of pathway, between the cottage and the river. This led to his sending me to the boathouse—and you know what happened afterwards. My master, as I suppose, is pumping Mr. Toller. That's all, sir, for to-night. When may I have the honor of expecting you to-morrow morning?"

I appointed an hour, and left the place.

As I entered the wood again, I found a man on the watch. He touched his hat, and said: "I'm the clerk, sir. Your gamekeeper is wanted for his own duties to-night; he will relieve me in the morning."

I went home with my mind in a ferment of doubt. If I could believe the servant, the Cur was as innocent of the abduction of Cristel as I was. But could I trust the servant?

The events of the next morning altered the whole complexion of affairs fatally for the worse.

Arriving at the cottage, I found a man prostate on the road, dead drunk—and the Cur's servant looking at him.

"May I ask something?" the man said. "Have you been having my master watched?"

"Yes."

"Bad news, in that case, sir. Your man there is a drunken vagabond; and my master has gone to London by the first train."

When I had recovered the shock, I denied, for the sake of my own credit, that the brute on the road could be a servant of mine.

"Why not, sir?"

"Do you think I should have been kept in ignorance of it, if my gamekeeper had been a drunkard? His fellow servants would have warned me."

The man smiled. "I'm afraid, sir, you don't know much about servants. It's a point of honor among us never to tell tales of each other to our masters."

I began to wish that I had never left Germany. The one course to take now was to tell the lawyer what had happened. I turned away to get back, and drive at once to the town. The servant remembered, what I had forgotten—the five pound note.

"Wait and hear my report, sir," he suggested.

The report informed me: First, that Mr. Toller was at the mill, and had been there for some time past. Secondly: that the Cur had been alone, for a while, on Mr. Toller's side of the cottage, in Mr. Toiler's absence—for what purpose his servant had not discovered. Thirdly: that the Cur had returned to his room in a hurry, and had packed a few things in his travelling-bag. Fourthly: that he had ordered the servant to follow, with his luggage, in a fly which he would send from the railway station, and to wait at the London terminus for further orders. Fifthly, and lastly: that it was impossible to say whether the drunkenness of the gamekeeper was due to his own habits, or to temptation privately offered by the very person whose movements he had been appointed to watch.

I paid the money. The man pocketed it, and paid me a compliment in return: "I wish I was your servant, sir."

CHAPTER XVII. UTTER FAILURE

My lawyer took a serious view of the disaster that had overtaken us. He would trust nobody but his head clerk to act in my interests, after the servant had been followed to the London terminus, and when it became a question of matching ourselves against the deadly cunning of the man who had escaped us.

Provided with money, and with a letter to the police authorities in London, the head clerk went to the station. I accompanied him to point out the servant (without being allowed to show myself), and then returned to wait for telegraphic information at the lawyer's office.

This was the first report transmitted by the telegram:

The Cur had been found waiting for his servant at the terminus; and the two had been easily followed to the railway hotel close by. The clerk had sent his letter of introduction to the police—had consulted with picked men who joined him at the hotel—had given the necessary instructions—and would return to us by the last train in the evening.

In two days, the second telegram arrived.

Our man had been traced to the Thames Yacht Club in Albemarle Street—had consulted a yachting list in the hall—and had then travelled to the Isle of Wight. There, he had made inquiries at the Squadron Yacht Club, and the Victoria Yacht Club—and had returned to London, and the railway hotel.

The third telegram announced the utter destruction of all our hopes. As far as Marseilles, the Cur had been followed successfully, and in that city the detective officers had lost sight of him.

My legal adviser insisted on having the men sent to him to explain themselves. Nothing came of it but one more repetition of an old discovery. When the detective police force encounters intelligence instead of stupidity, in seven cases out of ten the detective police force is beaten.

There were still two persons at our disposal. Lady Rachel might help us, as I believed, if she chose to do it. As for old Toller, I suggested (on reflection) that the lawyer should examine him. The lawyer declined to waste any more of my money. I called again on Lady Rachel. This time, I was let in. I found the noble lady smoking a cigarette and reading a French novel.

"This is going to be a disagreeable interview," she said. "Let us get it over, Mr. Roylake, as soon as possible. Tell me what you want—and speak as freely as if you were in the company of a man."

I obeyed her to the letter; and I got these replies:

"Yes; I did have a talk, in your best interests, with Miss Toller. She is as sensible as she is charming, and as good as she is sensible. We entirely agreed that the sacrifice must be on her side; and that it was due to her own self-respect to prevent a gentleman of your rank from ruining himself by marrying a miller's daughter."

The next reply was equally free from the smallest atom of sympathy on Lady Rachel's part.

"You are quite right—your deaf man was at his window when I went by. We recognized each other and had a long talk. If I remember correctly, he said you knew of his reasons for concealing his name. I gave my promise (being a matter of perfect indifference to me) to conceal it too. One thing led to another, and I discovered that you were his hated rival in the affections of Miss Toller. I proved worthy of his confidence in me. That is to say, I told him that Mrs. Roylake and I would be only too glad, as representing your interests, if he succeeded in winning the young lady. I asked if he had any plans. He said one of his plans had failed. What it was, and how it had failed, he did not mention. I asked if he could devise nothing else. He said, "Yes, if I was not a poor man." In my place, you would have offered, as I did, to find the money if the plan was approved of. He produced some manuscript story of an abduction of a lady, which he had written to amuse himself. The point of it was that the lover successfully carried away the lady, by means of a boat, while the furious father's attention was absorbed in watching the high road. It seemed to me to be a new idea. "If you think you can carry it out," I said, "send your estimate of expenses to me and Mrs. Roylake, and we will subscribe." We received the estimate. But the plan has failed, and the man is off. I am quite certain myself that Miss Toller has done what she promised to do. Wherever she may be now, she has sacrificed herself for your sake. When you have got over it, you will marry my sister. I wish you good morning."

Between Lady Rachel's hard insolence, and Mrs. Roylake's sentimental hypocrisy, I was in such a state of irritation that I left Trimley Deen the next morning, to find forgetfulness, as I rashly supposed, in the gay world of London.

I had been trying my experiment for something like three weeks, and was beginning to get heartily weary of it, when I received a letter from the lawyer.

"Dear Sir,—Your odd tenant, old Mr. Toller, has died suddenly of rupture of a blood-vessel on the brain, as the doctor thinks. There is to be an inquest, as I need hardly tell you. What do you say to having the report of the proceedings largely copied in the newspapers? If it catches his daughter's eye, important results may follow."

To speculate in this way on the impulse which might take its rise in my poor girl's grief—to surprise her, as it were, at her father's grave—revolted me. I directed the lawyer to take no steps whatever in the matter, and to pay the poor old fellow's funeral expenses, on my account. He had died intestate. The law took care of his money until his daughter appeared; and the mill, being my property, I gave to Toller's surviving partner—our good Gloody.

And what did I do next? I went away travelling; one of the wretchedest men who ever carried his misery with him to foreign countries. Go where I might on the continent of Europe, the dreadful idea pursued me that Cristel might be dead.

CHAPTER XVIII. THE MISTRESS OF TRIMLEY DEEN

Three weary months had passed, when a new idea was put into my head by an Englishman whom I met at Trieste. He advised turning my back on Europe, and trying the effect of scenes of life that would be new to me. I hired a vessel, and sailed out of the civilized world. When I next stood on terra firma, my feet were on the lovely beach of one of the Pacific Islands.

What I suffered I have not told yet, and do not design to tell. The bitterness of those days hid itself from view at the time—and shall keep its concealment still. Even if I could dwell on my sorrows with the eloquence of a practised writer, some obstinate inner reluctance would persist in holding me dumb.

More than a year had passed before I returned to Trimley Deen, and alarmed my stepmother by "looking like a foreign sailor."

The irregular nature of my later travels had made it impossible to forward the few letters that had arrived for me. They were neatly laid out on the library table.

The second letter that I took up bore the postmark of Genoa. I opened it, and discovered that the—

No! I cannot write of him by that mean name; and his own name is still unknown to me. Let me call him—and, oh, don't think that I am deceived again!—let me call him the Penitent.

The letter had been addressed to me from his deathbed, and had been written under dictation. It contained an extraordinary enclosure—a small torn fragment of paper with writing on it.

"Read the poor morsel that I send to you first" (the letter began). "My time on earth is short; you will save me explanations which may be too much for my strength."

On one side of the fragment, I found these words:

"... cruise to the Mediterranean for my wife's health. If Cristel isn't afraid of passing some months at sea..."

On the other side, there was a fragment of conclusion:

"... thoroughly understand. All ready. Write word what night, and what ... loving brother, Stephen Toller."

I instantly remembered the miller's rich brother; thinking of him for the first time since he had been in my mind for a moment, on the night of my meeting with Cristel. On the fourteenth page of this narrative Toller's brother will be found briefly alluded to in a few lines.

I returned eagerly to the letter. Thus it was continued:

"That bit of torn paper I found under the bed, while I was secretly searching Mr. Toller's room. I had previously suspected You. From my own examination of his face, when he refused to humor my deafness by writing what I asked him to tell me, I suspected Mr. Toller next. You will see in the fragment, what I saw—that Toller the brother had a yacht, and was going to the Mediterranean; and that Toller the miller had written, asking him to favour Cristel's escape. The rest, Cristel herself can tell you.

"I know you had me followed. At Marseilles, I got tired of it, and gave your men the slip. At every port in the Mediterranean I inquired for the yacht, and heard nothing of her. They must have changed their minds on board, and gone somewhere else. I refer you to Cristel again.

"Arrived at Genoa, on my way back to England, I met with a skilled Italian surgeon. He declared that he could restore my hearing—but he warned me that I was in a weak state of health, and he refused to answer for the result of the operation. Without hesitating for a moment, I told him to operate. I would have given fifty lives for one exquisite week of perfect hearing. I have had three weeks of perfect hearing. Otherwise, I have had a life of enjoyment before I die.

"It is useless to ask your pardon. My conduct was too infamous for that.

426

Will you remember the family taint, developed by a deaf man's isolation among his fellow-creatures? But I had some days when my mother's sweet nature tried to make itself felt in me, and did not wholly fail. I am going to my mother now: her spirit has been with me ever since my hearing was restored; her spirit said to me last night: "Atone, my son! Give the man whom you have wronged, the woman whom he loves." I had found out the uncle's address in England (which I now enclose) at one of the Yacht Clubs. I had intended to go to the house, and welcome her on her return. You must go instead of me; you will see that lovely face when I am in my grave. Good-bye, Roylake. The cold hand that touches us all, sooner or later, is very near to me. Be merciful to the next scoundrel you meet, for the sake of The Cur."

I say there was good in that suffering man; and I thank God I was not quite wrong about him after all. Arriving at Mr. Stephen Toller's country seat, by the earliest train that would take me there, I found a last trial of endurance in store for me. Cristel was away with her uncle, visiting some friends.

Cristel's aunt received me with kindness which I can never forget. "We have noticed lately that Cristel was in depressed spirits; no uncommon thing," Mrs. Stephen Toller continued, looking at me with a gentle smile, "since a parting which I know you must have felt deeply too. No, Mr. Roylake, she is not engaged to be married—and she will never be married, unless you forgive her. Ah, you forgive her because you love her! She thought of writing to tell you her motives, when she visited her father's grave on our return to England. But I was unable to obtain your address. Perhaps, I may speak for her now?"

I knew how Lady Rachel's interference had appealed to Cristel's sense of duty and sense of self-respect; I had heard from her own lips that she distrusted herself, if she allowed me to press her. But she had successfully concealed from me the terror with which she regarded her rejected lover, and the influence over her which her father had exercised. Always mindful of his own interests, the miller knew that he would be the person blamed if he allowed his daughter to marry me. "They will say I did it, with an eye to my son-in-law's money; and gentlefolks may ruin a man who lives by selling flour." That was how he expressed himself in a letter to his brother.

427

The whole of the correspondence was shown to me by Mrs. Stephen Toller.

After alluding to his wealthy brother's desire that he should retire from business, the miller continued as follows:

"What you are ready to do for me, I want you to do for Cristy. She is in danger, in more ways than one, and I am obliged to get her away from my house as if I was a smuggler, and my girl contraband goods. I am a bad hand at writing, so I leave Cristy to tell you the particulars. Will you receive her, brother Stephen? and take care of her? and do it as soon as possible?"

Mr. Stephen Toller's cordial reply mentioned that his vessel was ready to sail, and would pass the mouth of The Loke on her southward voyage. His brother caught at the idea thus suggested.

I have alluded to Giles Toller's sly look to his lodger, when I returned the manuscript of the confession. The old man's unscrupulous curiosity had already applied a second key to the cupboard in the lodger's room. There he had found the "criminal stories" mentioned in the journal—including the story of abduction referred to by Lady Rachel. This gave him the very idea which his lodger had already relied on for carrying Cristel away by the river (under the influence, of course, of a soporific drug), while her father was keeping watch on the road. The secreting of the oars with this purpose in view, had failed as a measure of security. The miller's knowledge of the stream, and his daughter's ready courage, had suggested the idea of letting the boat drift, with Cristel hidden in it. Two of the yacht's crew, hidden among the trees, watched the progress of the boat until it rounded the promontory, and struck the shore. There, the yacht's boat was waiting. The rocket was fired to re-assure her father; and Cristel was rowed to the mouth of the river, and safely received on board the yacht. Thus (with his good brother's help) the miller had made the River his Guilty accomplice in the abduction of his own child!

When I had read the correspondence, we spoke again of Cristel.

"To save time," Mrs. Stephen Toller said, "I will write to my husband to-day, by a mounted messenger. He shall only tell Cristel that you have come back to England, and you shall arrange to meet her in our grounds when she returns. I am a childless woman, Mr. Roylake—and I love her as I should have loved a daughter of my own. Where improvement (in external matters only) has seemed to be possible, it has been my delight to improve her. Your stepmother and Lady Rachel will acknowledge, even from their point of view, that there is a mistress who is worthy of her position at Trimley Deen."

When Cristel returned the next day, she found that her uncle had deserted her, and suddenly discovered a man in the shrubbery. What that man said and did, and what the result of it was, may be inferred if I relate a remarkable event. Mrs. Roylake has retired from the domestic superintendence of Trimley Deen.

About Author

Early life

Collins was born at 11 New Cavendish Street, Marylebone, London, the son of a well-known Royal Academician landscape painter, William Collins and his wife, Harriet Geddes. Named after his father, he swiftly became known by his middle name, which honoured his godfather, David Wilkie. The family moved to Pond Street, Hampstead, in 1826. In 1828 Collins's brother Charles Allston Collins was born. Between 1829 and 1830, the Collins family moved twice, first to Hampstead Square and then to Porchester Terrace, Bayswater. Wilkie and Charles received their early education from their mother at home. The Collins family were deeply religious, and Collins's mother enforced strict church attendance on her sons, which Wilkie disliked.

In 1835, Collins began attending school at the Maida Vale academy. From 1836 to 1838, he lived with his parents in Italy and France, which made a great impression on him. He learned Italian while the family was in Italy and began learning French, in which he would eventually become fluent. From 1838 to 1840, he attended the Reverend Cole's private boarding school in Highbury, where he was bullied by a boy who would force Collins to tell him a story before allowing him to go to sleep. "It was this brute who first awakened in me, his poor little victim, a power of which but for him I might never have been aware.... When I left school I continued story telling for my own pleasure", Collins later said.

In 1840 the family moved to 85 Oxford Terrace, Bayswater. In late 1840, he left school and was apprenticed as a clerk to the firm of tea merchants Antrobus & Co, owned by a friend of Wilkie's father. He disliked his clerical work but remained employed by the company for more than five years. Collins's first story The Last Stage Coachman, was published in the Illuminated Magazine in August 1843. In 1844 he travelled to Paris with Charles Ward. That same year he wrote his first novel, Iolani, or Tahiti as It Was; a Romance, which was submitted to Chapman and Hall but rejected in 1845. The novel remained unpublished during his lifetime. Collins said of it:

"My youthful imagination ran riot among the noble savages, in scenes which caused the respectable British publisher to declare that it was impossible to put his name on the title page of such a novel." It was during the writing of this novel that Collins's father first learned that his assumptions that Wilkie would follow him in becoming a painter were mistaken.

William Collins had intended Wilkie for a clergyman and was disappointed in his son's lack of interest. In 1846 he instead entered Lincoln's Inn to study law, on the initiative of his father, who wanted him to have a steady income. Wilkie showed only a slight interest in law and spent most of his time with friends and on working on a second novel, Antonina, or the Fall of Rome. After his father's death in 1847, Collins produced his first published book, Memoirs of the Life of William Collins, Esq., R. A., published in 1848. The family moved to 38 Blandford Square soon afterwards, where they used their drawing room for amateur theatricals. In 1849, Collins exhibited a painting, "The Smugglers' Retreat", at the Royal Academy summer exhibition. Antonina was published by Richard Bentley in February 1850. Collins went on a walking tour of Cornwall with artist Henry Brandling in July and August 1850. He managed to complete his legal studies and be called to the bar in 1851. Though he never formally practised, he used his legal knowledge in many of his novels.

Early writing career

An instrumental event in his career was an introduction in March 1851 to Charles Dickens by a mutual friend, through the painter Augustus Egg. They became lifelong friends and collaborators. In May of that year, Collins acted with Dickens in Edward Bulwer-Lytton's play Not So Bad As We Seem. Among the audience were Queen Victoria and Prince Albert. Collins's story "A Terribly Strange Bed," his first contribution to Household Words, appeared in April, 1852. In May 1852 he went on tour with Dickens's company of amateur actors, again performing Not So Bad As We Seem, but with a more substantial role. Collins's novel Basil was published by Bentley in November. During the writing of Hide and Seek, in early 1853, Collins suffered what was probably his first attack of gout, which would plague him for the rest of his life. He was ill from April to early July. After that he stayed with Dickens in Boulogne from July to September 1853, then toured Switzerland and Italy with Dickens and Egg from October to December. Collins published Hide and Seek in June 1854.

During this period Collins extended the variety of his writing, publishing articles in George Henry Lewes's paper The Leader, short stories and essays for Bentley's Miscellany, dramatic criticism and the travel book Rambles Beyond Railways. His first play, The Lighthouse, was performed by Dickens's theatrical company at Tavistock House, in 1855. His first collection of short stories, After Dark, was published by Smith, Elder in February 1856. His novel A Rogue's Life was serialised in Household Words in March 1856. Around then, Collins began using laudanum regularly to treat his gout. He became addicted and struggled with that problem later in life.

Collins joined the staff of Household Words in October 1856. In 1856–57 he collaborated closely with Dickens on a play, The Frozen Deep, first performed in Tavistock. Collins's novel The Dead Secret was serialised in Household Words from January to June 1857 and published in volume form by Bradbury and Evans. Collins's play The Lighthouse was performed at the Olympic Theatre in August. The Lazy Tour of Two Idle Apprentices, based on Dickens's and Collins's walking tour in the north of England, was serialised in Household Words in October 1857. In 1858 he collaborated with Dickens and other writers on the story "A House to Let".

1860s

According to biographer Melisa Klimaszewski, "The novels Collins published in the 1860s are the best and most enduring of his career. The Woman in White, No Name, Armadale, and The Moonstone, written in less than a decade, show Collins not just as a master of his craft, but as an innovater and provocateur. These four works, which secured him an international reputation, and sold in large numbers, ensured his financial stability, and allowed him to support many others".

The Woman in White was serialised in All the Year Round from November 1859 to August 1860 and was a great success. The novel was published in book form soon after serial publication ended, and it reached an eighth edition by November 1860. His increased stature as a writer made Collins resign his position with All the Year Round in 1862 to focus on novel writing. During the planning of his next novel, No Name, he continued to suffer from gout, and it now especially affected his eyes. Serial publication of No Name began in early 1862 and finished in 1863. By this time the laudanum he was taking for his continual gout became a serious problem.

At the beginning of 1863, he travelled to German spas and Italy for his health, with Caroline Graves. In 1864, he began work on his novel Armadale, travelling in August to do research for it. It was published serially in The Cornhill Magazine in 1864–66. His play No Thoroughfare, co-written with Dickens, was published as the 1867 Christmas number of All the Year Round and dramatised at the Adelphi Theatre on 26 December. It enjoyed a run of 200 nights before being taken on tour.

Collins's search for background information for Armadale took him to the Norfolk Broads and the small village of Winterton-on-Sea. His novel The Moonstone was serialised in All the Year Round from January to August 1868. His mother, Harriet Collins, died that year.

Later years

In 1870, his novel Man and Wife was published. This year also saw the death of Charles Dickens, which caused him great sadness. He said of their early days together, "We saw each other every day, and were as fond of each other as men could be."

The Woman in White was dramatised and produced at the Olympic Theatre in October 1871.

Collins's novel Poor Miss Finch was serialised in Cassell's Magazine from October to March 1872. His short novel Miss or Mrs? was published in the 1872 Christmas number of the Graphic. His novel The New Magdalen was serialised from October 1872 to July 1873. His younger brother, Charles Allston Collins, died later in 1873. Charles had married Dickens's younger daughter, Kate.

In 1873–74, Collins toured the United States and Canada, giving readings of his work. The American writers he met included Oliver Wendell Holmes, Sr., and Mark Twain, and he began a friendship with the photographer Napoleon Sarony, who took several portraits of him.

His novel The Law and the Lady, serialised in the Graphic from September to March 1875, was followed by a short novel, The Haunted Hotel, which was serialised from June to November 1878. His later novels include Jezebel's Daughter (1880), The Black Robe (1881), Heart and Science (1883) and The Evil Genius (1886). In 1884, Collins was elected Vice-President of the Society of Authors, which had been founded by his friend and fellow novelist Walter Besant.

The inconsistent quality of Collins's dramatic and fictional works in the last decade of his life was accompanied by a general decline in his health, including diminished eyesight. He was often unable to leave home and had difficulty writing. During these last years, he focused on mentoring younger writers, including the novelist Hall Caine, and helped to protect other writers from copyright infringement of their works. His writing became a way for him to fight his illness without allowing it to keep him bedridden. His step-daughter Harriet also served as an amanuensis for several years. His last novel, Blind Love, was finished posthumously by Walter Besant.

Death

Collins died at 82 Wimpole Street, following a paralytic stroke. He is buried in Kensal Green Cemetery, West London. His headstone describes him as the author of The Woman in White. Caroline Graves died in 1895 and was buried with Collins. Martha Rudd died in 1919.

Personal life

In 1858 Collins began living with Caroline Graves and her daughter Harriet. Caroline came from a humble family, having married young, had a child, and been widowed. Collins lived close to the small shop kept by Caroline, and the two may have met in the neighborhood in the mid–1850s. He treated Harriet, whom he called Carrie, as his own daughter, and helped to provide for her education. Excepting one short separation, they lived together for the rest of Collins's life. Collins disliked the institution of marriage, but remained dedicated to Caroline and Harriet, considering them to be his family. Caroline had wanted to marry Collins. She left him while he wrote The Moonstone and was suffering an attack of acute gout. She then married a younger man named Joseph Clow, but returned to Collins after two years.

In 1868, Collins met Martha Rudd in Winterton-on-Sea in Norfolk, and the two began a liaison. She was 19 years old and from a large, poor family. She moved to London to be closer to him a few years later. Their daughter Marian was born in 1869, their second daughter, Harriet Constance, in 1871 and their son, William Charles, in 1874. When he was with Martha he assumed the name William Dawson, and she and their children used the last name of Dawson themselves.

For the last 20 years of his life Collins divided his time between Caroline, who lived with him at his home in Gloucester Place, and Martha who was nearby.

Like his friend Charles Dickens, Collins was a professing Christian.

Works

Collins's works were classified at the time as "sensation novels", a genre seen nowadays as the precursor to detective and suspense fiction. He also wrote penetratingly on the plight of women and on the social and domestic issues of his time. For example, his 1854 Hide and Seek contained one of the first portrayals of a deaf character in English literature. As did many writers of his time, Collins published most of his novels as serials in magazines such as Dickens's All the Year Round and was known as a master of the form, creating just the right degree of suspense to keep his audience reading from week to week. Sales of All The Year Round increased when The Woman in White followed A Tale of Two Cities.

Collins enjoyed ten years of great success following publication of The Woman in White in 1859. His next novel, No Name combined social commentary – the absurdity of the law as it applied to children of unmarried parents (see Illegitimacy in fiction) – with a densely plotted revenge thriller.

436

Armadale, the first and only of Collins's major novels of the 1860s to be serialised in a magazine other than All the Year Round, provoked strong criticism, generally centred upon its transgressive villainess Lydia Gwilt, and provoked in part by Collins's typically confrontational preface. The novel was simultaneously a financial coup for its author and a comparative commercial failure: the sum paid by Cornhill for the serialisation rights was exceptional, eclipsing by a substantial margin the prices paid for the vast majority of similar novels, yet the novel failed to recoup its publisher's investment. The Moonstone, published in 1868, and the last novel of what is generally regarded as the most successful decade of its author's career, was, despite a somewhat cool reception from both Dickens and the critics, a significant return to form and reestablished the market value of an author whose success on the competitive Victorian literary market had been gradually waning in the wake of his first perceived masterpiece. Viewed by many to represent the advent of the detective story within the tradition of the English novel, The Moonstone remains one of Collins's most critically acclaimed productions, identified by T. S. Eliot as "the first, the longest, and the best of modern English detective novels... in a genre invented by Collins and not by Poe," and Dorothy L. Sayers referred to it as "probably the very finest detective story ever written".

After The Moonstone, Collins's novels contained fewer thriller elements and more social commentary. The subject matter continued to be sensational, but his popularity declined. The poet Algernon Charles Swinburne commented: "What brought good Wilkie's genius nigh perdition? / Some demon whispered—'Wilkie! have a mission.'"

Factors most often cited have been the death of Dickens in 1870, and with it the loss of his literary mentoring, Collins's increased dependence upon laudanum, and his penchant for using his fiction to rail against social injustices. His novels and novellas of the 1870s and 1880s are generally regarded as inferior to his previous productions and receive comparatively little critical attention today[when?].

The Woman in White and The Moonstone share an unusual narrative structure, somewhat resembling an epistolary novel, in which different portions of the book have different narrators, each with a distinct narrative voice. Armadale has this to a lesser extent through the correspondence between some characters. (Source: Wikipedia)

9 789390 171774